THE
CONDEMNED

KRISTY BERRIDGE

Kristy Berridge: writer, sometimes comedian, peanut butter addict, exercise junkie, vegan … woman.

There are many labels I go by, but not one can ever define me. Like all things in life, sometimes I commit 100% and other times I apply varying percentages to the effort and enthusiasm adopted.

To be a writer you must have passion and I have bucket loads, but I am human and sometimes I'd rather go cow-tipping or rob a Seven-Eleven than immerse myself in the written word.

The trick is to find balance. Between my love of keeping fit; outrunning my boyfriend to claim the television remote before being subjected to British drama and my clean-eating lifestyle; washing the plates before eating off of them, I sit down to write with a clear conscience.

Romance and horror are my general persuasions these days; not because my life is lacking, but who doesn't love a bit of blood and guts with a side of lip-locking? I've been drawn to both genres, even combining them more often than not.

The next stage in my journey is as unknown as the next paragraph in my forthcoming novels. It's better to live in the present, celebrate the small victories and of course, apply pen to paper whenever the inspiration may strike; a motto to live by.

Shadow Ink Press
P.O Box 352n, Cairns North, Queensland 4870 Australia
Email: admin@shadowinkpress.com.au

First published in Australia 2016 - This edition published 2016
Copyright © Kristy Berridge 2016
Cover design, typesetting: Shadow Ink Press
The right of Kristy Berridge to be identified as the Author of the Work has been asserted in accordance with the Copyright, Designs and Patents Act 1988.

Berridge, Kristy
The Condemned
ISBN: 9780995432703

Also by Kristy Berridge

The Hunted

The Damned

The Aligned

Diary of a Teenage Zombie

100 Days of Happiness

PREFACE

Darkness is a fearsome concept until eyes adjust and unknowns find explanation. It is the black of a raven's wing and the touch of obsidian silk spreading across the landscape like a blanket. Darkness covets well-kept secrets, hiding unexplored terrain until touched by the branching fingers of morning's first light. Eyes soon adjust, shadows become shapes, shapes become distinct and discernibility carves the landscape into something less apprehensive.

The dark was currently broken by pin-pricks of light—beacons of colour that marked the terrain as a city. Billboards flashed with vibrancy, highways were lit with the promise of safety and homes were touched by the invitation of warmth.

Before Araqiel's fall from grace, the angel had known no shadow. Learning to exist between the two extremes was now paramount, especially if he were to succeed with his plans: protecting Elena and saving the world.

Elena was no exception to the exploits of night's call. She explored darkness like an old friend, now entering a vampire neutral bar with an unfocused vampire at her side and an enemy at her heels. She invited death without fear of consequence, hiding behind the naivety of youth and calling it purpose.

'Purpose' was a word Araqiel was intimately familiar. Elena was his champion, the piece in a puzzle that could bind all pieces into a reconcilable image. She was light and dark—good and evil. She was

1

born vampire, but her blood was drenched in the innocence and purity of angels. Elena had the power to change everything with the Time Contract, ending Lucifer's influence over Earth.

At least, this was Araqiel's prayer.

'Is this spot taken?'

Araqiel smiled, looking up at Michael who towered above him. 'How did you find me?'

'I'm an Archangel, finding you wasn't difficult.'

'I am currently shielding.'

Smirking, Michael gripped Araqiel's shoulder for support and lowered himself onto the rooftop beside his angelic brother. He dangled his legs over the edge and glanced over the sparkling city as Araqiel had done for hours. 'My old powers have not yet deserted me.'

'You are lucky, Michael. Others would have been cast out for choosing the love of a mortal in lieu of serving heaven, but not you. You were always *his* favourite.'

Michael nodded, though his face remained impassive. 'What are you doing up here?'

'I'm watching.'

'Watching?'

'I watch because I can no longer feel.'

'I am sorry that being cast out has robbed you of such an integral part of existing on Earth.'

An echo of emotion whispered deep within Araqiel, though it was mostly a memory of what he had once felt. 'What are you doing here?' he said, dismissing the apology. 'I thought you were travelling further north to hunt and destroy the Alpha Vânătors,' he paused. 'Or *werewolves* as the humans prefer to call them.'

'I was. I am, but I picked up your immortal signature and thought perhaps we might talk.'

'Where will this discussion lead?'

Michael shrugged, casting his gaze over the piazza below. Tourists crowded the central monument. From this height they were merely shapeless figures within the dark. 'I need to know more about the Time Contract and Elena's part in its use.'

'Michael ...'

'Please, I gave up heaven and all of its comforts for this life and for her.'

'Was it worth becoming a vampire?'

Michael remained passively indifferent. 'Sometimes I doubt the decision, knowing what I have had to do to survive, but then I see her face and I remember.'

'Remember what?'

'How much I love her—how much I've always loved her. It's why I need to know how and why the Time Contract affects her.'

'It won't affect Elena alone, but everyone.'

Michael's face hardened. 'Enlighten me, brother. Last I heard, the Time Contract was in Lucifer's hands and you told me that I'm the bargaining chip for the exchange. Tell me now what it has to do with Elena?'

Araqiel considered the words, sighing as if the very weight of the world rested on his shoulders—an instinctive reaction. 'Protecting her has become difficult, Michael. I have interfered more times than the council approves. It is only by Samael's recent curiosity and wandering feet that I have been allowed this much grace.'

Michael's nostrils flared at the mere mention of the demon. 'Samael left Purgatory?'

'He's looking for clues that may lead to your whereabouts.'

'He seeks to destroy me.'

'No,' Araqiel murmured. 'He wishes to give Lucifer the opportunity.'

Michael's jaw snapped together, his teeth grinding in ire. 'All this time I have been right under Lucifer's nose, assuming the form of the creatures he created and yet—'

'They are close, Michael. They only wait for my order before the exchange is to be made.'

Michael's resigned breath was an echo of Araqiel's current thoughts. 'I am aware of the part I must play, but why Elena?'

'She is human but born of the master vampire and filled with the blood of the vânător and angel Uriel. She is the vessel for both light and dark, the only one the council will not ...' Araqiel stopped, voice fading.

'She's the only one that the council will not *what*?'

'I should not say.'

'If you know something, brother, speak to me.'

For the longest time, Araqiel was lost to the intensity of Michael's solemn eyes. The centre writhed grey to the gleaming brightness of silvered Christmas tinsel, but no twinge of conscience spoke to Araqiel's emotionless soul.

'This is your last chance, Michael. I would hate for it to end after so many millennia of trying to get it right.'

'You are changing the subject.'

'Regardless, I speak the truth. Time is of the essence. If you wish to have Elena, then I suggest you make it quick.' Araqiel gestured to the view before them. 'The darkness closes in, Michael. Find the Alpha wolves, destroy them and meet with your destiny.'

'You mean my ultimate death?'

Araqiel nodded, a vague memory of sadness scratching at the edges of his heart. 'I'm afraid so.'

Michael gripped the concrete edge of the roof, fracturing gritty pieces of mortar and terracotta tiling that quickly fell to the piazza below. The tourists remained unfazed by the granular rain, no more aware of the Archangel's tension-filled muscles than they were with the crumbling rooftop's descent. 'Will Elena live?'

'It is her choice.'

'I don't understand.'

Araqiel bowed his head, submitting to the rise in power swelling around Michael. 'I am sorry, but I am bound—as well you know.'

The cool night air was now thick with humidity and the crackle of energy. Lightning struck the horizon, cracking through the atmosphere in a hue matched only by Michael's eyes. Rain now kissed the horizon and then proceeded to coat their skin, moistening clothes and soaking them through. Michael's hair clung to his face, rivulets of water seeking escape. 'If anything happens to her,' he started to say, *'no one* will stop me from seeking vengeance.'

'You sound human, Michael. Archangels do not talk of vengeance. That notion is best left in the hands of Lucifer and his minions.'

'No Archangel has ever had so much to lose.'

Araqiel had the good grace to reflect sorrow, remembering its touch, particularly as he thought of the past and all he had lost or could, if he failed now. 'I am sorry, Michael. I can only promise you that if Elena is the person I believe she is, then everything will work out the way it should.'

'If I knew the purpose or intended result then perhaps I could trust in it.'

'Rules, Michael. You know these better than anyone.'

Michael laughed humourlessly, the easing rain the only indication his temper had subsided. 'The rules,' he mocked, shaking his head. 'I never thought I would be obstructed by those that bind me. I have no control and I hate that.'

Araqiel patted Michael endearingly on the shoulder. 'Speaking of control, you must avoid using the Ley-lines.'

'Why?'

'They are being watched by Samael and the other members of the council.'

'But without wings …'

'I am aware, but you must resist using these monitored corridors. You will leave a metaphysical footprint that any demon or angel can follow.'

'I know this.'

'Yet you risked coming here to speak with me.'

'I needed to pursue Elena's safety. I needed to know if my death would threaten her existence and I have still learnt nothing.'

Michael climbed slowly to his feet, mildly surprised that the tourists and locals previously enjoying the night were now gone, swept away by the sudden downpour. Perhaps they felt as dejected as he, cowering under temporary shelter in the hope that the tides would turn.

Michael took a shaky breath. How could he protect Elena against an unknown agenda and the upcoming war between vânătors and vampires with so little information?

'Araqiel, I cannot go to my death not knowing how Elena feels and I can't admit my feelings if I am to suffer rejection for an eternity in Purgatory.'

'Life is full of risk. It is why you chose to exist here. Elena is different this cycle—strong, independent—very much like Eimhir.'

Michael's eyes were hooded by memory as he recalled the Scottish version of Elena. Born in 8500BC, she was unlike anyone he'd encountered: beautiful, vivacious, perfect and the catalyst for his fall. 'I had noticed the similarities.'

'Then you know how she feels about you.'

Michael vehemently shook his head. 'I know she's attracted to me, but I don't know her heart.'

'Then ask.'

Michael wished it were that easy. 'Please watch over her, Araqiel. I do not know how long it will take to complete Lucius's task. If something should happen before I get my chance—'

'I will attempt to convey how you feel.'

Michael squeezed Araqiel's shoulder appreciatively. 'Thank you.'

'Do not thank me yet.'

Michael didn't linger. He dove from the side of the building, discussion at an end as his form converged with the darkness. His movements were fluid, like water through a faucet as he disappeared down a side alley, his glowing eyes leaving a lasting impression of a man resigned to the inevitability of death.

Back in the central piazza, people began to re-emerge, the rain a forgotten memory since Michael's departure. A child now squealed with delight, splashing in puddles with oversized yellow boots while simultaneously gobbling down a crimson scoop of gelato. Pigeons fluttered, shifting wings to release stubborn droplets, scaring those already posing for new photos in front of the cathedral.

For now, Milan was safe, protected by its ignorance, but three weeks hence, the city would be destroyed and every evil classified an illusion of darkness would come to life and strip the city bare.

In three weeks Milan would be host to a war between humans, vampire and vânător—the world forever changed. Michael would also be dead; an inevitable truth that darkness could no longer hide.

CHAPTER ONE: NEUTRAL

The flashing red neon sign blistered darkness with surreptitious invitation. Its deceptive words of welcome spelled salvation; otherwise known as a place to sample the illustrious versions of Synth Corp's packaged blood products.

Vampires preferred an open vein, but the master vampire—Lucius Valerius—forbade drinking from the source. Calling ourselves *civilised* was the token word of this century; hence the blood baggies and designated drinking zones.

This neutral bar's weather-beaten windows and doors, blackout curtains and all round lack of proprietor care repelled the general public. Its lacklustre exterior and seedy undertone promoted neglect—curiosity my only driving force to enter.

Tonight—though shit scared—I was going to sample the merchandise firsthand, immerse myself in this vampire culture and pray I wasn't added to the menu. Why? I'm *technically* still human and my blood is unfortunately craved by all with unnatural urges.

A cool arm snaked tentatively across my shoulders, directly followed by a sheepish grin emitted from a vampire with limited restraint. At first I found the weight of his arm comforting since I'd begun to label him a friend, but then I remembered that this *friend* would probably drain me dry if he thought he could get away with it. The bunched sleeves of his jacket were crisp and itchy against my nape as we walked; his palm limp like a dead herring as it hung in front of my chest, fingers up to no good as they grazed dangerously close to the edge of my breast.

Frowning, I peered into Caleb's mischievous blue eyes. He was armed with a lecherous wink that was quickly chased by a bone crushing embrace I could only assume was aimed at getting a better grope or perhaps greater access to my jugular.

'You might want to show some fang,' Caleb said, fingers slipping enough to finally earn him a slap.

Cheap cologne and the smell of soap permeated the air between us. His breath was frigid against my heated cheek, tainted with blood from what I presumed was an earlier feed. The icy tip of his nose brushed against my temple and pushed upon boundaries as he inhaled bliss he would hopefully never attempt to sample.

Caleb's slow releasing canines suggested that continued proximity was not healthy for either of us. His magnetic blue eyes were already darkening and his pale flesh bordered transparency, but when combined with a pink-tipped Mohawk, chipped, black fingernail polish and a clichéd death-metal shirt, taking Caleb serious proved difficult.

'Why do I need to show fang?' I supposed the obvious reason was to remind Caleb I was capable of biting him back.

He eyed me as though I were daft. 'I'm taking you into Rome's busiest neutral bar, Elena. With hungry vamps inside, you need to show that you're one of them—not on the menu.'

I snorted, unamused. I could never just be a *vampire*. My eighteenth birthday marked the date of actual transformation, but at sixteen, I was already a freak of nature. I'd inadvertently exchanged blood with two different supernatural entities and was now a fanged, blood-drinking vampire with super strength and telekinetic abilities. Oh and a werewolf with uncontrollable rages and a bloodlust that makes Genghis Khan look like a pussy.

'I'm not sure my fangs are really going to help,' I mused.

'Of course they will. They give off the *don't mess with me* vibe.'

'Don't be so sure.'

Two passing vamps approached, undoubtedly drawn by my scent. Their pace slowed reflecting interest, lips smacking together with anticipation. Canines were unleashed followed by an eager appreciation of my throbbing pulse points. I may share their DNA, but it was imperceptible, just like the vânător half I liked to keep hidden.

Caleb's fangs lengthened to extent, eyes filled with the obsidian darkness I'd come to recognise as the vampiric form. His skin; already translucent and showed pulsing veins eager for blood. His arm was still hooked around my neck, face close enough that I shivered at the thought of a lost moment of control and the consequences that could follow.

Caleb hissed at the two circling sharks. 'Back. Off.'

The vamps were either deaf or ignorant, darting forward to sniff at me like mongrel dogs. I was blinded by their speed, irritated that despite my talents, I could never be as fast or as strong as any vampire while still human.

'We can share her,' the first vampire offered. He had long black, greasy hair that swirled around his pallid face like sticky tentacles. He was turned, perhaps mid to late twenties at most, forever frozen in time due to a blood exchange with another vampire.

Although technically ageless, true death finds a turned vampire like any mortal. They reek of vulnerability and their ability to breed is tenuous at best. Born vampires are faster, stronger and capable of withstanding sunlight when avoiding direct rays. We also regenerate damaged flesh—a gift from birth and a form of protection until turning.

'Share her?' Caleb echoed, voice considering. Jesus. He was actually weighing up his options. Sebastian would have kicked his ass if he were here right now.

I frowned and kicked Caleb's instep, glowering as he undoubtedly continued to entertain fantasies of licking my bones clean.

'What?' he mouthed, claiming innocence.

My attention shifted back to Greasy-hair and partner. 'There will be no *sharing*,' I admonished. 'You're standing right outside a neutral bar. Go inside and grab a tetra pack like everyone else.'

Greasy-hair—that was what I was calling him now—craned his neck and sniffed. 'You smell far better than any of the packaged stuff on offer inside.'

'Let it go,' Caleb warned, finally stepping up to offer support.

'Let it go?' vampire number two answered, a small smile twisting his parched lips. 'I don't think we can … I don't think we want to.'

This troublemaker was also turned, nearing fifty and sporting red hair like Bozo the clown. I was likening his sharp teeth and deadly appetite to the red-nosed fiend Stephen King had already immortalised in fiction.

'Don't you want to taste her blood?' he persisted, eyeballing Caleb.

I was suddenly battling images of a donkey, taunted by a carrot dangling via a piece of string. Surprisingly, I was not the ass in this scenario.

'Go inside,' Caleb pressed, indicating the bar's decrepit, wooden door with a nod of his head. They seemed entirely unconvinced of their options. I pondered my durability in spite of my humanity.

Bozo started to laugh, a hiccup at first followed by a raucous assault on my ears that grated on my last nerve. 'What are you going to do about it? I bet if we slit her throat you wouldn't be able to help yourself.'

'Okay, time out,' I said, putting space between all three of them. 'We don't want to fight. It'll just end up in a bloody mess that neither of us really wants to explain to anyone.'

Perplexed, Bozo's eyes narrowed. 'What do you think you're going to do to stop us, *human*?'

There it was—pigeonholing—a colossal mistake of the untrained. Yes, I was still human, but I also grew fangs, shape-shifted and could probably bench press a Volkswagen.

'I *can* kill you,' I answered calmly, rationally. Did I mention I'm also telekinetic—a gift inadvertently handed down from the master vampire?

Greasy-hair thought I was thoroughly amusing, snorting as though it were flu season. 'What will you do? Talk us to death?'

'Oh, a comedian,' I mocked, applauding his efforts. With a tilt of my head, I gestured once again to the door. 'Come on, let's just go inside.'

'We don't want Synth Blood, anymore.'

Of course you don't. This was going to get ugly.

Greasy-hair stopped snickering, but continued to grin, circling me—studying me. Bozo teamed curiosity with a puffed chest and crooked finger aimed at invitation. Any intimidation I'd felt shattered as their gazes met mine and they burst into hysterics.

Was it something I said?

'This human is funny,' Greasy-hair spluttered. 'Are you going to try and stake us? Throw holy water on our skin or press a cross to our chests?'

I showed them the whites of my eyes. 'Do I look like Van Helsing?'

'No, you look like a tasty, helpless, little girl.'

'She's definitely not one of those,' Caleb mused.

That only seemed to make them laugh more. I was trying particularly hard not to be offended by the outright ridicule. 'They don't think I'm serious.'

'You're going to be in *serious* trouble if your dad finds out about this.'

'He won't.'

Caleb clucked his tongue, clearly doubting my ability to execute a clean getaway. 'I think you sometimes forget who you're dealing with, Elena. Lucius is the all-seeing eye.'

Bozo hissed, spitting his noxious irritation by the side of my foot. 'Stop talking!'

My lip curled in disgust as I studied my right shoelace, now coated in stinky, vampiric saliva. 'Say it, don't spray it.'

Brows crumpled, confusion once again setting in. 'Why aren't you afraid?'

'Because I bite back.'

'What?'

'I drink vampire blood.'

Another baffled look.

'Me predator, you prey,' I said, breaking it down for them. Caleb made gagging noises which I chose to ignore.

'Who are you?' Bozo queried, perhaps slightly smarter for his hesitation in pouncing.

'Elena Manory.'

'Who?'

'Lucius Valerius's daughter,' Caleb answered, sliding a finger threateningly across his throat. Apparently miming their demise was enough to stop both vampires in their tracks.

'Wait,' Bozo murmured, 'you're the daughter of the first and most powerful vampire in existence?'

'I usually just call him *Dad*.'

Bozo paled; quite a trick for the already pasty undead. Demonic eyes assessed exit points as his bottom lip began to tremble, betraying nerves. His flaming red hair was soon the only thing I saw as he bolted into the shadows of a nearby alley.

'What a chicken shit,' I said to no one in particular.

Caleb was visibly relieved. 'I'd say the odds are now in our favour.'

Greasy-hair was unfazed and immediately back on the prowl, circling with quiet regard. I admired his persistence, but still thought he was an idiot.

'You say you are Lucius's daughter?' he asked, eyeing me from head-to-toe. 'Prove it.'

'Sure, just let me pull that genealogy map from out of my butt right now ...'

Greasy-hair was in no joking mood, simply eager to pounce, driven by the desire for fresh blood. I could practically hear his thoughts as his tongue darted out to moisten the surface of his cracked and parted lips. *Taste her, taste her*, his eyes seemed to say. The exposed fangs currently on route to my arteries were a clear indication of intent.

Dodging his greedy, clawed-fingers, I spun, searching for a hand-hold and finding Dumbo-sized ears as consolation. Instead of landing a swift punch to his fleshy mid-section, I pulled on those ridiculously large lobes and hauled his vampiric ass over my shoulder.

Cobblestones fractured and wheezed offending motes of dust. Greasy-hair tried rolling away, but since I had him pinned with telekinesis, he remained a disgruntled resident in the womb of disturbed earth. A shallow grave? Several thunderous cracks and Greasy-hair's sudden silence suggested I'd been a little rough.

'Holy shit, I think I broke him.'

'That's the understatement of the century,' Caleb mused, vying for a closer look. I gathered from his pursed lips and Greasy-hair's shallow breathing and blood-stained lips, that the prognosis wasn't all that good.

'My bad.'

I stepped closer, leaning over the vampire to catalogue his injuries. I was no expert, but I figured the red stuff was bad and the blooms of purple were really going to hurt in the morning. 'What should I do?'

'Ask him,' Caleb shrugged, gesturing to the whimpering mass by my feet.

I released Greasy-hair from my telekinetic barrier, pleased with my humanitarian skills, though surprised that the idiot lunged for me again. Within seconds he was back to resting uncomfortably in his cobblestone grave. 'What the hell is wrong with you?'

Firing a foamy-wad of spit in my direction, Greasy-hair was ultimately taken down by Karma. His saliva slapped the telekinetic shield, bowed to the inevitable pull of gravity and landed right back in his face.

Epic fail.

'Now what?

'Well, we can't just leave him out here, can we?'

I gestured to the thrashing, fanged camel by our feet. 'Be my guest. Watch out though, he spits.'

Caleb pointed sternly at the vampire, warning him to settle before gingerly hoisting him into his arms. Blush-worthy curses erupted from both their mouths as Caleb was attacked and Greasy-hair went on the defensive. I'm not sure what happened after the attempted eye-gouging, but silence suspiciously greeted the night. Greasy-hair's unnaturally lolling head and sudden, vacant expression was worrying.

'I think I snapped his neck,' Caleb murmured, a sheepish look on his face.

'That's just great, Caleb.'

'Oh, so this is my fault now?' He dropped Greasy back to the ground like a sack of potatoes.

I winced at the callousness. 'No, but maybe—'

'Maybe *what*? Would it have been better to leave him or whip out cutlery and go all Hannibal Lector on his ass?'

'You're the one who snapped his neck!'

'And you tried to puree him via the cobblestones.'

'Whatever,' I grumbled, terminating any further finger-pointing. 'What do we do with him now?'

'Leave him.'

'Out in the open? Big mistake.'

Caleb groaned. 'What's the worst that could happen?'

'The locals toasting marshmallows over his flaming carcass come sunrise?' I painted a pretty picture. Of course, it was more likely that the alley would be cordoned off with yellow tape and stuffed with cops scratching their heads, discussing spontaneous human combustion.

Caleb sighed, grabbing one of Greasy-hair's arms and dragging him towards a nearby dumpster. It was head first followed by two

13

mangled legs. Caleb was dusting his hands off in no time. 'Who would have thought we'd be dumping a body tonight? First time for everything, hey?'

'Actually, this isn't my first rodeo.'

Confounded, Caleb's crooked grin slipped as quickly as it had appeared. 'Do I even want to know?'

I shrugged, recalling the pulverised vânător I'd dragged through a public toilet in Croatia, unceremoniously dumping him on a pile of rotting vegetables. 'Let's keep some mystery between us, shall we?'

* * *

Crossing the threshold of the dimly-lit bar, I noted at least thirty vampires within the premises. Most huddled in leather-lined booths skirting the nicotine-stained walls, while others gathered around sporadically placed wooden tables and chairs in the centre. The solitary jockeyed stools by the bar, sipping drinks and avoiding chatter.

My first few steps drew enough unwanted attention that Caleb swung a proprietary arm across my shoulders again. 'Show some fang,' he ordered, smiling wide enough that his own pointed arsenal was showing.

I thought I looked stupid, but complied, smiling like I'd won the lottery. Really, who cared if I had fangs? Most patrons were back to staring at their blood-filled beer mugs or harassing the barman for another. Apparently it worked.

Caleb directed me to a secluded booth at the back of the room. He positioned himself in the corner to keep eyes on the bar while I sat feeling small and ineffectual, hidden behind the bulky back rest. 'Can we swap seats?'

'No.'

I supposed we were both dead anyway if someone picked a fight. It didn't particularly matter if I could see them coming.

I smoothed my palms across the semi-damp wood of the table before me. 'It's not really that special,' I commented, eyes mapping what I could see of the bar.

Smirking and pointing at the ceiling, Caleb said, 'What did you think it would be like? Humans hanging from the ceiling like chandeliers?'

I shuddered at the thought. 'That's gross and no. I was going for cheesy. You know, coffins, bats—that kind of thing, just in case humans wandered in.'

Caleb scoffed, turning his smile on the approaching barman instead. He was in his early forties, hair as pale as his flesh and lips as red as a rose. He was rather pretty for a man, especially when combined with silken threads more fitting to the early twentieth century.

'What can I get you?' the barman asked, looking first at Caleb and then turning curious attentions on me. Those soulful brown eyes were surprisingly non-threatening when paired with his crimson-lipped smile. In fact, I was betting his warm and rather friendly approach earned him more than a few monetary tips at the bar.

'I'll have an A positive and B negative,' Caleb answered.

'Would you like them warmed or chilled?'

Caleb seemed to consider the offer or perhaps was as distracted by the barman's mellifluous voice as I was. 'Warmed, please.'

'And for your guest?'

'I don't know, ask her. I'm a vampire, not a mind-reader.'

I rubbed my eyes, certain the glistening pools of chocolate the barman appraised me with were not really hosting a fireworks show behind the retinas. Entranced, part of me slipped willingly into the soothing warmth of his gaze. I was no stranger to compulsion, but was surprised that when sanity surfaced, I was clutching the barman's arm, a hairsbreadth from his protruding fangs.

'Give me any blood,' I gasped, snapping back like rubber against the booth, shaken and decidedly annoyed that Caleb had allowed this situation to occur.

The barman straightened, reworking that charming smile from earlier. 'I just received a fresh batch of AB positive from Synth Corp today. It's particularly nice with a bit of ice—that is—if you *are* tempted by what we serve?'

Caleb rapped his knuckles on the table-top, focusing narrowed eyes on the pretty barman. 'She'll have one of those, an AB Positive. No, make it two.'

For several tense seconds, the barman stood mute, eyes downcast. 'Very good.' He retreated thereafter, the rest of the bar continuing prior business. I hadn't even noticed how quiet the other patrons had become.

'Thanks for watching my back,' I snapped at Caleb. He shrugged, having no apology to offer. I really shouldn't have expected more.

The barman returned with our drinks in record time. I mumbled my thanks and pulled the chilled glass to my lips. The metallic tang of blood met with my tongue, bitter at first and then just as quickly sweet.

Synth blood is a product manufactured by Synth Corp, derived from vast amounts of willing human donations and various synthetic compounds. It isn't as smooth or crisp in flavour like fresh blood, but it's satisfying. Target markets are hospitals, veterinarians, general practices and private recovery centres, but the main purpose is to provide neutral bars with a constant supply.

'Ahem …'

I peered over the rim of my glass. The barman hovered disturbingly close. I decided to avoid all eye contact, looking to Caleb for instruction. He seemed to be studying the menu with gusto, ignoring my raised eyebrow.

Again, the barman cleared his throat, now rubbing fingers together right underneath my upturned nose. He wanted cash and Caleb was a cheapskate.

'Keep the change,' I said, sliding a bill across the table, careful to avoid further contact. He lingered only long enough to pocket his earnings.

'You know, Caleb, only a douche bag invites girls to bars and then makes them pay for drinks,' I said, tapping my half-empty glass.

'This isn't a date.'

I scratched my forehead, resigned. Arguing with a tight-ass was a pointless exercise. 'At least tell me what you know. Give me my money's worth. What did you find out about The Protectors?'

To cut an extremely long story short, The Protectors are part of an organisation known as the IMI or Institute of Magical Intervention. Their intent is to protect themselves and human interest with the magical abilities they inherited from their Romanian ancestors who attempted to defeat vampires some three hundred years previous.

At present key members including my adopted family—*The Manory's*—have disappeared. Multiple divisions of the IMI have closed down or relocated; none of Lucius's contacts uncovering evidence of their whereabouts.

'There isn't much to tell,' Caleb answered, gulping down a mouthful of blood. He licked the red stain from his lips and leant across the table. 'I went back to your house in Cairns and tried to pick up your family's scent, but the place was deserted.'

'Sebastian and I discovered that weeks ago. What about travel routes? Did you find anything at the bus station or airport?'

Caleb suddenly looked rather pleased with himself. 'They flew to Melbourne.'

Great. Progress. I felt my excitement rising as I urged him on.

'I compelled a lovely girl at the check-in counter at the airport. She gave me passenger logs for the estimated routes your family might have travelled out of Cairns. It took a few hours of searching computer files but—'

I applauded his efforts. Caleb had discovered more than I. After finding an empty house, I'd lost hope and headed back to Rome under Sebastian's advice. It had been decided that the search for The Protectors and my brother would be put on hold until after the multi-coven gathering.

Thousands of vampires converged on Rome over a week ago to discuss the missing Protectors, the end of the alliance between us and of course, the Vânătors collectively building an army at every border.

'Caleb, this is great. I'm slowly getting closer to finding Lucas. What else have you got?'

Caleb frowned. 'Correct me if I'm wrong, but he's a Protector, Elena. How can you want to find him so badly after everything the IMI has done to you over the years?'

'Lucas may be a Protector, but he is still my brother.'

'Not by blood. Susan and George Manory are not your real parents.'

Bitterness seeped into my voice. 'Oh, I am very aware of that, thank you, Caleb.'

For sixteen years I'd considered the Manory's family before I'd learnt the truth.

I was the IMI's pet project; the compositionally perfect blood running through my veins their only vested interest. I'd been handed a one-way ticket to headquarters in Bucharest: The plan;

use my blood and abilities to manufacture a weapon to effect against vampires.

We were still trying to get to the bottom of that.

'Susan and George played their roles,' I mused, nowhere near as grieved over my upbringing, capture and escape as I used to be. 'Lucas is different. We grew up together, Caleb. We may not be related by blood, but he's still my brother and it's my fault he's trapped with them now.'

'Elena you can't—'

'No. When Lucas discovered that Chester and the other scientists had kept me hostage, drained me of blood and locked me up for the Vânătors to find, he decided to leave the IMI. He stayed *only* because I needed him to learn more about the serum and its effects. Now key members of the IMI have gone underground and he's been sent with them. I have to help.'

Caleb took another swig of his drink, cerulean eyes glued to my face. 'What will you do if the information I give you sends you straight to them?'

I frowned like the question was surely rhetorical. 'I'll go and get Lucas.'

Uncharacteristic worry lines settled around Caleb's mouth. He leaned back against the cracked leather booth, folding his arms over his chest. 'See, that's what I was afraid you'd say.'

'What did you think I'd do with the information?'

'Give it to Lucius, find someone else to extract your brother for you. Finding the IMI could be very dangerous.'

I mirrored Caleb's posture, snorting in the most unladylike manner. 'Since when do you really care if something happens to me?'

'I care.'

'You care about currency.'

'Aw, now that's not nice. I helped you and Sebastian break into the IMI headquarters—which FYI—we were almost killed by a pack of vânătors after *your* blood.'

'Sebastian paid you quite handsomely for that.'

'Semantics.' Caleb shrugged, uncrossing his arms to run a finger over the rim of his glass. 'The point is, being around you is good for business. I don't want anything to happen to you.'

I rolled my eyes and downed the rest of my drink. The second glass beckoned. 'So what else have you got? Or do I need to whip out my cheque book?'

'First, tell me about Sebastian. I want to know where he is.'

'I haven't spoken to him since before the multi-coven gathering.'

'Elena ...'

'Caleb, I'm serious. After the gathering, Lucius sent him away, told him not to return until he'd located and destroyed the last nineteen alphas.'

'And the rest of the vampire populace?'

I absently waved at the bar patrons. 'Apparently sitting here is action enough. They're supposed to be learning how to defend themselves and the borders. If we want to prevent war—'

'War is inevitable,' Caleb interrupted, tapping on the tabletop like a woodpecker. 'Humans will eventually notice that the Vânătors have amassed thousands to fight and now that the alliance between protector and vampire has ended, the Vânătors will take advantage and the Humans will be the ones to suffer most.'

I mostly agreed. 'The Vânătors have an agenda, figuring it out is the problem. Sebastian and I thought that the Vânătors might have made a deal with The Protectors given the timing of these attacks and The Protector's disappearance.'

A loud crash lifted our gazes to a cloaked vampire sitting hunched in a corner booth, directly opposite our own. His mug had shattered, spilling crimson life in every direction across the stone flooring. The clandestine figure made no attempt to help the barman clear his mess.

'Sebastian mentioned some of your theories,' Caleb continued, recapturing my attention. 'You still think The Protectors have manufactured a synthetic compound boasting infallibility?'

I shrugged. 'Why else would the Vânătors be planning an attack on the most powerful coven in the world? I can only assume there's a trade-off and it isn't coming from the Vampires.'

'Why would The Protectors—supposed saviours of the human race—end a three hundred year alliance with us only to make good with the Wolves?'

'It's best guess, Caleb. The Protectors forged the alliance out of necessity. The Vânătors are not easy to eradicate. Staying neutral with vampires has provided The Protectors with protection, and given them time to create a way to destroy us.'

'So …'

'So, think about it. If you turn two enemies against each other and wait for war, all The Protectors have to do is finish off the wounded and claim ultimate victory. At least, that's what I'd do.'

'Your theory makes sense, but doesn't make it true.'

'Hence why Lucius is covering all avenues, sending Sebastian to track and hunt the Alphas while the rest of us help fight what is already on our doorstep.'

'How is Sebastian supposed to hunt and kill nineteen alphas by himself? If it was that simple, it would have been accomplished centuries ago.'

No point mentioning that one of Lucius's weird-ass visions had stopped that from happening. He'd seen me, his future daughter, a perfect blending of species better to be protected than eradicated.

'Sebastian won't be alone,' I grumbled, sticking on point.

'I checked with Nicholas and Eric, they aren't with him.'

'I know,' I answered, trying not to look sour. I'd been informed that Sebastian would be paired with William, my former love interest and Sebastian's estranged brother. They'd probably try to kill each other before the Vânätors did.

'Who's helping him?' Caleb repeated.

'William.' I grimaced. 'Not an ideal partnership, right? But since Lucius ordered it—'

'They have no real choice,' Caleb finished.

Nodding, I sighed heavily. I'd been trying not to think about Sebastian and William, hunting among the masses of snarling werewolves. My heart couldn't fathom the two of them fighting a losing battle.

As I forced myself to toss aside these troubling thoughts, I saw Caleb's face beginning to wrinkle in confusion. He had questions, the type I probably couldn't or wouldn't answer.

'Okay, I understand why Lucius sent Sebastian; he's the best tracker we have. Why William?'

I fixed him a deadpan stare. 'I'm assuming it's because William has a skillset of his own. He was responsible for wiping out the entire London pack, you know.'

'But …'

'No buts. If anyone can complete this mission, it's those two. I just think ten or twenty extra vampires to help Sebastian and William wouldn't have hurt anyone.' A disgruntled breath chased my deepening frown. I'd wanted to be one of those extra vampires. No one would have watched their backs better than me. I supposed Lucius had his reasons for sending them on a suicide mission.

Caleb pressed a fresh, steaming glass to his lips. 'You really like him, don't you?'

I scoffed and looked away, inadvertently locking eyes with the cloaked figure. The darkness beneath his hood twisted facial features, but of what I could see, I still thought he was oddly familiar.

'Elena?'

'I'm not discussing my relationships with you, Caleb.'

'I know you like Sebastian.'

'I also like cinnamon donuts. What's your point?' Dealing with emotional crap was not my forte. I'd recently learnt that Sebastian and I were bound—soulmates with several thousand lifetimes under our belt.

Stranger than fiction, right?

And William? He'd introduced me to the world of vampires and also managed to alienate me. He'd lied about my father and abandoned me at the IMI. Sometimes I still felt driven by the urge to peg hard, metallic objects at his head.

'What else did you find out about The Protectors?' I said, attempting to change the subject.

'You haven't given me enough information on Sebastian.'

'What do you want? I don't know where he is, Caleb and neither of them are returning my calls.'

'Do you think they're okay?'

Bile burned at the back of my throat, so I downed the rest of my drink, subduing the acidic taste. 'Enough. Tell me what else you've uncovered.'

Caleb's lips pressed together in a dissatisfied line. 'I didn't learn anything else useful from Cairns, but Melbourne is another story.'

'Are The Protector's still there?'

'No, but after checking those passenger logs I was telling you about, their names came up along with quite a few others.'

'Such as?'

'Unimportant,' Caleb replied. 'What is important is that their party was joined by the Sydney faction of the IMI as well as the new boarding members in Melbourne.'

'Where did they go?'

'Are you ready for this?' Caleb teased, leaning forward conspiratorially. 'Hobart.'

'Hobart?' I echoed. 'What the hell?'

'I was hoping you had answers.'

'Did the trail go cold after that?'

Caleb nodded. 'No record of any outbound flights with any airline from that point on.'

'What about trains, buses—that kind of thing?'

'Zilch. I compelled everyone with transport logs, but couldn't uncover anything.'

'Are you sure they're still there?'

'Interesting you should say that,' Caleb remarked. 'I thought perhaps I was missing something, but on my way back to Rome, I asked Eric to meet me in Hong Kong. There are a few members of a faction of Protectors he knows that used to operate out of Kowloon, but even those associates have disappeared.'

'What about the faction's base of operations?'

'Still accounted for, but the Protectors that were present knew nothing of the current crisis or when and where the senior members of their faction had departed.'

'What does the Kowloon branch have to do with Cairns?'

He waved impatiently. 'Eric learned that a week before your Australian factions left for Hobart, the Kowloon clan also boarded a plane for the same destination. I then contacted a friend in Santiago who confirmed similar details.' He rapped on the table again to nail home his point. 'As far as I can tell, Elena, all branches have headed to Hobart.'

'Why?'

Caleb shrugged. 'Maybe lavender is an ingredient in the serum?'

I was unamused. 'No, my blood is the base ingredient.'

We were interrupted, yet again, as the cloaked vampire fumbled a second mug, its contents now strewn across the recently mopped floor. What was with this guy? Vampires are not clumsy; their reflexes too quick to drop anything by mistake.

Unease settled over me. 'I think we should get out of here,' I said to Caleb. 'I have a very bad feeling.'

'I think you could be right,' Caleb whispered. He stood abruptly, holding out his hand. 'I know you rode here on Sebastian's motorbike, but I think I should take you back to the villa via the underground tunnels.'

Across the room, those hooded eyes now watched me with baleful purpose. Thus I quickly slid my hand into Caleb's. 'I'm being hunted again, aren't I?'

'Let's just say that I think we should stick together until you're safe at home.'

'Lucius will hear us approach in the tunnels.'

Caleb yanked me to my feet. 'What would be worse: having your throat torn out by that weirdo in the cloak or Lucius yell at you?'

'Honestly?'

'Elena ...'

'Seriously, I'm leaning towards Option One.'

We were already heading for the door, eyes fixed on the deathly-still figure watching us unabashedly. 'Option One means you're dead.'

'Being mauled to death would actually be quicker and less painful.'

'You're only saying that because you're addicted to the adrenaline rush of riding Sebastian's motorbike.'

I tried to look outraged and failed. It was common knowledge how I felt about cars and motorbikes.

Back in the alley I evaded another attempt at a piggy-back ride despite Caleb's ongoing protestations.

I couldn't possibly leave Sebastian's bike in the middle of Rome, so I attempted renegotiation. 'I have to take the bike so I'll give you a lift wherever you need to go.'

Caleb was losing patience. 'Look, I usually don't give a shit, but if anything happens to you, I'm pretty sure my bank accounts will be drained and so will I.'

'Think about this logically. Lucius will hear us in the tunnels and figure out that a vampire helped me.'

'Wait, are you saying that if I don't help you ... again ... you'll turn me in, tell Lucius I took you to a neutral bar and helped you sneak out of the villa?'

'That's generally how blackmail works.'

Caleb scoffed, looking down at the top of his scuffed biker boots. 'You wouldn't.'

'I'm pretty sure I would if I have to.'

'I don't think I like you, Elena.'

'I don't like that you made me pay for drinks.'

Caleb cursed and kicked the edge of Greasy-hair's dumpster, finally looking back up at me with ire. 'Fine. Where the hell did you park the bike?!'

CHAPTER TWO: DECEPTION

Julius couldn't believe his luck. Never one to have fate shine upon him, it seemed auspicious being swept up in the hands of good fortune now. Julius had come to the neutral bar, wary of hunting humans with so much vampiric presence policing the city. He ached for the taste of freshly spilled blood, but had opted to slake his thirst by surrendering to conformity. He wasn't a fan of the rules set by his oldest adversary, but forsaking a beating pulse beneath his lips had proven providential.

Elena was here!

Julius pulled the grey cloak tighter around himself, hiding his face deeper in shadow. A smile formed at the corners of his lips. He was already counting the ways he could torture and kill her; the ultimate revenge against his long-time enemy, Lucius Valerius.

Two thousand years had passed since Lucius murdered Julius's wife. He would never forget the look in her eyes or the stench of combined fear as Lucius's blade plunged deep and true. Julius should have also fallen victim, but as a thrall, he was only vulnerable to direct sunlight, silver and beheading.

He would never stop seeking justice for all he had lost.

Julius tentatively clasped the lukewarm mug of blood he'd ordered. He craned his neck, blocking out all other sound as he focused solely on Elena's conversation.

'Apparently sitting here is action enough,' Elena said in a mocking tone. 'They're supposed to be learning how to defend themselves and the borders. If we want to prevent war—'

'War is inevitable,' the pink-haired vampire answered with certainty. He tapped the tabletop with black-painted fingernails. 'Humans will eventually notice that the Vânătors have amassed thousands to fight and now that the alliance between Protector and vampire has ended, the Vânătors will take advantage and the Humans will be the ones to suffer most.'

Julius released the full extent of his smile, pregnant with power. He was more knowledgeable than most, the instigator behind the brewing war. A deal had been made with the Alpha Roshan; the death of the Italian coven in exchange for Elena. Of course, Julius had no intention of giving Elena to the wolves. He now had nefarious plans of his own.

'The Vânătors have an agenda,' Elena continued. 'Figuring it out is the problem. Sebastian and I thought that the Vânătors might have made a deal with The Protectors given the timing of these attacks and The Protector's disappearance.'

What?!

Julius's mug met with the floor, broken pieces scattering far and wide. Blood seeped across the stone like a living thing, following nooks and crannies in the grout before the barman attempted to eradicate the spill. The action drew the attention of both Elena and her companion. They looked upon him as a stranger, unable to detect the menacing need for revenge that rode him.

Julius listened more closely as Elena and the pink-haired vampire settled back into uneasy conversation, Elena still watching him.

'Sebastian mentioned some of your theories. You still think The Protectors have manufactured a synthetic compound boasting infallibility?'

Elena finally looked away, focusing back on her companion. 'Why else would the Vânătors be planning an attack on the most powerful coven in the world? I can only assume there's a trade-off and it isn't coming from the Vampires.'

A trade off ... The thought whispered through Julius's mind. *Is it possible that The Protectors have invented a synthetic compound to make lesser beings as capable as vampires?*

26

The Protectors had been nothing but a trifling inconvenience to Julius in the past—a small bump on the road to vengeance. Now the possibility of their interference was troubling. He'd think on it some more later.

Julius listened intently to the rest of Elena's conversation, amused that Sebastian and William had been sent to their inevitable death, but also curious about Elena's origins. Julius certainly didn't expect to hear that she'd been raised by Protectors—a world away from Lucius. What had gone wrong?

'What does the Kowloon branch have to do with Cairns?' Elena asked, leaning forward, eagerness palpable.

The pink-haired vampire waved to silence her inquisitiveness. 'Eric learned that a week before your Australian factions left for Hobart, the Kowloon clan also boarded a plane for the same destination. I then contacted a friend in Santiago who confirmed similar details. As far as I can tell, Elena, all branches have headed to Hobart.'

'Hobart? What the hell?'

Julius smirked. Elena was nothing like her father. Certainly they shared similar looks: dark, chestnut hair and eyes that sparkled green and topaz, but her mouth was anything but resplendent. She spoke without care for consequence.

The pink-haired vampire shrugged. 'Maybe lavender is an ingredient in the serum?'

'No, my blood is the base ingredient.'

Shock saw a secondary mug find the floor. Its ceramic surface slipped through Julius's fingers like butter, reflexes failing him as the mug shattered, spilling the residual contents.

No wonder Roshan wants her!

The bar's patrons swivelled in their seats again, curious. The barman had rapidly progressed to annoyed, shaking his head and cursing what he believed to be a deliberate act. Vampires were not clumsy. Julius needed to leave, already drawing too much attention, but Elena and her companion made the first move, hurriedly leaving the bar, fear the stench that oozed from her pores.

Julius gave pause and then exited within seconds of their departure. He was vaguely surprised to find the alleyway deserted. A deep inhalation uncovered the faint smell of death, exhaust fumes and the lingering scent of the pink-haired vampire's cologne. He'd just missed them.

Throwing the grey, hooded cloak back from his face, Julius promptly took his leave all the while considering his next move. Hunting Elena would be a delight, but steeling himself for upcoming events was more practical. He urgently needed to find Roshan.

* * *

Roshan surveyed the sprawling city of Grenoble from his hotel window, beautiful and idyllic, it was nestled at the base of the Alps; nothing like Paris—the city of his past.

Elena, now at one with her vânător nature had destroyed any pleasant memories Roshan might have had of that city when she'd dispassionately dispatched every member of his pack. Commanding her as he'd done in the past via his alpha timbre had proven ineffectual. Her wolf was strong, determined and quite possibly his equal.

Roshan detested having no claim to a territory and sorely missed the Parisian pack he'd spent years populating and commanding. 'Typical,' he muttered, turning away from the picturesque setting outside. 'I should have *taken* her when I had the chance.'

'Taken who?' Elias asked, entering the hotel room and slamming the door behind him.

'No one.' Roshan snapped, having no intention of telling the other alphas about Elena and her ties to their kin. She was the first female of their kind—albeit half vampire—but capable of breeding the ultimate vânător. Besides, he wanted Elena for himself.

'It doesn't sound like it,' Elias persisted.

Roshan scrubbed a hand over his still swollen face, his last encounter with Elena proving almost fatal. 'I ignored the call of flesh last night and now I have regrets.'

Elias laughed, sinking into a nearby sofa. Tonight he embodied a young girl—his latest victim—her blood moulding his ability to shape-shift. Roshan never bothered with children—too small to be satisfying.

'There's always time for pleasure. That's how we build our armies. The more seed you release in human women, the more of us there will be.'

Roshan offered a droll look. 'I am aware of how the process works.'

'There's still time for another victim. The sun won't rise for two hours hence.'

Roshan shook his head, the long, dark threads of his hair brushing against his deeply tanned cheeks. 'No. I'm expecting company.'

Elias's delicate eyebrow rose. 'Who?'

'The vampire Julius. I've been informed that he attempted to cross the border a few hours ago. I presume he's trying to locate me.'

'Is that why you are here and not at the caves?' Elias asked, turning his nose up at the modest furnishings of the rented room.

'I won't risk our current location.'

'Excellent.' Elias relaxed further against the cushioning. 'What does the vampire want?'

'Probably the attacks to commence sooner rather than later.'

Elias nodded, small hands absently smoothing the blonde ponytails away from his creamy shoulders. 'The other alphas and I have our concerns about following this current path.'

Roshan tampered his outrage by cracking each knuckle in turn. *Crack, crack, crack.* Had they not been over this already? 'The goal is to obtain the ability to self-heal. Our immortality is flawed—our bodies weak and vulnerable.'

Elias nodded again, blonde pony tails bouncing with renewed vigour. 'Perhaps our reluctance stems from not understanding the vampire's role in this arrangement. The Protectors offered the serum before their disappearance, but—'

'Julius's goals are the same as ours.'

Elias persisted. 'What did the vampire offer you to initiate war in the first place?'

Roshan turned away, uncertain his eyes wouldn't betray him. Elena was a well-kept secret he had no reason to share. 'He offered me nothing.'

'Then why have you not killed him?'

'He could be useful.'

Elias looked understandably confused, but let the matter rest … for now. 'Are you certain the alliance has been severed between vampire and the IMI?'

'Of course,' Roshan barked. 'It was an uneasy alliance to begin with.'

'Aren't you worried *why* The Protectors offered the serum?' Elias was studying Roshan's reactions closely from behind feathery lashes.

'I'm not so naive to think that they will stick to their end of the bargain, but even you have to admit that if they do, the reward will be … priceless.'

Elias pried himself from the sofa cushions and joined Roshan by the window. 'Reluctant though some of us are, we will stand by you, brother.

We have not survived the last three hundred years by turning our backs on each other.' Elias clutched Roshan's bulky arm in his tiny hand. 'We just hope that you're telling us everything we need to know.'

Roshan patted Elias's hand. 'I speak the truth when I say that I fight for our immortality.' Anything else would have been a lie.

Elias pried his fingers free. 'Then I'll leave you to your meeting.' He made haste for the hotel door. 'We'll wait for you to report back at the den.'

Roshan's answering smile was contrived, cheeks pulled unnaturally tight as he waited for the door to close behind his pack mate. Taking a shaky breath did little to steady fraying nerves. Lying to his kin, wiping out the Italian coven, killing Julius, finding The Protectors and reclaiming Elena all made for a busy week.

Could he pull it all off?

Freshly laundered linens and spicy apples tugged at Roshan's nostrils. The vampire was close.

Roshan opted to sit on the sofa, uncertain if his wobbly knees would keep him upright. He ran nervous fingers back and forth across the rough fabric, absently picking at pilling as he waited.

Julius was suddenly perched beside him, blue eyes pulsing with the kind of madness that renders unease. 'I'm sorry; did I frighten you, Wolf?' Julius murmured, leaning close.

Roshan opened his mouth to speak, but abruptly pursed his lips. The rhythmic pounding of his startled heart was answer enough.

Julius pulled a leg towards his chest, resting his foot on the edge of the cushioning. His arm he draped casually across his knee.

'Shall I start? Fine. I hear you are busy making deals with The Protectors.'

Roshan—rendered momentarily speechless—couldn't disengage from the steely orbs of blue glaring back at him. He was shocked to learn that Julius knew of his double dealings and equally compelled to remain quiet as he didn't believe he owed the vampire explanation.

'You do not answer me, Roshan? Could this be confirmation that our accord has perished?'

'My pack mates are ready at the borders for an attack on Rome's covens as we speak. What more do you ask of me?'

'You have betrayed my trust.'

Roshan laughed. 'What trust is there between enemies?'

'That may be so, but we had an agreement.'

'The deal still stands.'

'Not if you are dealing with The Protectors.'

'I am upholding my end of the bargain,' Roshan growled. 'Whom else I talk to is not your concern.'

'I know about the serum,' Julius barked. 'I know why the IMI sought you out to kill the Vampires.'

'And?'

'And I think putting your faith in those that once had an alliance with my kind would be a mistake.'

'I believe the humans call it *hedging their bets*.'

Julius shook his head. 'Do you truly believe that the IMI will give you the serum?'

Roshan snorted. 'Of course they won't.'

'Then why the arrangement?'

'Sooner or later their representative *Chester* or someone else will seek us out to learn of our progress.'

'And you plan to kill them?'

'No, I plan to track them.'

Julius slid off the arm of the chair, dropping down rather inelegantly onto the cushioned seat. 'Smart, Wolf. I didn't expect you to be so clever.'

'And that, *Vampire*, is why you have underestimated *me*.'

Julius's returned smile was laced with wicked intent. 'Perhaps I have.' He began to drum his fingers upon the arm of the chair in which he'd previously resided, quiet in his contemplation. 'This is why you wait, is it not?'

Roshan stared blankly.

'I have seen your packs as I passed into France. You have more than enough to equally match the Vampires in battle.'

'What is your point?'

'I want this finished. The two vampires William Granville and his brother Sebastian Marcellus are currently tracking you—bad for business I would think.'

'They'll never find us.'

'Then you underestimate Sebastian's abilities.'

'I very much doubt that, but I will still not attack until I am ready.'

Julius's fingers continued to beat mercilessly upon the tattered upholstery. 'What if I told you that I know where the hidden Protectors are?'

Roshan's eyes narrowed to suspicious slits. 'I would say that you want something.'

'Yes, I want you to attack before Lucius has a chance to train the newly relegated vampires he has helping to fight his cause. In your delay to attack Rome, he summoned a multi-coven gathering and enlisted the help of many more of our kind.'

'A multi-coven gathering?'

Julius sighed, pinching the bridge of his nose in annoyance. 'Have you learnt nothing of your quarry over the last three hundred years?'

The growl that had steadily been building momentum within Roshan's throat finally erupted. 'I eat you. I don't study you!'

'Well, if you'd bothered to educate yourself and pack you'd know that a multi-coven gathering summons vampires worldwide—the most recent to discuss how best to combat you!'

Fangs now bared, Roshan leapt at Julius, taloned nails catching and ripping through any visibly exposed flesh, but the assault was fleeting, Roshan baulking at further attack as the pale hands now wrapped around his throat threatened to crush his windpipe. This was precisely why Roshan needed the serum; immortality a mere illusion while plagued by the fragility of irreparable flesh.

'Release me,' Roshan begged, gasping for breath.

'Why?'

'Without me this war will never begin.'

'Do you rule all the Alphas?' Julius asked, clasped fingers marginally easing around Roshan's jugular.

'At present they confer to me.'

Julius tossed Roshan aside, dusting his hands as if clearing garbage from the very surface of his pallid skin. Roshan gasped for air, massaging his swollen oesophagus. 'Be careful, Wolf,' Julius cautioned, lips pursed at the holes Roshan's talons had left in his clothing. 'I am not someone that you want to cross.'

'Noted,' Roshan rasped, humiliated as he reclaimed control over his vocal chords.

'Now, before I was so rudely interrupted,' Julius murmured, 'Lucius's multi-coven gathering has now made all vampires aware of your intentions. The longer you leave the attack; the more time they have to prepare for a defence of their cities.'

Eyes flashing with further defiance, Roshan said, 'Hurt me if you will, but I will not attack until I am ready.'

'Do not make me hit you across the nose with a rolled up newspaper, Wolf. Were you not listening when I told you that I know where The Protectors are?'

'Then where are they?'

'No. First we come to a new arrangement and then I tell you what you want to know.'

Roshan's nostrils flared though he kept his temper in check. 'What are your terms?'

'I want you to attack Rome as of tomorrow night—no more stalling.'

'And ...'

'Giving you Elena is off the table. She has become important to my own plans.'

'I will kill you to claim her.'

'Then pray you find her and the serum first. Your life expectancy just shortened considerably.'

Roshan snarled, protruding teeth chaffed the edges of his lower lip. Elena was a precious commodity, but the power of the serum was an equaliser difficult to surpass. 'Fine,' he answered, tone clipped. 'Give me the information I need.'

Julius was standing in an instant, straightening his partly shredded cloak as he made way for the exit. 'I'd start by looking in Hobart, Australia. It was their last known destination for all key members of the IMI.' He clasped the handle tightly and pulled. Light from the shabby exterior corridor spilled into the darkened room. 'Remember, I want the attacks to begin tomorrow night.'

Before Roshan could question Julius further he disappeared, the soft click of the closing door the only accompaniment to his departure.

Roshan melted into the sofa cushions, tension easing considerably in his rigidly set shoulders. He absently rubbed at his throat again, annoyed that the impending bruises would mark his submission to the rest of the packs.

He tested his voice again, the sound scratchy and vulnerable, but not enough to stop him from reaching into his back pocket, determined to investigate Julius's findings. Cell phone in hand, he began to organise a search group, relaying what little information he'd received to set this new plan in motion.

CHAPTER THREE: HUNTING

Sebastian crept silently through the trees, his footsteps feather light and eyes focused on the distance ahead. Leaves from protruding ground shrubs tickled the sides of his leather-clad legs while low hanging tree branches easily ensnared clothing or tangled in the silken locks of his sable hair.

Ignoring all distraction, Sebastian focused on cradling his vampiric self, expanding the parameters of capability. Skin translucent, talons drawn and eyes bleeding to black; he was without weakness, his agenda simply the hunt.

Under an absent moon the night was a suffocating blanket of darkness. Vampiric vision helped by opening his retinas beyond limitation and soon thick shadow morphed to a rich canvas of colour—leaves glowed with green iridescence and dirt moved in puffs of cinnamon coloured smoke at his feet.

'They're close,' William whispered, crouching beside him.

'I know.'

'There's more than usual.'

'No more than before, William.'

In a small clearing a mile ahead, the steady thrum of heartbeats laid a musical path directly to a party of vânǎtors. Sebastian and William had encountered small groups every few miles and had managed to avoid most, but there were some they hunted with purpose.

'We might get lucky this time.'

'Let's hope so,' Sebastian replied, placing his palms against the dry earth, feeling for even the slightest of vibrations.

Seventeen, eighteen vânători?

'What are you doing?' William asked him.

'Listening.'

William snorted his disbelief, but Sebastian ignored him, knowing that centuries of hunting various enemies had taught him numerous lessons. Patience, camouflage, anticipating movement and understanding their strengths and weaknesses were all important. He couldn't afford to rush now with so much at stake.

'Your techniques are slowing us down,' William complained.

'They are keeping us alive.'

'Debateable,' William added, studying the dried blood that coated his hands. His nose simultaneously wrinkled, a small breeze wafted the scent of death from the surface of their dirtied skin, swirling in the very air around them. He sought out the chain Sebastian had placed around his neck days earlier garnished with tufts of vânător fur, urine, blood and other questionable discharges. 'Is this necklace of death really necessary?'

Sebastian was hasty in his glance at William's dour face. 'It's disguising our own scents. I've explained this to you already.'

'I never needed this when I hunted John and the London pack.'

'That's probably why it took you two years,' Sebastian answered, focusing back on the movements in the clearing ahead.

William's nostrils flared, his anger a simmering emotion threatening to erupt in uncontrollable rage. His hands curled into fists and a growl sat snug in the back of his throat, but he wouldn't risk exposure simply for want of sibling pulverisation. 'So what are we looking at?' He snapped. 'What has the forest floor told you?'

'I feel seventeen,' Sebastian answered, choosing to ignore his brother's impertinent tone. He closed his eyes and listened once more. 'Make that eighteen. One of them is injured.'

'What do you want to do?'

'Right now they're distracted so we should be able to sneak fairly close.'

'You want me to create a diversion again, don't you?'

Sebastian nodded. 'The ones that follow you are useless to our cause—mere followers. We need to single out the more mature members of the packs. They'll be the ones that stay behind to finish eating what's left of their kill.'

William's scowl seemed to have taken up permanent residence. 'This plan didn't work last time.'

'No, but we did learn more about the hierarchy and what to expect from larger packs.'

William's uncontainable ire finally erupted, spittle flying from his lips as he snarled, 'you weren't the one that had a set of teeth buried an inch deep in your ass!'

Sebastian pretended to examine the surrounding earth with gusto, determined to hide the mile-wide grin that formed upon his lips. 'You healed.'

'Luckily!'

'Hopefully this time we'll find ourselves an alpha.'

William took a deep, audible breath to calm himself. 'Sebastian,' he started, voice still riddled with tension. 'We've been out here for a week and all we've managed to do is kill a few random groups of vânători and probably raise suspicion. I'm starting to think that the Alphas won't be hiding in the wilderness with their packs.'

'You think they're in the cities?'

'The cities make them harder to track. I don't think—'

'Look,' Sebastian interrupted, mirth finally shelved. 'I don't disagree with you. It makes sense, but we know from Elena's intel that the Alphas must be close in order to keep the pack submitting. Yes, there is loyalty and they will follow to some degree, but direct alpha command does not work over great distances.'

William flinched at the mention of Elena's name—everything still too raw and unresolved. 'Whatever. This is your show.'

'William, I do value—'

'No. Lucius put you in charge, so let's just get on with it. I'm not going to argue I just want this done so I can get back to her.'

Sebastian—only slightly more emotionally evolved than his brother—contained the shudder evoked when imagining Elena and William intimate. Elena—as far as he was concerned—was his, the very reason he had given up his status as the Archangel Michael and forsaken an eternity in paradise. 'Like I said,' Sebastian murmured, 'you create a diversion and I'll come in from behind.'

William nodded once, turning on his heels and disappearing into the tree line. Was it always going to be like this between them? Was William always going to blame Sebastian for his misguided actions in the past?

'Focus,' Sebastian muttered, dispelling all other thoughts. He was supposed to be hunting alphas!

In the distance, wolves that he could clearly see still periodically dipped their heads to feed on the fresh carcass of a brown bear. The two within immediate view coveted most of the kill, growling at one another over portion size. The subordinates—often blurred tufts of fur—darted in and out, tearing away pieces of meat and bone before scattering to safer distances.

Sebastian crept closer, one eye on the Vânătors and one on William already circling the perimeter, staying downwind and avoiding noisy foliage. The Vânătors remained engrossed in their kill, oblivious to impending threat.

An inevitable fight soon broke out amongst the frenzied feeders, marked by snapping snouts and the rabid clawing of flesh. Assertive growls of dominance settled most of the pack, the two gluttonous wolves at the helm not particularly open to sharing. It was William snapping a thick tree branch in the distance and throwing it against the forest floor with a *thud* that rendered the entire loitering pack into utter silence. Their pointed ears swivelled in all directions, hackles rising and paws tensed for attack.

Another branch crashed to the ground, a *thud* more determined than the last. Every vânător flinched, claws extending, eyes forward. The two dominates lifted their snouts and sniffed, flesh pulled back from their blood-covered muzzles revealing numerous rows of very sharp, pointed teeth.

William had been made.

Most sprung to their feet, spurred on by the sound of more tree branches crashing noisily to the ground. Snarls sounded in warning, a few tentative steps in William's direction the signal of their intent. As hind legs reared, muscles tensed and fangs were bared, the subordinates leapt into the brush leaving the two larger, more dominate wolves as expected.

Sebastian waited, listening. As the fading footfalls hit the five kilometre parameter, he decided to strike.

He stalked with purpose, the weight of his vampiric form barely disturbing the soil beneath his booted soles. Awareness seeped through every pore, his senses heightened—resolve unchallenged.

Sebastian could hear the warm fluids that dripped from their eager fangs onto blades of grass at their paws. He could smell the cloying aroma of blood and the stench of sweaty vânător fur as if inhaling perfume straight from the bottle. He could now see the plaque gathering at gum level and the tiny pieces of raw bear meat caught between fangs as well as taste the anticipation of hollow victory on his own tongue.

With only fifty feet between them now, Sebastian lowered back into a crouch and closed his eyes, praying for the soul of the creature he was about to kill. Before conscience could permit indecision, Sebastian sailed through the air and towards his intended victim.

Landing deftly next to the first of his prey, he snapped its neck before protest was even uttered. The second barely looked up before Sebastian was atop his hairy back, dislocating the wolf's shoulder and sending him sailing nose first into the dirt with a strangled howl.

'Be still,' Sebastian murmured, voice calm. He slowly dismounted the vânător, circling and studying him. Its eyes were wider than dollar coins, shiny and rimmed with a healthy dose of fear. Its breath came in putrid smelling wafts, tainted with the sweet smell of a fresh kill. 'Vânător ....' Sebastian said, injecting some authority. 'I want you to revert to human form so that I may speak freely with you.'

The wolf snarled, defiant despite its current physical shortcomings, but fear still swam in the murky depths of its black, soulless eyes.

'I will be forced to keep hurting you until you do tell me what I need to know.'

A howl of pack distress snapped both Sebastian's and the wolf's heads to the right. Both contemplated the moment as silence quickly pursued the initial outburst.

'Well,' Sebastian said, looking back down at his captive again, 'I wonder what that was all about?'

The vânător refocused on Sebastian, snarling louder and more defiantly than before. It tried gaining footing within the grass and dirt, but remained unsuccessful, the dislocated shoulder undoubtedly hampering its efforts.

'It's done,' William shouted as he cleared the trees, skidding to stop beside his brother and the injured wolf. 'What did I miss?'

Sebastian assessed the latest arrival. 'I see you are free of bite marks.'

William scoffed, circling the wolf, perhaps studying its weaknesses. 'Barely.'

'How long do we have before the rest of the pack circles back around?'

William smiled, a rather rare occurrence around Sebastian, so he must have been pleased with a certain turn in events. 'They won't be coming back.'

'No?'

'Let's just say that the Vânǎtors thought running after me over the edge of a particularly deep ravine was a good idea.' William toed the injured vânǎtor by their feet, the satisfied smile vanishing as he knelt close to whisper, 'Would you like to try it?'

The vânǎtor looked decidedly uneasy. One vampire had dislocated its shoulder and the other had apparently wiped sixteen members of its pack off the face of the earth.

'Last chance,' Sebastian said quietly. 'You know what we're capable of now.'

Black eyes drifted between each vampire. Surprisingly, uncertainty soon swayed to obstinacy and considering its current predicament, the vânǎtor was either a moron or a masochist. To be outnumbered and continue to defy? Not brave, simply stupid.

'So be it.' Sebastian stepped back to allow William opportunity to negotiate. Tracking was *his* speciality—everything else was William's department or so he'd made clear on numerous occasions of late.

A small silver blade was retrieved from the waistband of William's pants. He casually twirled the hilt between deft fingers, careful not to touch the blade as silver was just as harmful to vampires as to the creature huddled at his feet.

Three hundred years of extrication from family and the Roman Guard had made him bad-tempered and impatient and before Sebastian could protest this avenue of torture, William hastily claimed one of the wolf's long, pointed ears and sliced it clean from the base with one unceremonious flick of the wrist. It would never grow back. A vânǎtor could not self-heal.

The wolf cast its snout to the sky, howling loud enough that birds over a mile away took flight, searching for alternate shelter within the night. Insects and other animals clicked and brayed at the sound, cowering as they scampered deeper into the forest's cover.

William was remorseless. His actions were driven by the terror vânătors willingly inflicted on their victims. Even as he watched the bleeding, whimpering ball of fur in front of him, no moment of regret arose. 'Are you ready to talk yet? Or do I need to chop off something vital?'

Seconds without response and William was already kicking the wolf onto its side, breaking three ribs in the process and puncturing a lung. Strangled sounds of indescribable pain that were choked with vital fluids spilled from the beaten wolf's throat. Sebastian struggled to watch, flinching at the hasty brutality, knowing it was effective, but nevertheless soul-destroying.

William hunted around in its pelt with the pointed tip of his blade until he found the base of its reproductive organs. The Vânător stiffened, whimpering a reoccurring symphony of desired mercy. The tip now pierced flesh, drawing a meagre line of blood.

'William ...'

The wolf began to shed its fur, the muted grey morphing into the pinkish hue of humanity. Limbs extended and bones snapped and reformed. Arms and legs shaped themselves, transforming paws into hands and feet. Claws retracted and black eyes melted away, replaced with milky brown ones brimming with unshed tears.

Relentless, William kept the knife firmly in place despite evidence to suggest the mangled and beaten creature was not going anywhere. The vânător took deep gasping breaths, sucking air through its newly formed oesophagus and into its punctured lungs as best as it could.

'First you answer our questions and then I'll move the knife,' William said, purposely drawing more blood.

'Please,' the vânător wheezed. 'I can't run. I can't even move and I can barely breathe. I'm not going anywhere.'

William saw reason and lowered the knife, prompted by a pleading look from Sebastian. He tucked the bloodstained instrument of justice back into the waistband of his pants, not nearly as satisfied by the wolf's answer as Sebastian.

'Do you know why we are hunting you?' Sebastian asked, squatting to remain at eyelevel with his foe.

'The same reason your kind always hunts us—to exterminate our species.'

'Then you know what we are going to ask you?'

The vânător spat a mouthful of blood onto the ground before him, missing Sebastian's boot by an inch. He wiped a shaking hand across his trembling lips, nodding. 'You want to know where the Alphas are.'

'Very good, Wolf. Now tell us what we need to know,' William commanded.

The vânător twitched, looking uncertainly between its enemies. 'I c-can't.'

William viciously prodded its broken ribs with his steel-capped boot, eliciting a fresh round of pain-filled moans of protest. 'You don't know how much your life depends on answering our questions.' He patted the waistband of his pants to emphasise.

'You don't understand,' it pleaded. 'I literally *can't* tell you. My alpha commanded it. No one can know. The success of the war depends on it.'

'I'm getting tired of hearing that,' William muttered to no one in particular.

Sebastian could hardly disagree as he absently massaged his chin, deep in thought. He had a moment of self-depreciation where he considered his idiocy in not drawing conclusions sooner. 'Can you *show* us where they are?'

The Vânător's face crumpled in a myriad of conflicting emotions. Conformity urged it to zip its lips together; the threat of its life made it stutter with uncertainty. 'I ... w-what?'

'*Show* us where they are,' Sebastian repeated.

'I ...' It was obvious the vânător was at a loss, torn between protecting its alpha and saving its own skin. Its bindings of secrecy were not nearly as well tied as they should have been.

William was quick to act, mercilessly yanking the vânător to its feet. The wolf cried out, clasping a limp hand across its chest. 'I can't breathe,' it choked, staggering in William's hold.

'Do I look like I care?' William grunted. 'Start walking.'

The vânător was shoved into the underbrush where it fell to its knees, belching more blood and gasping for breath that struggled to come. It was vertical in an instant, William grabbing its good ear and jerking it upright. Its torturous cries could be heard for miles.

'William ...' Sebastian murmured. 'Have care.'

The cycle of pain was destined to repeat itself with William at the helm.

Sebastian shook his head, resigned to shadowing William and surrendering to patience.

They both remained in vampiric form, wary of the vânător's intentions, uncertain if it was leading them to the Alphas or into denser packs. Either way, death had been a likely proposition from the day they were set this task.

'If the creature leads us in the right direction there's still a very good chance we won't survive nineteen alphas,' Sebastian whispered in Latin—an old language that the vânător would hopefully be unfamiliar.

William appeared to agree. 'We don't have a choice. Lucius said we must keep going until the Alphas are dead. If we return with the task incomplete, then we might as well have died in this forest.'

Sebastian's brow creased. Did William still think so little of the master vampire? There was no denying the man had done evil over the centuries, but redemption was not beyond him—especially now. 'We have to stay strong and overcome the odds despite the fear.'

William remained impassive, eyes neatly fixed on the limping vânător ahead. 'Fear is a luxury I cannot afford.'

'Fear is a reasonable response to this situation, brother. I fear that I will not be able to protect you when the battle finally begins.'

William scoffed. 'I only fear what I'll lose if I'm no longer around to covet it.'

'What do you mean?'

'You should know this. Dying vampiric offers only a true death in the pits of hell. Our souls are damned and without opportunity for reincarnation.' He laughed, though it was humourless. 'Well … mine is.'

Sebastian bowed his head in acknowledgement, knowing that this too was his last time on Earth. Their chosen father—Tiberius—was one of Lucius's thralls, damned and no longer capable of repeating a cycle of existence. 'Don't you think we should make peace then?'

'What for?'

'We are brothers, William. What happened in the past is history; I don't want either of us leaving this plane of existence and not being united.'

'You are not my brother,' William spat. 'You know as well as I do that you never have been. Yes, you are always Tiberius's first born son, but it's not what you really are. You shouldn't even be here.'

Sebastian was rendered momentarily speechless. 'So you do know?'

'Of course I know.'

'How?'

'Araqiel told me what I needed to know and I deduced the rest. I guess he thought by telling me you were the Archangel Michael that I might back off from Elena and let you have her.'

'But you won't.'

'No.'

Sebastian could barely place one foot in front of the other let alone field an acceptable response. How could he possibly explain thirteen thousand years of rebirth and the fall from heaven just so that he could find Elena, the love of his immortal life and the very reason he'd come back time and time again?

'You know what the worst part is?' William finally said, burying his fisted hands deep inside his pockets. 'Araqiel told me what it was like for you. He explained what you had given up to be with her.'

Sebastian nodded, unsure how anyone could put into words the beauty and sense of peace heaven could bring. 'It was much.'

William's angry glare was instantly upon him, black eyes burning with a hatred Sebastian couldn't quite describe. 'You had *everything* you could possibly want. Your soul was intact and you had wings and an open passport in and out of paradise, but you were greedy for more, craving something that you had no right to claim.'

'William, I don't—'

'Elena has always been mortal, born to earth and thus meant for those of us that truly exist here. She is a part of *my* universe, *my* lifetime and yet I'm the one that always has to give her up because you're supposedly fated. You had everything, Sebastian and it still wasn't enough. Isn't it time that you go back to wherever you came from and leave her alone?'

'You don't understand,' Sebastian said glumly. 'I can't go back. When I chose Elena I gave up my angelic rights. I now choose whatever form Elena takes and pray that she falls in love with me as she has done for the last thirteen thousand years.'

'You're a selfish bastard.'

'Agreed, but I cannot deny my heart. Even as a transcended being I have my weaknesses like any other. What Araqiel told you was true. I did have everything, but it was no comparison to the warm and comforting embrace of her love. I may be selfish, William, but everything I do now, I always do for her.'

'What if she didn't choose you?'

'It's never come up.'

'But what if she doesn't?'

Sebastian's shoulders slumped as reality suffocated his upright posture into submission. Elena was different this cycle. Hardship and pain had hardened her heart, making it difficult for her to love and trust anyone, but like always, he would do what was in her best interests even if it killed him. 'My love for her is deeper than any ocean can fathom. Her happiness is more important than anything in my existence and thus if she wished it so, I would let her go.'

'And what happens to you?'

Sebastian chanced a look at his still furious brother, surprised that William would care enough to ask. 'I no longer exist. Life will go on without me.'

William was silent for several minutes, his pace slowing considerably, much to the relief of the vânător. 'Is it possible for her to choose me?' His voice was softer than before, weak and almost at breaking point. Sebastian could see him trying to reign in the strongest of his emotions, but was failing against the weight of unreciprocated love.

'Of course it's possible, but make no mistake, brother,' Sebastian said, grappling William's tense shoulders and attempting to pull him to a stop. 'Elena is everything to me and I won't walk away from her unless she asks me to. You may have a chance, but I'll always be there, watching, waiting and doing my part to fulfil her happiness even to the detriment of my own.'

William shrugged loose and jogged to catch up with the vânător. 'Do whatever you have to. I have no intention of fighting fair when it comes to Elena.'

'Did it not occur to you that perhaps your path lays elsewhere? Is it not possible that there is another girl out there for you?'

William either didn't hear him or chose not to answer. Either way, the silence between them stretched on. Sebastian feared they would never reconcile, two brothers torn apart by bad history and the affections of one girl—a typical cliché.

Twenty minutes passed before the vânător indicated they were in close proximity to another pack. It was probably scared enough of William's ever flaring temper to avoid leading them into a trap. Instead, they detoured through the trees and across a small stream before starting up the side of an unchartered mountain path. A small showing of snow on the upper peaks and the frigid air growing thinner the higher they climbed only prolonged the wolf's suffering.

In human form it was completely exposed to the February climate, no doubt wishing it could shape-shift to cover all exposed flesh with downy fur. Its broken body suggested that the transition might be painful—maybe impossible—so it soldiered on, occasionally whimpering.

Sebastian and William only felt the arctic tension that shifted between them, filling them both with resentment and discontent. Sebastian stayed only to fix the damage between them and figure out how to reconnect before the animosity became a vein that would not stop leeching unjustified anger. William stayed because the consequences of Lucius's wrath were immeasurable.

'Nearly there,' the vânător gasped. It was shaking now, arms around itself and hunched over, possibly consumed by pain or the sting of the winter chill. Clumps of dried blood collected around its neck and back, the missing ear nothing more than a bloodied crater within the side of its head.

'If you somehow warn them that we are coming, I will kill you,' William growled.

'You're going to kill me anyway.'

'Yes.'

Sebastian's earlier frown had not yet left his tired features. Hearing William's complete disregard for this creature's life urged him to employ new tactics. He always preached redemption; he had to allow for it when given the chance.

He made his way past William and fell into step beside the vânător. 'If you honour our trust and lead us to the Alphas without warning them, we will not kill you.'

'We won't?' William choked in surprise.

Sebastian ignored him, studying the milky brown eyes of the stunned vânător. It stopped limping, lips trembling and confusion evident. 'You have a choice. You help us get to the Alphas quietly and undetected and we will let you go.'

46

William snorted his disgust. 'Typical.'

'Do you mean that?' the vânător wheezed, scepticism pronounced.

Sebastian nodded. 'Once we let you go, you can either continue on the path that the Alphas have set for you, run the risk of being killed by the thousands of vampires we currently have residing in Rome ready and waiting for the war to begin or you can gather as many of your pack mates as you can, hold fast in these here mountains and align yourselves with the Vampires when they finally find you.'

'Sebastian what are you doing?'

The vânător shook his head. 'We cannot ignore the call of our alphas or the commands that they give us. Even when I do not wish to do what my alpha commands of me I have no choice.'

'If you are far enough away from the clutches of their sway and scent you are capable of remaining independent.'

The vânător blinked as if this was all foreign information. 'I am?'

'Not smart, Sebastian.'

He quietened William with a harsh look before refocusing on their quarry. 'Do you want to live in peace, go back to the ways of the wolf?'

The vânător's eyes widened. 'I would not know how. I have only known this life and if we do hide in the mountains, what will we gain by aligning with vampires?'

'Your life for one,' Sebastian answered patiently. 'As for the rest, if you remain quiet, stay here, feed off the wildlife and stick to your roots and avoid cities, you will be left alone.'

'Not hunted?'

'Correct. Then I will concentrate on finding you an alpha worthy of leading you. An alpha who will be fair and understanding of your needs, an alpha who will let you indulge those needs without getting you targeted for death.'

The vânător fell to its knees, tired and out of breath. 'I do not understand. You want to replace all the Alphas for just one?'

'Yes.'

'Sebastian, what are you talking about?' William demanded. 'We kill vân ators. That is what Lucius sent us here to do.'

'No,' Sebastian murmured, shaking his head. 'Lucius sent us to kill the Alphas and only those that oppose us.'

'Sebastian, what you're saying—'

'Everyone has a right to live, William. Yes, some die for the greater good and some are sacrificed to ensure others live. It's not always fair, but if you can save one, then you have to do it or at least try.'

'Ridiculous. These creatures rape women and feed off the unwilling.'

'Is that so different to vampirism? We rape the minds of those around us with our compulsion. We feed off the willing and unwilling. Yes, we may appear more civilised, creating neutral bars and blending in with society, but in the end we are darkness, too, no matter how we try to paint ourselves otherwise.'

William threw his hands in the air and turned away, disgusted. 'How do I know that you are not lying?'

'You don't,' Sebastian said, 'but even you must realise that the Vânătors do not stand a chance against vampires, no matter how many of you there are.'

'I can't believe you are offering them protection,' William mumbled from the rear. 'It's ludicrous.'

Sebastian continued to ignore him, holding a hand out to the vânător instead. 'Do you understand what I'm asking of you?'

The wolf curiously studied the outstretched hand. Its own fingers twitched, longing to grasp hope for the future of his kind, but equally unsure if the Vampires weren't leading it to death regardless. It could either run with the packs and face the war or hide in the mountains and live for eternity. The inclination towards option two was compelling.

Eventually, carefully, it took Sebastian's hand and shook it with unyielding suspicion. 'So you want me to gather as many packs as possible, hide in the mountains and await your return?'

'Unbelievable!' William hissed, tirade apparently far from over. 'Do you even realise what you have done?'

Sebastian peered over his shoulder, unfazed by the continuing outbursts.

'They are a product of their fathers. They were born to this life and not taught how to be responsible for their actions. Answer me this: should you be killed simply because you were born a vampire—a vampire that woke hungry and inadvertently killed your own—?'

'Don't you dare say it!' William roared. 'You have no right to talk about my mother!'

'Then you understand that not everything is black and white, William. We are killers as much as they are. The difference is, we know better and they do not. It is our responsibility to teach where there are those who are willing to listen.'

'Were you always this high and mighty in heaven?'

Sebastian smirked. 'Yes, I suppose I was.'

'I was not trying to flatter you,' William scolded.

Sebastian's smile faded as he helped the stumbling vânător climb back to its feet. It staggered a few steps and then continued on, Sebastian following quietly in its wake. 'I am aware, brother.'

'I'm not your brother.'

Silence ensued once again.

Half an hour later, the vânător cried uncle. Its injuries seriously impeded breathing and the cold had finally begun to seize its limbs. Sebastian carried him, once again verbally thrashed by his intolerant brother who would play no part in aiding the creature.

'We draw close now,' the vânător whispered, falling from Sebastian's arms to the solidness of the ground below.

'Where?' William barked.

The vânător pulled itself to its knees, a shaking arm now outstretched to give direction. 'Just over that ridge and partway down the mountain is the entry to a cave system. It is in there that you will find their den. Follow your nose. They have m-made no effort to disguise their scents. They are b-bloated with the certainty that they will win the war and that v-vampires would not be stupid enough to hunt them in such dangerous territory.'

William immediately took off, headed in the direction the vânător described, a backward glance a luxury that William would not afford anyone.

'What is your name?' Sebastian asked.

The vânător shrugged then winced with regret. 'I don't have one. I've only b-been alive for five years. When we are young, the Alphas d-don't bother naming us.'

'What would you like your name to be?'

The vânător looked perplexed, straightening up as Sebastian touched a gentle hand to its shoulder. Heat immediately radiated from his palm, pressing outwards and into the wounds that would take human time to heal—if ever. 'I-I've always l-liked T-toby,' it stuttered, heat bowing his spine.

Sebastian smiled. 'Then I'll call you Toby.'

Toby's muscles bunched and released, easing as the heat within sparked a flame without pain, flaring and then just as suddenly gone. He found himself breathing easy, his ribs re-set and shoulder now in the right position. Even his missing ear had somehow grown back. He scuttled away from the vampire's touch, scared, confused and yet, thoroughly grateful. 'What? How?' he managed to say.

'You agreed to help me, so now I've helped you. Please don't let me down. I've given you a second chance to change.' Sebastian nodded his head in the direction of the mountains behind them. 'Go now. Make sure you convince as many of your brothers as possible to follow you to this area. Someone will come for you after the war.'

Toby continued to blink, uncertain as he'd ever been, but the instinct for self-preservation was stronger than doubt. Sebastian watched as Toby quickly turned and bolted across the landscape, running down the path and finally disappearing into the trees.

'You let him go,' William said flatly as Sebastian re-joined him a few minutes later.

'Yes.'

'You're a fool.'

'Perhaps.'

William shook his head, increasing his stride to reflect his anger. 'He probably sent us in the wrong direction so that he could warn the Alphas.'

'I don't think so.'

'You always think you're right, don't you?'

Face impassive, Sebastian said, 'No, I don't think that, but I am older and I have seen things you can only imagine. Maybe you should give me the benefit of the doubt instead of judgement. Our goals are the same.'

'In more ways than one.'

Sebastian crouched, pulling William down with him, quickly cupping a hand around his fitful brother's mouth as the protests started ringing out. 'Do you hear that?' Sebastian whispered, holding fast.

William finally stilled and for a solid minute, he was actually quiet.

'The vânător was right,' Sebastian murmured, lowering his hand. 'Tread carefully. We want to catch them by surprise if we can.'

'And after?'

'After what?'

William turned in the loose embrace, serious concern playing out in the depths of his emerald eyes. 'What if we do die?'

Sebastian squeezed William's shoulder and then patted his back. 'I didn't say it would be easy.'

'It's my last chance, Sebastian.'

'This is true.'

'If I die, then I don't come back.'

'Neither do I.'

'But you won't go to hell, will you?'

'No.'

William rose slowly, Sebastian's comforting touch trailing across his arm and falling away. 'The true death is a concept I've only flirted with in the past. I could die tonight and never, ever come back.'

'I will do everything in my power not to let that happen, William.'

'And Elena?'

'She'll be waiting for us when we get back.'

William nodded, seemingly accepting fate and whatever it might bring. 'Then I suppose we should do this thing, kill the Alphas and end a problem that should have been dealt with three hundred years ago.'

Sebastian nodded and climbed back to his own feet, eyes now cast on the darkened shadows of the cave entrance below. 'Yes, I suppose that would be a good place to start.'

CHAPTER FOUR: CONTRACTS

Blood—fresh, slick and entirely too much of it covered my eyes with a crimson curtain I couldn't rub away. My nightmare was shifting to another level of gore—a permanent haze of unsettling images forever entrenched in my mind. I couldn't smell it or feel it, but I could see blood everywhere. Its red slickness coated the walls of some dank, dark cave like a spattered canvas of a Jackson Pollock original.

The copious amount of arterial spray was unsettling. I was drowning within its gathering momentum, terrified I would never have the ability to see past the hazardous hue again.

I took a hesitant step, stumbled on a rock and fell straight into a warm pool of crimson wetness that was entirely too determined to swallow me whole. Its murky essence rushed over my head, dragging me under and drowning me in the viscous soup of life and death.

I kicked my feet, swimming in the slimy substance, relieved as my fingers broke the surface and cool air touched my skin. I clawed at the air until dirt edges and things without description came to hand, but then I was sinking again, the surface I'd latched onto slippery with arterial grease. I gulped and gelatinous blood poured into my mouth; salty, stale—dead.

Inhalation proved pointless. I was drowning. Blood filled every crevice that took savage possession of my lungs, robbing me of final breaths that were uselessly choked and gasped. I sunk further and further down in the pool, no longer coloured but filled with the darkness of looming death.

Do something, Elena ... anything ...

My feet caressed something solid.

What is that?

With every last ounce of strength, I toed it again, hoping I could propel back towards the surface. Attempts were thwarted by a clawed hand grabbing at my ankle, talons tearing into my flesh as it pulled me further down into the abyss.

I screamed ...

'Elena! Elena, wake up!'

My eyes flew open, a desperate gasp escaping already parted lips. My entire body convulsed under the silken threads of my coverlet, back bowing unnaturally towards the ceiling. I tried to suck in oxygen, but the pain seemed to deprive me of all air. My fingers clenched the silk sheets until my knuckles were white and the tendons begged release. Sweat trickled down my forehead and my nightshirt clung to my clammy skin with insistence. I convulsed again, tortured by the burning flame from within.

What the hell is happening to me?

'Elena!'

I screamed, the pain indescribable; nothing like I'd ever felt before and that was saying something. In my not so distant past I'd been impaled to a tree, fractured bones and been drained of blood, but it didn't compare. 'I'm on fire!' I shrieked. 'Somebody help me!'

'Elena, you're not on fire,' a soothing voice answered. 'It was just a bad dream.'

Logically speaking I knew that I was in my bed, the sheets now tangled around my feet and the damp mattress beneath my back. I could hear the words my father spoke and I knew they had to be true, but the pain—the pain was real. I was on fire. I was sure of it. 'Help me!' I gasped, eyes wide.

Lucius caught my wrists and pinned them next to the pillow. 'You've just had a bad dream, Elena. That is all.'

My back arched, my toes curling painfully. Could no one see the fire? It was right there, golden like the sun, charring my insides with agonising persistence.

The door to my room burst open and more people entered. I was relieved. Maybe one of them would see that I was on fire?

Maybe they would try to help me instead of telling me it was just a bad dream?

'What's happening to her?' I heard Tiberius ask, concerned.

'I believe she had a bad dream,' my father answered. 'Now I'm not so sure.'

'Do you hear that?' This from Decimus.

'It's hard to hear much over her screaming,' Lucius countered.

'No, beyond that,' Decimus answered. 'Listen, you can just hear it.'

'Is that ... howling?' Tiberius asked.

'It's the Vânători,' Lucius breathed wearily, denial etched on his features. 'We shouldn't be able to hear that. They're either closer than we thought or howling as loud as Elena is screaming.'

'Some must be in the city,' Tiberius murmured.

'You know what that means,' Decimus answered. 'It means that the humans can hear it too.'

I felt eyes upon me as another burst of flame wracked my body from within, forcing yet more convulsions that tampered with my father's hold. I didn't care. His rough touch was the least of my concerns when coveting so much angst.

'Elena can you hear me?' Lucius asked, brushing gentle fingers through my damp hair, smoothing it away from my clammy forehead. 'She's burning up,' he said to the others.

'Is she ill?' Decimus demanded.

'I don't know. It would appear that way but she is a born vampire. We do not get sick as you know.'

'Then what is wrong with her?'

'Elena?' Lucius attempted again. 'Answer me ...'

'Put out the fire,' I moaned. 'The pain ...'

'I'll get some ice,' Tiberius suggested. 'We could put her in a cold bath. I remember having to do that for William once when he was a child.'

Lucius nodded, relinquishing his grip to slide his hands underneath my body and lift me off the bed. I cried out again as skin almost certainly ripped from muscle and tore from bone. 'It's okay, Elena,' he whispered in my ear, 'I'm here.'

A fat lot of good that was doing me!

Lucius lowered me into the ceramic tub and turned on the faucet. Cold water poured a temporarily calming embrace over my feet and legs. Steam rose from my butchered limbs, curling up in tendrils that smelled of ash and burning barbeque meat.

Tiberius hurried back armed with a bucket of ice and a face full of worry lines. He dumped the ice into the tub, disappeared and then returned a few seconds later with another.

'Is it working?' Decimus asked, shuffling from side to side, all nerves.

'I don't know.' Lucius touched a wet hand to my forehead. 'She's still burning up.' He turned the faucet to high. The water gurgled around me until it was up to my chest. I felt like I was sitting in a hot pool. Steam was rising all around me and the ice was rapidly melting, swallowed by the heat of the flames that continued to burn.

'The ice is melting as quickly as I add it to the water,' Tiberius complained after his fifth bucket-load.

'I can see that,' Lucius sighed, turning off the tap. 'Whatever this is, it's definitely metaphysical.'

'This has to be vânător related,' Tiberius remarked, tone somewhat speculative.

'How do you mean?' Lucius enquired.

'Well this kind of behaviour is unheard of in vampires except on the night of their turning. You don't think—'

'No. It's too soon. She's not even seventeen yet.'

'Just as I thought. If not her turning and her immunity to human sickness—being born vampire—then it must be her other half. Lucius, she has been altered by two different blood exchanges. It's possible that whatever is currently afflicting the Vânǎtors is affecting her too.'

'It's possible.'

'Her screams match their howls, Lucius.'

My father turned his decidedly worried gaze upon me, wiping a chilled cloth against my heated forehead for the second time in as many minutes. His bottom lip trembled ever so slightly, quickly hidden behind a jaw that clenched tight. His fingers flicked at the water by my arm, perhaps a nervous tick.

'We've run out of ice,' Tiberius said, coming back for trip six and a fresh bucket.

'I don't know what else to do to help her,' Lucius murmured.

Kill me!

Not exactly realistic and hardly a solution given my afterlife plans in the burning underworld, but I contemplated the ease of a swift release over the smarting that presently licked at every appendage. Ironically, as I slipped further under the water's surface to flood my charred lungs and hopefully shut myself up, everything stopped. The fires that burned and writhed mercilessly promptly disappeared and all pain ceased.

I shivered, an unexpected chill now laying claim. 'I'm cold. Get me out of the tub.' My lips began to tremble and my previously heated flesh broke out in a rash of goose pimples.

'What the hell?' Decimus enquired, having been mostly quiet during the entire ordeal. Thankfully he actually helped me climb to my feet and handed me a towel while Tiberius and Lucius simply stared.

I relieved the plug, moving away from the swirling whirlpool while I concentrated on getting myself warm and dry. 'I'm fine now, I think.'

I squealed as Lucius abruptly gripped my face between strong, calloused hands. He squeezed tight, hypnotising me like a snake charmer, searching for answers while attempting to avoid my venomous bite. The speckled green and topaz of his eyes captivated and for a second, I forgot to shield my mind from his determined probing. If I thought he'd taken a sneak peek before, I had been wrong.

His eyes glazed over whilst colours flashed behind the retinas. My memories were reflected back at me, a motion picture of private moments exposed as he scoured through each encounter and every thought I'd ever had. Impassive though his face remained, when his eyes bled black, I knew I was in all kinds of trouble.

He released me as though stung. Shock was a fleeting emotion quickly chased by the dangerous cloud of confusion and anger. I had been keeping an awful lot to myself lately; my feelings for Sebastian, my second transition into becoming vânător and of course, my visit with Araqiel—an angel intent on helping me get my brother back.

Shit. Shit. Shit.

Lucius collapsed on the edge of my bed, head now buried in his shaking hands. I stood motionless, draped in a damp towel, dripping from the waist down. I figured if I stood still for long enough, he just might forget I was there.

'What is it?' Decimus pleaded, glancing uncertainly between me and his master.

'Can we do something?' Tiberius countered.

When the minutes dragged on in silence, I dared to move, exiting the tub and darting behind my changing screen.

I stood uncertain for several more minutes, my own brand of shakiness claiming my limbs before I shook off the nerves and peeled myself out of the wet night clothes.

I pulled my long, wet hair into a messy bun, ribbons of water still trying to escape. I slipped on a long sleeved shirt and my favourite pair of skinny jeans, not to be fashionable, but to keep warm. I took my time putting on my socks and boots because I really didn't want to come out from behind the screen. I knew that made me some kind of pussy, but my father was a damn scary man and ...

Double shit! He knows I snuck out with Caleb last night!

Shit! Shit! Shit!

'Elena.'

Shit!!!

I took a deep breath, pulled on the remaining boot and stepped out from behind the screen. There was no more hiding. 'Yes, Lucius?'

'We need to talk.'

'Talk?'

'Yes, talk, Elena.'

Perhaps that activity wouldn't sound so bad if it weren't for the look suggesting Sebastian's wandering hands and my sometimes hairy back didn't have him all worked up. Yes, I'd practiced shape-shifting when he'd made me promise not to. Yes, I'd disobeyed direct orders to stay at the villa and under guard. Yes, I'd had late night chats with an angel. Yes, I'd ...

Yeah. I'd stuffed up a lot.

I perched opposite my father on the end of chaise lounge. I figured if he wanted to strangle me then at least I'd see him coming and attempt to flee.

'Decimus, Tiberius. Would you give us a few minutes alone please?'

Shit.

Solemn, they both nodded and left the room, a rather pointless exercise considering their incredible hearing and undoubtable urge to eavesdrop meant separate geography within the house meant little. Hell, they could probably go the neighbour's house for brunch and still get the four-one-one.

The brush of Lucius's telekinetic energy caressed my skin.

I knew he was creating the privacy he'd asked for, sealing us inside a barrier that would allow either of us to speak freely without risk of being overheard. Tiberius and Decimus would be pissed.

'I thought privacy would be best,' Lucius said. 'What we need to speak of does not need to be heard by everyone in the house.'

'What is it you're going to grill me for first?'

Lucius shook his head, the stubborn curls at his nape unfurling from the movement. 'It's quite a list, isn't it?'

I didn't wait for him to start cataloguing them all. 'Look, Lucius, I know I say this a lot, but I'm sorry. I didn't mean for you to—'

'What are you sorry for?'

Confused by his abrupt interruption I said, 'Um, what?'

'Why are you apologising?'

Something was off. I expected him to be tearing strips off of me right about now. There had to be some kind of mistake. 'What did you see?'

Lucius sighed, pressing his hands over the top of his knees, massaging them gently as he spoke. 'I know everything. I saw you and Sebastian, I saw you turning vânător and I know you snuck out with Caleb last night.'

'O-kay,' I enunciated slowly. 'Then why aren't you breaking the sound barrier right now?'

'Is that what you think of me?'

'Well, you do kind of yell at me a lot.'

Lucius meticulously cracked each knuckle in turn, answerless.

I cleared my throat, nervous as hell. 'On a scale of one to ten how mad are you right now?'

'Elena, I'm livid, but your deviations from my rules are not what have me worried.'

'I promise that what happened just then was not some attention seeking act. I don't know what the hell it was, but I'll figure it out and—'

'No. I realise there is more to your dream and your connection to the Vânǎtors, but I'm more concerned about other factors in this instant.'

I shuffled through earlier thoughts, ticking off my mental list of recent imprudent decisions—Sebastian, vânǎtors, neutral bars …. 'Oh,' I finally answered, 'oh, *that.*'

Lucius moved so that he was closer to me, the bedsprings groaning in protest. At present he kept his flexing knuckles and fingers either against his thighs or unfurling to grip his kneecaps. Controlled though he appeared to be, his face was a road map of rage. 'Yes, *that.* When were you going to tell me that you encountered an angel?'

Never. 'Soon.'

'You're lying to me, Elena.'

I cringed. 'Okay, maybe just a little, but what was I supposed to say? "Hey, guess what? I just had a deep and meaningful chat with a Calvin Klein model sporting a halo, feathers and white tracky-dacks?"'

'What are *tracky-dacks?*'

Was that really relevant right now? 'Tell me what I should have done?'

'Told the truth.'

'The truth involves me finding Lucas and you won't let me leave the villa.'

'That did not seem to stop you last night.' The slight flare of his nostrils suggested Caleb would also eventually receive the sharp end of his tongue.

'I guess not.'

'You should have told me that an angel was in my house!'

Curious as to his intense reaction, I leaned back into the downy cushioning of the chaise and folded my arms across my chest. I looked more confident than I felt. 'What difference would it have made?'

'They are the opposite of everything we are.'

'That's not an answer, Lucius.'

Wide eyes filled with a sense of hopelessness met with mine across the divide. 'Nothing good awaits me in hell.'

Lucius had once been human, a Roman General and a senate member, blessed with a son named Lucius and a beautiful wife named Selena—pregnant with his second child—a girl.

One night, just over two thousand years ago while Lucius was away on senate business, thieves broke into the villa. They raped, tortured and killed Selena and drowned little Lucius in his own bathwater. When my father returned and found the remains, he tried easing his pain with suicide, earning him a one-way ticket to the fiery pits of hell.

Ever vengeful, he struck a deal with Lucifer to seek his own justice, unaware he would remain earthbound as a vampire with no soul for all eternity.

'You wanted to talk to him, didn't you?' I murmured, leaning forward to reach for his hands, hoping he would take mine. He did, his shoulders slumping as he curled large fingers in my palms, squeezing tight. 'You wanted to ask him if he'd seen your family.'

Lucius bowed his head, grief pulling him away from me as he began to swipe frantically at blood-stained cheeks.

'They are safe and happy, Lucius. You have to believe that.'

'How do you know?' he rasped, voice choked with tears. 'The way they died …'

'If heaven is the opposite of hell then you should be happy that they are forever bound to a place that gives them peace and love.'

'But I will never be with them.'

I shook my head, taking a shaky breath. I wasn't sure what to do with my hands now that they were absent of his touch. I curled them in my lap instead, squeezing them together between my knees. 'I don't believe that. I'm sure—in fact I'm certain—we will find a way for you to see them again.'

'I am damned, Elena.'

'Apparently so am I, but I choose not to let that stop me from doing everything I can to change it.'

Lucius wiped blood-stained palms across the top of his pants, leaving immovable paint-like smears across the tan coloured fabric. 'It's different for you.'

'I don't think so.'

'No, Elena, it is. There has to be a reason why everything that has happened from past to present revolves around you.'

I couldn't help the snort of cynicism that bubbled in my throat.

Lucius listed his reasons deliberately and without pause. 'Julius has chosen you as his tool for revenge against me. The Protectors chose your blood as the champion for some synthetic compound that will undoubtedly change the face of vampirism. You are tied to

Lucas and in turn he is tied to the IMI. Both Sebastian and William are drawn to you—two powerful vampires that would die in your name and your body houses every drop of blood that makes us unique on this earth. Elena, you are the best of all of us, watched and protected by an angel that comes to you in dreams and in life and you are also my daughter—descendant from the master vampire. Tell me that doesn't mean something?'

'I'm no prodigy.'

'There are too many coincidences, Elena. There's a reason I saved the Vânători from extinction all those years ago. There's a reason Sebastian became a vampire when he should have stayed human and there's a reason why you were born to me—the little girl I never had.'

'I'm not sure what you want me to say—what I'm supposed to do …'

'I think everything you already do is par for the course. You are the tie that binds us all, perhaps even …' Lucius paused, scrubbing a hand through the stubble on his chin, his topaz eyes thoroughly focused on my face whilst deep in thought. 'If anything were to happen to you …'

'Lucius …' I reached for him again, sensing raw emotion once again destined to spill in tears of blood.

'Just promise me you'll be careful, Elena—not so trusting. I can't … I can't lose any more children.'

I squeezed the hand now clasped in mine and moved to sit next to him, our shoulders bumping and my eyes firmly fixed on the floor. 'So you're not really angry with me, you're worried about me?'

'I thought I'd made how I feel about you perfectly clear.'

Companionable silence followed. I nibbled my lower lip contemplating his words whilst he awaited my response. 'I might have a solution to your ongoing concerns about my current involvement in the dark and dangerous and my obvious fragility.'

The arm Lucius had been about to wrap around my shoulders paused mid-air, his palm slapping the mattress a second later, his glare icy. 'No.'

I sighed, turning just enough to rest my knee on the bed between us. It wasn't nearly enough space to avoid dawning malice. 'You don't even know what I was going to say.'

'Elena, I said no.'

'Lucius, you have to turn me. You just listed most of the reasons why this makes sense.'

His head shook manically from side to side, his curls all but loose from the gelled hold he'd set in place earlier that day. 'You don't understand, Elena. What you're asking is irreversible—damning!'

'What? And I'm safe now?'

'When you're with me at the villa—yes.'

'I'm going to become whatever it is I'm supposed to become on my eighteenth birthday anyway and that's only a year away.'

'You should treasure your lingering humanity, Elena.'

I scoffed, annoyed by his close-minded perceptions. 'Are you serious? Maybe I'm essentially human, but I lost what that really meant the second I drank that alpha's blood and grew stronger. I lost it again when I shared blood with William and I became telekinetic and gained the thirst. All I'm asking is that you finish what I started so I have the strength and the stamina to rescue Lucas and put things right.'

'No.'

I fought the urge to stamp my foot like a four year old as I endeavoured to get my point across. 'Lucius, you and I know that your bite and blood are as powerful as what the born vampire would receive on their eighteenth birthday. If you turn me, I would be as strong as you. Plus, there's a good chance I'll be able to control my vânător side better.'

'No.'

'Gah!' I shouted, all frustration. 'You're not listening to me.'

'I hear you just fine, Elena. It's you who isn't listening.'

'I'm a liability around the Vânătors unless I shape-shift. I can't defend myself properly against a thrall or a born vampire because they are stronger and faster than me and you and I both know that Julius will come looking for me again soon. Plus, there's the vânător war to consider,' I said, prattling off a few of my current concerns.

Lucius took less than a minute to think about his response. 'I can protect you from all of that.'

'I want to be able to defend myself!'

'You don't have to be scared.'

I screwed my face up, only terrified that this argument may digress into a full-blown hissy fit. Scared? After everything I'd been through, the devil himself could jump out of a closet and scream 'boo' and I'd probably just roll my eyes. 'I'm not scared, Lucius. I'm being practical.'

'Practical?' Lucius barked, rubbing at the bridge of his nose in agitation. 'Turning someone—anyone is not something I take lightly. I have caused enough damage to the nineteen souls that now belong to Lucifer. Would you have me do the same to you?'

A million highly inappropriate expletives begged release, but I managed to keep the insults in check, punishing the mattress with my fists instead. 'People are trying to kill me, Lucius. Julius wants a piece because he seeks revenge. Roshan undoubtedly wants to rape and then slaughter me for killing his pack and The Protectors have already shown their complete disregard for my wellbeing. How many people do I need to be running from before you realise that turning me protects me?'

'I can handle Julius,' he said, smothering my balled fists in his grip. 'And I can take care of the alpha. Roshan will never touch another hair on your head as long as I live.'

I let him attempt to quiet my aggression by forcefully cradling my hands in his. My thoughts had already turned in the direction of my earlier episode and the unexplained phenomena behind it. 'You can't protect me from everything.'

'I can try.'

I rolled my eyes, unmoved by the sentimentality. I was trying to be practical and he was trying to be a good dad. 'Will you at least think about this?'

'No.'

I yanked back my hands, hurriedly shoving them under my armpits and crossing my arms over my chest. I felt rebuked and somewhat childish and almost certainly unsatisfied by our conversation. 'You don't know how much I want to punch you right now.'

Lucius pursed his lips, left eye twitching slightly in the corner. Pushing my luck? Undoubtedly. 'Let me make myself perfectly clear. If I do this for you, if I make you a thrall, your name will appear on my contract and my protection will be for naught.'

'What are you talking about?' I mumbled.

'If I give you what you're asking for, Elena, your name will appear on the contract holding not only my soul, but the souls of the nineteen men I originally turned. You'll be marked and Lucifer will always know where you are and how to find you. I won't be able to protect you from him.'

'So we'll just add him to the list of people out to get me.' Sarcasm was doing me no favours.

'Do not be so naïve!' he snapped. 'Your humanity is the only thing currently protecting you from the worst kind of evil.'

'It also makes me weak.'

'Have you not been listening to anything I've said?'

'Of course I have.'

'Then you're merely choosing to ignore my warnings, much like you did last night when you snuck out with Caleb.'

I squared my shoulders and sat resolute, arms still crossed. 'Are you going to punish Caleb?'

'I haven't decided.'

'It wasn't his fault.'

'Of this I am more than aware.' Lucius's features suddenly softened, the lines around his eyes etched with concern. 'I'm worried about you, Elena. You're quick to anger and acts of violence and apparently you have a death wish.'

'That's not true.'

'I'm also concerned about your duel nature and your flippant attitude towards the danger it brings.' He gently tapped his temple, giving me a knowing look. 'I've seen your bloodlust first-hand and your lack of control not to mention your zealous approach to inappropriate sexual activity.'

'What?' I screeched, anger quickly dissolving into throbbing humiliation. Why did I suddenly feel no more virtuous than a prostitute teaching the values of abstinence at a local church group?

'Making you like me not only puts you on the devil's radar, it heightens everything you already think and feel. I'm worried that your rash and hormone-driven decisions may lead you—'

'Into a blood-fuelled orgy!' I squawked, jumping off the bed no longer capable of sitting still. I began to pace, livid and mortified—an unsettling combination.

'I'm only trying to look out for you.'

I continued to pace, quietly seething and secretly appalled that my father—in a roundabout way—might have thought I was a slut.

'Now, about the angel,' he continued in an effort to change topics. 'If you see him again you should call for me.'

'Araqiel is the least of my concerns.'

'Perhaps,' Lucius mused, seemingly unconvinced. 'I'm sure he has an agenda.'

'Don't we all?' I snapped, turning face and resuming pace to the French doors and back again.

Lucius maintained his patience, my brutish tone undoubtedly tiresome. 'A halo does not necessarily rob them of nefarious intent.'

'What's the worst that could happen? They throw some feathers at us?'

'No. They throw Michael at us, the Archangel that cast Lucifer out of heaven and banished him to hell. If he's involved in any way, Elena, it won't be long before Lucifer's eyes are on you, anyway.'

'Hang about,' I said, coming to a stop by the armoire. 'Michael's real?'

'Is it truly that much of a stretch for you to believe in one more supernatural being? Knowing what you already know and your connection to everyone around you, it would be no coincidence if that plot unfolded.'

I was about to fire a round of questions when the door to my room burst open and Marcus ran in like his pants had suddenly caught fire. He hit the outer wall of Lucius's telekinetic shield and rebounded backwards, sliding across the landing and taking half of the stair banister with him.

Wound up tighter than a spinning top, I quickly succumbed to the unexpected slapstick routine and laughed so hard that tears ran down my face and I began to hiccup. Watching Marcus blow backwards and destroy half the stairwell was a million times better than watching the comedy channel. If only I'd had a camera.

Lucius remained impervious, focused on dropping his shields and allowing outside communication. Marcus could now be heard cursing, undoubtedly picking himself up from the rubble. I could also hear the television blaring from the media room and the baritone conversations between the other thralls. 'Marcus?' Lucius said, dashing into the passage outside my room. 'What's wrong?'

I followed, still sucking in fresh air to calm my ill-timed burst of amusement. Naturally Marcus was scowling at me by the time I peeked over the balcony; picking banister from his butt almost made me forget the nightmare and Lucius's reluctance to concede my point on vampirism.

'I think you should come downstairs,' Marcus muttered, dusting off his pants. 'There's something that you both need to see.

CHAPTER FIVE: EXPOSED

I rallied with the vampires back in the media room. Decimus, Maximus and Tiberius were already huddled on the big sofa, facing the television, eyes wide and alert. It was vaguely reminiscent of the time cable flipped out and gave them free-to-air pornography. This incident, however, was more serious; a news report had stolen their attention the same way free naked flesh could.

I checked what all the fuss was about. There were in fact multiple news reports being aired, but because Marcus was a channel surfer and couldn't pick just one, I watching indeterminable fragments. 'Can we pick a bloody channel already?' I chastised, settling onto the arm of the sofa next to Maximus.

'Language,' Lucius warned.

Marcus growled, channel surfed for several more minutes just to be a dick and then finally stopped on the Italian news.

I rolled my eyes. 'Can we please pick a channel that I can understand?'

Thankfully Decimus snagged the remote. Whatever had happened was getting international coverage.

Oh boy …

I slipped off the arm of the sofa and almost fell into Maximus's lap. He steadied me as I focused only on staring blankly at the screen. Photos highlighting the news story were prominent—a wallpaper of snarling vânătors.

'This is Carol Brennan reporting for CPB. Good Morning.'

The reporter habitually shuffled her papers and then glanced back at the teleprompter, face stern. 'Well, when you plan for a holiday in the south of France, one might expect to revel in the luxury of the varied ski resorts, rustic towns or to sample the warmer waters of Marseille and Nice. What you don't plan for is a confrontation with a monstrous pack of enraged wolves.'

A myriad of beastly wolf pictures dotted the screen. 'Unfortunately for American, Mark Porter—award-winning photographer for National Geographic magazine—that's exactly what happened. Mr Porter has survived such an ordeal and even captured his experience on camera.

In Grenoble, France, we now go live to Cindy Driver who was one of the first reporters on the scene after Mark Porter's harrowing escape.'

The picture changed from the short, dark-haired desk girl incessantly shuffling papers to a live reporter rugged up in some sort of fluffy ensemble paired with a ridiculous pink beanie. 'Hi, Carol, yes it's true. I'm standing here now in Grenoble, outside of the local hospital waiting on some definitive information regarding Mr. Porter's health. So far doctors have confirmed that he is understandably shaken by his ordeal, but lucky enough to have only escaped with a few minor cuts and bruises.'

The picture cut back to the studio. 'Do we know how this footage was released so quickly?' Carol asked.

Cindy nodded, holding a finger to her ear as if listening through some sort of special device. 'Yes. I have confirmed reports that the paramedics that pulled Mr. Porter from the scene found a small camcorder in his hand. When they saw the footage of the wolves in question it was immediately released to the local authorities who then passed it onto the media to help warn locals and tourists to avoid the area. From earlier conversations I had with the authorities, it's clear that this infestation is cause for concern and might even be a contributing factor to the number of missing person cases surrounding this region at present.'

'Do we have any confirmation on that?' Carol asked.

Cindy was shaking her head. 'It's all speculation, but the police and local wildlife authorities are working together to uncover answers for the public.'

The camera was back on Carol in an instant. 'Thank you, Cindy. We'll come back to you later for an update.'

'Thank you, Carol.'

Carol needed to be forcibly restrained with all that paper shuffling she was doing. 'That was Cindy Driver reporting live for CPB.' She paused, looking back into the teleprompter. 'The footage we are about to show you from Mr. Porter's encounter with the Wolves has truly taken the world by storm. As we have reported to you live in the past, the Italian, French, Swiss and Slovenian governments along with local law enforcement agencies have been undeniably swamped with reports of missing people. As of yet there has been no indication as to what may have caused the influx of so many similar cases, but now we might have an answer.'

The screen went blank and then the camera started rolling. It was shaky, a little hard to see until figures started looming in the darkness, but soon it was impossible to miss the giant cluster of wolves or more precisely—the Vânători.

I blinked as the camera switched to reflect the dodgy night vision that all personal camcorders seemed to be equipped with these days. A hazy green tint lit the television and also made locating the Vânători in the dark and on film that much easier. Their eyes even glowed as the camera captured each in turn, teeth somehow whiter, longer and more dangerous.

'I'm currently in Vanoise National Park,' Mark whispered into the camera as he sunk down, hiding behind some sort of embankment. 'I've come to this area for several days, finding left over carcasses and trails in the earth all congruent with a large group of predators. I have traipsed through here during daylight and found no sign of wildlife large enough to decimate so much prey in such a short space of time. Now, I have returned at night, finally stumbling upon the elusive wolves that have been terrorising this landscape.' He said a few cuss words highlighting his forgetfulness regarding a certain telephoto lens, but they were *bleeped* out by the news team.

Mark fell quiet instantly; a few of the Vânător's ears pointed in his direction, their eyes settling eerily on the camera, their muzzles pulling back to emit vicious snarls. 'I think they might have figured out I'm here,' he whispered, making no attempt to move. 'If I keep perfectly still, they might go about their business and continue to let me film them.'

Not likely. I thought to myself.

The Vânători began to move towards him, padding slowing and purposefully in his direction, head down and eyes forward; not just one, but at least seven or eight. There would be others behind him too. It was like watching a train wreck. You knew it was going to be bad, but you just couldn't look away.

'There are at least eight approaching me now,' he breathed into the camera's microphone.

He suddenly sounded a little bit shakier than he had a second before. He swivelled the camera slightly to the right and took in another area below the ridge. He swore again. It was longer this time and required a few more bleeps from CPB. 'There are at least another fifteen to twenty over there.' He then spun the camera to the left, past the approaching wolves and over to the other side. 'Another ten over there.'

Those vânători had started to approach him too.

Mark started to back up slowly, pulling the camera off the outcrop and slowly edging his way to ... well, I had no idea. I didn't think there was anywhere safe from the Vânători.

When he lifted the viewfinder to eye level again, the Vânători were crowded around him, hunched forward on their front legs and gazing at him menacingly with those eerie, glowing eyes. That's when they started snarling and snapping their snouts at him.

His screaming didn't help.

By now the camera shook so badly that all you could see was fur and the occasional glowing eyeball. I had no idea why they didn't launch into full assault or why they never did, but I was sure the answer was coming.

And just like that, the ones closest dropped first, followed by the rest gathered; they fell to the earth in doggie piles. Limbs twitched uncontrollably and backs arched into unnatural positions, hoisted off the ground by invisible chest strings. The twisting piles of flesh became a cacophony of torturous howls. Eruptions of agonising barks and yips escaped every whiskered snout, piercing the silence of night and making for bloody good television.

I turned to find my father and the thralls looking at me. Surely they weren't thinking what I was thinking? Was it possible that what happened to me an hour ago was connected to this footage?

I turned back, watching in mind-numbing horror as Mark had trampled some of his fear and was now actively filming the episode. I was reluctant to believe that whatever had happened to the Vânătors had also happened to me, but the proof was irrefutable. Even the time and date stamp on the bottom of the footage suggested we had all been actively feeling sorry for ourselves at precisely the same time.

Mark slowly stood, cautiously. Wolves still wreathed and contorted near his feet. Some of them had shredded the lower half of his jeans with their claws, drawing what looked like blood. He stepped over them, careful to avoid the twitching limbs and snapping snouts that still bellowed their pain.

He made it to another nearby outcrop, pulling himself up with grunts and groans before standing at full height, surveying the area around him. From this vantage point there was no mistaking the numbers and no mistaking why this footage was being plastered all over the news.

There were hundreds of them.

'Mother fuc—'

'Indeed,' Maximus said, cutting me off before I could follow through. Mark pretty much summed it up for me. Even CPB couldn't *bleep* out everything.

'I've never seen that many,' I continued. 'Not even Roshan's pack was that large.'

'I suspect this may be a few packs,' Decimus answered.

'What's happening to them?'

No one answered me. No one knew.

As I glanced back at the screen, the Vânătors were still wildly thrashing about, howling loudly and scratching at their own fur. Some were so distressed that they were diving over the edge of a nearby precipice, committing mass suicide. Was I to assume that their skin had burned as mine had? And if so, what was the connection?

'I don't know what's happening here,' Mark said, voice shaky. 'But I'm getting out of here!'

The camera went black and the screen focused back on Carol in the news room. Her face was ashen and her habitual paper shuffling seemed to have been forgotten as she gripped them tightly in her hands.

Decimus changed the channel.

This time the reporting focused on a gathering of local wildlife experts on some sort of British morning talk show. They were debating the issue of whether the wolves should be culled immediately and what sort of detrimental environmental effects a pack that size would have on the national park wildlife.

On another channel, the French tourism minister rattled off that it was perfectly safe for tourists to visit. Back on CPB they were now debating whether the Serbian President would be re-elected in the polls today. On the sport channels, talk was rife about moving the French Open in May to Australia, just in case the wolves became a problem and decided to overrun Paris.

I would ordinarily think that comical and say that movie had already been done, but this was serious stuff. The Vânǎtors had inadvertently elevated themselves to national headlines and exposed themselves to humans in just over an hour. Thank God none of them had been shape-shifting at the time!

Decimus finally switched the television off and handed the remote back to Marcus who threw it onto the coffee table in front of him with a grunt. 'What now?' Decimus said.

Every single one of us shrugged. 'I don't know,' my father answered honestly. 'But whatever it is, it has to be done soon.'

'Having The Protectors on our side right now would be useful,' Marcus countered bitterly.

'Well, they're not anymore,' Tiberius muttered. 'There's no point pretending or wishing that they were.'

'How are we supposed to clear this up with the humans?' Decimus piped in. 'The Protectors have always taken care of such measures in the past.'

I frowned. 'Can't you guys just do some sort of mass compulsion or something? Let people know that the footage was, I don't know, falsified?'

'Elena, it doesn't work that way,' Lucius answered. 'Compulsion only works when face to face with people. Besides, the footage is the least of our problems. It's the humans that are now going to investigate the area that we have to worry about. Copious amounts of people have already gone missing. If more venture into the Vânǎtor's territory and don't return, it's going to turn into mass hysteria. It won't matter if we can somehow convince various news stations that the initial reports were false if people start dropping like flies.'

'So what do we do?'

'We need to find The Protectors. This is their job. They are the human liaisons. If we can just get some of them to agree to help…'

'Yes, but what is it that they can do that we can't?' I felt frustrated, like I was missing some vital piece of information about the people I had grown up with.

For sixteen years I had lived with a family of Protectors. I'd even bonded with their child and formed deep sibling affection for him. I thought there was nothing I didn't know about them.

I had seen their spells and watched them practice. Hell, I was even trained to fight like them in the hopes that one day I'd be a kick-ass vampire slayer.

It didn't work out that way of course, but I still couldn't fathom what they could do to make a difference now. How could they change world opinion that the Vânǎtors existed? Their magic was good, but not that good.

Lucius shook his head as Marcus smirked. 'Have you never wondered why we have not been exposed until now?'

'Not really. I guess I just figured that you all didn't want to become lab rats, so you kept to yourselves.'

'There is truth in that statement,' Lucius said gently. 'The real terms of the accord, however, took into account their ability to hide things from the human eye.'

'You're talking about the *Revatarus* spell. It makes objects and people invisible.'

He looked pleased by my knowledge. 'No matter how fast, strong and compelling we can be, we cannot—as vampires—hide the combatant results of a fray with the Vânǎtors.'

'Are you saying that for the last three hundred years, Protectors and vampires have been working together to cover up evidence from the Humans?'

He nodded. 'This is not the first war Elena. On numerous occasions the Vânǎtors have tried to take over various cities throughout the world. With the protection of the IMI's magic, we've been able to hide our supernatural dealings and clean up the mess at leisure. The Humans have been none the wiser.'

I leant back into the cushioning and propped my feet up on the coffee table. 'Well, the answer is simple then, isn't it?'

Everyone looked at me expectantly. I loved how in this household everyone actually listened to what I had to say even if my ideas were sometimes stupid or unstructured. Marcus, of course was the exception; he thought I was an idiot twenty-four-seven.

'What is it, Elena?'

I held up a pausing finger. 'First you need to turn me.'

There was an audible gasp from everyone. Even Marcus looked more stunned by my suggestion than my own father who I at least thought would have expected me to try this angle.

'Hear me out—I have a plan.'

'Elena, we are trying to figure out how to proceed with the Vânǎtors,' Lucius chided. 'We don't have time for you to air your ideals about becoming a vampire.'

'Gimme a break would you? What I have to say makes sense. Listen first, then you can judge.'

'Just hear her out, Lucius,' Tiberius piped in. 'Elena's very rarely been wrong in the past. She's the reason we know the IMI abandoned us and the reason we know about the serum.'

I blinked. I really wished I could get that in writing.

Everyone sat expectant, my father less than impressed. 'Granted there are things about me that are controversial,' I began. 'I know you are all worried that when I turn I might not be able to control my vânǎtor half. I'm scared about that too, but Sebastian helped me to gain control during my last shift and I was able to remain coherent during and after the transformation.'

Lucius started to interrupt, but I cut him off. 'I know how to reign in the dark side now and if you turn me, I have a feeling that control will be even easier.'

'You can shape-shift?' Marcus interrupted.

'Try to keep up.'

Marcus made motions of reaching out to throttle me, but Tiberius pulled him back. 'How do you know you have control?' Marcus scoffed. 'You can't even control the things that come out of your mouth.'

I ignored his dig. 'If I become a vampire, then none of you will have to worry about me anymore. Julius won't be as big a threat. I'm hoping Roshan won't be able to control me and I'll be able to track The Protectors.'

'Elena, what part do you want to play, exactly?' Maximus asked.

'I'll go and look for the controlling members of the IMI. I have some solid leads regarding their whereabouts. In the meantime, you guys can sort out the Vânǎtors and pray that Sebastian and William have slaughtered enough alphas to delay the war.'

By now Lucius was cradling his head in his hands. 'This does not change the fact that you will be on Lucifer's contract!'

I looked to Maximus, passive as always beside me. 'Does the devil bother you on a daily basis?'

'I have never encountered him.'

'And you, Decimus?'

He shook his head, the short brown curls bobbing from side to side. 'No. I have not seen him.'

'Tiberius?'

'Nor I.'

'Marcus?'

'And if I say yes?'

'Well, it would certainly explain a lot about you.'

I suspected Marcus was considering strangulation as a form of punishment again judging by the baleful glare on his face.

I hid my grin by pretending to rub an itching nose. 'Look, eventually I will be a fully-fledged vampire. You're only prolonging the inevitable. These guys have been with you for two thousand years and Lucifer hasn't bothered them once.'

'They aren't my daughter! They aren't being protected by angels that Lucifer hates!'

More intakes of breath. 'You have to move past this. What I'm suggesting makes sense. While I search for The Protectors, you can deal with the Vânătors and the thousands of untrained vampires still waiting to gain your expertise before the war breaks out. I won't be vulnerable anymore and if I find them, I can bring them back to help.'

'How do you even know where they are?' Marcus asked snidely.

'Caleb did some research for Sebastian.'

'Sebastian put Caleb up to this?' Tiberius sputtered.

I nodded. 'He was trying to help me. Wherever the key members of the IMI are now, Lucas is with them. I need to get him out of there and if nothing else, he *can* help us.'

'Just where is *there*?' Decimus asked.

'At the moment, Hobart. It is the last incoming destination for all factions recorded. If they aren't there, then they have to be somewhere nearby.'

Lucius was a flurry of activity, every part of his body shaking with rage. He no longer cradled his head, but wrapped his arms around himself to contain whatever outburst was building. 'And if you find them? What are you going to do? Even if you are a vampire, what makes you think they'll help you?'

I shrugged. I honestly hadn't thought that far ahead. My plan thus far was this: become a vampire, find the IMI and get Lucas back. What happened after that? Well, I'd wing it like I always did.

'They have no reason to help us,' Decimus argued. 'We have drawn enough conclusions to realise that the IMI's only interest now is to ensure that all vânători and vampires destroy each other.'

'They surely still care about humanity?' Tiberius murmured. 'Their life's work has been about protecting those we preyed on in the past. How can they ignore this cry for help now?'

'Because their objective is to no longer *beat* us, but to *be* us,' I added confidently. 'To become immortal is far more important than protecting human life.'

Maximus flexed his fingers, cracking each knuckle in turn. 'So we have nothing to offer them if we find them.'

Everyone sat in silent contemplation. It was Marcus that moved, rising from the sofa to pace the length of the media room's floor. He moved back and forth in a torrential tornado, pacing only mildly slower than an Olympic runner. Occasionally he glanced in my direction, his lips twitching. When he spoke it surprised everyone but me. I think for once we might have been on the same page. 'That's not exactly true.'

I grinned at him, nodding maniacally. 'It could work.'

He returned my smile, but it was by no means attractive or warm. Considering we were finally agreeing on something, it was a good place to start. 'Yes, I think it would.'

The others looked to us for some sort of elaboration. Evidently it was uncommon for Marcus and I to grin at each other like idiots.

'What's going on?' Lucius demanded.

Marcus nodded his head at me to take the lead, mostly because Lucius would probably kill him for even suggesting to offer me up as a sacrifice to The Protectors. I gave him a starring role anyway— for old times' sake.

'Marcus and I believe that the IMI might offer assistance in this matter if I were to agree to remain in their custody until after they perfected the serum, whatever it may be.'

'No!' Lucius roared. 'That is simply unacceptable!'

'Elena, we don't want The Protectors to perfect the serum,' Tiberius reminded me.

'I don't care about that!' Lucius growled, bolting forward and out of his seat. His very presence filled the room with a sense of malice, causing everyone to shrink back in their seats and Marcus to retreat into the corner of the room. 'I only care about Elena and I will not see her martyr herself again!'

Marcus and I shared panicked expressions. 'That wasn't the entire plan, Lucius. I wouldn't actually be giving myself up. It would be a ruse.'

Marcus's expression turned to bewilderment. 'It would?'

'I would go to them and—' I'd just caught on, stopping my explanation mid-thought. 'What? You mean you would have let me ...' I sighed, rearranging my features to reflect calm. I should not have been surprised that the temporary alliance between us was at an end. 'Never mind. *Lucius*, the trade would just be a distraction, a way to get their help.'

Lucius was adamant I'd play no part. 'End of discussion, Elena. I'm not turning you and you're not going to go running around looking for the IMI. We have enough to deal with here in Rome.'

'But, Lucius ...'

'No,' he finished sharply. 'I have nothing more to say.'

I watched him, my mouth gaping as he left the room. I still had plenty left to say. Apparently that was irrelevant.

Tiberius, Decimus and Maximus left about three seconds after my father. Marcus was the only one that lingered. At first I thought he wanted to have a go at me too, but then I realised he was staring longingly at the television. It was just about time for Project Runway to start. Usually I would mouth some snappy remark about his sexual orientation, but today I just didn't have it in me.

'Elena?'

'Yes, Marcus?'

'I still think looking for The Protectors is a good idea.'

I nodded. 'So do I.'

'You want to find your brother.'

'Well yeah, but if The Protectors can help, then I think that they should.'

'Likewise.'

I wasn't exactly sure what he wanted me to add to that given the abrupt end to the previous conversation. So I shrugged and headed for the door.

'Elena?'

I spun, finding him close enough to make me jump. He seemed to take pleasure in my discomfort. 'Yes, Marcus?'

'I think you should do it.'

'Excuse me?'

He pressed a finger against his lips and then cupped his ear and pointed towards the door. I understood the undercurrent of intent and quickly used my telekinesis to form a protective barrier around us. It wasn't as large as the one my father had used to sound proof the entire bedroom earlier, but good enough.

'I think you should leave the villa and go and look for your brother.'

'Did you just hear what Lucius said?'

'I did.'

'Do you remember how much he yells and screams when I disobey him?'

'He won't even know that you are gone.'

'How?'

Marcus smirked. 'I will convince Lucius that he should still send out a team to look for the IMI, a small contingent like Caleb, Nicholas and Eric. They are trusted vampires and I suspect we can manage here without them.'

'Go on.'

'I will speak with them and tell them to wait back for you until the war breaks out—'

'Then I'll sneak off during all the commotion and Lucius is none the wiser,' I finished for him.

Marcus smiled his encouragement. 'He will be too busy directing the intentions of the guard to check on you. He will undoubtedly leave one of us at the villa to watch over you. I will make sure that person is me.'

'What if Caleb and the others don't agree to it?'

'Everyone has a price.'

I was well rehearsed in Caleb's particular penchant for money. If the others didn't agree, then relying on Caleb's greed was a certainty that would get me back to Australia. 'That's a good plan.'

Marcus chuckled. 'Of course it is. I thought of it.'

All I ever did was fight to contain eye rolls around this vampire. 'Okay, so I guess you'll give me the details as soon as you know anything.'

Marcus agreed. 'May I suggest having a packed bag ready? It could be any day now, particularly given that the Vânǎtors have been exposed.'

'Sure.'

I dropped the telekinetic shield around us and made my way back to the door again.

'You know, I underestimated you, Elena.'

I did my pirouette again.

'I've always thought you were a bratty teenager, a thorn in my side, but today you've shown me that you can be grown up if you want to be.'

I frowned, uncertain where the compliment was in that last remark. 'Thanks, I think.'

He inclined his head as if he'd bestowed some great honour upon me. 'Perhaps as the centuries roll by, you and I may even learn to tolerate one another, particularly if you can keep that attitude of yours in check.'

'Marcus, I have no words.'

Nice ones, anyway.

'A pleasant change.'

I snorted, a million retorts sitting on the tip of my tongue that I held in check. After all, he was right. I did have an attitude and wore it like a comfy sweater you never want to remove. 'Just make sure this plan works, Marcus.' Not disagreeing with him felt like chewing through a box of waxy crayons.

'There's one more thing ...'

'Yes?' My feet were already edging towards the door, his hand creeping towards the remote control.

'I would appreciate it if you stopped making innuendoes regarding my sexual orientation. I do not have a preference for men. I'm merely cultured.'

I chewed on my lower lip to hide the rising smirk. Sure. Cultured.

'Elena?'

'Uh huh?'

'I mean it.'

'Okay. I'll make no comment about the pink shirt you're wearing, either.' I fired a devilish grin over my shoulder as I exited the room. 'By the way, you're missing Project Runway.'

The shriek he made while fumbling for the remote kept me laughing until dinner.

CHAPTER SIX: WAR

My packed bag was an asset I was glad to have pre-prepared. The inevitable had happened.

War!

I'd been sitting in the kitchen with Maria—our housekeeper—munching on a bowl of pasta and discussing our respective days'. Lucius had burst into the kitchen and scared the crap out of both of us. He was supposed to have been at Synth Corp making preparations for extra blood supplies to be facilitated to the neutral bars throughout the city.

'Maria, it's time for you to leave now,' he'd said, panic choking the usual calm from his voice.

'Ma, Signore Valerius, che cosa è?'

'Go home, Maria,' he'd repeated in English. *'Take your husband and any family you can think of and hide in the basement. Don't come out until daylight.'*

Her rumpled, already significantly lined brow signified her confusion. *'Is it vampire?'*

Lucius had shaken his head. *'No, Maria. It is much worse.'*

She'd nodded as if she understood and hadn't wasted another second trying to interpret my father's wishes. She'd bolted from the kitchen, unravelling her apron and tossing it onto the oak counter before she left.

'What's happened?' It was a stupid thing to say. Even before the words had left my mouth I'd known the war had begun.

'The Vânâtors have advanced. The Vampires I sent to Milan have reported sightings and in areas past the cities, they are already engaging those who oppose them.'

I remember dropping the fork I'd been holding; it crashed noisily into the ceramic bowl of half-eaten spaghetti. *'We have to stop them before they breach the cities. People are already frightened thanks to the news stories. They're going to be extra vigilant for anything amiss.'*

Lucius had agreed. *'I've already sent everyone I can spare. I still need the major cities to be protected; there are three thousand going to the borders to assist as we speak.'*

'You're worried it's not enough, though.'

He'd grimaced. *'It's hard to know what to expect from the Vânâtors. That stunt on the news this morning and your connection have me worried. I need to be there so I can watch for any significant changes in the packs. I also have skills that the others do not; I can't be killed.'*

'So go. Do what you have to do.'

One dark eyebrow had arched towards the ceiling, reflecting his scepticism for my new-found agreeability. *'Why aren't you asking me if you can assist?'*

'Do you want me to?'

'No, of course not. It's far too dangerous.'

'So what's the problem?'

I still remember the touch of his hand on my shoulder as he'd reached out and held me tightly. I'd been quick to wrap a shield around my mind, hiding my thoughts from him. The last thing I'd needed was him privy to what Marcus and I had discussed earlier.

'There is no problem. I just don't believe that I can leave you behind—not after everything. Between the angels, Julius and this latest connection you seem to have with the Vânâtors it seems ... risky.'

'Are you saying you want me to go with you?'

'No.'

'Then what are you saying?'

The weight of his hand on my shoulder had lightened, his fingers very pointedly tapping on the side of my temple. *'You're shielding. You only do that when you want to hide things from me.'*

'I don't like it when you shuffle through my head like a deck of cards.'

'There is also the matter of leaving you unattended.'

'Why don't you leave one of the thralls to watch over me if you're worried? You can't stay here if you could be more useful elsewhere. Like you said earlier, your number one concern right now is preventing this war. Well, it's happened. Now you have to try and stop it from escalating.'

When he conceded, I'd nearly smiled … nearly. *'Marcus has offered to watch over you.'*

I'd pulled an ugly face to represent my displeasure at the proposition of alone time with Marcus despite our temporary truce and underhanded workings about to unfold. I'd rather have poked my own eyes out than spend any length of time with Marcus, but these were exceptional circumstances.

Lucius had been appeased by my response. *'You should know that I considered some of your ideas today. I have sent Caleb and the others to look for the IMI on the off chance that some Protectors may be willing to lend their support.'*

'I think that's a good idea,' I'd murmured. *'If you can keep the wolves away from the towns and cities we may be free and clear, but if they invade them, we might need The Protector's help.'*

'Agreed.'

'Well, good luck then.'

I'd never forget the look that had possessed his face—sad and haunted by the vicious memories of his past.

'I have to go now.'

'Sure.'

He turned to leave. I'd almost gotten rid of him, but I'd grabbed him by the shirt sleeve and held him steady. I was scared for him, yes, but also been scared for Sebastian and William all week. Not hearing from them while they hunted the Alphas was driving me crazy.

'What is it, Elena?'

'Do you know if something has happened to William or Sebastian? They haven't contacted any of us. Now that war has erupted, I'm worried and I was hoping—'

'That my blood would know when one of our kin has died?'

'I was gonna say, "hoping that one of them contacted you", but yeah, that works too.'

'William is fine.'

'How do you know? Did he call?'

'I just do.'

'And Sebastian?'

'Sebastian's different. He chose to become a vampire. That's unprecedented in our kind and never ...'

Inexplicable emotions warred with my father's features, pulling him from the brink of confusion to perfect understanding. I had no idea what had run through his mind, but I'd known that every part of his thought process had centred on my dark warrior.

'Lucifer ...' he'd whispered, voice barely audible. 'How did I not draw the connection until now?'

'Lucius, what are you talking about? What connection?'

'I have to go.'

His lips were a memory against the flesh of my forehead. I'd been forced to release his shirt sleeve, the wind of his swift exit pulling him from my grasp. By the time I'd found my feet to chase him down, he was already gone.

That was why I now stood at the bottom of the stairs, my back pack over one shoulder and gazing into the expectant faces of my friends. The war had begun, The Protectors needed to be found and my father was gone, taking the intrigue of his words with him.

'Hey, Elena,' Caleb said, wandering up to pat me endearingly on the head. 'Did you get into much trouble for sneaking out with me the other night?'

I waved in acknowledgment to Eric and Nicholas in the background. 'Lucius had other things on his mind at the time.'

'No wonder he's hesitant to leave you unattended. You simply can't be trusted!' Marcus goaded.

'Especially if there's a man around.'

I peered over Caleb's shoulder, searching for the face that belonged to that last mumbled comment.

Marianne.

I couldn't believe she was here. The last time I'd seen her I was living in Cairns. We weren't exactly friendly, mostly because she was in love with the guy who was chasing after me—William. 'What are you doing here?'

William, Marianne and her twin brother Thomas (William's best friend) had tracked the alpha John to Australian shores by way of London. As a courtesy of the alliance, they had introduced themselves to the local members of the IMI. Mine and Lucas's curiosity had drawn an acquaintance between them all. William and

I had moved beyond friendship and Marianne had been less than thrilled.

'She's with us,' Caleb answered.

I could feel a monumental frown. 'How do you even know her?'

'We met at the multi-coven gathering,' Eric answered. 'Marianne and Thomas had come in the hopes that William would be there. It's been many months since they have seen him.'

'Since he dumped us back in London, anyway,' Marianne moaned.

'Yeah, but why are you *here*?'

Thomas, who I hadn't noticed, unfurled himself from one of our courtyard deck chairs, looking exactly as I remembered him: blonde hair, sapphire blue eyes and a smile that robbed me of breath. 'Because we want to help find Lucas.'

My frown was instantly extinguished. I rushed forward to give him a hug. Unlike his sister, I was a fan. 'I'm glad you're here, Thomas.'

'Whoa,' Thomas chuckled, wrapping his thick arms around me in a rock-solid embrace. The tiny peck he planted on the crown of my head indicated he was pleased to see me too.

Marianne chortled. 'Now you make a play for my brother too?'

I pulled back, embarrassed. 'What is your problem?'

'You.'

'You came all this way just to tell me you hate me?'

'Don't be so naive,' she spat. 'Do you think I care if you like me or not? I'm three hundred and seventy years old! You're a spec in my existence, Elena. Lucas is my friend and wherever he is right now, it's nowhere good. He needs our help and you were the best one to contact.'

That stopped me from offloading a bitter retort. It appeared we were on the same team for once. I had this strange feeling that I was blinking like a Cindy doll regardless. You know, the ones you turn on its head to open and close its eyes?

'When did you strike up a friendship with Lucas?'

'Since you and William started whatever it is that you have.'

'I thought you thought Lucas was an idiot?'

'I did at first, but then he grew on me.'

'He does that.'

She started to smile, forcing me to blink several more times from sheer shock alone and to clear my eyesight. Was she actually grinning?

I looked to Thomas for a little bit of help. He shrugged. 'He flatters her with his compliments.'

'It's not just that!' she shrieked, now angry again. 'We, um, well, we talk.'

I'd managed to stop catching flies with my mouth, but my eyes were still as wide as dinner plates.

'Lucas saw *me* when you and William couldn't keep your hands off each other and forgot that the rest of us existed.'

I blushed—a rarity. I avoided embarrassing sentiments in most instances as blushing around vampires was equivalent to lighting up my arteries like Fourth of July fireworks—dangerous and emotionally telling.

Caleb swallowed, taking several steps back. Thomas was not too dissimilar in his actions; Marianne also took a step back. Eric and Nicholas—past five hundred years of age—remained tolerant of the flush of blood beneath skin. As for Marcus, he'd grown bored by our conversation and left the room or there was a Village People concert somewhere that he was missing.

'We should be going,' Nicholas said, glancing at the watch strapped to his wrist. 'We don't have time for any of this right now.'

Eric nodded in agreement. 'I will take Elena, the rest of you follow the plan.'

'What plan?' I said as Eric paced towards me like a deadly jungle cat. With waist-length dark hair, tanned skin, serious features and dark eyes that were almost black, it was easy to think of him as a feline predator.

'A plan I will explain to you shortly.'

He scooped me up into his arms despite protests. I did not like this method of vampire transport. I liked walking. I was good at it—had lots of practice. Yet despite best efforts, he ignored me.

In the past, Nicholas and Eric had played an integral role in helping me escape a very bad situation with The Protectors. Not to mention various other mini dramas that had cropped up since I'd been welcomed into this coven. They were also close friends of Sebastian's.

Nicholas took my back pack and shouldered it. 'We have a flight leaving from the airstrip in about an hour. We need to make sure we're on it.'

Caleb sidled up next to us, looking forlorn. He toed the ground with his big, black combat boot and picked at his raven coloured fingernail polish like the end of the world was approaching. I doubted he empathised with my desire to be free of Eric's arms, so I said, 'What's up?'

'I wanted you to know that I'm doing this because I like you, Elena. No one is paying me to help this time.'

My lips twitched at the virtual impossibility of such a prospect. Caleb without compensation or motive? Yeah right. 'That's nice, Caleb.'

'Nice?'

'Yeah, unexpected, *unbelievable*, but nice.'

Eric shuffled me around in his arms until we were both comfortable, following behind Marianne as she smoothed her blonde curls and adjusted her own little blue back pack. She led the way through the courtyard, towards the front door, Nicholas behind us. Thomas pulled his blonde hair back from his face with a rubber band, while Caleb moped, keeping pace with Eric.

'Was there something else you wanted to add?' I asked Caleb.

He stopped staring at his fingernails to scratch the back of his neck instead. 'Um, well, yeah.'

'Okay, out with it.'

'I still haven't been paid for the last job yet.'

Eric and Nicholas groaned, the two of them pulling the group to a stop as Caleb began to toe at the ground again with his shoe, delaying departure.

'I thought you just said this wasn't about the money?'

'This job isn't, but I haven't forgotten about the three grand Sebastian promised me for the information that's making this trip possible.'

'Sebastian will sort that out when he gets back. You know he's good for it.'

'What if he doesn't come back?'

'Caleb—' Eric started to say before I interrupted him.

'Sebastian *will* come back.'

Caleb still looked unconvinced.

'What if we upgrade you to first class on the plane?'

'Really? First class?' Caleb was smiling again, probably negotiating a way to cash in that elusive first class ticket for a coach seat just to make some extra dollars.

* * *

An hour later we were *all* strapped into our 'first class' seats, gliding down the runway in my father's private jet.

'Elena, this is bullshit,' Caleb scolded from three seats behind. 'The whole plane is first class.'

Nicholas and I shared a smile from across the aisle. Eric was chuckling to himself beside me. I didn't bother with an answer. Caleb was already mumbling something about stealing the headsets as compensation. 'So, we have twelve hours until we get to Singapore,' Nicholas murmured. 'What do you want to do?'

I reclined my chair, waiting until I was almost horizontal before I closed my eyes. 'Well, I don't know about you lot, but the human needs to sleep.' I cracked one of my eyes open and whispered to Eric, 'Can you keep an eye on Caleb for me?'

'Why?'

'He likes my blood a little more than he should.'

'You trust me?'

'Sebastian trusts you. That says everything.'

Eric inclined his head. 'Then I will watch over you.'

'Thanks.'

* * *

I must have been tired, because the next thing I knew, the landing gear was coming down and I was waking up to a darkened cabin with all the vampires standing in the centre of the aisle. 'What's going on?'

'We are preparing for landing.' Nicholas nodded to the windows. 'The shades need to be pulled up as per the pilot's instructions, but we cannot stray into the sunlight for long.'

I yawned, nodded and then sluggishly set about opening all the window shades. Sleep caked my eyes like sticky sand and my muscles suffered the momentary stiffness of the cramped conditions. I was certain my breath smelt like the rear end of a donkey, but it was nothing compared to the startling awareness that

I'd slept for twelve uninterrupted hours. The nightmare and connection I shared with the Vânătors must have knocked me for six. I still hadn't really considered what had happened yet. How do I begin to explain the seeming reality of flesh covered in a metaphysical flame, tortured by an unknown source that just happened to also affect my enemies?

'Elena? Is something wrong?' Nicholas asked.

They were all staring, but to be honest, they'd never stopped since I woke up. I was beginning to wonder if I'd farted in my sleep. 'Nothing any of you can help me with.'

'Are you ill?'

'No, I'm fine. How long are we in Singapore?' I asked, changing the subject.

Nicholas checked his wrist watch again. 'Just enough time to re-fuel and then we'll be up in the air again.'

'How long will that take?'

'Half hour I expect.'

'Shouldn't we get off the plane?'

'Why would we need to?'

'To investigate possible leads from any IMI clans here in Singapore.'

'I've already done all the legwork, Elena,' Caleb reminded me. 'My research extended further than Kowloon and Santiago. There's no Protectors left here of any benefit. They've had their minds hazed by magic.'

'Right.' I blew out a frustrated breath, squinting through the shards of bright sunlight streaming into the cabin. The vamps still loitered in the aisle, packed like sardines in a can.

'We have roughly eight hours before we land in Melbourne,' Nicholas started. 'We need to figure out what we are going to do when we get there.'

'I thought we had to go to Hobart?'

'We need to re-check the information Caleb came up with, make sure nothing was missed.'

'But you just said we weren't checking Singapore for that very reason.'

'Melbourne has records of The Protector's travel arrangements. There is no evidence to support incoming clans moving through Singapore that weren't consistently transient.'

'Caleb said the trail leads to Hobart. There's no need to waste time in Melbourne. If you trust him enough to surpass questioning those still living here, then you should trust that Hobart was the last port of call.'

'Gee, thanks,' Caleb muttered.

I shot him a questioning look. 'What? I'm being supportive!' Caleb snorted.

'I wonder why Australia?' Marianne commented, altering the course of the discussion.

'What do you mean?' I asked, eyes narrowing.

'Well, I just can't picture cultured and intelligent scientists from Europe holing up in—'

My intense eyeballing and erect middle finger stopped her mid-thought. I was offended that the rustic nature and wholesome spirit of the country I grew up in was being underestimated as a viable base of operations for a magical clan hell bent on pushing the envelope of conspiracy. Australia cultivated some of the world's leading scientists, agriculture and art. Sure we wore thongs and singlets on weekends and threw shrimp on the barbie at Christmas, so why couldn't we play host to psychopathic magic users vying for a bit of open space?

Australia was nothing if not diverse.

Thomas attempted to extinguish the fire. 'I think what Marianne is trying to suggest is, *why that particular city in Australia*? Hobart is not exactly a Mecca for supernatural activity.'

She rolled her eyes. 'That is *not* what I meant.'

I ignored her. 'I don't know why they chose Hobart, Thomas, but there has to be a good reason. A lot of Protectors and their families have divided the factions. If they've congregated, they would need somewhere large enough to house them all—somewhere inconspicuous.'

'I still think we need to look into Melbourne,' Eric protested.

'The trail leads to Hobart.'

Nicholas and Eric passed looks between them; a common accompaniment to my objections. Just because they were six hundred years old—or something gross like that—didn't mean they knew what was best. 'Flying into Hobart could have been a ruse.'

'Why choose such an unlikely destination? You two are already turning your noses up at the prospect of the IMI settling into such a small community. Perhaps that was the plan all along?'

They looked doubtful. 'Where do you think they are hiding? Cradle mountain?'

The sarcasm was not lost on me. 'Maybe.'

Eric turned to Caleb. 'Are you sure your information is solid?'

'Granted I'm a penny-pinching, blood-thirsty vampire, but I'm not a liar. My sources are good. Most of my information came directly from flight logs. I followed the entire Manory family to Hobart.'

Nicholas and Eric both looked thoughtful. 'You don't suppose—'

'What?' I interrupted. 'You don't suppose what?'

Eric waved me off, perhaps considering his own thoughts absurd. I urged him on regardless. 'Do you think it's possible that the IMI knew you would come looking for Lucas?'

'It's not out of the realms of possibility. Why?'

'Perhaps the IMI put up a few roadblocks to ensure that wouldn't happen.'

'It seems a little elaborate to deflect one person to this extent. Caleb said their names were on the passenger lists. Airlines don't seat imaginary travellers. Isn't that a counter-terrorism measure now since nine-eleven?'

'True,' Nicholas agreed. 'But they do have the power to implant memories and suggestions with their spells, the same way we use compulsion.'

'The *Defenacus* charm is for memory loss. They wouldn't have been able to amend an entire passenger log without putting spells on several staff members. I mean, I get where you're coming from, Nicholas, but I don't think it's likely and I don't think they believe I'm a serious threat.'

'Elena's right,' Caleb agreed. 'Even if the IMI created a diversion to stop her from finding Lucas, it doesn't explain everything else. An IMI faction still left Hong Kong for Hobart and a friend I have in Santiago confirmed that members of his faction also boarded a plane heading for Australia.'

'Where was the scheduled arrival for the Chile contingent?' Thomas asked.

'Melbourne,' Caleb answered.

Nicholas and Eric were passing around those *I told you so* looks again.

'Fine,' I said calmly, bracing a seat back as the plane touched down. 'I have an idea that will satisfy everyone.'

'And what is that?' Eric's slender eyebrow rose exponentially. He grabbed my seatbelt and buckled me up as the secondary contact bounce on the tarmac raised me off my chair. The flashing *fasten your seatbelt* sign near the cock pit door indicated I should have been restrained long ago.

'How about you and Nicholas go to Melbourne? Actually, you can all go to Melbourne if you think it's a good idea, but I'm taking the jet to Hobart.'

'I'm coming with you,' Caleb said, pointing at my forehead like he was picking out countries on a map. I absently rubbed at the sweet spot. There was nothing there.

'You know I'm going to go with you, Elena,' Thomas murmured. 'William would want me to watch out for you.'

Marianne sighed so loudly that we all had to look at her for fear of a tantrum. She rolled her eyes and pouted her lips in displeasure. 'Well, of course I'm going to go with you because my brother is and because the pink-haired vampire behind me said it's the last stop.'

'I have a name.'

Marianne ignored Caleb. 'I want to find Lucas. I'm going to go where my instincts take me and they're telling me to follow you.'

I half smiled at her. 'Thanks ... I think.'

'Elena, splitting up is not a good idea. Marcus specifically requested that we keep an eye on you,' Eric chided.

I scoffed. 'Marcus also thinks orange is the new pink and that gay pride is an African wildebeest.'

'Are you suggesting that Marcus is—?'

'I'm not suggesting anything. I'm just frustrated and I know Marcus doesn't really care about my wellbeing.'

Caleb slapped the top of his thigh, smirking. 'I knew it. Pink shirts and hair product—it's a bit of a giveaway.'

Everyone studied Caleb from head to toe, in particular, the black fingernail polish and spiky pink and blonde hair creatively styled into a Mohawk.

'Have you looked in the mirror today?' Marianne teased. 'Finger polish and eyeliner aside, your hair is better tended than mine and you're giving Marcus crap?'

'What's wrong with my hair?' Caleb said, plucking at the stiff strands.

I kept my face as neutral as possible. 'Nothing, Caleb. Absolutely nothing.'

We all let rip after that, a much needed bit of levity in the face of what was to come. Even Caleb was good-humoured enough to admit that his hair was the perfect broom to sweep the cabin floor, but the black fingernail polish? He argued that it was not makeup or gothic suggestion, but simply necessary for scaring away encroaching small children.

The argument regarding our destination and research parties had temporarily desisted. I was taking the jet to Hobart and the others could do what they thought was right. The jet was my father's and there was a MasterCard in my wallet with no limit— the ultimate decider. If that didn't work, then there was always my old friend Visa.

What is it that they say on the commercials?
Oh yeah ... priceless.
We were going to freaking Hobart.

CHAPTER SEVEN: PLANS

It was after midnight when the aircraft touched down in Melbourne. It was another twenty minutes after that before I managed to dump Eric and Nicholas on the tarmac; the two of them protesting my flight plans. Thirty minutes saw us slamming the cabin door in their faces, but it was the preceding hour that saw the rest of us land in Hobart.

'I'm going to try and gain access to the flight logs again,' Caleb said, heading for the flight door and stairs.

'I'll come with you,' Thomas shouted after him.

They disappeared in a blur. Re-checking the flight logs did seem like a solid idea, the only problem was ...

I turned to look at Marianne. She'd realised, as I had done, that we'd been left alone. Not such a great plan. 'Well ...' I started to say, but stopped. Usually I opened my mouth and words poured out like proverbial diarrhoea. Now that we had arrived, I had no real idea how to proceed. My partial turning and earlier training with the IMI suggested I had useful skills in my repertoire, but I couldn't track and scent. All I had to work with while trying to find my brother was instincts and deductive reasoning—neither came with a GPS.

'Oh my God,' Marianne muttered, studying the blank expression on my face. 'You have no idea what you're doing, do you?'

'Define *no idea*.' I grimaced, turning to collect my bag from the seat next to me. I headed quickly down the aeroplane steps, following my legs to the rear of the hanger. I could hear Marianne behind me, but hoped she'd opt to run after the guys and assist them instead. I should be so lucky.

'I'm guessing,' she said, mustering as much sarcasm as the universe would allow. 'That when we landed here you thought someone would wave a big old sign in front of your face that said 'Protectors this way'.'

'That's just stupid.'

But would honestly be very helpful right now.

'It is stupid,' Marianne agreed. 'But I'm starting to think you run with stupid ideas until one of them works out for you.'

'I resent that. Vampires wouldn't have known the war was coming if it wasn't for some of my so called *stupid* ideas.'

'The fate of the entire world does not rest on your shoulders, Elena. Vampires have survived for thousands of years before your arrival and we'll live long after you depart.'

'Look, I'm just following Caleb's lead, trusting my gut and hoping I find Lucas. If you don't like how I do things, then go back to Rome. They could use the extra hands there at the moment.'

'Rome?'

'Yeah, there's a war, remember? You could help fight the Vânători.'

'I don't involve myself in such lunacy.'

'Oh that's right,' I said, tone mocking. 'You like to bark like you're a vicious dog, but in the end, you're a bloody Chihuahua.'

She hissed at me. 'You don't know the first thing about me!'

'Where were you when John established a new pack in Cairns and I was abducted? I remember Thomas and William helping to hunt and destroy the pack, but I never saw you.'

'I didn't want—'

'Even though I do sometimes make stupid choices, I'm always prepared for the consequences of my actions, even that means my own life may be at stake. I don't have any real leads to find Lucas, but I won't stop until I do. Protecting the people I love is more important to me than saving face in front of you.'

I stopped walking, turning to look at Marianne who was just shy of my heels. Her eyes were fixed on the distance ahead, her mouth set in an immovable line. She was not a happy chappy.

I began walking again, momentum making my stride purposeful. My impromptu tongue lashing had given me hope that I would find the answers I needed. I didn't have a masterful plan, but ideas were starting to trickle in about where we should start.

'Maybe instead of verbally bashing each other we could focus on finding Lucas.'

She snorted. 'So you've developed a strategy in the last few minutes?'

Oh my God. I don't think she can help being a bitch.

'We should investigate the transport services offered here at the airport; you never know if we're going to get lucky.

We also need to find Thomas and Caleb and book a hotel to dump our things. I'm going to need to eat and sleep again soon and I'd like to do some research given that most hotels have internet access.'

'Then what?'

I have no idea.

'Then we'll follow where those leads take us. If The Protectors did move through Hobart on any form of transportation besides foot, we'll find it. We can also look into building and freight companies. A couple of hundred Protectors and their families don't just move into a new location without needing supplies—be it food or materials.'

'And if we don't find anything?'

'Then Caleb was wrong. Eric and Nicholas were right and—'

'You look like a giant fool.'

I took a deep breath to calm myself. 'At least I can say I tried.'

Marianne caught up to me, her shoulder nudging mine as we both tried to simultaneously squeeze through the hanger door. 'What are the likely scenarios?'

I adjusted my back pack, Marianne now leading the way into the terminal. 'I guess that depends on whether they were transit passengers or hanging around.'

'Let's say they were hanging around. What options do we have from this airport?'

I shrugged. 'The usual: taxis, limousine services, buses, trains, hire cars ...'

'Thomas and Goth boy are taking care of transit possibilities; you and I need to look at the other options.'

I continued to follow the blonde bombshell in front of me as we hit security and were requested to present our passports and travel papers. Well, I was questioned and had my bag inspected while Marianne blew through the customs line like a fart in the wind.

'What took so long?' she moaned as I finally emerged into the arrivals lounge.

'I can't compel my way through security or run like hell to avoid it.'

'Well what good are you?'

I ignored the urge to kick her in the shins. 'Did you do anything useful while you were waiting?'

She stared blankly.

'Did you think to check with that hire car company over there to see if they had any records of the Manory family hiring vehicles? For that matter, what about the limo service next door or the other hire company after that?'

Now she was sheepish, her gaze drifting between the car rental booths lined up against the wall. I savoured the vestiges of Marianne having to eat her words. 'Um, no.'

'Then what good are you?'

I headed to the first rental place. A man with short blonde hair, a small goatee and a grey pinstriped suit jacket sat behind the counter reading a men's health magazine.

'Can I help you?' he asked, lowering his reading material as we approached. He'd been reading an article relating to premature ejaculation.

'I hope so. I'm looking for—'

Marianne shoved me aside, leant across the counter and grabbed the man by his lapels to pull him closer. I stumbled, gripping the edge of the counter for support. 'What the—'

'Shut up,' she told me. 'This will be faster.'

The blonde man started to protest, but as soon as he looked into her eyes, he went limp, the battle lost. He had been eaten up by Marianne's sapphire gaze and her pungent scent of citrus sorbet.

'I need you to look through your records for the last ... two months,' she started to say. 'I want you to tell me the names of any particularly large parties that have hired vehicles from you. This includes buses or limousine services. Do you understand?'

He nodded.

'Do it now.' Marianne made sure to keep eye contact where possible or hit him with the suggestive nature of her scent. Rental guy was busy tapping away on the keyboard, occasionally looking back up at Marianne for confirmation of subservience.

'Do you want me to print it out?' he asked.

'No, just turn the screen around so that we can look at it.' Her voice still held that authoritarian tone—part of her compulsion.

Her scent touched the edges of my being, stroking my skin without obvious effect. I had no doubt that her compulsion would rattle me if she turned the full force of it upon me.

We skimmed through the list of hires. There were plenty—too many for me to look through with haste.

'What sort of names am I looking for here?' Marianne asked.

'Essentially *Manory*. George was the leader of the Cairns faction so he might have used his name, but then again, if they were trying to stay inconspicuous then perhaps they didn't use their own names at all. Just try looking for decent size groups that booked continuously over the two month period. Not all of The Protectors would have arrived on the same day, so there might be a steady influx of rentals. Oh and check for bus hire too.'

She nodded and went back to skimming the screen at warp speed. Every ten seconds she indicated she wanted the page refreshed. I'd only read through about six or seven names before she'd finished an entire list. 'There's nothing,' she muttered, pushing the screen back towards the zombie-like rental guy.

'Are you sure?'

'Yes.'

'Okay, we should try the next hire company.'

She agreed. 'Thank you ... Wallace,' she murmured, glancing at our helper's name tag. 'You may continue what you were doing before we arrived and you will forget that you ever encountered us.'

Marianne moved to leave, but then stopped, reaching out to touch Wallace's hand as he reached for the magazine again. 'By the way, Wallace, you don't need that magazine. The problem is all in your head.'

Wallace acknowledged the suggestion by throwing the magazine into the rubbish bin by his desk, a satisfied smile spreading across his lips. Meanwhile, Marianne dragged me by the backpack to the next counter along, uncaring whether I stumbled and fell against her.

'What if you've inadvertently damaged him with your Jedi mind tricks?'

'Unlikely'

I slapped at her hand to release me, muttering under my breath, 'The poor guy probably has jammed up pipes now.'

Marianne eyed me curiously, still gripping my back pack despite the persistent slapping from my end. Short of a smack down in the airport, she wasn't letting go until she was ready.

She released me as we reached the next rental company; back to business as she begun repeating the process with the next sales clerk, equally as helpful as Wallace under duress. Unfortunately, the new information did not yield any results either. We pestered several companies in the terminal, exhausting all avenues.

'What now?' Marianne grumbled, gnashing her teeth together in frustration.

'Taxis?' I suggested.

She shook her head. 'That will be impossible to narrow down. They don't take names, just drive you to your destination.'

'They take your name if you ring in advance and book a pick up.'

'That's true,' she conceded. 'I don't think they let you book taxis at the airport because there is always a steady stream of them coming and going. It's just not necessary.'

'So it's a good way to move through the city without being traced.'

Caleb and Thomas appeared at our sides, startling me. Caleb ignored my sharp intake of breath and swung a proprietary arm around my shoulders, burying his nose in my hair. 'Wow,' he said, grinning down at me. 'You always smell so good.'

I shucked his arm and then shoved him. 'Keep your distance.'

'Did you find anything?' Marianne interrupted, pulling us back on topic.

Thomas scrubbed a hand across his smooth chin. 'Caleb was right. There's been no outbound flights for the last two months from Hobart with the name *Manory* attached to the passenger lists.'

'What about group bookings?' I asked.

Caleb was looking down at his feet, scuffing one toe of his black combat boot with the other. 'There were a few, but nothing suspicious.'

'Did those group bookings happen to repeat themselves?'

'No, like I said, Elena, nothing suspicious, mostly just Japanese tourists.'

'What about you two?' Thomas asked, appraising us. 'Did you find out anything interesting?'

'Only that Wallace over there has premature—.'

'Can we focus, please?' I was not a fan of any conversation that may have led to ongoing discussions regarding *anyone's* sex life. 'While you were both gathering info on the flight logs, Marianne raided the databases of every car rental place in here, but there's nothing to report.'

Caleb asked a relevant question. 'What about van hire?'

'Nothing,' Marianne said in frustration. 'I searched everything I could think of and linked every connection. There's nothing. Elena and I considered that perhaps they took taxis from the area.'

'That would mean they are virtually untraceable,' Thomas replied.

'Not necessarily,' Caleb answered, 'Although it would be exceedingly difficult to gain headway. We'd have to find photos and interview the drivers, but that could take weeks.'

'We don't have weeks,' Marianne complained. 'We won't be able to keep the Vânători out of the cities forever.'

Outside the terminal windows a bus pulled to a stop in front of the curb. I groaned, realising there was yet another avenue difficult to trace.

'What is it, Elena?' Thomas cooed, touching my forearm in concern.

I pointed to the airport shuttle bus holding up traffic outside. 'They could have left here using that too. In fact, there's any number of ways they could have left the airport without leaving a trail.'

'And it's been too long to try and scent them now,' Thomas agreed. 'We'll have to think of something else.'

Everyone looked to me as if I had the answer. Usually I thought I did, but tonight I was at a loss as to what to do.

'Let's stick to Elena's original plan,' Marianne explained. 'We'll book into a hotel, find our feet and figure out what to do next.'

Caleb bobbed his head at the shuttle bus outside. 'Do you want to take that while it's already here?'

'Are any of you capable of carrying me without being tempted by my blood?'

Thomas and Caleb shook their heads guiltily. Marianne nodded, but an evil grin on her lips suggested she'd either rip my throat out while in transit or drop me in front of moving traffic. I decided to take my chances with public transport. 'We'll use the bus.'

'Chicken.' I thought I heard her murmur under her breath. The look on Caleb and Thomas's face suggested I was accurate.

* * *

As per the advice of our kindly driver, we were dropped in front of one of Hobart's most exclusive hotels boasting views of Mount Wellington and the Derwent River. At another time I might have been persuaded to revel in the beauty that this small city had to offer, but at present, I was unable to partake. My sole focus was to find the missing members of the IMI and to get Lucas home.

Finding my brother had tormented me for weeks, particularly since returning to our childhood home and finding the place completely deserted. Lucas had a mobile device containing documents and letters between the IMI's head scientist, Chester and our father, George. I wasn't the only one the IMI had experimented on. Lucas had been caught in the crossfire.

The information had been lacklustre, outlining results I had already discovered myself. The IMI had planned to raise me, nurture me and then butcher me, using my body and blood to harvest a serum that I now truly believed replicated vampirism. When it came to Lucas's involvement, it was all just best guess.

'Elena? Are you coming?'

I blinked a couple of times, shaking myself from my reverie. I smiled at Thomas who was looking at me expectantly. 'Yeah, I'm coming.'

* * *

After we checked in and headed up to our suite, we assembled in the lounge to hash out a plan. Marianne drew the shades while Caleb rifled through his back pack, searching for Synth Blood. He tossed each of us a bag, but I shook my head, handing it back to him. 'I'm good. I had some before we left.'

He grinned at me broadly. 'That's right. How could I forget?'

Thomas and Marianne wanted in on the private joke. 'What's going on?'

Caleb, settling down onto the couch next to me, jammed the straw into the foil at the top of the tetra pack, greedily slurping it down. He stopped only so he could speak. 'I took Elena to a neutral bar and she made a pig of herself.'

I gasped. 'Excuse me?'

Caleb shrugged. 'And roughed up a random vamp that tried to get a fang in.'

'I'm pretty sure it ended differently.' I eyeballed the big-mouthed murderer next to me, hoping he didn't mention my penchant for vampiric blood.

'If I hadn't broken his neck and thrown him in the dumpster, she'd have made a meal of him!'

'Caleb!'

'What? So you're a cannibal vamp.'

I slapped a hand over Caleb's gaping hole of escaping hot air, praying Marianne and Thomas didn't intend to stake me. 'Let me explain …'

Caleb shot me an apologetic look, perhaps realising his overshare of personal information.

'I …' Thomas stopped. 'I … I didn't realise that you drank vampire blood.'

'Only on weekends.'

'Caleb!'

Remorse all but a distant memory, Caleb smirked at his ill-timed joke. 'Look, you know Elena's half vânător. What did you expect?'

'I honestly don't know,' Thomas continued. 'William never mentioned anything about your dining habits.'

'I didn't have any the last time we were all together. Blood's only become a staple in my diet since our blood exchange in Bucharest.'

'Wait, you exchanged blood with William?'

'Long story. It's not something I like to advertise.'

Thomas and Marianne still looked uneasy. Caleb was no longer afflicted by any form of guilt.

'I only have to feed from blood once a week and I can drink whatever I want. Vampire blood tastes good, but I don't make a habit of it.'

'I should think not,' Marianne muttered. 'It's disgusting.'

'I can't help what I am any more than you can control your bloodlust. Let's not point fingers. We came here to find Lucas.'

'Great, so what's the plan?' Caleb murmured in between slurps of blood.

'Well, it's been over two and a half hours since we dumped Nicholas and Eric in Melbourne. I'll give them a call and see what they know. If it turns out we were wrong about this place then we won't have to waste our time looking for Lucas here.' I fished my mobile from my back pack; two missed calls—one from Lucius, the other from Marcus. I decided to call Marcus first. I wasn't ready to deal with my father just yet, particularly if he had discovered I had left the villa ... again.

'Buonasera?'

'Marcus it's me.'

'Who is *me*?'

'It's Elena. How many other Australian teenagers do you know?'

'This century or the last?'

Okay ...

'You rang me. I'm calling back to see what you wanted.'

'Your father called. He was looking for you.'

'What did you say?'

'I told him that you were on a plane heading for Australia.'

I slapped a hand to my face, groaning out loud. 'What the hell did you do that for?'

'I do not lie to my maker.'

'You said you would cover for me!' I was squealing like a crazed lunatic, but at this point it really didn't matter. Lucius was going to go wild.

Marcus clicked his tongue. 'I did try and cover for you.' He paused. 'At least until I logged into my e-mail account and saw that you had signed me up for the *Men versus Men* dating website. Now you're on your own.' He disconnected the phone while I sat there speechless, wondering if I'd taken my jokes just a little too far.

'You signed him up for all-male dating?' Caleb asked with spectacular enthusiasm. I should have known with vampire hearing he wouldn't have missed a beat.

I shrugged and tossed the phone aside. 'I did that like a week ago. He'd made some sort of comment about wanting to see Celine Dion in concert and I couldn't help myself.'

Caleb chuckled and slapped me on the back. 'Sebastian would have loved to hear that.'

'Sebastian will hear that!' I snapped. 'Stop talking about him in the past tense. He's fine. Everything is going to be fine.'

Caleb removed his hand from my back, holding it up in surrender. 'I didn't mean anything.'

'Whatever.'

I reached for the discarded device again and dialled Eric's number. I didn't see the point in calling my father. Avoidance was a good plan and he would only flip out until we had viable evidence that proved The Protectors were in the area.

'Elena?'

'Hey, Eric. Any news?'

'No. It appears Caleb may have been right. Passenger logs indicate your family boarded a plane to Hobart along with several other factions of the IMI. There was a large group from Sydney as well as Melbourne. Plus, the week before was an arrival from Santiago—at least thirty-three of them.'

'Nicholas and I are going to head to you now. We should be there within the hour.'

'Sorry you have to catch another flight.'

'We will be running.'

'There's quite a big stretch of ocean between the Australian coast and Tasmania.'

Eric chuckled. 'We'll jump most of it and swim the rest. What hotel are you booked into?'

I gave him the details and hung up shortly after. They were antsy about leaving me alone with the others, especially Caleb. I'd reassured Eric they'd brought blood which they'd been happily sipping on instead of opening one of my veins.

Marianne clapped. 'So, they both back Goth boy's evidence that the IMI is here?'

'It's *Caleb*,' he muttered, clearly not a fan of the nickname.

I nodded. 'It would seem that way.'

'So what's the next step?'

'Well, transport from the airport was a write off, but there are still several car hire companies that we could no doubt contact. Not to mention the local hotels they might have booked or freight companies used to transport their belongings—amongst other things.'

'What other things?' Caleb asked.

'Elena has this theory that they would have had to order supplies for a hideout as large as the one required to house such a vast group of Protectors,' Marianne quoted.

Thomas shook his head. 'Even if we managed to cross a likely trail, what if they used that spell to mess with people's minds?'

'They couldn't use it to wipe a paper trail, could they?' Caleb asked, looking in turn at each of our faces.

I reluctantly nodded. 'It's no different to your compulsion. All they would have to do is ask whoever they had mind-meddled to delete the records.'

'Then what hope do we have of finding them?' Marianne grumbled. 'If they can cover their tracks as well as we can, finding them could be impossible.'

'They made a slip with the passenger lists on the planes. If they forgot to edit those out, then they must have made other mistakes too. We just need to find them.'

Caleb bounced off the sofa and snatched a room key off the table. 'I'm going down to the computers in the lobby to see what research I can do into all the local transport companies.'

Marianne and Thomas stood up too. 'We'll help,' Thomas offered. 'Marianne can start looking through freight companies and I'll look at local building contractors for the last several years. Wherever they moved, it has to be big. Someone built it, so there would have to be a record.'

'That's a great idea, guys.' I yawned loudly, noticing the current time. It was almost four o'clock in the morning. 'I'm sorry, but I have to get some sleep again.'

'No worries,' Caleb and Thomas chorused. 'Just come down when you're ready.

'Wake me up at ten; otherwise you won't see me for days.'

'Who gets that honour?' Caleb enquired. Surely my reputation as a terrible morning person had not escaped the sanctity of the household?

I hauled my backside off the couch and headed for one of the bedrooms. 'Just bring coffee and sugar when you do.'

I face-planted the sumptuous mattress before my eyes had even closed.

CHAPTER EIGHT: ADMISSION

I stumbled from the bedroom a little after nine o'clock, groggy and not altogether human. I fumbled like a blind man, trying to find purchase on the objects around me. My eyes were resolute in remaining closed, my feet stubbornly tripping me up in the plush pile of the hotel carpet.

Heavy drapery pulled across the windows made the rooms darker than necessary, but the sun beat down on the panes from outside, vying to gain entrance. Imagining its warmth upon my skin almost settled me back to soothing dreams, but something wasn't quite right. For one, I was awake before noon; two, the imagined warmth from beyond the curtained windows was starting to feel a little *too* warm for my liking.

My whole body itched. At first it was a hum of static across my flesh, growing in intensity. Imaginary bugs crawled across my bones in roving masses, scurrying like moving currents within, securing my lungs in their pincer grip. Biting, they stole breath. A burning behind my eyes would not abate no matter how much I rubbed at them. The result was a sleep-caked face and blurred vision.

I scanned the lounge area of the suite with hooded eyes. Deserted, I assumed the others were still in the lobby doing research. Good. I couldn't stay upright, my bearings all messed up. Was I ill? Not possible. I could self-heal.

A shower. That's what I need. I'm just tired, stressed and worried about everything.

I staggered back into the bedroom, heading straight for the ensuite. My feet continued to disobey my forward movements and dragged like lead weights. I tripped up twice, various pieces of sporadic furniture keeping me upright. I hit my head on the TV cabinet. The second time I twisted my ankle, but no permanent damage.

In the ensuite there was a marbled spa bath in the corner. I imagined warm soapy water, invigorating and therapeutic. Logic dictated that immersing myself in this state was not a good idea.

I stuck to the shower, hoping the steaming hot water would ease some of my growing aches and pains.

It didn't. If anything, I felt worse.

I got out, hastily dried off, dressed and then grabbed my phone. I had an inkling about what was to come and an idea that may serve purpose at the frontlines.

I dropped onto the edge of the bed, feeling particularly dizzy. I clutched at the sheets and with the other hand, dialled my father's number. I knew—no matter how angry—he would want to know I was alright. I was most definitely *not* alright.

My eyes burned and the itching under my skin was turning into a simmering fire that I was beginning to recognise.

'Elena?'

I clutched the phone gratefully and closed my eyes. 'Yeah, Lucius, it's me.' In the background I heard sounds of a struggle. Growling and snarling came through the line, followed by shouts of direction from strangers and the accompaniment of hissing that defined angry vampires.

Lucius had to be near the frontlines, wrangling with the Vânători to keep them out of the cities and towns. I felt guilty I wasn't there, but grateful. I had faced vânători in the past and I had won, but fighting with thousands of them, watching comrades fall beside me? I wasn't so sure I could do that.

'Elena, now's not a good time. I'm in the middle of—' Lucius's voice cut out. A few grunts, snarls and pain-filled howls echoed down the line—tearing flesh the accompaniment; strange that I would recognise that sound.

'Lucius,' I grunted, knowing he would hear me anyway, 'something's happening to me and I think you should know because—'

Snarls and then the sound of silence breathed down the line. I gasped for air. My throat felt like it was closing over—not an allergic reaction. Heat had begun to sweep across my body. I did not want to go through this again, especially not knowing the reasons why or when it would end.

'Are you in danger?' Lucius yelled. His voice sounded distant, almost remote as if he'd put the phone down and walked away.

'It's like before, but not as sudden.' My cheeks burned with the steam from my tears.

'I can feel it coming and I don't know how to stop it.' Sobs began to wrack my entire frame. I felt stupid, but experience told me this would not be pleasant. My memories of being burned alive were particularly vivid.

'Elena,' Lucius said gently from the other end. 'What can I do?'

I was hoping he had the answer. We weren't even sure that this fever related to the Vânătors or why, but it was—despite my current discomfort—the perfect time to see if we were *all* afflicted.

Choking and gasping sounds followed by a grunt from my father and a large crack to be equated with breaking bones drowned out the sound of my shallow breaths. I needed his guidance, but I also hoped to impart my marvellous idea before unconsciousness.

'Did you have the dream again?'

I shook my head and then remembered he couldn't see me, so answered accordingly.

'Are you somewhere safe?'

'Yes!' I gasped. 'But you have to act quickly, Lucius. The burning is happening again.' I tried for another breath and failed. 'Call all vampires … to borders. Kill them while … Ahhhhhhh!'

I dropped the phone as if it were a burning piece of coal. I slid off the edge of the bed and collapsed onto the carpet, the sounds of my father yelling my name distant and unhelpful.

I screamed. My entire body burst into flames, engulfing me from head to foot. They danced across the top of my skin like liquid heat, singeing every inch of me with unforgotten agony.

As I opened my mouth to scream again, heat poured down my throat like molten lava, burning my air passages and melting my insides. It was excruciating. It was everything I remembered and then some.

'Elena!'

My eyes rolled, but I caught a glimpse of Eric, Nicholas and the others as they came cascading into the bedroom. Eric attempted to move me, but I was resolute in remaining, a scream halting his movements. My throat was a melted globule of skin and ooze, sounds emitted like wet gurgles.

'Don't touch her!' my father screamed through the phone.

Eric fumbled with the device, switching it to loud speaker. 'What's happening to her? We heard her screaming from the lobby and came as quickly as we could.'

'It has something to do with the Vânătors,' Lucius answered.

My back arched off the floor, contorting my body into unspeakable shapes. Another wave of fire engulfed me. My vision was now filtered with images of all things red. I thought my eyes were bleeding, but then realised the blood I saw belonged to those that wished to dominate, to those with fur and fangs and knowledge of my weaknesses.

'It's happening to the Vânătors here,' my father continued. 'Elena called for my help and to warn me. We're taking advantage of the situation now and killing as many as we can while incapacitated.'

'What does it mean?' Nicholas asked. 'Elena looks like she's dying.'

'I don't know,' Lucius replied. 'But it has to do with the connection they all share.'

'What do they all have in common?'

'The Alphas!' I spluttered, immediately sure it was true.

A sense of loss flooded through me and at the same time, a deluge of power washed against my burning skin. I'd felt a trickle of that loss and power when John had died, but that was before my last blood exchange, before I'd been able to shape-shift and harness my vânător nature.

Eric tried to restrain me. His hands felt like they were tearing the flesh right off my bones. I vowed to hang him by his short and curlies later!

'Stop trying to touch her!' Lucius shouted. 'It will pass.'

'This has happened before?' Nicholas asked.

'Sunday morning—the same time the Vânătors exposed themselves to that photographer in France.'

Caleb leant forward, his face blocking my vision. 'Elena? Can you hear me? Is something happening to the Alphas right now?'

I moaned, wallowing in my own self-pity. Everything hurt. I didn't care about anything right now, especially answering questions.

'What's happening?' Lucius asked via phone.

'She's unresponsive,' Caleb continued, 'but I think Sebastian and William must have been successful. I mean, if this connection is resultant of the alpha bond, maybe the two of them have killed some of them. That *could* be what's sending her crazy.'

'A connection being severed,' Lucius murmured. 'You might be right, Caleb.' He paused. 'Wait, something is happening here. The Vânătors are coming to.'

My back hit the ground, arms grew slack and panting subsided. The flames disappeared and I was released—anticlimactic after such a big stage show.

My eyes shuttered and breathing returned to normal. A slight sheen of sweat glossed my skin, but otherwise I was fine. There was a little bit of emotional trauma I'd have to wade through, but now was not the time to get wet. My cheeks were still streaked with tears and my eyes puffy, but all was quiet in Hobart and at the frontlines with Lucius.

I sat up slowly, the previous wave of dizziness beginning to dissipate. I was going to live—a much better prospect than five minutes before.

'Elena, are you okay?' Eric asked me.

'Yeah, I'm okay *now*.'

'You gave us quite a scare,' Nicholas said, touching my leg gently. 'We didn't know how to help you.'

'Apparently it's one of those freaky vânător things.' I meant it as a joke, but my voice came out tortured and breathy. I wasn't fooling anyone, even as I swiped angrily at my tear-stained face.

I grabbed the phone, took it off loud speaker and pressed it back against my ear. 'Lucius? Are you there?'

'I'm here, are you alright?'

'I'm fine. The Vânătors?'

'We killed a few.'

'I gather the war continues.'

The sound of renewed fighting confirmed it.

'There are so many, Elena. Our side has suffered. The turned vampires are not holding up. I just hope Caleb's theory is right that the connection between the Alphas and offspring severs on the death of the blood line.'

I wasn't exactly sure what that would mean for me or my continued existence. 'I can't go through that again, Lucius.'

'I'm sorry, Elena, but the pain will not be ending here.'

I gulped. 'How do you know?' He had to be guessing. The connection idea had been born five minutes ago. He had no facts, no confirmation of alpha death and no idea where and if Sebastian and William had been successful.

'We have other issues to address—namely your disobedience.'

'Oh.' He was really considering this now? Surely this seemingly repeated metaphysical occurrence begged full attention?

'Yes, Elena. I am not so distracted by the war that I have forgotten you left the villa after I expressly asked you not to. My only concern is for your safety and yet you constantly disobey me.'

Shit. In trouble again? I wonder when I'll try something original?

I started to make static noises with my throat. Not a great plan, but one that would get him off my back for now. 'Sorry, Lucius, I missed that … I think you're breaking up.' I made more static sounds.

'Elena …'

'I can't … hear you. I'll call back … later.' I hung up the phone. Nicholas and Eric were shaking their heads at me.

'Don't start,' I said, pulling myself to my feet. 'If I'm going to get it from him, I don't need it from you too.'

Eric's phone started to ring.

'If that's my father and you answer it, I'll kill you myself.'

Eric checked the display, smirked and then tucked the phone back into his pants.

'Do you really think you could be connected to the Alphas?' Caleb asked as he climbed back to his own feet.

'I don't know, Caleb. All I remember is the fire.'

Furrowed brows spoke of their confusion. 'What fire?'

'No one can see the flames, but it feels like I'm on fire. I feel every second of whatever is happening through these apparent bonds; whether real or not.'

Caleb was thoughtful. 'Do you think Sebastian's alright?'

I sighed, pinching the bridge of my nose in an act to ward off any tears that dared to slip past my control. 'I don't know, but if you're right and my little breakdown is because one of the Alphas is being injured or killed, then I guess that's positive.'

I may not have known how it would ultimately affect me, but it surely would be a representation of the boy's success?

'What does Sebastian mean to you?' Marianne asked, suspicion pinching her delicate features. 'You talk about him like he's your boyfriend which confuses me since I thought you were with William.'

I stilled, thrown completely off-guard. A second ago I had been on fire. Now I was being asked questions about my relationship with Sebastian and William. How had I evaded one fire only to be thrown blindly into another?

'What did you just say?' Asking me what colour my undies were or what colour my poop was would have been less disturbing. I never discussed my personal life or *feelings* with anyone—not even with the men in question.

'I want to know. You know how I feel about William, yet you dangle him from a hook while you appear to be busy reeling in his brother. What's your angle?'

'No angle.'

'Then what relationship do you have with William's brother?'

'None of your business.'

'William is *my* business.'

I studied the carpet for as long as possible, finally moving into the lounge room as if I had purpose. When I got there however; I was at a loose end. 'Is this really the time to be having this conversation?'

'No, it's not,' Thomas agreed, entering the room with the others. 'We've found some information that might help to locate the IMI.'

Marianne pressed a manicured hand to her brother's broad chest. 'No. That can wait a minute. I need to know what Elena is playing at.'

'Let's play a new violin. I'm getting real tired of this song and I'm desperate to find my brother.'

'Too bad, I'm asking the questions and I want some answers. You can't run away this time.'

Thomas, Eric, Nicholas and Caleb couldn't have looked further from comfortable if they tried.

I dropped onto the sofa, Caleb setting up residence beside me. His shoulder brushed mine—a show of solidarity perhaps?

'Is that what you think I did when I went to Bucharest, run away?'

'I would *never* have left William, no matter what.'

'The Vânătors discovered what I was, Marianne. They knew my location in Cairns and sent another alpha to scout for me. I was protecting my family—protecting Lucas!'

She shook her head. 'You should have run away with William. It didn't even cross your mind to put your trust in him.'

'Okay. Sure. Whatever you say. Are we done now?'

'I hope so,' Thomas chimed in, echoed by nods of agreement from the others.

'No. I want to know what your ultimate goal is.'

'Why?' My hands were suddenly knotted within the confines of my lap. Punching her in the face seemed like a good idea in theory, but her granite skin would undoubtedly just break my hand.

'William will never look at me if you keep offering him hope.'

Unbelievable.

'William and I aren't together,' I said as calmly as possible. 'We never really were.'

'Yet you're stringing him along even though it's clear there's someone else you're interested in. You don't think I haven't seen how many times you've pulled out your phone and dialled Sebastian's number or looked at the photos you have in your gallery?'

Blood vied for a party across my cheeks. I was so embarrassed right now I could barely even think straight.

'Have you even called William?'

'I ... yes ... ' Kill me.

The boy's eyes moved from my face to Marianne's as if caught up watching a particularly trying tennis match. Not one of them said a word as Eric and Nicholas moved to flank either side of the sofa and Thomas shadowed Marianne, encircling one of her wrists with his thick fingers.

They were preparing for an all-out bitch fight. I was more likely to pull the window drapes open and fry her like a piece of BBQ steak—minimum effort required.

Enough of this.

I slapped my hands against my thighs. 'Right, I think we're done here. Thomas, why don't you tell me what you found?'

He nodded and started to speak, but Marianne slapped a hand against his mouth. 'We are not finished.'

'Yes we are.'

Eric and Nicholas sighed audibly, Caleb eyeing us all with a supercilious grin.

'Is it easier for you to run away from this conversation and pretend that you're not playing with William's heart?'

'How many times do I have to tell everyone I'm not with William?'

'William is in love you, yet you're openly affectionate with your feelings for his brother.'

'Sebastian is ...'

Can I kill her and make it look like an accident?

I was still coming to terms with what Sebastian meant to me; friend, soulmate ... We'd kissed on several occasions, even admitted we had some warm fuzzies for each other, but I'd forbidden it to go further, scared of my own reactions and feelings. It was typical behaviour for me to hide in an emotionally exempt bubble and to deny, deny, deny.

Marianne scoffed. 'Let me guess? Friends? Don't you mean, friends with benefits?'

I took a deep, calming breath, envisioning Marianne bursting into flames as I threw open the window drapes, but then my conscience grabbed hold, reminding me of my own experience. I immediately regretted my urges; a terrible fate; even for a vampire bitch determined to lay my personal life bare.

'Marianne, back off. I'm not with either of them—both are free to be with whoever they want. I've never given either of them any indication that I wanted something more, so can we move on to finding Lucas now?'

Admitting to anyone how I truly felt was simply not an option. I kept those emotions locked up tight so I wouldn't have to face making a decision and dealing with the consequences they evoked. I certainly didn't owe Blondie an explanation when I couldn't even be honest with myself. The affections of my heart were superfluous compared to the warranted actions of everything else happening around us.

Marianne shifted closer, Thomas still restraining. I could tell she was getting ready to launch into another tirade. 'Does William know that you say his brother's name in your sleep?'

Now I was livid. 'I'm so ready to stake you! We can deal with this after the war!' I was shouting now. Any moment hotel security would be beating on our door.

'No. We can deal with this now. You need to admit it.'

All faces looked at me expectantly. I should have charged admission. 'Admit what?'

'That you're in love with Sebastian.'

I violently disagreed by wildly shaking my head. My fingers clenched and my skin itched with irritability. If she wasn't careful, I'd shape-shift and chew her bloody face off.

'You're wrong about everything.'

'You can't ignore their feelings!'

'I'm not!'

'I can't have William if he's in love with you!' She was so loud and animated that her blonde curls bounced around her ire-ridden face to tangle with her tongue.

'I didn't ask him to love me! I just want to get on with my life! I just want to save my brother!'

She moved like a jungle cat ready to pounce on their prey. Her teeth gnashed together and her canines had begun to extend. 'Do you think your little declaration changes anything? William still lays his life on the line for you.'

'What do you want me to do about it?' I roared, rising to my feet to meet her gaze. My fists were curled into tight balls by my sides, the knuckles white and the skin stretched taught across the bone. 'I've told him that I don't reciprocate the intensity of his feelings. I even asked if we could be friends, but he won't listen. I want him to stop because I know he'll never be happy with me because I can never really be truly happy with him!'

'Because you're in love with Sebastian!' Marianne shouted in my face, spittle spraying the end of my nose.

'Yes!' I fired back.

The room went instantly silent.

Oh crap.

I slapped my hands around my gaping mouth, thoroughly humiliated. What had I just admitted to?

I fell back onto the sofa, my knees suddenly weak and giving out. My breath came in short, sharp gasps as I struggled to pull in air. I wanted to take back those words so badly that I could feel the bile on my tongue ready to burn the admission from existence.

What have I done?

'I knew it,' Marianne said smugly. 'I knew from the first time I met you that William wasn't the one that you saw.'

'Enough Marianne,' Thomas chided. 'Enough.'

Eric and Nicholas intervened by guiding Marianne into the adjacent room. She protested, but Thomas pushed her from behind. She'd said her piece and now the damage was done.

Caleb took my fisted hands in his and smoothed the knuckles until I uncoiled the nails piercing the flesh of my palm. 'He loves you too, you know,' he said quietly.

'I don't want to talk about it.'

Caleb persisted. 'Last year, when he and I were helping you to break back into headquarters and Roshan and his pack ambushed us, everything changed. I saw it in his eyes when he was faced with the idea of having to let you go.'

'I said I don't want to hear it, Caleb.' I tried to yank my hands free of his grasp, but he held tight.

'I've known Sebastian for forty years. It's short compared to Nicholas and Eric, but they didn't see the look of despair in his eyes as he bloodied his fists between Bucharest to Paris because he couldn't find you. They didn't see the look on his face the night he finally found you again and you dived into his arms. They didn't see how he closed his eyes and savoured your scent like a man terrified to lose what he had all over again. He—'

'Don't say it, Caleb,' I urged, voice pitiful.

'He loves you.'

I managed to push him away and climb back to my feet. I started to pace to keep calm. 'It's a mistake.'

'What is it that you're afraid of?'

'I'm not afraid of anything anymore.'

'You're being a coward about this.'

'You don't know me well enough to judge!' I shouted.

'You're terrified that he's going to hurt you—reject you.'

'You don't know anything,' I spat.

'Don't I?' His voice was bitter. 'You're not the only one to have had a bad childhood where shitty things happened. Your

121

experiences should have made you stronger and more appreciative of the loved ones you do have, not closed off and scared to take chances. Sebastian is your match and you deny him because you're too afraid to experience anything real because you might get hurt. Life is about experience. It's about change, love, hate, pain and pleasure. It's time you grew up and realised this, otherwise you're going to miss out on everything worthwhile.'

I turned my back, not wanting him to see my fresh trail of tears. His words were a slap to the face, ringing truer than any bell. I'd been naive to think I could skate through life, never having to feel anything unless I truly wanted to. I was missing something vital; I could see the big picture around me, but wasn't ready to admire the view. Falling in love with Sebastian was not something I could take lightly nor was it something I could ignore.

I swiped fingers across my cheeks and shelved this subject in my mind for later perusal. For now, I really needed to focus on my brother. I didn't come halfway across the globe to admit feelings that made me blush, argue with Marianne and get a tongue-lashing from Caleb.

Caleb stood and made a play for my chin, ensuring my gaze was drawn to his. 'Elena?'

'I heard you, Caleb. Are we done now?'

He could do no more than nod before he released me.

I drew in a quick breath, put on my business face and called the other vamps back. It was hard given they'd just overheard Caleb's lecture. Marianne was itching to rub my face in it, but Thomas had gripped her upper arms, squeezing painfully enough to elicit a pained expression.

Eric and Nicholas remained impassive. I busied my fingers, pulling forward a stack of papers they had printed and left on the coffee table. There was a lot to go through, therefore no reason to risk locking gazes with any of them. I could feel Caleb's eyes upon me, but I refused to bow to pressure and look up. Perhaps that did make me a coward, but right now, I didn't give a crap.

I coughed. The tension in the room was palpable; filled with the weight of what everyone was *not* saying and everything I was thinking. 'What did you find that could be useful, Thomas?' I murmured, still studying the strewn paperwork.

He leant forward, tapping a finger on the top sheet of paper. 'Where should I begin?'

CHAPTER NINE: MUTINY

Karina gnawed her fingernails until they were bleeding, sore and little more than stumps. She'd decided the punishing behaviour was a physical consequence and constant reminder of her betrayal. It had been almost three weeks since Lucas had been drugged and hauled down to the IMI's laboratories without consent; her actions leading to his imprisonment somewhere in the facility.

What have I done?

She moved to add another digit to her mouth before realising there was nothing left to chew. Tattered skin; ripped and bleeding, Karina needed to torture herself to ease the burden of guilt.

She curled her hand into a fist and struck the wall in front of her. Pain coursed through every knuckle, reverberating through her forearm with jolting discomfort. The skin opened, releasing a steady flow of blood that dribbled through her fingers and down her wrist. A wet path trailed to stain her shirt sleeves, but she didn't care. If Lucas was suffering right now because of her; she deserved to suffer too.

Karina struck the wall a second time, opening the wounds further. Blood flowed anew; thick and fast.

'Lucas is becoming unpredictable,' Chester had said to her. *'He needs to be taken to the lab for treatment and analysis.'*

'But why? I can see that he's definitely better than a few months ago with spell-wielding, but he's still just boring, old Lucas.'

'There are things about Lucas you don't know,' George had answered.

'I've known him my entire life. He's just a goof. He's not dangerous or anything.'

'Nevertheless, we need you to do something for us—something for the IMI.'

That had sparked her interest. Karina had always tried to be a model Protector; studied hard, finished her studies with shining results and trained as vigorously as possible. If the IMI's most valuable employees were asking for a favour, who was she to turn it down?

'What do you need me to do?'

'We need you to inject Lucas with this.'

Karina remembered looking down at Chester's hand. The head scientist for the IMI held a syringe between his fingers. She hadn't realised enlisted help meant drug pushing. Did she really want to be a part of this when she had no idea what they intended to do with Lucas?

'What is it?'

'A sedative. It will just put him to sleep.'

'And then what?'

'Then we take him to the lab and figure out what has changed. He'll be back in training before you know it. You won't even have a chance to miss him.'

'If something strange is going on, maybe he'll be willing to help you work it out. Lucas is nothing if not agreeable.'

Karina hadn't missed the impatience. 'We have tried explaining to Lucas the reason he must stay, but he is still determined to go,' George had retorted.

'Wait, you just said he was changing or could be sick. You didn't say that he was trying to leave the IMI!'

Chester had waved a hand to silence her. 'A slip of the tongue. Lucas isn't going anywhere.'

Karina had shied from the outstretched hand and syringe. 'I don't know ...'

'Think of it this way,' George had said, narrowing his powder blue eyes upon her. 'You will be doing the IMI a big favour that will not be forgotten in a hurry, but if you choose to say no ...'

Karina had shaken her head. 'I don't understand. You're offering me a choice, but also threatening me?'

'*We don't threaten,*' Chester had said, showing off the gold crown at the front of his teeth. '*We just expect certain results from our most promising members of the IMI.*'

'*You think I'm promising?*'

'Oh yes,' Chester had said, nodding his head.

Karina understood now that he had been appealing to her overachieving nature and it had worked. She had always wanted to do well as a Protector and to hear Chester say that she was promising was a highlight.

Karina had shuddered at her lack of reluctance.

She'd plucked the syringe from Chester's fingers and only briefly wondered if Lucas would ever forgive her. '*How am I supposed to get this into him?*'

Chester had patted her shoulder in a condescending gesture. '*Distract him.*'

'*How am I supposed to do that? We haven't talked much since we got here.*'

'*Use your imagination. You have certain ... assets that I'm sure will draw his attentions long enough for you to inject him with the sedative.*'

Karina had snorted. '*He'll think I'm an idiot if I try hitting on him now after seventeen years of knowing one another and only being friends.*'

George had participated with a shrug. '*He's still a man and you are very beautiful, Karina. It would not be difficult for you to figure something out.*'

Oh, she'd figured something out alright. She'd ambushed Lucas in the passages connecting to his sleeping quarters; followed him to his bunk and tried inflating his ego with complements about his magical skills. When that hadn't worked, she'd forced herself on him. It wasn't until she'd begun kissing him and making him think that certain *other* activities were going to eventuate, did he actually relax enough for her to inject him.

Then he'd gotten mad—really, really mad.

Karina punched the wall again, moaning as blood flowed more freely—the pain a constant companion. She hoped self-inflicted distress would overwhelm her guilt, but nothing seemed to be working. Maybe if Lucas was an asshole who repulsed her, it would be easier to ignore what she had done, but Lucas was handsome, faithful, funny and honest. He would never have done to her what she did to him.

'My God! Karina? Are you okay?'

It was Annabel; one of The Protectors that had greeted her Cairns faction at the Melbourne airport. They didn't know each other very well, but were on a first name basis.

'Yeah, I'm okay.'

Annabel reached for her battered hands, studying them and the sight of the bloodied wall. 'I think you should go see the nurse. It looks like you need stitches.'

Karina braved a look. Oh yeah, she needed stitches. Her hands were a mangled, swollen mess.

'What were you thinking?'

Karina shrugged. 'Cabin fever, I guess. We've been here for a month and I've never been outside.'

Annabel settled hands upon her thick hips. 'Do you need to talk to someone?' She pointedly looked at the blood again. She might as well have said, '*only the unhinged take on steel and hope to win*'.

'Do you think I'm crazy?'

'It's not normal to bloody yourself up unless something is bothering you, Karina. I've been watching you, you're miserable. If you won't talk to me about this, then please talk to someone else.'

'I'm fine.'

Annabel's eyes narrowed. 'No you're not. People who are *fine* don't try to break their hands.'

'I'll go to the nurse now.'

Annabel nodded, satisfied. 'I'll come with you.'

Karina kept her face neutral. 'Are you worried I won't go if you don't follow me?'

'Frankly … yes. From what I hear from your father, this isn't your usual behaviour.'

You mean the usual selfish bitch that only cares about herself?

Karina nodded in acknowledgement, following Annabel. She couldn't argue with the truth. She hadn't felt like herself for weeks and ironically, she wasn't sure if she wanted to. Her actions had forced her to take a long hard look at herself. She wasn't sure she liked her reflection anymore and was uncertain how to change it.

The walk to the nurse's station didn't take long. With all the passages and intersections in this place, it only took five minutes. The wall Karina had pounded was outside the laboratories where Lucas might have been held; the nurse's station only a hop skip and a jump from those restricted areas.

Alba—the IMI's designated nurse—sat in front of her computer typing notes. She immediately looked up as they entered, eyes zeroing in on the bloodied hands that hung limply by Karina's side. 'My goodness! What happened?' she said, rushing to her medical supply cabinets and pulling out various dressings and ointments.

'I ... um ... I ...'

'I stumbled upon her pounding walls,' Annabel answered, manner reproachful.

'If you were trying to get to China, you need to go down.'

Alba's attempt at a joke?

'I'll leave you both to it,' Annabel said, smiling first at Alba and then directing negative attention back to Karina. 'I'll let Malcolm know you're here.'

Karina shook her head. 'Please don't tell dad. He'll just worry.'

'And rightly so,' Annabel muttered, making a beeline for the exit.

'Please, Annabel. I won't do this again. I don't even know what I was thinking.'

'I think the question is why did you do it in the first place?' Alba murmured as she began to dab antiseptic over the abrasions. Karina winced, but welcomed the pain.

Annabel studied her thoughtfully before swiping the panel to re-open the door. One last look was cast over her shoulder on exit. She wouldn't let the matter rest for long, but Karina would act happy if needed. After all, she'd been convincing enough to let Lucas think she was going to bed him.

Ugh.

'You must have been pretty angry to want to hurt yourself like this.' Alba unfurled Karina's fingers and studied the chewed stubs. 'Or you're self-harming.' She then pulled back the long sleeves of Karina's shirt, running her fingers over the pale skin.

Karina snatched her arms back. 'I'm not self-harming. I just ...'

'What is it, Karina? You know that you can talk to me, right? As your physician, I'm bound to keep what you say between us.'

That didn't make Karina feel any better.

'Karina?'

'I'm not self-harming,' she repeated. 'I feel guilty.'

'Guilty?' Alba's brows narrowed over her expressive eyes. 'What does someone your age have to feel guilty about?' Next she snapped on a pair of latex gloves.

'Lots of things.'

'Such as?'

'Betraying a friend's trust.'

'I see.' She focused on a syringe packet, unsheathed it, then plunged the needle into the end of a bottle. The syringe brought back a deluge of memories, namely the look on Lucas's face when he realised he'd been played.

Alba noticed Karina's quick withdrawal and soothed her arm. 'It will sting a little, but I do need to numb you up so I can suture. I promise I'll be gentle.'

'I don't want to be numb, I need to feel it.'

Alba shook her head, extracted the needle, flicked it to remove air bubbles and then moved to begin injections. 'Why don't you tell me who the friend was that you think you betrayed?'

The question caught Karina off-guard. 'What does that matter?'

Alba shrugged, stashing the empty syringe and used gauze into contaminated waste bins. A second later she started to assemble her suture kit. 'Okay, no names. Tell me how you betrayed your friend's trust then?'

'I lied to him. I used him to further myself within the IMI.'

'I see.'

Karina felt the skin around her knuckles pull taught then relax as each cotton thread repaired torn flesh; there was no more pain. 'How can you possibly see?'

Alba smiled. 'You aren't the first woman to break a man's heart.'

'I didn't break his heart! I used him!'

'He will forgive you eventually.'

Karina snorted. 'No he won't. My actions got him sent away.'

'There aren't too many places someone can be sent here, Karina. He will be back.' Her eyebrows narrowed further; either her sutures required complex thought or something about her own response had her concerned.

'That's what they told me,' Karina answered bitterly. 'They said he'd be back in training before I knew it.'

Alba was actually frowning now. 'Who are we talking about, Karina?'

128

'I already told you, it doesn't matter.'

She picked up the scissors and cut the string on the last suture. 'You're referring to Lucas Manory, aren't you?'

'How do you know that?'

'He's a patient of mine. I fixed some cuts and bruises after his last training session with Beryx, but haven't seen him since.'

Alba hurriedly cleaned away the bloodied instruments and sourced more ointments as well as a bandage.

'They took him to the laboratories, you know,' Karina continued meekly. There was no point pretending they weren't discussing the same person. 'Chester said he was changing, that something was wrong with him.'

Alba shrugged. 'It's possible. We've all seen what he's capable of in a training session.'

'Yeah, but three weeks in the lab? What are they doing to him? Chester promised he'd be in and out. He missed his birthday.'

'He did?'

'Yes. I truly believed he'd be gone a few days at the most.'

'What part did you play, Karina?'

'I injected him with a sedative. George said he wasn't compliant about getting checked out.'

'Lucas's father instigated this?'

'And Chester.'

Alba focused solely on bandaging up her hands. 'He seemed fine when I saw him last.' She paused then looked up at Karina. 'I've been in the laboratories. I haven't seen Lucas.'

'Where else could he be? I've been to his bunk. I check the training rooms daily. He isn't anywhere.'

'This is a big place. Perhaps you just keep missing him?' Alba seemed convinced that had to be the explanation, even nodding at her own suggestion.

'I don't think so. They've locked him up somewhere—I'm sure of it.'

Disbelief warred with Alba's features. 'The IMI is about protecting people. You don't lock up members and experiment on them. If Chester has Lucas in the labs then he is probably sick and in quarantine. In which case, they'll be taking very good care of him.'

'I guess you're right.'

'Tell you what,' Alba said, smiling again. 'I have to pick up pathology results for another patient this afternoon. I could talk to Stephanie, Chester's assistant and ask if Lucas is there and if he's okay.'

'Could you do it now?'

'I don't really have the time. I have a stack of paperwork to get through.'

'Please. It will only take a minute and if I know, then I can stop hurting myself.' Karina knew she was playing on Alba's duty-of-care, but if she knew for certain Lucas was okay, perhaps she could hate herself a little bit less.

Alba sighed. 'Wait right here. I'll be back soon.'

Karina started grinning, nodding her head vigorously. 'I won't move a muscle.'

'Good.'

Karina was true to her word. She sat on the chair in which Alba had allocated and studied her fingernails. They were a disaster and a reflection of her current self-loathing. She also noted that she'd given up on washing her long, dark hair, wearing make-up and had lost a couple of kilos that her already slender frame couldn't afford. She just hoped Lucas was okay. If he was being held against his will, then she'd never, ever be able to forgive herself.

Karina looked up as Alba returned, the nurse's expression relatively neutral. 'Did you find him?' She jumped to her feet, a positive response her only hope.

Alba deposited samples on the workbench and then threw a pile of files onto the desk by the computer. 'He is there,' she said darkly, a storm brewing in her eyes now. 'It's not what I expected.'

'Is he okay? Is he sick? Is he in quarantine?'

'No. I don't think he is.'

'Tell me.'

'I don't know if ... Look, I have to re-evaluate some things before I can figure out what I just saw.'

'What did you see?'

Alba flopped into the chair behind her desk. She folded her hands in her lap then proceeded to twist her fingers into knots while deliberating. What she had just seen had changed her perceptions of the IMI. She was uncertain if she could be part of an organisation that held a healthy child against their will.

'Alba? What's happened to Lucas?'

'I can't discuss it,' she said, shaking her head. 'It's beyond anything I had expected to find.'

'Tell me what you saw. Please.'

Alba now busied her fingers with the hem on her skirt. 'I need to get him out of here.'

Karina was taken aback. 'What do you mean? We follow orders, we don't leave. No one would *really* hurt him. George knows about this.'

'You don't understand. What they are doing to him, it's not right. He's just a boy.'

'What are they doing to him?'

Alba took a deep breath, closing her eyes in an effort to dispel the image of Lucas in her head. 'I can't.'

'Tell me!' Karina shouted. 'Or I'll go there myself!'

Alba was too shocked to process that telling one child about another's predicament was probably not a wise decision. 'He's shackled to a gurney in one of the rear labs. He's conscious, but they've got him gagged. There are tubes everywhere attached to some sort of machine that's filtering his blood.'

'So maybe he's really sick and they're giving him blood transfusions.' Her voice sounded weak and uncertain, searching for plausibility in a situation that sounded grossly surreal.

'Then why is he gagged and restrained?'

Karina slumped against the wall, devastated that her fears were plausible.

'He saw me through the door,' Alba continued, haunted. 'I could see it in his eyes—he wanted me to help. No one should be treated like that.'

'Are you sure that's what you saw?' Karina needed some sort of assurance.

'He is handcuffed to the gurney, Karina. He can't get away and he can't yell for help. I don't care if we've all been rallied here for some sort of inoculation that will protect us against the Vampires and vânători, I can't witness this blatant abuse and do nothing.'

'They have a chemical deterrent against vamps and werewolves?'

Alba came back to the present. 'It's what my husband was told.'

'What can we do?' Karina murmured. 'I don't know what the IMI have planned for us, but you're implying that Lucas is suffering some form of torture—'

'We have to get him out.'

'How do we do that?'

'I don't know. I have access to the labs because I use some of the equipment, but there is always someone watching.'

Karina moved away from the wall and sat back down on the chair across from Alba's desk. 'How did you find Lucas now without someone watching?'

'Stephanie went to get my pathology results. I did a quick scout of the rooms I'd never seen.'

'That was sneaky.'

'I honestly don't know what came over me.' She stopped fidgeting with her hemline and rested her hands on the desk in front of her instead. 'I shouldn't have said anything. I know you care for Lucas, but you're also a child—a child that does not need to concern herself with such adult matters.'

'They involved me when they asked me to sedate him. It's my fault he's in there now how do we get him out?'

She hesitated, conflicted only momentarily. 'Even if I can get Lucas out of the labs, there's nowhere to go. He's too young, it's too far and he'll never make it back to Casey Station without freezing to death first.'

'How else can you leave here?'

'There's a light aircraft that travels here once a month to drop off supplies.'

'How do you know that?'

'My husband's one of the forklift drivers in the dock. He has access to their scheduled arrivals and departures.'

'So we make sure Lucas escapes from the lab the same day the plane arrives.'

'Exactly.'

'When does that happen?'

'Tomorrow.'

'Well, that's cutting things a bit fine.'

'It's either that or wait another month.'

'Okay, supposing we get Lucas into the dock area and onto the plane, what then? He has no money, no passports and no place to go.'

'Does he have friends he can trust that are outside the IMI?'

'Just his sister Elena, but she's long gone.'

Alba rocked back in her chair in quiet contemplation. 'You're talking about the half-breed, aren't you? The girl that the Manory's allowed to grow up in their household?'

Karina pulled a face. 'It's weird hearing people talk about her like that. I didn't even know until a few years ago. Before that she was just Elena—Lucas's little sister.'

'What happened to her?'

'I don't really know. A few months ago she was still in Cairns. Some vânǎtors set up a new den in our town; Elena was abducted by the alpha and we had to rescue her. After that, the Manory's decided it would be better for her to move to headquarters—you know—because an alpha had been killed and others would come looking.'

'Why was that significant?'

'She's half vânǎtor. The alpha we killed thought he could start some sort of super pack with Elena so everyone was worried that when others came looking they would think the same thing.'

'Were you sad to see her go?'

'Not really. Elena was okay, but she was kind of a show off. She was always getting into trouble and dragging Lucas into it with her.'

'So we can't rely on her to help get him out?'

'If she knew what was happening to Lucas right now, she'd flip her lid and be here in a heartbeat. They were always really close.'

Alba started to frown again. 'Why didn't she come with the rest of The Protectors from the Bucharest division when they moved here?'

'Something must have happened. Maybe she ran away or decided to stay in Europe?' Karina felt her own brow crumple. Something definitely wasn't right. She was certain Elena would be here now if she knew, but since she wasn't, then where the hell was she?

'Are you sure you can't get in contact with her?' Alba said, interrupting Karina's train of thought.

'I wouldn't have a clue where to start.'

Alba sighed. 'Then I guess we have to hope that Lucas is resourceful enough to look after himself.'

'I could go with him.'

Alba didn't answer for several seconds, staring at Karina as if she had gone completely mad. She blinked several times, her mouth slightly ajar as shock shaped her lips and halted her words. 'You can't do that.'

'Why not?' Karina protested. 'I got him into this mess. The least I can do is get him out of it.'

'You have a father that would miss you terribly. Not to mention you'd become an outcast from this society and either shunned or hunted. I may not be a Protector, but my husband has explained how this society works.'

Karina tried to swallow the giant knot forming in her throat. Talking brave was one thing, but acting on it was something else entirely. 'I have to make up for what I've done.'

'No.'

'You can't possibly understand what it feels like to be a part of this clan only to realise it could have all been built on lies. You can walk away—you're human. If I walk away, I walk away from everything I've ever known, but it'll be my choice.'

Alba streaked a hand through her hair, tugging on the roots with her slim fingers in exasperation. 'I can't believe I'm going to be a part of this. What kind of responsible adult am I?'

'The kind that's going to get to the bottom of what's going on in this place and then tell everyone that you can.'

'Mutiny?'

Karina grimaced. 'I never believed the IMI could be capable of this, but Lucas is proof.'

Alba finally released her hair, some of the ends unsettled and now standing at attention. 'We're really doing this, aren't we? I'm going to break into the labs, defy protocol and help two teenagers escape into a world outside that neither of them is prepared for.' She sounded tired all of a sudden.

'Give us a little credit,' Karina muttered. 'Lucas and I both excelled in our training and academic studies. We'll think of something.'

'Why does that not make me feel any better?'

Karina swallowed back her lump of rising bile. 'Try not to think about it too deeply. It's what's stopping me from throwing up all over your desk.'

'Really?'

'No. Hand me a bucket. I'm gonna blow.'

CHAPTER TEN: CLUES

My cheeks hurt. In fact, my entire face hurt. I'd been grinning like an idiot for ten minutes. I should have lowered my lips and covered every exposed molar, but it wasn't likely considering my mood; I was psyched.

A little foot shuffle ensued as a rented silver Hummer gleamed at me from valet parking, beckoning with eighteen-inch chrome wheels and ground clearance that would allow you to mow down a buffalo and call it a speed bump.

The shuffle transitioned into an awkward dance with too much hip movement and random head-banging. I looked incredibly stupid and people were staring, but I remained unfazed.

Caleb appeared next to me, dangling keys from his outstretched fingers.

I snatched them up. 'I've never driven a Hummer before.'

'Do you have your licence?'

I snorted. 'A licence is just a suggestion.'

'But you *can* drive, right?'

I rolled my eyes. 'Probably better than you.'

Eric arrived with the others in tow. 'Shall we go?'

'Are we seriously letting her drive?' Marianne whined.

'Funny. You can ride in the boot.'

Piling into the car, I made sure the windows were up and sunroof closed. These vamps were born, not turned, but sun was still a major issue. 'Where are we going, Thomas?'

'First stop is a wholesale food outlet in a place called Derwent Park.' He gave me the address which I quickly entered into the on-board GPS—another awesome feature.

I placed the keys in the ignition. 'Everyone ready?' Murmured responses were followed by me pulling the car out of the valet area and onto the main road. With great enthusiasm, I started bouncing up and down in my seat, head lolling from side to side.

'Elena, what are you doing?'

I smiled at Caleb who eyeballed my idiocy. He wasn't the only one. 'I'm Jim Carey from that movie *Ace Ventura Pet Detective*.'

Blank stares greeted me so I stopped bouncing and focused on my driving. I still managed to overcorrect, spin the wheel and drive up onto the median strip.

'Are you sure you don't need a license?' Caleb muttered.

'Do you want to sit in the back with Marianne?'

'Hey!' she squawked from the rear.

Caleb grabbed the hand rail as I floored it, ploughed through the red light and narrowly missed more oncoming traffic. Marianne's admonishments from the rear were endless.

Fifteen minutes later, I'd endured a barrage of ongoing discussion regarding my driving techniques. The Hummer was completely unscathed and we'd all arrived safely at our destination. I had no idea what all the fuss was about.

I parked as close to the front doors as possible given everyone's affliction to sunlight, yet by the time I entered the wholesaler, the others were already speaking with the cashier, intense expressions targeted to compel. A manager was requested; a simple task with simple instructions. Asking nicely would have done the trick too.

A fit looking guy in his forties bounded down a flight of stairs beside me. I darted out of his way as he rounded the landing.

'What can I do for you folks?' He seemed nice enough, although, he did pass the cashier a brief look of displeasure. I suspected it had something to do with his name repeatedly parroted over the loud speaker.

Marianne snatched the microphone from the eager cashier's hands and then whispered in her ear. The cashier shook her head, rubbed her eyes and promptly went back to her previous task.

'We need some information.' Thomas said, suffusing his compulsion scent of lemon myrtle within the vicinity.

'What sort of information?'

'We'd like to know your biggest account holders and access their delivery addresses and contact numbers please.' At least his compulsion was polite.

The manager nodded, compliance his only option. 'Certainly. If you would follow me to my office?'

Twenty minutes later we had addresses for several food outlets and a few smaller companies.

We crossed off the big name corporations like Woolworths or Coles supermarkets. However, smaller companies seemed viable, so we decided to look into them to be on the safe side. The IMI would need food; we had a starting point.

We piled into the car again and headed to the suburb of Kingston. The addresses turned out to be for a sporting complex and several primary and high schools in the local area. We scouted each location, checked for scents or physical trails, but were soon back in the car again, chalking up the failure.

Thomas had several other wholesalers to try, so we spent the rest of the morning and most of the afternoon searching for a valid connection to the IMI. Unfortunately, we came up empty at every turn. If the IMI were in Hobart or anywhere else in Tasmania, we would eventually find them by sourcing their food supplier.

We headed back to the hotel feeling underwhelmed by our lacklustre day. My thoughts fell to Sebastian and the morning's declaration of emotion. It was the first time all day that I'd had enough quiet time to ponder my admittance of love.

I'd succeeded in keeping focused on the task of admiring the Hummer and the various destinations we'd scoured, but now it was difficult to maintain deflection. I was circling back to Caleb's lecture and obsessing over proclamations of Sebastian's mirrored affections. Could I really believe that? Could Sebastian love me the way that I loved him?

'Elena, you missed the turn,' Caleb piped up, rousing me from inner speculation.

I observed the GPS. Sure enough, it ordered me to perform a U-Turn. I'd be driving the Hummer into the water if I didn't about face in the very near future.

'Hang on a second,' Caleb said, now gripping my arm tightly. 'Head in that direction.'

137

I slowed to a stop, leaning across the steering column to see where he was pointing. 'Holy crap,' I muttered. 'I never even considered boats.'

'New Zealand, Antarctica; there are ships that travel to South America from here too,' Nicholas added.

I steadied my hands on the wheel, looking back down at the GPS.

I hadn't just missed one turn off to arrive at this point, but several.

Caleb's eyes narrowed as he tapped the route map display on the dash, perhaps as confused as me. 'I see multiple missed turns. How could that happen?'

'Surely we all couldn't have missed it?' Thomas added. 'Although, it's fortuitous regardless!'

'Well don't blame me,' Marianne chided. 'I'm in the back.'

'No one is even talking to you,' Thomas answered, shaking his head. I imagined that he'd probably rolled his eyes too, much to everyone's amusement and Marianne's disgust.

The Hobart docks loomed before us. Ships and small boats bobbed up and down in the water, distorting the view of the falling sun. I didn't believe in fate. I was the first person to call bullshit, yet it was hard to deny the series of events realised by a distracted, unlicensed teen driving in the wrong direction.

At least my preoccupied state had given Caleb fresh ideas to find The Protectors. These new ideas also contained possibilities of the IMI travelling beyond the Hobart region and leaving Australia altogether!

I started to shake, wondering if I hadn't led everyone on a wild goose chase. Hobart might have been a transit city after all; the thought of wasting so much time made me sick to my stomach.

'I know what you're thinking, Elena,' Eric said over my shoulder, 'but we still need to exhaust all possibilities including alternate methods of transport.'

'This will be a good chance for us to explore other transportation avenues too,' Nicholas agreed. 'We can't exactly track travel via taxis and buses, but we can still look into boats.'

'There are freight companies that operate from the area. I can double-check whether they have distributed food supplies recently,' Thomas added with injected positivity.

'So our efforts are still productive,' I breathed, hoping the words were true.

'Yes,' Eric answered. 'I wouldn't have driven around all day if I didn't think we were on the right track.'

'But if they moved on from Hobart, they wouldn't necessarily be getting food from here.'

'Which is why Nicholas will explore other avenues The Protectors may have used to vacate the area.'

I sniffed. 'Okay.'

Caleb directed my attentions to a road leading down the side of some warehouses and shipping slips. I checked my mirrors before pulling back onto the road and driving the short trip down narrow side streets and into an unmanned loading zone.

'We'll get a ticket ...' Marianne mused.

'I don't see anywhere else to park.'

'Over there,' Nicholas said, shoving a rigid finger past my peripherals. 'There's a bay next to the side of that shed.'

Re-joining the afternoon traffic invited a forklift driver with a full load of cargo to toot at me. It's true what they say about checking your blind spot.

'I'll go with Nicholas,' I stated, finally finding the safety of the parking bay and switching off the engine. 'Nicholas and Lucas look very similar. It might spark memories in combination with photographs.'

Nicholas jumped out and immediately opened my door. I smiled, taking his offered hand. The car had since emptied, everyone else off on their own missions.

'May I carry you? It would be preferable to avoid sun and move with haste.'

'Oh sure, whatever you need.'

He quickly scooped me into his arms and dashed for cover. It was anticlimactic; the wind barely blew my hair nor the sun touch my skin before we were hiding in shadow again. I supposed that was the entire point.

Nicholas followed as I pushed the creaky metal doors of a Derwent River tour operator open. I didn't hold high hopes for tracking The Protectors this way, but it was better than nothing.

'Hello,' the lady at the desk said as we walked in. 'How can we help you today?'

She looked friendly; dimples and kind, brown eyes glistened with warmth.

'My friend and I wanted to ask some questions if that's okay?'

'Sure, honey. What would you like to know?'

'Does your company offer tours to other areas besides the Derwent River?'

'No. We do Lunch and dinner cruises taking in views of Mount Wellington, but we don't venture into the open sea if that's what you're asking.'

'Do you know any operators that do?'

She retrieved a notepad and pen from a desk draw. 'Where is it that you want to go?'

I laughed. 'I'm not sure exactly. I wanted to know if there were any nearby Islands that were habitable or cruises between here and New Zealand or South America.'

She made notes on the pad in front of her. 'You're better off trying the private charter companies. Some travel to New Zealand if their fares are willing to pay top dollar. There are larger companies that do cruises too, but go through a travel agent for that. As far as islands go, there are a few little ones, nothing tourists would be especially interested in. If you're after a bit of adventure, you could try the research vessels that travel to Antarctica. The season ends in May, I think, so you should be able to book tours if you want.' She ripped out the piece of paper she was writing on and handed it to me. 'These are private charter companies that I know of. If you decide to do the Antarctica thing, then follow this strip and you'll find their offices.'

I reflected her genuine smile. 'Thank you. You've been really helpful.'

'My pleasure. Now are you sure I can't interest you in a dinner cruise this evening?'

My smile dimmed. 'Sorry.'

She waved goodbye as Nicholas led the way back outside again.

'Okay, let's try this place.' I was still pointing at the paper as he swept me off my feet and hit the ground running.

* * *

An hour later and the sun had sunk low enough in the sky that Nicholas no longer bothered carrying me around like a backpack.

We had made progress thanks to his speed and though no one had been specifically helpful, we'd eliminated a lot of lost causes.

Nicholas and I consulted the piece of paper again. The last name was a deep-sea fishing company offering week-long trips into the Southern Ocean. It was a long shot, but the alternative was jumping aboard every moored vessel and asking if they had seen my brother—a last resort.

Deep Blue Fishing Charters was easy to find. A massive fibreglass fish was affixed to the roof of their offices—an even bigger sign said as much.

'Crap,' I said, tugging on the locked door for good measure. 'They close at five-thirty.'

'We'll come back tomorrow,' Nicholas answered calmly. He was always so level-headed. I wondered how I could master his Jedi skills.

'Can I help you folks?'

A man dressed in flannel and a pair of heavily stained overalls stood next to the adjacent building, holding a bucket of fish goo in one hand and a lit cigarette in the other. He looked as if he'd had a long day and judging by the bucket and the unloaded boat behind him, it wasn't over yet.

I coughed; a wreath of cigarette smoke encircled me. 'Do you know if anyone who works here is still around? It's just hit five-thirty and they're locked up tight.'

'This is my place.'

'Oh, great, well, the lady at Derwent River Cruises gave us your details. She said you might be able to help us.'

He took a long drag on his cigarette, swallowed it down like the tough guys on TV and expelled it painful slow through his bulbous nose. 'What do you need?'

'Do you ever travel to any other mainland—like nearby Islands, for example?'

'We sail so we can still see the coast and anchor where the fishing is good. We take a crew of six with us and enjoy the spoils.'

He jabbed a thumb over his shoulder at the boat. 'Has a nice little kitchen, a couple of bedrooms below deck and an entertainment space if the fishing gets a bit much. Why? Are you interested?' He looked me up and down slowly. Judging by the creased brow, he'd realised that these feet didn't leave land unless they had to.

'No. We don't want to book a charter. Sorry.'

He started to walk off, shrugging his shoulders to indicate the end of his part in the conversation.

'Hang on a sec,' I said, digging into my back pocket for my mobile.

I'd transferred all the documents Lucas had left for me in Cairns as well as photos of us. 'Would you mind taking a look at these?'

I held the photo of Lucas for him to inspect. 'Do you recognise this guy?'

He shook his head, the breeze rustling his thinning hair, wafting the distinct smell of 'fishy ashtray' in my direction.

'What about these two?' I scrolled through until I found one of Susan and George.

He shook his head again. 'Are they lost?'

'It's my family. I'm trying to find them.'

'Well, good luck with that, lady.'

'Excuse me, sir,' Nicholas said, stepping in front of the fisherman's path. 'Do you know of any other tour companies or charter boats that cater to particularly large groups?'

The fisherman tried to unsuccessfully side-step Nicholas. 'There are always large groups of people milling around here.'

'This group would have been carrying luggage. They might have been here three weeks ago, possibly eighty to one hundred of them.'

He suckled his cigarette until the whittled butt warmed his fingers enough for him to toss it into the waters behind him. 'Doesn't ring a bell. Now if you'll excuse me, I'm busy.'

Hope waned with the setting sun and now all that was left was to wander from boat to boat, hoping someone had seen any of them.

Finding Lucas is like finding a needle in a haystack.

'Um, excuse me?'

Nicholas and I pivoted, drawn by a meek voice behind us. A boy—no more than twelve or thirteen—was on hands and knees, scrubbing at the fisherman's deck with a bucket of soapy water. I was sure he had not been there a second ago.

'Hey there,' I said, wandering over.

He smiled shyly. 'Sorry. My dad can be really rude sometimes. I'm Tim.' He scratched at his freckled nose and then dumped the sponge into the bucket, spilling water everywhere. 'I heard you talking. Dad wouldn't know anything about that big group you were talking about because he was on a charter that week.'

Nicholas and I passed a look between us. 'Are you telling us you saw a group like my friend just described?'

Tim's head bounced up and down eagerly, his floppy, auburn hair falling into his eyes. 'They arrived in taxis carrying lots of luggage. They looked kind of funny too.'

'What do you mean?' I asked, drawing nearer.

He sniffed, assaulting his nose again with grotty fingernails. 'They were carrying big jackets and gloves.' He shrugged. 'It's summer here—too hot for the stuff my nana makes me wear in winter.'

I navigated my mobile again and flicked through photos of Lucas. 'Do you recognise him?'

'Not really. I mean, there were heaps of them with long, blonde hair like that.' He pointed at a photo of George. 'I remember him, though. He looked really grumpy. His face kept going beetroot red.'

I suppressed a giggle. It certainly sounded like George, so I closed my eyes and silently sent up thanks. When I opened them, Tim was staring at me.

'What are you doing?'

'Saying a little prayer of gratitude.'

'Why?'

Were kids always this inquisitive?

'For meeting you, I suppose.'

He beamed. 'That's weird.'

'Maybe,' I agreed with a shrug, 'but you might have just helped me find my brother. Do you have any idea where they went when they arrived?'

'Oh sure,' he said, grinning now. 'That's easy. They followed the pier down past the Antarctic expeditions and got on the private ship.'

'Private ship?'

He was nodding vigorously, more wild tufts of hair falling in front of his eyes. He tried to brush it away, but remained unsuccessful in pinning it behind his tiny ears.

'Do you know what they are called?'

'Beyond something ...'

'Beyond The Blue Shipping?' Nicholas quoted.

'That's it!'

Nicholas smiled. 'We passed it on the way in. It's near the Hummer.'

'Cool! You have a Hummer?' Tim was bouncing up and down like an excited puppy.

'Well, thanks for your help, Tim. You're a life saver.'

His grin shaped into something more mature, eyes now filled with a light shaped by experience and age. 'I've been known to be called that in the past.'

I frowned, confused by the shift in inference and presence; such an odd thing for a kid to say. Glancing back at Nicholas, I wondered if he had thought so too, but he was already heading towards the car, eager to explore the next avenue of information.

'Could you stay and talk for a while?' Tim asked, a knowing smile still toying with his innocent features.

I studied that hopeful expression and the thatch of tangled hair that kept attacking his vision. Something had changed, but I couldn't put my finger on it. I really wanted to catch Nicholas and find out where this last piece of information led—preferable to staying and solving the mystery that was Tim.

I turned to leave. 'I really do have to go. I appreciate your help, though.'

'I should hope so. I'll be penalised for this.'

A very adult voice from behind shot my brows skyward. I was shocked to turn around and find Araqiel standing in Tim's place. I hadn't seen the angel since the multi-coven gathering when he'd told me to concentrate on finding Lucas. Seeing him again after my father's warnings to stay away was unsettling, yet I couldn't exactly make myself run in the other direction. Curiosity had cemented my feet in place.

'Surprise,' he sung, spinning on the spot. 'I bet you didn't expect to see me again so soon.'

'What the hell?'

Araqiel crooked a finger at me, admonishing. 'Language. Please.'

I took an automatic step back.

He seemed momentarily confused by my retreat. 'You're afraid of me.'

'No, just cautious.'

'I won't hurt you, Elena.'

'Said the angel to the vampire half-breed.'

'Touché.'

I wondered why Nicholas had not glanced in my direction.

'He won't look for you and can't hear you,' Araqiel said, suddenly appearing beside me.

I squealed, backing up far enough to slam into the side of the charter office. 'Don't sneak up on me like that!'

'I thought you were used to the fast pace of the Vampires and vânǎtors?'

'I can usually still see them coming.'

'I will consider that for future reference.'

'Try wearing a bell.'

Araqiel wasn't wearing a bell, but instead, his all-white suit again. No dirty marks or wrinkle lines marred the outfit; pressed and perfect, it was absent of the scent of fish and all that had clung to the boy's skin before. Should I have expected anything less of an angel? An angel with big, soft, beautiful ...

I reached out to fondle the feather-soft wings again before I realised what I was doing and snatched my hand back.

'You can touch them as long as you don't rip my feathers out like you did during our last encounter.'

'I was making sure they were real.'

'And now?'

I straightened up, determined not to be intimidated or distracted. 'Why are you here?'

'I want to help.'

'I still don't understand why. Are you a fallen angel—in league with Lucifer?'

Araqiel's lips puckered. 'I am *not* in league with Lucifer. In the beginning I found his rebellious reasons relatable—even stood with him against my brothers and sisters, but he took things too far. He went on to create and lead evil, to claim the souls of those tortured and in pain. I could not be a part of that.'

'So what do you want? I'm trying to find Lucas. Are you here now to throw me off the scent or are you here to help me?'

'Always to help, Elena.'

'So this information you/Tim just gave me, it's legit?'

'Legitimate enough that I will be punished for offering any form of support.'

'Punished?'

Araqiel shook his head, golden hair spilling around him in a proverbial halo. 'It's not for you to concern yourself with.'

'I'm not concerned, I'm curious. Between the two of us, I think your odds of avoiding eternal damnation are higher.'

'The wings do not represent innocence, Elena nor do I get a free pass into utopia because of them.'

'No matter how good I try to be, I still have a non-refundable, one-way ticket south.' I wasn't bitter, merely accepting of facts.

'You are not damned, Elena. You have choices.'

I scoffed. 'Since when?' This was the first I'd heard about it.

'Every decision you make is a choice and those choices are what determine your—'

'Please don't say fate or I'll swear at you again.'

'You don't believe in fate?'

I crossed my arms in front of my chest and moved from the office wall, putting space between us. 'I don't believe in a lot of things. Now tell me what you really want?'

Araqiel's angelic smile faded. 'Why are you suddenly so wary?'

'Rather than playing these cloak and dagger games and throwing me dog bone clues, why don't you just finish what you started and tell me where Lucas is?'

'I cannot, Elena. As an angel, I have rules I must follow.'

'I'm hearing that a lot lately.'

'Rules are what stop light from becoming dark and day becoming night.'

'And probably the reason my father told me to avoid you.' I could feel my knotted brow and pursed lips. I was in no mood to continue on with these antics.

'Ah.' Araqiel nodded in understanding. 'But what does he really know of angels?'

'Cut the crap. What do you really want?'

Araqiel mirrored my pose, folding his arms across his chest and ruffling his wings behind him. 'Your safety and the safety of those you love are very important.'

'Why?'

'Your choices having meaning—effect change.'

'Why?'

'You are unique, a travelling soul born of both darkness and light, a soul capable of choosing her own path of life and death.'

'Stop speaking in riddles and just tell me what you mean.'

'You are not listening.'

I fought the urge to stamp my foot and punch him in the head. 'I'm listening, Araqiel. You're just not making any sense as per usual.'

Araqiel's face remained neutral, though his eyes held caution, slightly pinched at the corners. 'I cannot directly reveal Lucas's whereabouts, but know this; when I cannot help, my brother is always near.'

'Brother?'

'Yes.'

'Another angel like you?'

'He is much more than I, someone you are very familiar with.'

I drummed impatient fingers upon my crossed arms. 'Are we playing twenty questions here?'

'This is not a game, Elena. Michael is on his last legs. Purgatory awaits him if death becomes him in this life.'

'Wait. Back up,' I said, disbelieving. 'Did you just say, *Michael*—as in—the *Archangel Michael?*'

Araqiel's eyes flashed silver in their sapphire depths. 'I did.'

'Shit ...'

'Language.'

I swallowed the dry lump forming in my throat. 'That's why Lucius wants me to stay away from you.' I shook my head, still shocked. 'I've studied Michael. He is an enemy of Lucifer. My father believes that if I associate with him or with you that I will fall under Lucifer's evil radar.'

'You are both naive if you think that Lucifer does not already know of your existence. You are the reincarnated soul of his unborn daughter—destined for great things. You have a chance in this time and life to change everything from the past because—'

'Wait, wait, wait. Back up again. I'm who?' I sputtered, eyes the size of dinner plates as a fresh wave of shock rocked me to the core.

'Were you not aware of your origins?'

'Isn't being a half-breed enough?'

Araqiel remained unapologetic. 'I would have thought that you would have made the connection by now.'

'The connection? What, between my father's pregnant wife murdered over two thousand years ago and my birth in the twentieth century? How could I have possibly known I was her unborn child reincarnated?!'

'Are you not aware of your past lives?'

'Sebastian only revealed our past a few weeks ago. No one else knows about our connection.'

Araqiel appeared beside me again, hand gripping my shoulder. I ducked the presumed extension of comfort and backed away. 'Please don't touch me.'

'I'm sorry.'

'He told you, didn't he?'

'Who?'

'Sebastian,' I said, shuffling another step back. 'You told me Sebastian was *other*. He must have told you about us.'

'We have talked.'

'Suppose I believe you want to help me, what is your connection to Sebastian?'

'I think deep down you already know, Elena.'

'No, I don't.'

'Think through everything he has ever said to you—moments he might have tried to open himself to you. I know the answer will come.'

'Sebastian always says how many rules he's bound by and ...' I stopped talking, wildly searching Araqiel's deep blue eyes for the recognisable flash of silver in their depths.

Could it really be possible?

'No.'

'The answer is right there, Elena—always right in front of you.'

'No, it's too crazy to consider.'

Araqiel made motions to leave, wings slowly unfurling to accept the last touch of warmth from the setting sun. 'Suit yourself. I have done all I can to help you today.'

'Wait,' I choked, trying to process a million thoughts all at once. Why Sebastian might be tied to Araqiel and the reason they had a vested interest in me was becoming very clear, but I was too chicken shit to acknowledge it. I was however, going to clarify William's part in everything. He was the only other vampire I had ever heard use Araqiel's name and who had actively pursued me.

'What is it, Elena? Are you ready to see the truth?'

'No. I can't think ... I can't ...' I hesitated for what felt like an eon, doubt and confusion catching my tongue in a vice-like grip.

'What can't you—'

'Why did you appear to William?'

'Avoidance will get you nowhere, Elena.'

'Answer the damn question!'

Araqiel allowed his wings to droop, but did not fold them away. He wasn't planning on lingering. 'I asked him to watch over you.'

'Why? Does William know what you are?'

'He does.'

'When did you recruit him?'

'After he arrived in Cairns, the moment he was first captivated as you danced on the beach. Fate had blown him in your direction and thus, I could not ignore that he would lead you to Michael.'

My hands balled into fists at my sides. I felt betrayed and irate that every past encounter with William was based on coercion. 'And were his feelings towards me real?'

'They were unexpected and I did everything in my power to persuade him not to fall in love with you.'

I exhaled a breath I hadn't realised I'd been holding. I may not have reciprocated William's deep affections, but it would have hurt to know his feelings might have been tailored. 'And Michael?'

'What about him?'

'Where is he?'

Araqiel hazed me with a look so intense I had no choice but to break eye contact. 'He fights to save the world, Elena—nothing short of what he's always tried to do for humanity, but you already know exactly where he is, don't you?'

I flexed my stiff fingers, releasing them from their fisted prison. 'Is he safe?' I whispered, words struggling to leave my trembling lips.

'For now.'

I took another shuddering breath, terrified that conclusions I'd begun to draw were nowhere near correct. 'If I asked you the same question about Sebastian, would I get the same answer?'

'Apples and oranges, Elena. They appear different, but in the end, they are both still fruit.'

'No,' I said, shaking my head in denial yet again. 'It just can't be.'

'Take care of yourself, Elena. I don't want to have to see you again under a different set of circumstances.'

'Wait! I'm not finished! I need to know if—'

And then he was gone.

Could I be any more damned for wanting to strangle an angel to death?

CHAPTER ELEVEN: FRUIT

Apples and oranges. Well, shit. How had I not drawn a connection until now? How could I have been so blinded by the truth?

I glanced at the empty spot Araqiel had vacated, head spinning with speculation and churning with disbelief. Not only had I discovered I was the reincarnation of my father's two thousand year old unborn daughter, but that Sebastian was …

Dots had finally been joined; starting as messy scrawl work and ending in a straight line, drawing the only possible conclusion.

Sebastian was Michael or Michael was Sebastian.

Either way, Sebastian *was* the Archangel, something I was having trouble swallowing, regardless of the fruit analogies.

I nibbled my bottom lip as it started to quiver. What were the odds of such a conviction being true? Sebastian an angel? He was a bloody vampire! At least, I'd thought so until now or at the very least, a remodelled version of one.

Ha! An angel, as if!

'Elena?'

Nicholas had doubled back to check on me. His eyebrows were furrowed in concern. 'Is something wrong? I turned and you weren't behind me.'

'How long did it take you to realise that?'

His brows buried themselves further in the etched lines of his forehead. 'Only a second or two, why?'

'No reason.'

151

Nothing I can really explain.

'You seem upset.'

'Um, no, just really confused.'

'About the information that kid just gave us?'

'So you remember that?'

He now looked at me as if I were a barking lunatic. 'We just finished talking to him. He was right ...' Nicholas pointed at the boat, but Tim was of course no longer there. 'Where did he go?'

'Long story.'

'Care to share?'

'I don't think you'd believe me even if I did.'

'There's very little that surprises me anymore, Elena.'

I scoffed, certain of this truth's shock value. 'I'm pretty sure this little gem would knock you off your feet.'

'Tell me.'

Tell me. He made it sound so simple. I'd been asking the same of everyone lately with zero result. 'You'll laugh at me.'

'Elena ...'

'Okay, fine! I just found out from an angel—which by the way was Tim—that I'm the reincarnation of my father's unborn daughter and Sebastian's the Archangel Michael.'

Nicholas wrinkled his nose. 'I'm sorry I asked.'

'I thought you might be.'

'Should I call Lucius?'

I waved away his suggestion. 'No. He told me not to talk to angels.'

A second later I lost it, laughing hysterically at the absurdity of the situation and its meaning.

Nicholas eyed me with renewed concern. I was yet to cease laughing. 'You don't seem like yourself.'

'How would you know?' I spluttered. 'No one around here is who they say they are. I'm not me and Sebastian's not Sebastian. Are you sure you're not really Elvis, Nicholas?'

'I can safely say that I am not.'

'Attila the Hun maybe?'

'No.'

'Winston Churchill?'

'No, Elena. I am Nicholas.'

'You don't even want to pretend to be Brad Pitt?'

'No.'

He rested his hands on my shoulders, an attempt to settle me down. 'You are Elena Manory, daughter of Lucius Valerius.'

'I'm also reincarnated and half vânător.'

'Sebastian is definitely *not* an angel, though.'

'No, he's the Archangel Michael. You had better get that part right—don't want to be smited now, do you?' I was starting to sound jaded and just a little hysterical. Laughing about this new discovery seemed infinitely better than believing it.

Nicholas was becoming visibly irritated. 'Sebastian is not Michael. Angels are fictitious!'

I sobered, feeling less humorous by the second. 'I'm not making this up, Nicholas. It's not the first time I've met Araqiel.'

'I remember that name,' Nicholas whispered, calming down. 'Your friend William mentioned it when he and Sebastian came to blows after your abduction from the Vânǎtors.'

'I know. I was there.'

He shook his head. I could tell he wanted to frolic as long as possible in the wonderful land of denial. It was my favourite place. 'Even so, Sebastian is one of us.'

'Except with wings and a halo,' I added, laughing again. I'd always known Sebastian was different, but to think of him as the divine illustrated creature on the cover of my favourite book in my father's library—hilarious, but apparently not impossible.

Vexed, Nicholas pulled out his mobile phone, drafting a text quicker than I could read. When the others arrived less than a minute later, I realised he must have felt out of his depth and called in reinforcements.

'Elena?' Thomas murmured, all concern. 'What has happened?'

'She believes she's encountered an angel,' Nicholas answered for me. 'She also thinks Sebastian is the Archangel Michael.'

Caleb erupted into hysterics much the same as I had. 'We are talking about Sebastian Marcellus, aren't we?'

I nodded, not trusting myself to speak just yet.

'That's stupid!' Caleb wheezed. 'Sebastian's the biggest sinner of us all.'

I followed through with a shrug. It was hard to reconcile.

Thomas gave me a little shake. Perhaps I appeared dazed and confused which wasn't actually that far off the mark. 'How do you know it was an angel that came to you?'

'The wings gave him away, but this isn't the first time, Thomas. I know who and what he is. I'm just having trouble digesting what he's served me.'

'What is his name?'

'Araqiel, why?'

Thomas released me suddenly, recognition pinching his features. I closed the distance between us again. 'You know him, don't you?'

'I do not know him. I know of him.'

'What?' Marianne barked. 'What are you talking about?'

He turned to address his sister. 'Elena is of sound mind.'

'Thank you, Thomas,' I answered sarcastically. 'I'm fully aware of that fact.'

He ignored me. 'William told me about Araqiel. The angel came to him shortly after we arrived in Cairns. He told William that Elena needed to be protected and returned to her family.'

'Angels are fictitious,' Nicholas repeated.

'I used to think so,' Thomas agreed, nodding, 'but that was before I met Elena and certain events unfolded.'

'Why don't I remember any of this?' Marianne interrupted.

'Because no one told you.'

'Why not?'

I groaned. This was so not the time for sibling rivalry. 'So I was supposed to be taken to Lucius then? This is something that William knew and chose to ignore?'

'William fell in love with you. It was not part of the plan.' Thomas grimaced. 'As a protector he did fail you. William knew that if he returned you to your father you would meet his brother. William didn't have enough faith in your affections not to be swayed by Sebastian's charms.'

I frowned, raw anger lapping at the edges of my patience anew. 'I could have avoided Roshan, Julius, the IMI—everything.'

'I'm sorry, Elena. What can I say? William is my best friend. I wasn't going to interfere. You both seemed happy.'

I started to pace. 'How could William know that I'd be attracted to Sebastian? He gave me some sob story about the cruel intentions of my father and I believed him.'

Thomas remained sheepish. 'According to William, everyone is attracted to Sebastian.'

Caleb scoffed. 'That's true enough. Sebastian has some seriously weird mojo.'

'Thomas, were William's instructions to take me to my father or take me to Sebastian?'

'It's one in the same,' Caleb answered. 'Sebastian's always where your father is.'

'William knew that,' Thomas finally responded. 'I suppose he thought he was protecting you from a man he considered dangerous and a man who could steal your heart.'

'Does William know that Sebastian might not just be his brother?'

Thomas shrugged. 'I honestly do not know.'

Caleb made some sort of snort of disbelief. 'Do you truly think Araqiel led William to Elena to find Sebastian because Sebastian is really Michael? If Sebastian is an angel, why didn't Araqiel just tell him where Elena was?'

'We should put this conversation on hold,' Nicholas suggested. 'We are speculating.'

'I think the most pertinent question,' Marianne muttered as she studied her fingers with disinterest, 'is why would an angel choose to be a vampire—or if he didn't—why the act?'

'An excellent question,' Eric responded.

Yes it is. I thought to myself.

Sebastian was born human and chose to become a vampire—private knowledge I'd recently unearthed. He was turned, but not through a mutual blood exchange. Sebastian remained as strong, if not stronger than the other born vampires around him and also adopted a few minor quirks—namely his desire to drink vampiric blood.

Tiberius (Sebastian and William's father), was made a vampire thrall long after Sebastian's birth therefore making passing on the vampiric gene impossible. Now knowing that he might have had a little divine intervention made the situation seem more plausible. Then there was Marianne's question to consider. If Sebastian was still legitimately an angel and pretending to be one of us, why the hell did he turn vampiric?

'I have another question,' Marianne continued. 'Regardless of whether or not William's brother is an angel, why would Araqiel go to all this trouble to protect Elena?' She released her cuticles from her intense gaze to look pointedly at me. 'No offence, but you aren't anything special.'

I bristled, offended regardless and prepared to stake her.

'Let's put this conversation to rest,' Nicholas interjected. 'We have a solid lead on The Protectors now. We need to keep moving.'

'So you found someone with useful information?' Thomas quizzed.

Nicholas nodded enthusiastically. 'A small boy. He witnessed their arrival and boarding onto a private freighter.'

'That small boy was Araqiel.'

Nicholas seemed irritated regarding my insistence of this point and angelic existence. 'Why did I not sense the fact that he was *other*?'

'Who cares?' Marianne griped. 'Let's find Lucas!'

I couldn't argue. I wanted to find Lucas too. Araqiel had spun my world into turmoil, but he'd also given me what I hoped to be sound advice.

As the others left, following behind Nicholas, Thomas cinched my waist, holding me back. 'Are you really okay?' he whispered.

If the others truly wanted to listen in on us, whispering would make little difference. 'I'm having trouble digesting everything, but I'm okay.'

Thomas nodded thoughtfully, blonde hair brushing the tops of his shoulders. His concern was genuine and I was honestly touched. His great advice was to chew slowly—not bad considering my current indigestion. It earned him a smile.

'Can you do me a favour?'

My smile faded, favours were dangerous.

'Please go easy on William when you see him again. He knows that keeping you from your family was a mistake, but acted out of love. He was blinded by his feelings and forgot to look at the bigger picture.'

'That's not an excuse.'

'I know,' Thomas said, releasing me to plunge his hands into his pockets. 'William is my friend. I feel I must somehow defend his actions.'

'If William hadn't kept me from my family, there's a good chance The Protectors may never have been able to manufacture the serum and I might have avoided capture and torture by Roshan.'

'He carries that guilt with him, Elena. He knows that he has wronged you. What would you have done if the situation was reversed?'

'I would have told him the truth—made sure he could choose whether he wanted to meet his father or stay with me.'

Thomas tugged on my elbow, pulling me along to keep up. The others were quite far ahead, but I had a feeling they'd be listening regardless. 'Are you sure?'

'Of course I'm sure.'

'What if it was Sebastian? Are you so sure you would still do the right thing if it meant losing the person you loved?'

My heart constricted at the thought; I almost despised Sebastian for making me feel so vulnerable. 'I would still make the same choices.'

'Then you are stronger than most.'

'Strength has nothing to do with it. Don't you see? If you truly love someone, then you let them choose their own path. If Sebastian picked someone else that he wanted to love, then I'd never deny him happiness. How could I say I love him if I wasn't willing to let him go?'

'You do not believe that William loves you?' I could tell he was afflicted by shock.

I smiled sadly. 'I think William loves the idea of me. Deep down he knows I'm not the one. It's why he fights so hard to keep us together. It's almost like he doesn't want to prove himself wrong.'

'How can you be sure?'

'He doesn't see the real me.'

'And Sebastian does?'

I shrugged.

'So there is no chance that you and William will pick up where you left off?'

I nudged him as we walked, trying to bring him some comfort. I wasn't out to destroy the soul of his best friend, merely retain some personal integrity and honesty. 'We'd both be lying to ourselves. Now that I know the truth, I'm beginning to think that I'm just the toy that William doesn't want Sebastian to have.'

Thomas's jaw stiffened, but he conceded my point with a curt nod. He then peeled a hand from his pocket and wrapped his arm around my shoulder. 'Sometimes you seem wiser than your sixteen years.' He squeezed, forgiveness in the gentle exertion his fingertips imbued upon my skin.

I rolled my eyes and found myself suppressing a smile. 'Apparently I'm a little over two thousand years old.'

'Do you really think you are Lucius's unborn child?'

'Who knows? Araqiel believes it to be true, but I'll have to talk to Lucius. It's not like the information changes anything though, does it?'

'I suppose not.'

I laced my fingers through Thomas's, his arm still casually draped around my shoulder. He smiled, sapphire eyes glistening against the faded sun now hiding beyond the horizon. 'No matter what happens between William and I, we'll still be friends, won't we?'

With his other hand, he ruffled the top of my hair like a young child. Though I despised it, I knew he meant well. 'Of course we will.'

'Except Marianne,' I said, screwing up my nose. 'We don't need to get friendly.'

'I heard that!' she shouted from several hundred meters in front.

'Good!' I whispered to a delighted Thomas. 'I didn't want to have to shout.'

We grinned at each other as we hurried to catch up with the others.

* * *

Beyond The Blue Shipping Charters was located exactly where Tim (Araqiel), said it would be. A large vessel with a battered red hull was anchored to the side of the pier in front of a small shack we assumed doubled as offices. The sign above the door's entrance indicated as much, but presumably they weren't drumming up much business from walk by's, judging by the dilapidated appearance.

Thomas and Eric had begun to study the ship. Marianne was following up the rear, looking for a way onto the vessel without being noticed. Caleb circled the shack, sniffing the air and sorting scents, while Nicholas and I took the more direct approach and headed for the door.

It was locked. It was well after six and according to the sign on the front door, they conducted business between the hours of seven and five.

'We'll have to come back tomorrow,' I said, stating the obvious.

Nicholas agreed, now signalling to Caleb. 'Anything?'

Caleb appeared, shaking his head. 'The sun, wind and rain have long since diluted useable scents.'

Nicholas sniffed the air himself. 'Maybe we'll learn more from the ship?'

I glanced over just in time to see Marianne, Thomas and Eric bound on board the deck and then promptly disappear from sight.

'Are you coming, Elena?' Caleb asked, realising I was not following their lead.

'No. You two go ahead.'

Nicholas tugged on my shirt sleeve, insistent. 'What are you going to do? Break into the premises while we are gone?'

I grinned, wishing I'd thought of the criminal activity first. 'I *was* just going to wait here, but that sounds like a better idea.'

'How will you get in?' Nicholas enquired.

I pulled my arm back and rammed my elbow through the glass. It shattered, falling to the ground in uneven shards of glittery sand. The noise was telling, but no one was around to hear, so I slipped my hand through the gap and unlocked the door.

Nicholas sighed, turning to head for the ship. 'I shouldn't have asked.'

I snickered, waving them off as I let myself inside. It was dark; not enough that I couldn't see, but turning on lights would alert some sort of local surveillance to my unauthorised presence. I was just going to have to manage.

I wondered if I should wear gloves or wipe down surfaces after touching them. I saw an episode of CSI where they convicted a guy of murder because he sneezed on the dumpster next to the victim, leaving behind trace amounts of DNA. I wasn't about to spit all over the room, but I was pretty sure leaving my fingerprints was just as stupid.

On a wooden counter in the centre of the room sat a box of tissues. They weren't latex gloves, but they would do under the circumstances. This criminal plucked a few and went back to wipe the door handle. I did the outside too, remembering that I had tried to open the door before this genius plan had unhatched.

Once satisfied my digit smudges had been erased, I headed back to the counter and fired up the computer. While waiting for the archaic setup to load, I headed to a bunch of filing cabinets in the corner.

There was no one here I could question, so I needed to get answers for myself.

Using tissues again, I yanked open the first draw and looked over the tabs. Employee information, superannuation records and payroll groupings. The chances of recognising names would be slim and not purposeful in this instance.

I moved onto the second draw.

This one was loaded with client files, indiscriminate in choice of venture. Beyond the Blue appeared to ship an assortment of items to many different places. Food, fishing equipment for trawlers, building supplies and even scientific crews bound for the Antarctic were among client listings. They also ventured into the tourism market during off season, loading their ship with tour groups wanting views of ice caps, polar bears and penguins; an eighteen day roundabout excursion of Antarctica. Talk about cashing in on every opportunity.

I flipped through the files more closely, focusing specifically on pickups and drop offs for food deliveries. Quite a few were scheduled for delivery to Casey Station, but I didn't consider that unusual; the scientists had to eat.

I stopped only when I heard the front computer finish loading. It made a weird kind of beeping noise that I assumed meant it was a piece of crap that needed upgrading.

I left the files and headed to the counter. The screen had a picture of rolling lavender fields in the background and a few icons pertinent to client files. I would have searched those first, but noticed a scheduling program in the left hand corner. I prayed it had records of the Manory's departure from Hobart.

The information slowly materialised. Across the top listed time and date with two separate columns indicating the ship's loading schedule as well as an affiliate.

I clicked on today's schedule; a box appeared with all the relevant details. It translated as being still in port, listed for onsite maintenance and repairs. Scrolling further I could see it was due to depart in two days—another tour group headed for the Antarctic. The programme was thorough, even giving me a full list of the names, deposits paid and which cabin they were being allocated.

'Found anything?' Marianne asked, sneaking up on me despite the glass shards scattered across the threshold.

'No. Not yet,' I muttered.

She wandered around the counter and stood beside me. She smelt like freshly squeezed oranges and vanilla bean ice cream. I kinda wished that I smelt like a French dessert. 'The boys are still checking the boat, but it's clear The Protectors have not travelled that route for a while.'

'You picked up a scent?'

She nodded, smiling—a rarity to be sure. 'It was faint, but there in the cabins.'

'Lucas?'

'It's hard to say,' she replied. 'Protectors are a little like vânātors. They may be human, but the magic makes them smell like battery acid or burning electrical wires. If I get close, I can smell the base scent of an individual, but it's all too faint now to pick up Lucas's scent.'

'Okay, well at least we know they were on that ship.'

'Yes, but where did they go? That is the question.'

'I'm trying to figure that out.' I turned my attention back to the screen, scrolling through dates until I was nearer the time frame that Lucas had presumably been in the area.

'They seem like a legitimate shipping company,' Marianne remarked.

'The IMI is good with legitimate,' I answered, giving her a wry look. 'Have you ever been to headquarters in Bucharest?'

She shook her head.

'It's a five star hotel. The top three floors were used for research, development, weapons manufacture, scientific experimentation—you name it. The rest was a tourist mecca.'

'And now?'

I shrugged. 'The last time I was there I trashed the place. I don't know what they are using those last three floors as now.'

'Should I ask?'

'Probably not. Long story, but these projects are what funded their research and development of items like the serum.'

'You're referring to that biological weapon Lucas mentioned a few months back?'

'Did William give you recent details?'

She looked away and scratched at her nose. 'He's been distracted.'

By me you mean.

I cleared my throat. 'The serum is a compound that has been manufactured from my blood. From what we can gather from the Vânâtors interest and certain documents uncovered by Lucas, the serum either turns humans into vampires or cures vampirism. I don't know for sure, but neither one is really good when the Vânâtors have started a war. This is why I'm frantic about getting Lucas out of there. I don't think he realised what he was getting into when he agreed to stay and spy on them.'

'So this is your fault,' she said mercilessly.

I had enough guilt to last a lifetime. I didn't need her to force feed me anymore. 'Yes, I should have pulled him out when I realised The Protectors were not who they claimed to be.'

'Why your blood? Is it because you're a half-breed?'

'That might have something to do with it, but it's more likely that my blood is genetically perfect.'

Marianne snorted, disbelief abundantly clear. 'You really do think you're special, don't you?'

My lips puckered, but I managed to restrain from punching her in the head or being overly flippant. 'No, I don't. My blood is defect free. There are no trace diseases present, no genetic markers for any future ailments—nothing that could deteriorate my body as a human.'

'Why?' She continued to mock me with her very mannerism.

'Stephanie believed it was because of Lucius.'

'Who is Stephanie?'

'Stephanie is one of the nicer Protectors I met during my stay at headquarters. She believed my blood was perfect because I had inherited it. Since Lucius is the original vampire, it makes sense.'

'Lucius *was* human once.'

'True, but Lucifer took his soul and re-birthed him to this life. He's not human anymore, not since the deal was made.'

Marianne looked at me through narrowed eyes for the longest time before responding. 'If that is true, then what does that make you?'

I'd asked myself the same question so many times. 'I honestly don't know.'

We stopped talking after that. I didn't have the energy to tell Marianne the sordid details of my time with the IMI or my capture by Roshan. The fact that she hadn't contemplated the serum's ramifications told me how much vampires had underestimated the underhandedness of The Protectors and the resourcefulness of the Vânǎtors.

'I think that's it there,' Marianne said impatiently, pointing repeatedly at the screen. 'Bring up the passenger list.'

I did as she said, not because of her tone which leaned heavily towards bossy, but because our objective was the same; to find Lucas alive and well. I did wonder, as she kept fingering the screen, how my brother found time to make friends with a bitchy blonde who was in love with her own reflection while he played double agent under the IMI's umbrella.

'Let me try,' she said, pushing me out of the way.

'You know,' I muttered, gripping the edge of the counter to steady myself, 'I was born in the technological age. When were you born? When they first developed irrigation? What do you know about computers?'

She gave me an equally icy stare. 'It's called higher education. If your intellect matched mine you'd know that irrigation has been around for thousands of years, substantially longer than I.'

'Were you this nasty when you were human too?'

She shrugged, eyes never leaving the screen. As far as I was concerned, she was clicking the mouse exactly as I'd been doing it before. She was no more successful opening passenger logs than I had been.

'It keeps saying that the passenger list has been altered or deleted.'

It was my turn to shove her out of the way and commandeer the mouse. 'Maybe it has been deleted?'

She elbowed me in the ribs; the equivalent to being prodded with a crowbar. It took everything not to wince.

'Try entering their names into the customer database and see what happens,' she said, aiming for the: *I accidentally kicked your ankle* manoeuvre.

I tried the: *whoops, was that your toe I just stood on?* trick, but I might as well have caressed her foot with a feather.

Only the slight rise of her blonde brow told me she'd felt my efforts. 'There's no Manory's listed.'

'What about the other members of your faction?'

'They aren't listed either. Araqiel must have been wrong.'

Marianne's look was reproachful. 'The entire passenger list for this particular day is wiped or inaccessible. That has to tell you something!'

I smacked the keyboard aggressively. 'It tells me this is a heap of crap computer that has probably dropped files.'

Marianne snatched the mouse back again and scrolled through other scheduled tours and shipments. 'Then why is every other passenger list including crew accompaniment found on every other journey?'

I shook my head and pointed to the exceptions. 'There are several tours missing passenger lists. Look.'

She held the cursor over the blank areas in the schedule. 'When did certain factions of the IMI go underground, Elena?'

'Headquarters was abandoned when Caleb, Sebastian and I were there before Christmas.'

She opened the schedule several months beforehand. As the computer struggled to keep up with her movements, I watched her eyes dart across the information like lightening. She opened and closed files so fast that I couldn't read them or figure out what she was looking for.

'What do you see?' I said.

'They appear to keep excellent track of their shipping schedule. There isn't any detail that is missed. I can only find discrepancies on the tours from here to Antarctica. Some are detailed—right down to how much luggage the individual was taking on board the ship. In other instances, it's blanked to allow travel time in the schedule, but nothing more.'

'The Protectors could have used the *Defenacus* charm on the employees to hide permanent records of their comings and goings.'

'Do you really think they would honestly go to Antarctica?'

'I don't know. You said that's where the discrepancies are.'

'Come on, Elena,' Marianne said with a nervous laugh. 'Be serious. For six months of the year that place is covered in darkness and practically uninhabitable. Why would they move headquarters there?'

'It's the last place anyone would think to look.'

164

'How could they go unnoticed?'

'The *Revatarus* spell. They have the resources, money and know-how to do these things. Setting up shop on the coldest continent on Earth is merely another surmountable challenge.'

'There's nothing smart about frostbite. Trust me, I lived in Russia after I first turned.'

I frowned, vaguely curious where this conversation may lead, but more eager to find Lucas. I went back to studying the computer screen. 'So what's this affiliate used for?' I pointed to the second column which spent most of its scheduling time blank except for once a month when it was blocked off for a couple of hours at a time. 'Look, Marianne. There's another company that operates under Beyond the Blue's umbrella.'

She double-clicked a blocked time to bring up the information. 'It just says *Blue Horizons Charters*.'

'Another ship?'

'I don't think so. Not unless it can fly.'

I licked my suddenly dry lips. 'They have an aeroplane too?'

'It looks like it.'

I scanned the information. 'It has the departure time and flight duration. Does it list where it leaves from or the destination?'

'Hang on. Let me see if I can look more closely through the files.' I took off for the filing cabinets again and leafed through the top draw. I knew most of it was gibberish, but I recalled it was full of employee records.

'What are you doing?'

'Searching for info on the pilot.' I pulled out the manila folder and went back to the counter so Marianne could read it too. 'Here it is.'

'It just has his personal information. It doesn't tell us about the air charters themselves.'

'Double-click on the inventory button,' I said, nodding in the direction of the screen. 'I want to see what comes up.'

'I already told you it's—' She stopped mid-sentence as a caption opened with the much needed information we had been searching for. Sometimes the Gods shine upon you and other times they crap all over you. Today I was as clean as a whistle and forever in Araqiel's debt.

'Well looky here,' I said, grinning. 'Someone forgot to delete some vital information.'

'It's The Protectors,' Marianne murmured. 'We found them.'

'Thomas did say they had to eat sometime.'

Marianne scrolled back until she landed on tomorrow's schedule. 'It looks like we've found their next date of shipment too.' She smiled at me for the second time since our re-acquaintance. 'We're actually going to be able to find Lucas.'

'We just need to figure out where the aircraft departs from and then we're all set.'

'How do you plan on doing that? The computer and the files offer us no more information than what we already have.'

I tucked the pilot's file under my arm, patting it smugly. 'We're going to pay Mr. Walters a little visit.'

CHAPTER TWELVE: TIME CONTRACT

Araqiel settled his feet upon the hardened earth of Purgatory, the crusted dirt cracking and crumbling under the soles of his shoes. He studied his footprints, amazed that Purgatory was the only place that revealed his presence. Here he was just like any other, a soul with no past, present or future.

'Have you been up to no good again, Araqiel?'

The angel exhaled, breath as solemn as his mood. It was tiresome dealing with the devil's minions. 'Have you been following me again, Samael?'

'Now why would you think that?'

Araqiel turned, finding the demon at his back. The half-goat was smiling, whiskered lips pulled back to reveal too many teeth. 'I'm starting to think it may be a hobby of yours.'

'You flatter yourself, Araqiel. Do you not remember what happened the last time I followed you?'

Of course he did. Samael was one of the four council members required to pass judgement on those that entered Purgatory. He'd broken the rules by leaving and following the angel's path. The council members were meant to be impartial; the decisions made on earth and in heaven or hell respectively were irrelevant to the undertakings in Purgatory.

Now—thanks to Samael's indiscretion—he'd helped Elena get back to her family through vision and established a deal for the

Time Contract which would inevitably alter everything already come to pass.

'I remember that you were warned against following me again, Samael. If this is true, then why are you here now?'

Samael snorted. 'Purgatory is my domain. It is me that should be asking that question of you.'

'Appearing in the Desert lands as opposed to the Lakelands has proven my suspicions—you monitoring me. You had to have been watching which Ley-line I used to get here.'

Samael stamped a hoof against the crusted earth, plumes of dust emerging. 'Do not play with me, Angel!'

'I do not play, Samael. I am merely stating facts. You have been watching me.'

'With good reason! You have been contacting the half-breed again and I know that you are urging her to find her human sibling. What are your motives?'

'I do not need to explain myself to you.'

'No, but you do need to explain it to the rest of us.'

Araqiel stiffened as the other three council members came into being. Two were angels: Munkar and Nakir—divine entities like himself. The other was Mammon, a demon like Samael with flesh the colour of blood, constantly slicked with sweat and the acrid smell of death.

'You came here with a purpose, Araqiel,' Nakir stated, voice like a chorus of melodic church bells. 'You must explain yourself, if for no other reason than you have once again interfered when not permitted.'

'Yes,' Mammon agreed. 'Why do you urge the girl to find her sibling? What is the purpose?'

'It's a distraction,' Araqiel answered with calm consideration. He didn't want to give too much information to the demons.

'I do not understand,' Nakir murmured. He looked to the others for possible explanation.

'Tell us, brother,' Munkar pleaded. 'What is this distraction you speak of?'

'Her brother *is* the distraction and in direct relation to the deal made last time I was here.'

Mammon and Samael frowned, but appeared to be catching on. 'Michael's life in exchange for the Time Contract?'

'Does that offer still stand?'

'Of course. What petty distractions you make with the half-breed and those around her matter little compared to having Michael back in Purgatory. Lucifer anticipates his arrival even as we speak.'

Nakir and Munkar looked incredibly uncomfortable. The thought of selling the Archangel out simply to have the power to reverse time was unsettling.

'The Time Contract is with Lucifer. He waits for you to uphold your end of the bargain.'

'And I will,' Araqiel countered. 'You will see Michael before this week is through.'

Samael rubbed his hands together and grinned at his demon counterpart. 'So soon, Angel. I am impressed.'

'This is most excellent news,' Mammon agreed. 'We must go to Lucifer now, tell him of this turn in events.'

Araqiel was pleased. He'd distracted the demons once again from his greater purpose; to mention Michael's name was to derail the thoughts of those easily misled.

'Wait,' Nakir yelled as both demons turned to leave. 'Have you not forgotten something?'

'No,' they answered in unison.

Araqiel cringed inwardly, hoping the honesty of his brothers didn't re-tip the scales.

'Michael's soul is bound to this place. No matter how much Lucifer wants him, Michael has a long-standing deal with *our* head of house. Michael will die on Earth, but his soul is to be contained within Purgatory for the rest of eternity until such time other arrangements can be made.'

Samael snorted, mucous spewing from the end of his snout. 'Our dark lord knows the restrictions on Michael's soul, but there are no rules against his treatment in Purgatory.'

'This place is neutral,' Munkar argued.

Mammon's goading smile matched that of the demon beside him. 'You cannot watch Michael all of the time.'

'Are you suggesting that you will torment him when our backs are turned?'

Both demons snickered, making Araqiel feel sick to the stomach. 'Eventually Michael will beg to be released from this place and when he does, where do you think he will go without renewed entry into heaven?'

Nakir and Munkar shot Araqiel panicked expressions. 'Do you really want this for your brother?' Munkar pleaded.

Araqiel shook his head. 'Of course not, but Michael's been on Earth for thousands of years and had the opportunity to prevent so much—the Vampires and vânătors the biggest plight of all. Now I have a chance to undo some of the damage his unwillingness to interfere has created.'

'All at the cost of Michael's freedom and possibly his soul?'

'It's what has to be done.'

Samael gleefully clapped. 'Let us go, Mammon. Lucifer will be pleased with this news.' He pointed straight at Araqiel. 'I'll be watching you, Angel.'

'Then what has changed?'

And then they were gone.

Munkar and Nakir closed in on Araqiel, the neutral expressions they wore for the demons vanishing under the weight of fear they carried for their brother. 'What have you done,' Nakir murmured, shaking his head. 'You have condemned Michael to an eternity of torment.'

'I have not,' he responded, folding his wings around himself for comfort.

'Then why are you doing this?' Munkar prodded, determined to unearth the truth.

'Elena can change everything; you both know this.'

'She is a born vampire and half vânător, Araqiel. There are no guarantees that she will overcome her dark nature.'

Araqiel was disappointed by his brother's narrow-mindedness. 'She also has Uriel's blood in her veins—angel blood.'

'We are aware that Uriel possessed her mother at the time of conception, but how does this work in our favour?'

'She cannot be judged here.'

Both angels took a moment to think about that.

'Do you understand what that means?' Araqiel pressed. 'She is born of both darkness and light. She cannot rest her soul in either place.'

'So she must choose to stay in purgatory or she must go back to Earth.'

Araqiel smiled as understanding finally dawned on the others. 'Yes, my brothers. That is exactly what will happen.'

'And the Time Contract?'

'Will be placed in her hands to decide the fate of us all.'

'Araqiel ...'

'I believe Michael will not suffer for long as she will make all the right choices. I can feel it.'

'That is a lot of pressure for a sixteen-year-old girl.'

'Look at what she has had to overcome so far? Elena Manory is no ordinary teenage girl.'

'And this distraction you have arranged?' Munkar asked. 'How will it change things?'

'Her brother will change nothing, but he will give her comfort and reason to choose Earth over Purgatory.'

'Michael may persuade her to stay.'

Certainty gripped Araqiel as he shook his head, blonde hair crowding his eyes. 'No, she won't. She may love Michael and she may want to stay, but she will always choose what is right—what is needed which is why I sent Elena to look for Lucas. If she were to stay in Rome, help fight in this war, she would try to save Michael.'

'Mammon and Samael cannot kill him, it would be against the rules,' Nakir interjected.

'It is not the demons who will mark him for death.'

'Then who?' Nakir pressed.

Araqiel's eyes widened ever so slightly. 'Have neither of you been watching unfolding events, taking note of all of those that oppose Elena's existence or even those that she cares about?'

Munkar bristled, shoulders stiffening and jaw pulsing under the sudden brutal clench of teeth. 'We are busy here in Purgatory, Araqiel. We do not have time to observe every human from on high.'

'I apologise,' Araqiel conceded. 'I meant no offence.'

Munkar's jaw relaxed, defiance and self-righteousness all but a distant memory. 'I simply worry for Michael and his stake in this. He not only loses his life, but the love he has fallen for time and time again. He gave up everything he was to be with her and you're telling us that she would disregard that to save the human race. It is hard to swallow. No one can resist Michael's charms indefinitely.'

'Elena is very different in this cycle, very independent. I have faith in her.'

'I hope so, Araqiel,' Nakir murmured. 'For all our sakes and Michael's, I really hope that you are not wrong about this.'

'Me too.'

171

CHAPTER THIRTEEN: SUCCESS

William knelt beside an icy creek bed, careful to avoid the rays of mid-morning sunshine overhead. He revelled in the feel of the frigid, hardened earth beneath his toes and the tiny tendrils of ice that kissed the edge of the water.

As he delved blood-soaked hands deep into the icy creek, the water stained red, spreading a crimson cloud beneath the rippling surface. It would disperse, mingle with open water and eventually disappear, washing not only his hands, but his conscience clean too.

He moved on to his arms, scrubbing his exposed flesh. The blood had dried, making it difficult to remove. His hair was worse, dripping into his eyes and dribbling to his lips. He could still taste the blood of his enemy.

William moved from his knees and waded further into the icy depths, soaking his entire body clean. He'd remained unbathed for over a week, the odour he was emitting—unimaginable, but entirely necessary to his hunt.

He ducked under the water, rinsing his sticky hair clean. From beneath the surface he saw Sebastian's blurred figure, sitting in the dense shade of a nearby tree, eyes closed and hands clasped across his stomach. He was still covered in blood, seemingly uninterested in rinsing clean.

William broke the surface, water cascading down his naked torso and over his well-soaked jeans. 'Come and get clean,' he ordered, the smell radiating from Sebastian almost as fetid as his own had been.

'In a minute.'

'You smell.'

'I am aware.'

William ran fingers through his hair, rinsing excess water that insisted on dripping in his eyes. Sebastian remained motionless, eyes closed and hands clutching his stomach as if in pain. It was only the slight furrow of his brows that gave him away. 'What's wrong with you?'

'It's nothing.' Sebastian pried opened his eyes, affording William a view of unending darkness completely absent of life.

Deep purple bruises marked the pale, delicate and seemingly papery flesh of his angular cheekbones. He clutched himself tighter, returning to the peace of closed lids.

'You're driven by thirst, aren't you?' William said, recognising the signs. He left the water and went and knelt beside him. He parted Sebastian's slightly parched lips; his fangs had unsheathed and his skin became translucent.

William was incredulous. 'We have plenty of tetra packs with us, surely during this last week you have fed?'

Sebastian shook his head. 'I cannot drink vânător blood.'

William fell silent, listening to the wind and the sounds of the forest carried upon it. 'There are animals nearby that you can feed on. If you are too weak I could fetch one for you.'

Sebastian seized William's wrist between bloodied fingers. 'I cannot feed from any life.'

William rolled back on his heels, studying the brother he had never truly understood. He'd judged the perception Sebastian wished to portray; a playboy and creature with low morality, but now he wasn't so sure.

He was confused, conflicted and eager to clarify his brother's agenda and the role he played in Araqiel and Elena's life. Sebastian was a vampire—all outward appearances indicating as much—yet William had never seen Sebastian feed, never seen him lose control and never knew he associated with angels. What was the connection? Surely it wasn't as outrageous as his mind suggested?

'You need to feed, Sebastian, otherwise eventually you will die.'

Sebastian moaned, head lolling to one side. 'I don't think I will make it back to Rome.'

'Are you so self-serving that you will only feed from human blood? Is that what this is about?' William returned to his feet, pacing the ground in front of them, irritated.

'I have no choice, William. I am not bound by the same rules as a vampire that you are.'

'Why is that?' William demanded.

Sebastian shrugged, determined to remain close-lipped which only seemed to irritate William more.

'Why won't you be honest!?' William pounded the trunk of the tree behind Sebastian's head.

His fist went clean through the centre, scattering bark and leaf debris.

Sebastian's eyes snapped open. The emptiness of the raven's depths reflected William's surprised expression. Sebastian was suddenly very alert, everything about him screamed hungry vampire.

William stumbled in his pacing. 'Why are you looking at me like dinner?'

'I'm famished.'

William's mouth gaped. 'You drink vampire blood?' He shook his head, the very idea preposterous. 'It's unheard of; not even the Vânătors eat their own. Elena is the first born vampire I've met that drinks all blood, but I figured that's because she's a half-breed. What are you?'

'It's irrelevant.'

'I am your brother, Sebastian. You owe me an explanation if it is my blood that you wish to feed from.'

Sebastian attempted to smile, but it was evident it took real effort to dismiss the pain currently felt. 'So now you recognise me as your sibling?'

'Sebastian ...'

'William, I have always called you brother. I protected you, I loved you and I always stood by your side. When you left the Roman Guard to pursue your own agenda, I tried to make you understand the misgivings driving your anger. I wanted to understand your misplaced hostility and explain that I had never betrayed you, but you never gave me the chance. You condemned me along with everyone else even though it was you who had made the error in judgement.'

175

'Is this little speech supposed to endear me to opening a vein for you?'

Sebastian shook his weary head. 'No. I just wanted you to know that I had not given up on you.'

'And that you want my blood ...'

'It would help, but I will not force you to help me.'

'Are you saying you could?'

'For years you have watched how vampiric women and even men reacted to me. Did you simply assume that I was bedding all of them?'

'It made more sense than *this*.' William gave a theatrical shudder. 'Why vampiric blood?'

'Vampiric blood is dead blood—darkness. It sustains this form and at the same time, I am not robbing anyone or anything of life to take it.'

'So you have chosen cannibalism to support your life for what? The taste? Self-indulgence?'

Sebastian pulled himself more upright, teeth clenched as another vicious cramp assaulted him. 'Would you let me die?'

Sebastian would usually take exactly what he needed, compel his intended victim and leave them empty of the memory, but with William he wanted to know if he'd offer himself freely, wanted to know if he still cared at all.

Surely a trick question? 'I hate you and I don't understand the first thing about you, but I don't want to see the look on Elena's face if I told her that I let you die.'

The very thought of Elena softened Sebastian's features, lips curving awkwardly into a goofy, pain-filled smile.

'Take my blood,' William pressed. 'It's what Elena would want.'

Sebastian's smile widened to reveal his pointed fangs again. 'Thank you.'

William grunted as Sebastian pulled him carelessly and greedily across his lap, pale and bony fingers yanking his head to the side, sharp fangs piercing his neck. He could taste his brother's need for blood like a fever across his tongue, veins aching as life force flowed through in haste to satisfy hunger. The fingers that gripped him were relentless in their partnership to acquire blood, lips suctioning against William's flesh like warm pillows protecting hidden knives.

William struggled at first, listless against the seemingly uncharacteristic strength of a vampire in blood lust. He'd bucked under the assault, teeth clenched and his own fingers finding purchase, digging into Sebastian's shoulders and clawing wherever possible.

It didn't last.

A welcoming warmth that William could not ignore spread from neck to the tips of his fingers and toes. It wrapped him in a blanket of safety, comfort and oddly enough, partial arousal.

Arousal?

'Are you okay?'

William blinked, opening his eyes. He couldn't remember why he'd closed them. He wasn't tired or thirsty and vampires definitely did not need sleep and yet here he lay, dazed and confused. Sebastian now stood above him, studying him with concern. He was clean, clothes wet from bathing in the creek, water still trickling from the length of his sable hair.

'I said, *are you okay?*' Sebastian waved a hand in front of his face.

He slapped it away. 'Of course I'm okay. What are you talking about?'

Sebastian shrugged and straightened, a small smile teasing the edges of his supple mouth. He didn't bother to respond, merely watched blooming confusion upon William's features.

William accepted Sebastian's hand to pull him to his unsteady feet. Why couldn't he recall the last few minutes? 'I could have sworn we were just having a conversation about your poor health,' William said warily, looking his seemingly healthy brother over again. Perhaps he'd been mistaken.

'I don't know. Something doesn't feel quite right.' He brushed fingers down his neck and came away with blood on his fingertips.

'Looks like you missed some,' Sebastian noted.

William rubbed the tips of his fingers together, inhaling the scent. 'This is my blood.'

'It happens in a fight.'

William nodded, but knew his brows were furrowed, unconvinced.

'We need to get back to Rome. If Roshan was ever going to take a risk again then it would be to find Elena.'

'You think she is in danger?'

Sebastian's unexpected laughter startled half of the local wildlife and William too. 'This is Elena we are talking about. When is she not in any danger?'

William was inclined to agree and reluctantly smiled, wiping his stained fingers across his damp jeans. 'Lucius will not be happy that we have returned unsuccessful.'

Sebastian looked puzzled. 'We *have* been successful.

We killed all the Alphas except Roshan and we are coming back to Rome because we know this is where he will eventually look for Elena.'

'How do we know that?'

'I would think by now he has realised that she is important to the Roman coven.'

'And Lucius?'

'Leave Lucius to me. He will see the sense of this plan once I explain it to him.'

'And if he doesn't?'

Sebastian sighed. 'Then I'll know he sent me away to hunt the Alphas to keep me at arm's length from Elena.'

William sneered. 'You just have to keep rubbing it in, don't you?'

'From now on we won't discuss Elena at all. I can see that it bothers you.'

'No, what bothers me is that she is blinded to all else but you.'

Sebastian rolled his eyes, turned and walked away, bored by the repetitiveness of this conversation and its cyclic inevitability.

'That's it? You're just walking away?'

'What else is there?'

William shook his head, hurrying to catch up.

CHAPTER FOURTEEN: SCENTS

Roshan groaned loudly, rolling over in the darkness, paw groping the surface of the cave floor looking for the source of the insistent ringing disturbing his slumber. The phone was procured from a particularly appetising wildlife authority stupidly venturing into the park to investigate the recent expansion in the wolf population. Roshan had had his fill, stolen the phone and wedged it between small rocks on the cave floor the previous day.

The burly man had made a nice little meal, sustaining his appetite since. The phone had also come in handy for monitoring the pack he'd sent to Australia to investigate the likely travel of The Protectors. The only problem; the phone rang regularly and not with news from his pack.

Roshan pried open bleary eyes, cursing the insistent ringtone. It was the wife calling again. Didn't she know it was the middle of the day?

He concentrated on the taste of the man he'd ingested, morphing slowly into his shape and adapting his vocal chords to suit. He made sure he was what the wife would expect to hear before answering.

'Philippe, c'est que vous?'

'Yes, it is me,' Roshan replied in French.

'Are you still in Écrins?'

'Yes.'

'When are you coming home?' his wife asked. 'The children and I are worried about you. You have never been away from us for this long before. I thought you were just investigating the scene from the news program?'

Roshan frowned. He didn't follow human broadcasting, so he wasn't sure what she was talking about. 'I am,' he answered hesitantly. 'But there have been some further developments.'

'When can we expect you home?'

Never.

'In a few days.'

'A few days! Philippe, this is madness! The park is filled with wolves; you could get killed.'

'I think not.'

She started to rant. It was about at this point in the conversation that Roshan usually hung up on her.

He rolled his eyes, yawning. 'Okay, love to the pups, I mean kids,' he corrected. 'I'll see you soon.'

'Philippe!'

Roshan disconnected. It started to ring again, but he ignored it. He hoped that when he found Elena, tamed her and integrated her with his pack, that she would not be a whiner. He could not listen to *that* twenty-four-seven. Roshan knew she would protest capture, but eventually realise she was half vânător—an inescapable truth that made her destined to be his mate. He'd tried to be reasonable in the past, but now that she could shape-shift and ignore his alpha commands, he was going to have to dominate.

He rolled again, stretching out his newly transformed limbs, wishing he could reach out now and find Elena by his side. He missed her—the feel of her and the taste of her. There was no other creature like her on this Earth and sometimes, he wanted her so badly that his whole body ached with need.

The phone started to ring again.

He cursed, looking down at the screen. It was not the wife this time, a pleasant change. She called so often that he'd memorised the number. He kept answering her calls because he didn't want a search party on his tail or the phone service cancelled. 'What?'

'Roshan?'

He breathed a sigh of relief. 'Yes, Wolf, I'm listening.'

'We have something to share—something you might find interesting.'

Roshan pushed the phone tighter against his ear. 'You found the magical ones?'

'No, but we believe they must be near.'

'You have found a scent trail?'

There was a brief moment of pause on the other end. 'Yes, but not from The Protectors. Vampires; five in total; four males and one female.'

'Interesting,' Roshan mused. 'They must be looking for The Protectors too.'

'We think so.'

'Follow them.'

'There is also a sixth scent that we cannot identify. It smells mostly human, but there is something wrong with it.'

Roshan moved into an upright position, clutching the phone tightly. 'Describe it.'

Another long pause. 'It's sweet—very sweet. In fact, it's more alluring than the Vampire's scents. It's not exactly definable, but it's ... pure, untainted, a one of a kind aroma that can't be compared with anything else.'

Elena ...

'I want you to keep following them,' Roshan commanded, his whole body snapping to attention. 'Whatever you do, stay out of their scope. We cannot risk the Vampires becoming aware of your presence.'

'And what of The Protectors?'

'The Vampires will undoubtedly lead you in their direction. I do wish to know where the magical ones are hiding, but I also want at least one or two of you to keep a constant watch on the sixth scent. I must know where it goes.'

'Yes, Roshan.'

'Don't let me down, Wolf.'

'I will not.'

Roshan snapped the phone shut with a barely suppressed smile. It appeared that Elena was entangled with a vampiric search party. He wondered what her interest in finding them could be or if it was simply to seek revenge on the man who had kept her caged and half-starved in Bucharest.

Elena was going to make a perfect addition to his pack, ruling the Vânătors at his side, the only two alphas left. It was starting to look like everything would work out the way he wanted.

How very fortunate.

CHAPTER FIFTEEN: STRATEGIES

The drive to New Norfolk took thirty minutes. I concentrated on following directions from the GPS while listening to the hastened conversation flowing from the backseat. According to the map we were a few minutes from the destination.

I turned onto a street with neatly manicured lawns, trimmed hedges and well-tended homesteads. The picket fences were freshly painted and yards were raked and tidy. Judging by the growth of the surrounding landscape, this area was well established. The houses weren't shabby though; most constructed from hand-carved sandstone, fitted with wrap around porches and iron roofs built to sustain the tough weather conditions Australia often delivered.

I pulled over; destination reached. I looked out the window, studying the darkened street. A few dogs skirmished their front yards and an old man a few doors down watered roses hanging over a trellis by his entry. Nothing spectacularly exciting.

'Are we all going in?' I asked, locking the car after we'd all piled out.

Eric shook his head. 'Thomas, Marianne and Caleb will surround the house in case the guy tries anything sneaky.'

'Why would he?'

'What do you smell, Elena?'

A test for sure, so I inhaled deeply, sucking in the various scents around me and sorting through them one by one. 'Someone's having steak for dinner.' I screwed up my face. 'And a cucumber salad. Yuck. Someone's baking a roast, someone's having potato bake I think and ... ooh, chocolate.'

Eric was nothing, if not patient. 'Do you smell Protector?'

'I've never been able to. I can smell artificial aromas—perfumes, deodorants, your compulsion and I can smell the Vânåtors now, but I can't smell humans.'

Eric gestured to the house. 'Well, this pilot is a Protector and we can't be too careful. Nicholas and I are going in because we are more in control of our compulsion.'

'He's going to know that you are both vampires the minute he opens the front door.'

Eric and Nicholas appeared baffled.

I was going to have to break it down for these pretty boys. 'You may not realise this about yourselves, but vampires are beautiful. Your skin is impossibly perfect, eyes more intense in colour and you move too fast.'

Caleb grinned. 'You think I'm beautiful?'

'You all are.'

Marianne touched her chest, lips parted in surprise. 'That could be the nicest words that ever came out of your mouth.'

'So maybe you should let me knock on the door.'

'You aren't exactly ugly either,' Marianne murmured. I suspected despite her delight in my comment, it might have hurt her a fraction to admit anything semi-wondrous about me.

I focused back on Eric. 'So I'll talk to the pilot, get him to let me inside and then you guys can come in after me.'

'What will you say? Protectors can be suspicious.'

I shrugged. 'I'll think of something.' I pushed past Eric and Nicholas and headed for the front door. I could hear the others moving into designated positions around the house; clambering up drainpipes and onto the roof, dispersing into trees and hiding in the back yard. Eric and Nicholas remained close but out of sight.

My hurried knock induced footsteps on the other side of the door. The peep hole darkened momentarily before the locks disengaged. I mustn't have looked threatening. I didn't know whether to be insulted or pleased with my camouflage.

A tall, dark-haired man with beady black eyes poked his head out from behind the door. He was in his forties, possibly early fifties judging by his grey thatch of balding hair. His breath smelt like stale ale and in the background I could hear the drone of mindless television. Judging by the silk boxers and singlet he wore, I'd caught him settling in for the night. 'What do you want?'

I acted nervous, widening my eyes so I had that deer caught in the headlights look. 'Um, are you, um, Ian Walters?'

'Who's asking?'

'I'm ... Betty.'

'Betty?'

Don't you dare say Boop.

'I'm Betty Ford.'

Great, now I'm a drug and rehabilitation centre.

'Why are you on my porch?'

'Would you mind letting me in so we can talk privately?'

He closed the door further, eyes wary and the only thing now visible through the slight opening. I spotted Caleb on the roof, clutching his stomach and trying not to laugh. I imagined Marianne rolling her eyes, Thomas slapping his forehead in despair and Nicholas and Eric exchanging that *look* they often reserved for my antics.

'I'm sorry,' I said, shuffling from foot-to-foot. 'I don't really know how to say this.'

'Say what?' the pilot said, curiosity once again ignited.

I conjured my waterworks; challenging since I didn't cry often. I had to remind myself that if I stuffed this up, I might not ever see Lucas again. That worked a charm and tears soon welled.

'Aw, come on,' the pilot said, opening the door wider. 'I don't have a cat that you could have run over. What could possibly make a pretty young girl like you cry?'

'I didn't kill your cat,' I said, hiccupping for effect. 'I think that you're my father.'

The pilot stumbled, swallowing imagined razor blades. 'What did you say?'

'I think you're my dad.'

He was silent as he eyed me up and down. I could tell that he was drawing comparisons between us and at the same time, cycling through his life and wondering how the hell it could have happened.

Eventually he scrubbed a hand over his face, shoulders slumping in defeat. He held the door open a little wider, inviting me in. 'I knew that trip to Thailand was going to come back and bite me on the ass someday.'

And just like that I was inside and so were Nicholas and Eric who blew in straight after me.

'So, you think I'm your father? Who is your mother?'

I sat down on the sofa, making myself at home. It smelt faintly of moth balls and had definitely seen better days. 'No one you know.'

'Then I don't understand.'

'Have a seat,' I said, gesturing to the armchair in front of me.

His brow rumpled as he looked between me and the empty, well-worn armchair, deciding the best course of action. 'What's going on?' he demanded, lowering himself into the chair. I didn't miss the crackle of blue light encased within his palms.

'My friends and I need to ask you a couple of questions.'

'What friends?'

'These friends,' Nicholas said, appearing right beside him.

The pilot attempted to bolt, but I captured him in a prison of telekinetic energy, forcing him back into a sitting position. He couldn't move his arms or legs, but could still converse.

'What happened?' Eric prompted.

'Relax,' I said. 'I inherited a few of Lucius's skills. You can now question him and he can't cast magic.'

Nicholas fingered the telekinetic barrier. It shimmered where his flesh touched the surface, rippling as if constructed of moving water. 'Amazing.'

'Why didn't you tell us about this earlier?' Eric chastised.

'It's not like I needed it until now.'

'Your father keeps making out that you need protection, yet it's quite clear that you are more than capable of taking care of yourself.'

'Have I not been saying that for months now?' I slapped the side of the chair. 'Why doesn't anyone ever listen to me?'

'Lucius is not to be ignored.'

'Whatever.' I contained a customary eye-roll and gestured to the pilot. 'Just find out where Lucas is so we can go home.'

* * *

After twenty minutes of *compelling* interrogation, the pilot—Ian Walters—spilled the beans on the IMI's location. South of Casey Station in the Antarctic region was a hub with facilities large enough to support at least five hundred Protectors. According to Ian, they ran a legitimate research station accounting for any unannounced visitors or scientists in the area. The rest of the facility had been built over the last fifty or sixty years, comprising of multiple buildings designed to blend with the landscape, some hidden by the Revatarus spell.

Ian's job was to ensure that the affiliate airline—Beyond the Blue Airways—was capable to deliver food to the IMI depot monthly without detection.

The rest of the time it was grounded at a private airfield, where none of us had thought to check for inbound or outbound flights. Although Beyond the Blue Shipping was owned by the IMI, the employees were human—bar one that helped Ian to alter records regularly and ensure important information was erased.

We left his home a little after eight, armed with the information that his flight left tomorrow at ten. Nicholas and Eric's compulsion was such that he happily agreed to wait until we arrived before take-off, also offering to lower the internal shades for the Vampires in the cargo hold. Most importantly, he believed it a threat to national security to divulge anything discussed.

'Only a few hours until I see Lucas again,' I cheered, throwing the car keys at the valet attendant on the way into the hotel.

Marianne sidled up beside me. 'I wonder how different he will be? A lot has happened. His parents have not made life easy for him.'

I nodded sadly. 'I know, but Lucas is a survivor like me.'

'Still … living with people that oppressive can't have been easy on him. He did also mention he was worried they had been conducting secret experiments on him.'

My nostrils flared at the thought. 'Just how often did you and Lucas converse before the IMI disbanded?'

She shrugged. 'To begin with, he called nearly every day. Thomas gave him my cell number because he thought Lucas would drive me crazy.'

'I gather it worked?'

She smiled reluctantly. 'At first I wanted to kill him, but then I realised something.'

'What did you realise?'

Marianne glanced at me only briefly, detecting her emotions almost impossible. 'I realised that Lucas was the first person I had met in a long time that was actually pursuing *me*.'

The others were huddled behind us talking excitedly and ignorant of our conversation. 'Don't you have men throwing themselves at you all of the time?'

Her lips twitched. 'Lucas wanted to know the real me, content just to talk on the phone for hours and ask me how my day was.'

'Oh, I get it, you care because he took the time to care about you?'

Her short burst of amusement morphed quickly into a grim smile. 'Something like that. It's complicated.'

'What's complicated about being friends?'

We'd reached the elevators, cutting our conversation short. The others had also caught up to us, immediately running ideas past us about how we were going to get into the IMI. I had to remind them repeatedly that The Protectors would not leave the place unguarded and that sneaking into a complex housing five hundred would not be easy. They'd laughed, practically pounded their chests in enthusiasm. It was only Marianne that could see my logic and the danger of running in without a decent plan.

As we poured out the elevator, my phone vibrated. I fished into my back pocket and flipped it open, the name flashing across the display stopped me in my tracks.

'Elena?' Marianne asked, genuinely concerned. 'What is it?'

'It's Sebastian.'

She took one look at my face and quickly ushered the boys into the hotel room, leaving me standing in the corridor alone. The fact that she recognised the importance of this moment elevated her character considerably. Though the others protested her bossy impatience, I knew they'd be eavesdropping anyway.

I accepted the call, my back finding the corridor wall as I slid to the floor, landing hard on my backside. It had to be the shock. 'Sebastian?'

'Yes, Baby Vamp, it's me.'

I closed my eyes, relief flooding through every vein and artery within. I'd missed the way he spoke—every word always a feather-light caress of seduction as they left his lips. 'You're alive.'

'Of course I'm alive. I'm very good at what I do.'

I re-opened my eyes, entirely overwhelmed by the reassurance of his safety.

'Were you thinking about me?'

'I was actually.'

'That sounds promising.'

'Sebastian, I have so much to tell you.'

He chuckled. 'Marcus informed me that you took a little trip to Hobart.'

'What else did he say?'

'That Lucius didn't like it.'

'No. Lucius was not happy, but I think he understands that Lucas is my top priority.'

'So you found him?' There was a hint of surprise in his voice.

'We did, but we had a little help.' I paused. 'That's one of the things that I need to talk to you about.'

'So tell me.'

I shook my head and then remembered he couldn't see me. 'No, I don't want to do this over the phone. I-I need to see your face.'

'Are you thinking you'll be able to catch me in a lie?'

'I never can tell with you, Sebastian.'

He laughed again—warm and syrupy. 'That is certainly true.'

'Tell him that you love him!' Caleb shouted, banging the wall at my back.

I covered the mouth piece and rammed the wall with my elbow. 'Shut up, you idiot, he can hear you!'

'Just tell him!'

'Caleb, be quiet!' Marianne hissed. 'If you don't shut up she'll go down to the lobby where none of us can hear her.'

'Are you trying to give her ideas?' came Caleb's muffled reply.

I jumped to my feet and headed back to the elevator. I'd need to thank Marianne for that later.

'Elena?'

'Sorry,' I murmured, pressing the phone to my ear again. 'Caleb was being a dork.'

'I know, I heard.'

'You did?' My forehead prickled with panicked perspiration. I was saved by the distraction of the elevator doors opening. I stepped inside the silver cube. 'I might lose you for a few minutes. If the phone cuts out, call me back.'

No reply.

When the doors re-opened in the lobby, I settled into a lounge chair in the corner of the bar. 'Can you hear me?'

'Yes.'

'So are you back at the villa? What happened?'

'Yes I'm back home and the hunt was a success; we killed all the Alphas. Well, everyone except Roshan. He was not at the den with the others. I came back to the villa to find you because at some point during this war he will come looking for you again.'

'I'm pretty sure I'm safe here.'

'I agree.'

'Sebastian?'

'Yes, Baby Vamp?'

'When exactly did you kill the Alphas?'

'Why do you ask?'

I took a deep breath. 'Caleb has a theory based on things I said while I was ... well, burning to death.'

'What has happened, tell me everything.'

I gave him a brief overview of my nightmares and the burning black out both at the villa and in the hotel room.

'We think I might be connected to the Alphas. I'm sure Marcus gave you a heads up, but did you know about Sunday's news reports?'

'Something about a photographer amongst a bunch of vânǎtors and living to tell the tale?'

'It's true. The photographer caught it all on video. The French are in uproar thinking that their southern national parks have been overrun by killer wolves. The thing is, we know that part is true. It's the fact that the Vânǎtors had some kind of fit like me that had us making connections. At precisely the same time the Vânǎtors writhed across the forest floor and committed mass suicide, I had an experience of my own, possibly the severed link between alpha and pack.'

'It's possible, but what's the relevance?'

'That we can't be certain how it will affect me in the long-term; we're speculating as per usual.'

'Well, for accuracy, we found their den earlier this morning. We killed seventeen at approximately one or two o'clock.'

I mentally calculated the time difference between Australia and France. They were roughly ten hours behind. 'That puts my second episode down to the same time you were killing them. Caleb might well be right that I was experiencing the death of the Alphas.'

'Do you feel any different?'

I clicked my tongue and buried myself deeper into the softness of the chair. 'No, but it hurt. I felt like I was dying, Sebastian. My whole body was engulfed by flames that no one else could see or feel.'

'Elena, I'm so sorry.'

'It's not your fault you didn't know.'

'Yes, but I should be protecting you.' There was audible regret and barely masked pain in his voice. My heart clenched painfully. I toyed with the notion of debating his archangel status, but decided against it at the last moment. We could dodge that minefield later.

'What are you going to do now?' I asked, changing the subject instead.

'About what?'

'Well, I can see that your plan is obviously to use me as bait to get to Roshan. I'm not there to help you out with that, so what are you going to do while I'm away?'

'Pine for you, of course.'

I smirked. 'You will not.'

'You're right. Perhaps I should assist your father?'

'Did you see him on your way back into Rome?'

'No. He's more towards Milan. He's trying to keep the humans from discovering the truth.'

'What's it like out there at the moment?'

'Contained, but barely. The wolves are aggressive, but we are lucky they are fallible. One good hit and they do not get up again. Now that the Alphas are gone bar Roshan, re-establishing pack numbers will be difficult. What about you? What are your plans for getting Lucas back now that you are aware of the IMI's location?'

I sighed, picking at a loose thread on my jeans. 'I don't know, Sebastian. Five hundred against six is not great odds. Eric and the others are tossing around ideas as we speak, but I don't think there's going to be an easy way in or out.'

'Do you need me?'

'I always need you.' I slapped my forehead as he started to chuckle. 'I just meant that you are older and wiser than some of the other guys. Plus, you track really well and—'

'Elena, it's okay. I miss you too.'

'You do?'

'Of course. I've been thinking about the last time we were together—'

'That's it! Give me the phone, Sebastian,' William's muffled voice could be heard quite distinctly in the background.

I bolted upright in the chair, guilty. Sebastian and I had been talking for almost fifteen minutes and I hadn't once thought of enquiring about William's wellbeing. What kind of person did that make me? I was in love with Sebastian, but that did not mean I'd stopped caring about William.

'Excuse me, Elena.' There was a muffled sound. I presumed Sebastian attempted to cover the mouthpiece. 'I said I would hand you over the minute your name was mentioned and it hasn't come up yet.'

I groaned, intolerant of the childish games these two attempted despite my constant reprisal of their behaviour. 'Sebastian?'

'Yes, Elena?'

'Put William on.'

Sebastian grunted followed by a momentary pause where defeat had obviously overcome him and he passed the mobile over.

'Elena?'

'Hi, William.'

'Are you okay?' he said, sounding slightly frantic. 'I heard most of your conversation with Sebastian. I'm sorry I was not there for you.'

'You know, I can look after myself. I'm glad that you are both alive and unharmed.'

'It wasn't easy at times, but it has been worth it. There's only one left to kill.'

'We'll get him.'

'No, Sebastian and I will get him. You will stay safe. I can't go on worrying about you all the time.'

I started to laugh. He should have known me better than that by now. 'You know, from the minute we met, William, you've been trying to save me—even from myself.'

'Why is that wrong?'

'You can't save me—no one can. I do pretty much whatever the hell I want whether I ask someone's permission or not.'

He groaned. 'That's why you are always in trouble.'

'Maybe,' I agreed. 'Perhaps it's also the reason I'm still alive. I follow my instincts, William. I trust my heart and I hope it takes me the distance.'

'What are you saying?'

'I'm saying that I love you for trying to love me. It can't be easy chasing after me all the time, but I think it's time you looked for a girl that actually wants to be rescued.'

'You finally admit that you love me and now you want to break up with me?'

I smiled because of the stubborn streak we both seemed to share. 'Come on, William, you know we were never together—not really. I told you from the beginning I just want to have fun. You raised your own expectations of our relationship.'

'I don't understand. You just said you love me.'

'I do, just not the way you want me to love you or how you deserve to be loved.'

I could feel his resignation in every disparaged breath or sigh emitted. 'I feel like we've had this conversation before.'

'We have.'

'How can we be friends after everything that's happened? Elena, we've done things that friends don't do.'

I blushed, thinking through those *things* in which my mind so vividly recreated. 'Nothing really changes the fact that we're attracted to each other, but that doesn't mean we're right for each other either.'

There was a lengthy pause, both of us turning inwards to reflect. Finally, William broke the silence. 'So what now?'

'Now you wait for the girl that takes your breath away.'

'That was you.'

'So wait for the one that makes you never want it back.'

Silence again.

'I love you, Elena.'

'I know.'

'I'm going to hang up now.'

'Sure.'

'When will we be seeing you again?'

I looked out the glass windows and over the Derwent river, the water shimmered, caressed by the thousands of sparkling night lights around the city. 'Soon I think.'

'You found Lucas.'

'Yes.'

'And you're going to get him back.'

I snorted. 'Obviously.'

He sighed again, tension threaded through the very timbre of his voice. 'Then I suppose I should wish you luck.'

'William, I don't need luck.'

'What do you need?'

'A good pair of boots so I can seriously kick some ass!'

He laughed and somehow I knew that everything was going to be okay between us. 'With or without the new shoes you'll get Lucas back.'

'I know that,' I said assuredly.

'So I shouldn't wish you luck?'

'No.'

'Then I better hang up.'

I slipped the disconnected phone back into my pocket and sat there for a little while longer, looking out over the Derwent River, smiling and contemplating. Despite my episode earlier this morning, the failed attempts to track The Protectors, breaking and entering, mind control games with a pilot and a disjointed conversation with my two love interests, I was fairly content in the knowledge that by this time tomorrow night my brother would be sitting in the chair beside me—safe.

Of course, reality dictated that everything was likely to blow up in my face, but a girl's got to dream. It was no longer acceptable to admit that finding and rescuing Lucas from The Protectors was unachievable. It simply had to be done or I would die trying.

Famous last words from a reckless sixteen-year-old.

Watch this space.

CHAPTER SIXTEEN: HOPE

'Alba, I don't know if this is going to work,' Karina murmured in despair, running to catch up with the nurse.

'It has to,' she tossed firmly over her shoulders. 'This is Lucas's last chance. If we get caught it's all over for all of us and if we don't do it today, there's another month before the plane comes back to drop off more supplies.' She shook her head from side to side. 'I don't want to have to think about him chained to a gurney helpless and alone for another month.'

'I don't either, but I don't know if I'm brave enough to do this.'

Alba stopped her rampage of the passage and turned to look at her. Karina was already dressed in her thermals, jeans, sweaters and carrying her snow jacket over one arm. Over the other shoulder sat her back pack, loaded with personal possessions and whatever money she could find. After today, she would never see her father again and she would never re-enter the IMI without being persecuted. From this point onwards, Karina would forever be an outcast and a runaway.

Alba's features softened as she drew Karina into an embrace. The girl was only seventeen yet had willingly taken on the responsibility of an adult twice her age. 'Everything is going to work out fine,' Alba reassured. 'Lucas is going to be okay and so will you, but if you're scared and change your mind, I will work something out with my husband.'

Karina shook her head. 'You can't—he's a Protector. Leaving this place and the clans will destroy him.'

'And you?'

Karina swiped an escaped tear that had begun the steady decent down damp cheeks. 'I owe Lucas.'

'You don't owe him your life, Karina.'

'Are you trying to talk me out of this?'

Alba squeezed Karina's shoulders reassuringly. 'No, I just ... You're both so young.'

Karina sniffed and then hiccupped, attempting to compose herself. 'Lucas needs me; there's no one else. I don't even know if Elena is looking for him and if she is, she'd never find him here.'

Alba nodded numbly. 'You are right.' She patted the side of Karina's cheeks and forced a smile. 'Are you ready?'

'I have to be.'

Alba grabbed Karina's hand, leading her up the stairs towards the loading bay. When they got to the door, she peeped through the window, motioned for Karina's back pack and snow jacket and then opened the door. She slipped just inside, tossed the items into the corner and then shut the door behind her. 'Okay, faze one complete.'

They both jogged back down the stairs and into the passages again. 'I guess I better go and do my part,' Karina said, breaking from Alba and heading for the mess hall.

'Be safe.'

Karina waved. 'I'm just going to try to not get caught.'

As they each went in separate directions, Karina sprinted to the mess hall. She passed a lot of Protectors on the way, many of whom she'd never met. She hastened her pace, pushing people out of the way where necessary and tearing through the passages as quickly as her legs could carry her. Many called out for her to slow down, but she didn't listen. She needed to do her part and meet Alba at the labs as soon as she could.

As the mess hall came into view with its sweeping expanse of space and cafeteria style feel, Karina felt a twang of guilt. Some of these people were bound to be innocent, but part of correcting her error in judgement would come from dashing past their tables to enter the air filtration room. They would never believe that one of their own had sabotaged the oxygen supply, tripping the switch that generated fresh, warm air for the entire facility. They would never think to look for a perpetrator or check the cameras until it was too late; they would never suspect a child.

Not Karina; the good little girl from Cairns who had never put a foot wrong until now.

The alarm started quietly at first, growing louder with her footfalls as she ran down the passages towards the labs. Minor panic ensued. People were suddenly everywhere, running not for the docking bay, but for the rear exit of the facility, the only door not requiring security clearance to evacuate during an emergency.

Everything was going according to plan.

The steel doors to the labs appeared a minute later.

Alba was standing right outside, holding a spare lab coat which she promptly handed to Karina. She slipped it on, waiting patiently as Alba used her ID tag to open the doors. They rushed in, doors whirring closed behind them, the smell of bleach and other chemicals ripe in the air.

'He's this way,' Alba said, taking Karina's hand firmly in hers. She was shaking. 'Try not to be too frightened by what you see.'

'Where is everyone?'

'I watched for Chester, Anica and a few of the others to leave the lab. The alarm sounded and they mobilized, responding just as we imagined.'

'Are there others?'

'I hope not.'

They hurried through the labs, a maze of tiny rooms, most filled with equipment and refrigerators. A few were empty, only a singular gurney in the centre, most with restraints.

'What do they do here?'

'I don't want to know,' Alba responded. She pulled Karina along to the last door. There was a small glass window in it; Karina could now see Lucas.

'Oh my god!' she gasped. 'What have they done to him?'

In the centre of the room was Lucas, strapped to a gurney, bound by both ankles and wrists. His head was firmly held with a leather strap and in his mouth a gag was pulled tight around his neck and lips. There was nothing else except two different IV's hooked to each arm. One held clear fluid that dripped slowly into the catchment and dribbled into the connecting tube; the second was a red concoction.

As Alba finally managed to get her ID tag to open the door, Karina rushed past. 'Lucas? Can you hear me?' She questioned Alba with wide eyes, hands fluttering uselessly over his body. 'What are they doing to him?'

Alba rounded the gurney, studying the IV fluid. 'It's a sedative. It's not strong, just enough to make him drowsy.'

'And this?' Karina said, pointing to the red fluid.

Alba shook her head, perplexed. 'I don't know. It's unmarked. I thought it was blood.'

Lucas slowly peeled his eyes open, glancing from one to the other before closing them again.

'We have to snap him out of this. Can you unplug him or whatever?'

Alba nodded. She went to work extracting the needle from each arm while Karina started to unfasten all of his restraints including the gag.

'Lucas?' Karina slapped him gently. 'Lucas, you have to wake up, we're going to get you out of here.'

He dragged his eyes open again, fluttering the drowsy lids like butterfly's wings. He licked his lips. They were parched and red where the gag had been placed, but it did not stop him from trying to move them. His throat bobbed as he swallowed, raspy sounds coming from the back of his throat.

Karina couldn't translate his noises, so leaned in closer but to no avail.

'Get him some water,' Alba commanded. 'I saw a cup with a straw on the table by the metal sink outside. While you're at it, check the closet next to the room before this one. They keep the emergency oxygen masks there and there should be a spare lab coat for Lucas.'

'Got it.' Karina raced out of the room, starting with the closet first. She commandeered a lab coat, grabbed the masks Alba had mentioned and raced back to the sink where she did find the water cup on the shelf *above* the sink.

Close enough. She thought to herself as she raced back into the room. 'Here they are.'

'Good. Now give him some water and then help me sit him up.'

Karina dumped the gear onto the floor and then bent the straw so Lucas could take a sip. He sucked at it timidly, eyes darting backwards and forwards between the two women, unsure of what their motives were.

Karina tentatively touched the top of his head. He flinched, lips dropping the straw as he strained to pull away from her.

Tears begun to well in her wide, green eyes.

He's frightened of me.

'I'm so sorry, Lucas. I didn't know this was what they were going to do to you. They told me you were sick, they threatened my future with the IMI.' Her voice lowered to a whisper as the tears streamed thick and fast. 'I didn't know. Please forgive me. I'm here to help get you out of this place.'

'Y-you t-tricked me,' he rasped.

'I know. I was wrong. I see that now. It's why I'm going to get you away from here.'

'Y-you're lying.'

Karina shook her head vigorously. 'No more lies, Lucas. I will get you away from here if it's the last thing I do. We'll go together, we'll even look for Elena and run as far away as you like. Whatever you want to do, I'll help you.'

Lucas sought confirmation from Alba.

'She's telling the truth.' She nodded at Karina, more concerned with the current task than conversing. 'Help me to sit him up. The oxygen level in here is dropping and I don't think we'll have much time before someone comes back, realising what has happened.'

While Karina propped Lucas upright, Alba concentrated on quickly massaging the muscles in his feet, calves and thighs.

'Do you think you can stand, Lucas?'

'I don't know.'

'You have to try, Lucas. Our window of opportunity is small.'

He nodded, head lolling awkwardly to the side as he looked back at Karina. Through her shining eyes she smiled at him hopefully. Forgiveness was going to be tough. He was going to have to dig particularly deep to find the will to ever smile back.

Lucas concentrated on his fingers instead, trying to coordinate them to grip the edge of the gurney. Both Karina and Alba supported his mid-section as he attempted to shimmy off the edge and onto the floor. His toes curled awkwardly and the bed sheet got in the way, twisting around his calves until they seized painfully. He was too weak to support his own weight and consequently fell.

'He's naked,' Karina gushed, surprise evident. 'I've never seen anyone naked before.'

Alba frowned at her over the top of Lucas's head. 'Maybe you should grab that lab coat now.'

Karina paused, studying him a minute longer, watching as his back muscles twitched and tightened under the strain of trying to pull himself upright again. Alba busied herself with the task of detangling the sheet and covering his naked form. He was shaking uncontrollably.

'Karina?'

'I'm going.' She spun on her heels, grabbing the coat off the floor. She hastily tossed it at Lucas, turning while he clumsily gathered it around himself, Alba helping him to button up. 'I don't think that's going to keep him warm.'

'Please tell me that your p-plan involves not going outside in the s-snow?' Lucas attempted to pull himself to his feet again. This time he was a little more successful thanks to Alba's support.

'We're smuggling you out on the aeroplane that delivers our food supplies every month. It should be a standard twenty-two degrees on the aircraft and probably a blanket or two on board. The only outside exposure you'll have to endure is in the cargo bay and as you know it's quite comfortable in there.'

'And she's coming with me?' Lucas said, jabbing a shaky thumb in Karina's direction.

Alba nodded, resting a firm hand on his arm. 'She's giving up her entire life and her standing with the IMI to repent for what she has done to you.'

Karina blushed. 'Alba, don't do that—don't make him feel like he owes me thanks.' Karina focused on Lucas, waiting for acknowledgement. 'I owe *you* everything after what I've done.'

Lucas's frown deepened. He wasn't sure what to make of this development and simply responded with, 'Just get me out of here.'

Karina returned to the door and fetched the oxygen masks while Lucas tried to stand unassisted. She hadn't expected his forgiveness. Hell, she wasn't sure she would forgive him if the situation were reversed. She was just grateful he was giving her the chance to make amends.

'They would have worked out that the supply has been turned off by now. We've probably only got minutes before a lab tech heads back this way.' Alba was reminding everyone of the seriousness of the current situation.

'What do we do?' Lucas asked, sliding the mask over his face and sucking in some much needed oxygen.

'We need to look like we are trying to help,' Alba replied. She raced to the corner, returning with a small fire extinguisher which she handed to Karina. She also grabbed what looked like a tool kit. 'Okay, Lucas. You need to focus on walking straight. Do you think you can do that?'

He started to put one foot in front of the other, still unstable on legs unused for over three weeks and woozy from the lingering effects of the sedative. 'I'm trying, but my vision is still blurry and my legs won't do what I tell them.' He stumbled forward and Karina caught him.

'Let me use the *Levitartium* spell on him. I've perfected it now. I should be able to hover him all the way back to the cargo hold.'

Lucas paled, stumbling until he found the wall for support. 'I don't know ...'

'Please, Lucas. I know this is really hard for you to do right now, but I need you to trust me. I'm just trying to help you get out.'

Hands balled into fists at his sides, knuckles flexing and the skin stretched taught across the bone. The muscle in the side of his jaw matched the stiffness of his posture, ticking uncontrollably as he clenched his teeth. Even through the mask, distrust was written across his face.

'Please, Lucas.'

'Alright, but I swear to God, Karina, if you betray me again, I'll probably kill you.'

Karina's bottom lip quivered, surprised by the conviction in his tone; robbed of his innocence and tortured for three weeks, it was no wonder his usually agreeable demeanour had altered. 'You have my word, Lucas.'

'Which means very little to me right now,' he said, sneering.

She nodded, understanding his reluctance. She waited for his approval before holding up the hand unencumbered by the extinguisher. '*Levitartium*,' she uttered, commanding the spell with both voice and mind. She poured every bit of her will into making Lucas levitate just a few inches off the ground to remain inconspicuous.

'Very good, Karina,' Alba encouraged. 'Now let's get going.'

Alba ran ahead through the labs, carrying the tool kit by her side and appearing purposeful in her stride. Karina stayed behind Lucas, concentrating on his direction and the speed at which his body was propelled forward. Lucas swung his arms by his sides, pretending that he moved on his own accord, even if his feet remained stationary. It wasn't perfect, but would hopefully work regardless.

When they reached the outer labs and entered the passages, Karina breathed a small sigh of relief. There was next to no one around, only a few stragglers that hadn't heeded the warnings.

A few security personnel bolted past on their way towards the mess hall. A couple waved, probably assuming the three lab coats were technical support. The main priority was getting the filtration system operating again; a couple of loose lab techs were of little consequence to their task.

As they reached the stairs to the cargo hold, Karina held her hand steady, making sure that Lucas ascended safely above the treads. It was cooler by a couple of degrees in this area and he'd pulled the lab coat tighter around him, shivering and looking longingly towards freedom.

'I can see the plane,' Alba said excitedly. 'They've just opened the cargo doors to allow it inside to unload.'

'When do we move?'

'After the forklift removes the first load. They'll be busy offloading it to the back of the warehouse storage. By the time he returns, you'll already be on the plane.' Alba turned suddenly and hugged Lucas fiercely. 'You look after yourself.'

Lucas's wrapped tentative arms around her tiny frame. 'I have to say I'm surprised that you of all people decided to help me, but I'm grateful anyway. We only met once.'

'You're a good person, Lucas. Anyone of sound mind could see what they were doing to you was wrong. I'm just sorry I wasn't made aware of your situation sooner.'

Lucas ended the embrace, too tempted to burst into tears and hold her longer. 'What will you do when they discover your involvement?'

She shrugged. 'Time will tell I suppose. I'd much rather cop the punishment they dish out than live with my guilty conscience.'

'I can't thank you enough for this.'

'I'm just doing what's right. We both are.'

'You don't have to come with me, Karina. I can do this on my own.'

'You can barely walk and yes I do.'

'You'll never be allowed to come back.'

'It doesn't matter anymore. This place isn't what I thought it was.'

Lucas expelled a raspy breath. 'It's good to hear someone else finally admit that. I feel like I've been the only one on the outside looking in for so long that it might be nice to have company for a change.'

'Even if it's me?'

Alba tapped Karina's shoulder. 'You need to get going. The forklift is almost finished loading up and I don't want Keith to see me. He'll start asking questions.'

They both nodded.

'Don't forget your things by the door and remember—look after each other.'

Karina nodded and Lucas looked away, unable to commit to the idea of looking out for the girl who'd seen him suffer for three weeks solid.

They stole one last look at the nurse as she slammed the door behind them. There was no going back now. Life was about to fundamentally change for the both of them. When had everything become so complicated?

Lucas didn't have the answer, but Karina was now willing to figure it out with him. He supposed that was a good place to start.

CHAPTER SEVENTEEN: SHOWTIME

The following morning, Ian Walters stood next to his aircraft, looking like the cat that caught the canary. Driven by compulsion, he'd gone to every extreme in order to help the Vampires avoid the mid-morning sun; even decked the inside of the cargo bay with blankets and cushions—comfort in mind.

Shrink-wrapped crates of food were also set for delivery; secured by belts hooked into wall fastenings and nets acting as a secondary catch point should all other fastenings fail. Where seats would've been there was empty space, presumably to allow for more storage. After all, this wasn't a passenger jet. It had been gutted to suit the IMI's needs.

Ian was pleased by our arrival, vigorously shaking everyone's hand like we were celebrities.

'What the hell did you do to him?' Marianne asked, settling onto a cushion and folding down the shade flaps closest to her.

'I merely suggested we were important cargo,' Eric murmured, also closing the remaining shades.

Nicholas snorted, clearly amused. 'You told the man we were important diplomats.'

Eric waved a dismissive hand. 'It was necessary.'

'Are you sure he isn't just acting the part?' I asked. Ian waved at me merrily, bowing as he secured the aircraft door. For all we knew it could have been an excellent trick.

'My compulsion has never failed me.'

'Never?'

'Are you challenging me?'

As if I'd challenge the much older and stronger carrier of razor-sharp teeth. I could definitely handle myself, but why bait a shark? 'I'm not. The Protectors are pretty powerful—not usually this susceptible.'

'Everyone is susceptible to compulsion, even some of our own.'

I had to admit I was curious. Over the last few days they'd compelled many. I'd smelt their scents, felt the influence, but never been tempted or coaxed into undertaking anything untoward. Sebastian was the only vampire whose compulsion had ever affected me on multiple levels. I now knew why that was.

I did wonder what would transpire should I allow Eric to test my boundaries. He wasn't Sebastian, but he was old. I *could* wake up in a bathtub full of ice with my kidneys missing, but it seemed unlikely—possibly my eyebrows missing instead.

'I'm probably going to regret this, but I am curious to see what you can do and what affect it might have on me.'

Eric looked genuinely surprised. 'Are you sure?'

I shrugged, unconcerned. It's never really worked on me before.'

'It may not work now because of your genetic dispositions, but it should be interesting.'

'Okay, so do it.'

Eric smiled, rubbing his hands together. I wasn't sure the mischievous glint in his ebony eyes was necessary, but felt confident I'd remain relatively unaffected.

I couldn't recall what happened next, but I was suddenly very aware that I was dancing around the cabin mid-flight, a bra strapped to my head and singing 'I feel pretty' from Westside Story.

'What the hell?' I cried, outraged as I ripped the offending garment off my head and glared at the hysterical faces of my *supposed* friends.

Eric clutched his stomach, shaking. Caleb snorted, slapping the cabin floor. Tears of blood ran down Marianne's cheeks and Nicholas and Thomas continued to laugh hard enough to wake even the dead.

Great. I didn't want to ask what the hell they'd made me do.

I looked at the bra I still fondled. 'How long have I been out?'

'Almost the entire flight.'

'We had to hold you down during take-off because you were trying to tap dance,' Nicholas remarked, refusing or incapable of ceasing his boisterous laughter. 'Once we were in the air we let you go for it.'

'Why did I stop?'

A sense of seriousness finally overshadowed Eric's amusement and calmed the others into rationality. 'I think you have more control over your vampiric half than first believed. You snapped out of my mind's caress unprompted. I have never seen a human do it, but we all know you're a hybrid.

Eventually you might become entirely immune, just as it was possible for you to ignore the alpha sway when a vânător.'

'You know about that?'

'Sebastian gave us an edited version.'

'I didn't want Sebastian to tell anyone about my shape-shifting.'

Eric and Nicholas passed a speculative glance between them. 'Sebastian merely said you could get hostile as a wolf.'

Hostile … yeah.

I didn't want everyone knowing I'd lost complete control twice, killed a den of vânători and nearly gutted Sebastian. Calling me *hostile* in my vânător form didn't quite begin to cover it.

'You know, Elena,' Caleb joked, 'irrespective of your alter ego, nothing seems to help your singing voice. If you weren't so damn funny and a halfway decent dancer, I might have tried skydiving.'

I put my hands on my hips, more annoyed that they'd made a joke at my expense that had wasted precious time. 'We could have been strategizing about how we are going to break Lucas out of the IMI!'

'We have it covered,' Nicholas answered.

'Did anyone think that maybe I would like to bear witness to that decision?'

Caleb chuckled. 'You were too busy serenading Thomas.'

I groaned. 'I'm seriously going to go postal if you all don't stop it.'

Nicholas, sensing my obvious disdain, patted the cushions beside him. 'We don't know what we are looking at until we get there, Elena. Ian gave us some helpful information about general layout and security, but even he was unaware how many people will be in the cargo hold when the plane arrives.'

'We can try to compel as many people as we can, but it could still turn into a fight,' Eric added.

I nodded thoughtfully. 'Ian mentioned something about access cards. If I know Chester, Lucas will either be in the labs or very near to them; somewhere heavily monitored and secure.' I studied each of them in turn; porcelain skin, perfect bodies and iridescent eyes. 'Now I think of it, I don't believe any of you can leave the plane either.'

'Elena, what are you asking of us?' Nicholas asked, eyes narrowing.

'Stay in the hold. I'll steal an access card from a cargo worker and then find Lucas. I know who to steer clear of and how to blend in.'

'We can blend,' Eric protested. 'And we can move faster!'

I fingered Nicholas's shirt for emphasis. 'You all look like you're going to Fiji with your jeans and t-shirts.' I wrestled with the heavy coat and extra sweater beside me. 'I'm the only one prepared for the cold weather and its implications—the only one who looks human.'

'Elena, it's dangerous,' Eric warned. 'Lucius would not approve of this plan.'

'Lucius doesn't approve of any plan he didn't come up with himself.'

'So you want us to sit back and let you wander around a Protector infested facility by yourself?' Marianne muttered. 'It's a stupid plan. You'll get caught.'

I couldn't disagree as she was most probably right so I remained mute.

'She could sing at everyone. That ought to clear a path,' Caleb said, grinning again.

He chose to ignore the reproachful look I delivered across the divide.

'Elena, your skills are limited,' Eric stated, blunt and cutting with his version of honesty. He had no idea what I was truly capable of—none of them did.

Anger consumed me one drop at a time. My whole life I'd been underestimated and underappreciated and I was tired of being second-guessed, studied or shut down by those around me. I was a different person now; changed by blood, time and experience. Was I the only one that noticed the difference?

'I have offended you,' Eric said slowly, angling for forgiveness.

Instead of answering, I focused my burning ire on manipulating air particles into tangible hands likened to steel, radiating a form of power that the Vampires could never match.

Once harnessed, I slammed the hefty waves of energy to knock each of them off their cushions and send them flying to the back of the aircraft. They slammed against the rear, arms and legs were plastered by an invisible force, holding them suspended and without mobility. Canned goods spewed forth, covering the floor in a sticky mess of erupted food.

I paced the length of the plane, stopping right in front of a spread-eagled Eric. 'Try and get free,' I baited, kneeling down to look him in the eyes.

The others were deadly silent, enthralled and somewhat confused by the turn in events.

'I'm trying,' he whispered, perhaps embarrassed by his lack of control and the others baring witness.

'Don't hold back.'

His dark eyes narrowed, fangs protruding. His lips trembled and limbs quivered with attempted exertion. 'I am, Elena.'

'Do you know how long I can keep you like this?'

'No.'

'Longer than you can imagine. The more I practice, the better at it I get.'

'I understand the point you are trying to make, Elena.'

'We all do,' Nicholas echoed.

I released the shimmery net wrapped around each of them, allowing operation of their limbs again. 'You are vampires; one hundred times faster and stronger than a Protector—stronger and faster than me, but for a few minutes you were helpless. I have a lot of flaws, but I can handle myself. I need you to know that.'

'But compulsion—'

'I allowed you to compel me, Eric. When using my abilities my weaknesses lessen. I doubt even The Protectors could use magic against me now.'

Eric fixed his hair and straightened his rumpled shirt. 'I should not have doubted you, I'm sorry.'

'Thank you.'

'We will no longer assume your limitations.'

'I'd appreciate it if you didn't make me sing show tunes again either.'

His lips twitched ever so slightly. 'I think I can remember that.'

I looked at the bra I still clutched. 'Um, where did this bra come from?' A quick inspection of my own chest assured me I was still wrapped and packed with underwire and elastin.

Marianne sheepishly wiggled her hand in the air. 'It's mine.'

I shivered, got the 'ickies' like you do when you're five years old and threw the lacy number back at her. 'Why was I wearing your bra on my head anyway?'

She smirked. 'Do you really want to know?'

I ran through a lot of options, none legitimate or sensible and most potentially upsetting for my future mental health. Sometimes, ignorance is bliss. 'Let's not and say we did.'

Everyone agreed to the end of that conversation with a smile.

* * *

Fifteen minutes later, the plane landed with a disturbing skid upon the ice. It wobbled, bounced several times and at one point slid too far to the left before the pilot regained control. The cabin had already filled with a chill that saw me slip on my extra sweater and snow jacket. My nose was cold, cheeks flushed and breath expelled in icy clouds.

I scooted over to a window and opened the visor for a better view. The Vamps were huddled at the back of the plane amongst the crates, concerned that when the doors opened, sun would pour in and burn them alive—entirely possible in this icy, reflective continent.

'What do you see, Elena?' Nicholas asked, voice muffled by packets of lentils and beans.

'Ice, ice, and can you believe it, more ice?'

'Is there any ice?' Caleb called out. He was snickering so I knew he was just being as big a dick as me.

'Wait. I see some buildings—not many—they look like shipping containers.'

'What about the cargo hold?'

I shook my head. 'No, nothing.'

'What's that noise?' Eric said to the others.

'Doors maybe?' Thomas replied.

'I don't hear anything,' I said. 'Just the plane engines.'

'It might be out of your scope,' Nicholas replied. 'It sounds like automated doors. I can hear a small mechanical engine whirr.'

I shut the shade on that window and quickly dashed to the other side to get a different perspective. 'Wow.'

'What is it?' They all asked.

'They are using the '*Revatarus*' spell on a massive level.'

Marianne crept forward, hoping to catch a glimpse through my window.

'It's like they threw an invisible blanket over the facility and I'm getting to peek under the covers now the doors are opening.'

'What else do you see?'

'Not much. It's so bright outside that the cargo hold looks black. My eyes are having trouble adjusting to the contrast.'

'Maybe you should come back here with us, at least until they begin to unload. You don't want to risk someone seeing you from the outside.'

'Good point,' I said, shutting my shade and heading for the back of the plane to hide out with the others.

We all stood patiently behind the shrink-wrapped crates, waiting for the aircraft to come to a standstill. Adrenaline surged through my veins, my palms starting to sweat and my cheeks flushed. I could taste anticipation in the air and I swallowed it down, hoping it would instil me with the drive I needed to get in, get out and save my brother.

We heard voices. Eric said there were six. Nicholas mentioned that five were Protectors based on their scents. All I could smell was engine fuel, chewing tobacco and stale aftershave, but I wasn't about to doubt a vampire.

The cabin doors disengaged. Three men climbed on board. One was carrying a clipboard, another rubbed his gloved hands together to keep warm and the third headed towards us. He reached for the fasteners and nets, fingers sure. He'd done this many times before and so had Eric.

He grabbed the man by the face, squeezing his cheeks and angling his chin to meet with The Protector's gaze. He never had a chance to struggle or call for help.

Whispered words were exchanged—words I couldn't hear, but served our purpose. The Protector continued his job, face blank and eyes empty—blind to our presence.

Clipboard man began calling out batch numbers, pen in hand, eyes downcast. Nicholas moved fast, capturing him in much the same way that Eric had done. Simultaneously, Thomas engaged the man with cold hands and a lacklustre enthusiasm for his job. Surprise rode him momentarily until compulsion hit home.

'We can move freely now,' Eric mouthed against my ear. 'These men are unaware of our presence, but be careful not to touch them or talk too loudly. We have only touched their eyes.'

I nodded, side-stepping the first guy who now tore excitedly through the shrink-wrapped packages, cursing the spilled cans and ingredients on the cabin floor.

'There's one on the forklift outside. I'll get him,' Marianne whispered, slipping past and heading for the door.

I followed, stopping only because Thomas flung an arm across my chest, quickly pointing out another man on direct course towards us—something I should have noticed.

Focus, Elena.

Thomas then used signalling techniques I might have seen in a movie once. I had no idea what it meant as he fisted the air, pointed outside the plane and then tugged on his left ear. He disappeared a second later, leaving me to stare after him like an idiot.

Eric followed, pointing to his eyes with both fingers, fisting the air and then pointing outside the plane as Thomas had done. I was off to a fantastic start. At this rate they'd all be back with Lucas before I'd even removed the thumb up my butt.

'They're securing the area for you,' Nicholas whispered. 'They want you to hold fast, listen and keep your eyes peeled.'

'I thought we were playing charades.'

'What?'

I shook my head, sarcasm wasted. 'Can I go yet or what?'

'No, two more Protectors just entered the hold.'

We retreated as the men behind rolled the shrink-wrapped crates to the cabin door. The waiting forklift hoisted heavy steel arms into the cabin, accepted the goods before reversing, lowering the payload and driving off.

Outside the aeroplane was a singular scream, muffled by the sound of grinding gears and the ever-present dulling aircraft noises. The workers hadn't seemed to notice.

'That can't be good.'

Nicholas looked panicked. 'Two Protectors just made us.'

We rushed to the cabin door, jumped down and ran towards the disturbance. Nicholas was gone before I'd made any real progress.

'Eric stop!' I heard Thomas shout.

By the time I rounded the corner—past a mountain of food stock and snow vehicles—I spotted the blurred outline of Nicholas grabbing Eric, trying to hold him back. Marianne hissed at a Protector whose hands were alight with the power of their magic, another lay crumpled, wounded from what I imagined was the initial attack.

'What's going o—' I skidded to a stop, my breath leaving me in a rush as I sunk to my knees, surprised, happy and downright relieved.

I started to crawl, my hands frigid and screaming in protest as they slapped against ice and concrete, barely finding purchase as I crawled faster and faster towards the fallen Protector who tried against all odds to heave himself upright. I finally touched his back; muscles that had never been there before now tightened under the pressure of my fingers. His shoulders had broadened and arms thickened. His hands were larger and more powerful than I remembered, but there was no mistaking his identity.

He craned his neck, the pulse in his throat jumping as powder-blue eyes met mine. 'Elena?' he croaked.

The tears that had filled my eyes spilled over and I threw myself at him, arms tangling around his neck, sending him crashing back against the hardened ground again. 'Lucas!'

'Lucas?' Eric, Nicholas and Caleb repeated, looking at one another in puzzlement. It was like they couldn't quite believe the good luck of it. Hell, even I couldn't believe it had been that easy. The difference was, in that moment, I didn't give two shits.

'You're okay,' I gasped, sobbing like a baby.

'I am now,' Lucas replied, voice equally gravelly.

'What are you doing out here?'

'I'm escaping,' he said, patting the back of my head.

'But I'm here to rescue you!'

'You're about three weeks too late. Karina's been helping me try to bust out this joint, but I think your friends ruined it.'

'Karina?' I looked over my shoulder at the other Protector. Her face was finally coming into focus. It was a wonder I hadn't noticed her before, but then again, my brother had been a welcomed distraction.

Marianne hissed again, edging forward, saliva dripping from her already extended fangs. Her talons had grown too, shaping her fuchsia painted nails into sharp, black daggers.

'Marianne, I know her, it's okay,' I said, reaching out and touching her leg.

She straightened, eyes swivelling to the reassuring hand that still grappled with her shin. She hissed, but did as I asked and backed off, fangs slowly receding. Marianne's attentions quickly turned to Lucas. Unknown emotion flirted with her hardened features, erasing the harsh lines of her vampiric half. Her feet inched towards us; a giveaway to her intent. She was suddenly at his side, fingers gentle on his shoulder then fluttering uselessly an inch above his body as she assessed him from every conceivable angle.

'Elena,' Eric interrupted, startling me, 'if this is your brother, then I implore that we leave this place immediately.' He looked over his shoulder. 'There are cameras everywhere. It will not be long before someone monitors this reunion.'

'Help me up,' Lucas said, patting my head again.

I gave him one final squeeze and helped return him to his feet, Marianne assisting. He could barely stand, even with the support, so I swept him up into my arms, making use of my strength.

'I forgot how strong you are,' he said, resting his head against my shoulder. His eyes were heavy with fatigue and body limp like lettuce in my embrace. He attempted to wiggle free. 'I can walk.'

'You're a wreck, Lucas.'

He attempted an eye roll. 'Thanks, E.'

'Just let me look after you.'

'Carrying me does absolutely nothing for my image with the ladies.'

I smiled at him through my relentless stream of tears, a hiccup escaping.

'We need to leave, Elena,' Nicholas urged. He focused solely on a steel access door in the corner of the room. 'People are talking about Lucas in the corridors beyond.'

I nodded, shifting Lucas's weight so I could keep an eye on his weary self. I could measure and happily hold accountable by way of death those that had etched every shadow and line that marred his features. Bruises dusted the soft tissue under his eyes, his skin sallow and hair missing. Whether by choice or the IMI's hand, the beautiful blond locks that once dusted the top of his shoulders had now been shaved clean. I yearned to question the radical change in appearance, but concluded the timing was off. We needed to get out first.

Marianne's repeat guttural hissing slowed my retreat back to the plane. I stopped and turned, Lucas craning his neck to get a better look behind us.

'I want to come with you!' Karina shouted at her, though wisely keeping her distance from the pointy end.

'You are not welcome,' Marianne shouted back.

'Keep it down!' I chided.

Karina circled wide to avoid Marianne, edging her way closer to me and Lucas. 'I want to come with you.'

'Back up,' I said, shaking my head, wondering how I'd even forgotten she was there. 'What are you doing, Karina?'

'I'm coming with you. Lucas and I were planning on escaping via the aeroplane.'

'We came on the aeroplane,' Marianne spat.

Karina glared at her. 'I owe Lucas. I promised him that I would get him out of here safely.'

'And I will, Karina, you know that,' I said sympathetically.

'No, you don't understand. I have to come too. I can't go back now. I'm a traitor.'

'Or a spy.'

'Elena, we don't have time for this,' Nicholas said, reaffirming trouble beyond the door in the corner.

'I'm not a spy. I swear it, Elena. I'm an outcast now, condemned to a life outside the IMI and its protective umbrella. My father will never forgive me for helping Lucas escape.'

I sighed, too tired to start an argument on logistics. 'Fine. Get on the plane, but if you betray us or endanger Lucas in any way, I'll kill you myself.'

She took a perceptible step back, her face a riot of shock. 'Bloody hell, Elena! When did you become so brutal?'

'When The Protectors decided to drain me of blood, torture me and leave me defenceless against an alpha vânător. Get the picture?'

She gulped, nodded and proceeded forward again—much to Marianne's disgust. I never would have pegged Karina for being brave or stupid and she was simultaneously pulling off both. 'I

215

promise you no tricks. My whole life just got flushed down the toilet. Making sure Lucas is safe is my only priority now. It's the only way I'll be able to look at myself in the mirror again.'

Marianne scoffed and rolled her eyes—my usual reaction in moments of disbelief. However, in this instance Karina looked defeated, weary, but still somehow resolute in her appeal for understanding. She reminded me of myself—stubborn, determined and entirely too stupid for her own good. Leaving the IMI spelt alienation—undoubtedly the cause of her usually vibrant green eyes being dulled and ringed with sadness. Yet here she was, standing in front of me, pleading.

Shit.

A resigned breath escaped my ice cold lips. 'Let's go, Karina. Don't stuff this up.'

'I won't.'

'She will,' Marianne muttered under her breath.

We double-timed it back to the aircraft. The compelled men had just finished unloading the last crate and had started stacking and itemising the products that had been ordered. Ian sat patiently in the cockpit, awaiting our orders.

Thomas helped Lucas into the cargo hold and settled him comfortably amongst the cushions where he promptly passed out. Marianne gave me the boost I needed to get back into the cabin and Nicholas helped Karina by securing one wrist between deft fingers and hauling her inside. Neither protested about having to touch the other, Karina didn't dare complain about being man-handled.

'Wait,' I said as Eric began to close the cabin doors.

'What is it, Elena?'

'We didn't just come here for Lucas. We came for a few Protectors to help us win the war.'

'What do you need?' Karina asked. She had already settled on a cushion in the corner, aiming for inconspicuous, but remained nevertheless present with her nosey question.

'How much do you know about The Protectors and their betrayal of humanity and the alliance between vampires? Did you know that a war with the Vânätors has broken out too?'

Karina's brows furrowed, her confusion abundant. 'War?'

I nodded, watching as Caleb tapped on the wall between the cockpit and cargo hold, probably alerting Ian to our very dire need to leave the ground as soon as possible. 'The packs banded together forcing a mass attack on Italy. We're barely able to contain the borders and stop the carnage from spilling into the cities.'

She was shaking her head. 'I don't understand. I don't know anything about that.'

'Malcolm never mentioned anything—the reason why you came here?'

'No, dad—' She caught her breath on a sob, hand trembling as she covered her mouth. 'Dad never said anything,' she finally finished, attempting to hide her grief.

'We need Protectors to perform the '*Revatarus*' charm wherever necessary to keep public inspection at a minimum. The Vânǎtors have already caused a global sensation by outing themselves to a photographer from National Geographic. We were hoping some of you with consciences may help.'

She looked back, eyes impossibly wide and brimming with additional tears to add to her already sodden cheeks. 'We've been locked up like fish in a tank. I don't know what's going on in the outside world, but I'm pretty sure that Lucas and I can help you when he's feeling better.'

'Just the two of you?' Thomas sounded as doubtful as I was cynical.

'Lucas has changed a lot since you left, Elena. I don't know what's happened exactly, but he can do things that other Protectors can't. He alone could probably cast the spells you need to help the war go unnoticed by humans.'

We all glanced at each other and then at Lucas, now curled on a pile of cushions sleeping peacefully. 'What have they done to him?'

Fresh tears gathered momentum. I wondered if at some point she would dehydrate. 'I don't know, but it's all my fault.'

'How can that be?' I said, attempting to be more sympathetic despite wanting to slaughter anyone who may have had a hand in my brother's current condition.

She looked up at me, eyes as wide as the wheel on a penny-farthing bicycle. 'I'm the one that got him captured in the first place. If it wasn't for me, he would have left this place weeks ago.'

'I'm sure Chester and George probably had something to do with it.'

'They did, but I injected him with the sedative that saw him strapped to a gurney and pumped with drugs.'

I stilled. My heart rate increased and blood boiled in my veins. I hoped I'd heard incorrectly. 'They did what to him?'

Caleb took one look at my stormy expression and gulped. 'Careful,' he murmured to Karina, urging her with passive hand gestures to proceed with caution.

Karina pressed on, determined to unload. 'He's been hooked to various IV's for the last three weeks. When I found him he was barely conscious—couldn't even walk or hold his head up.'

'Not good,' Caleb reaffirmed, shaking his head. 'Not good at all.'

My fists curled into tight balls, the knuckles stretched taught and the nails pierced the flesh of my palms. The thrum of the aircraft engine kicked to life, fuelling the beat of anger within and the pulse that ticked in my jaw. I was shaking, thinking about my brother subject to unknown experimentation. He had lain on a cold steel table, shackled, unable to speak and unable to move. The thought was horrifying—the reality tantamount to going postal and inducing a shift. I recognised the signs.

'Elena?'

'Everyone needs to find a good hiding spot as quickly as they can.'

Caleb was the only one that moved to give me space, knowing me much better than the others. Eric did the opposite, boxing me in and aggravating the wolf within.

'Elena? What's going on here?'

'I'm serious, Eric. Everyone get away from me.'

'Elena? We don't understand,' Eric pressed. 'We want to help.'

I closed my eyes and tried incredibly hard not to let the anger consume me. It was impossible. This was my brother we were talking about and everything I had feared for myself had happened to him. My wolf found it simply unacceptable.

I opened my eyes again to find focus where I could. 'Do you remember those certain *skills* that we were discussing earlier?'

'You mean besides telekinesis,' Marianne said, wisely beginning to back up towards the rear of the plane. My wolf began to acknowledge her as prey. Not good.

I shook my head. 'This is much worse.'

'Are we in trouble?' Nicholas asked warily, following Marianne's lead and grabbing a handful of Eric's shirt as he passed.

'Let's just say that putting up those nets as quickly as you can and concealing yourselves from me would be a really good idea.'

'Shit,' Caleb muttered for the final time, wedging himself between two panels, 'she's going to shift and we're all going to die.'

And then everything went black.

CHAPTER EIGHTEEN: SURPRISE?

A high pitched scream cut through the nervous tension in the cabin. It echoed through my head—background noise as I rapidly began my decent into dissolved humanity. Muffled by the sound of the aircraft roaring down the runway, I was suddenly immersed in the sound of snapping bones, tearing muscles and personal torment.

I was turning.

Instantaneous to those watching, it was a process of suspended torture; limbs lengthened, contracted and bones broke and rearranged themselves into the shape of my wolf form. Nails sprouted, sharpened and then morphed fingers into paws—the same with my contorting feet. The clothes I wore disintegrated and my usually flawless skin was soon covered with a myriad of soft, black hair.

In this period of metamorphosis, I smelt fear and uncertainty—saw it on my friend's faces like never before. It was now that I could choose to gain control or choose to let my inner beast run free. If I didn't gain control now, the people I cared about would die and that included Lucas.

During my first shift darkness had overcome me. I had become the physical manifestation of my angry emotions. I had killed, I had fed and I had enjoyed it. The second time Sebastian helped me through it, putting his own life at risk while I'd clawed at him and tore out his throat.

He had believed in my strength to overcome the trappings of my wolf form. He showed me how to find the reigns that harnessed my raw emotions and how to hold them in check. I prayed that I remembered how.

I concentrated hard; I wanted choice not carnage. I wanted the presence of mind to rein the metaphysical tethers of my conscience and control my actions before I killed my friends.

Through the darkness was a glimmer of hope, within reach and glowing with the prospect of control and ability to see through eyes untainted with malice. If I could grab hold, squeeze my mental grip and find my way through the haze of emotions to gain control, I would be alright—so would everyone else.

I came back to myself more slowly than expected. The struggle was real as I continued to find focus with every blink. It had taken too long to wade through the dark and find the light. The cargo safety net was shredded beneath my claws. Eric, Thomas, Caleb and Nicholas were already crouched in a position of attack, their fangs bared and talons released. Behind them Karina and Marianne protected an unconscious Lucas, the fear that radiated from them was appealing to the predator within.

I forced myself into submission—to ignore my beast. I lowered my talons and took several steps back to reveal the return to self. The wolf within was now supressed and I felt confident I was safe to be around.

'What's she doing?' Nicholas murmured.

'She's gained control,' Eric responded.

'But for how long?' Thomas asked.

Eric appeared uncertain, fidgeting in his confined hiding spot between the cargo. 'I have no idea.'

I spotted Caleb creeping forward, taloned hand outstretched. I growled, uncertain of his intent. I hadn't meant to frighten him, but waving sharp objects in front of my face was always going to illicit such results.

'Careful, Caleb.'

'Retract your talons, Caleb,' Thomas offered, 'perhaps the wolf finds them offensive.'

'What if it's a trap?' Eric mused. 'What if we lower our defences and she attacks us again?'

I wound the mental cord tightly around sensibility and prayed I wouldn't lose control again. I kept my head bowed and moved slowly to where Thomas crouched. As expected he stiffened, fingers unsure as they hunted the soft fur of the coat by my neck. I resented resorting to these sorts of tactics, but as his movements left tentative in their exploration, I knew he'd accepted my peace-offering.

'Why did the shape-shift occur?' Eric mused. He slowly began to straighten, fangs and claws retracting. He still kept a close eye on me, unsure if I was to be trusted. Nicholas obviously agreed.

'Karina made her angry,' Caleb correctly guessed. 'Her eyes started going black the minute it was mentioned that Lucas was strapped to a gurney and—'

Nicholas slapped a hand across Caleb's mouth. 'Let's not incense her further, shall we?'

Caleb nodded, pulling away.

'I wasn't trying to make her angry,' Karina squeaked from behind Thomas. 'I just felt so guilty. I wanted to tell her everything. I had no idea Elena could turn vânător.'

'Now we all do,' Marianne murmured.

Caleb knelt beside me, our eyes now level. 'How do you get back to being you?' He rubbed the top of my head while Thomas continued to bury his fingers in the pelt by my neck and back. Judging by my swinging tail, I was starting to think I enjoyed it.

'Not that I don't like the new you,' Caleb continued, 'but it would be nice to be able to communicate.'

I attempted to try and yawn, unsure what that would look like with my wolfy snout and sharp fangs. The only way I knew how to convert back was by going to sleep.

'Is she hungry?' Thomas asked. He stopped stroking me almost immediately. I wished I were that intimidating in my human form.

I shook my head slowly from side to side, hoping it was clear. I then lowered myself to the ground, laying on my side and closing my eyes. I waited a few seconds for it to sink in and then got back up again.

'She needs to sleep,' Marianne answered.

I barked my agreement.

'It makes sense,' Thomas added. 'When she sleeps she's just herself—not vampiric or vânător. Both forms require emotion to circumvent change.'

'How long can you maintain this control?' Marianne asked, eyes flitting quickly across my entire form.

I attempted a shrug, unsure of its success until Thomas said, 'She doesn't know.'

'I thought you were going to kill us for a moment there,' Caleb said, never faltering in his need to run his fingers through my fur. But then he suddenly stopped as if burned. 'Is it inappropriate to be patting you like this?'

The others attempted to hide their smiles. I didn't know which parts were what in this form.

For all I knew he was patting my ass now that his touch had moved from my back and down to my wagging tail. Overanalysing the enjoyment of the sensation would only lead to a freak out.

Lucas stirred and drew my attention. Marianne had left defence mode and now sat cross-legged in a more open section between the crates, Lucas's head resting in her lap. She ran her fingers gently down the side of his cheek, eyes watchful as she covered him with a blanket to keep him warm.

I left Caleb's touch, curious as to her intentions. Karina shrieked as I approached, pushing pallets and crates aside to get to my brother. Her fingers crackled with the blue light of her power.

'It's Elena,' Thomas said, tentatively touching her wrist, perhaps concerned he'd bear the brunt of retaliation if he frightened her further. 'She has gained control. You don't have to be afraid.'

Karina shook her head, glancing at me warily. 'She was going to kill us.'

'She's doing her best.'

Karina scowled and scooted back further. She allowed the magic to fade, but still kept herself at the ready should I flip out again.

I hunkered down next to Lucas, effectively pushing Marianne a little further out of the picture so I could use the warmth of my fur and body to heat his frozen limbs. It appeared he'd left in a hurry, wearing a lab coat and little of anything else. If I had been in human form I would have clothed him by now, a consideration the weather-impervious vampires had little regard for.

'Karina,' Thomas Beckoned, 'why don't you tell us why the IMI ended the alliance and established this facility?'

Her ongoing scowl morphed to incredulous. 'You want to talk about that now while Elena's barely in control? It'll just make her angry again!'

'It's okay, Karina.'

She strongly disagreed. 'I don't even know who any of you are.'

'I'm sorry. It has been a few months. You obviously do not remember me.'

'That's because we haven't met.'

'We have actually—not formally of course.' He held out his hand to her, crouching between crates and dodging splinters. 'I'm Thomas Woodland and this is my twin sister Marianne.'

Karina looked at his hand but, did not shake it. Old habits die hard. She had been raised a Protector—vampires supposedly the enemy; a plight on humanity and a disease that would one day be erased.

Thomas lowered his offered hand. He didn't appear overly offended. 'We came to Cairns a few months back hunting an alpha from London that strayed into your area. My friend William and I were the ones that helped get Elena back after she was taken.'

'That was you?' Karina gasped. She looked him over with a critical eye. 'You look different now.'

Thomas smiled, his sapphire eyes shining with amusement. 'I assure you I am exactly the same. Our vampiric forms just take some getting used to and I suspect that was the only form you have seen me covet.'

She nodded at everyone else. 'Who are they?'

'They are Elena's friends.' He pointed them out individually. 'This is Eric, Nicholas, and Caleb.'

Karina looked at Caleb and screwed up her nose. 'You have pink hair.'

'Observant …' he muttered sarcastically.

'I thought vampires couldn't change their appearance.'

'If we cut our hair, limbs or fingernails it will grow back,' Eric answered. 'Hair dye, makeup, clothes—it's all superficial, made for surface application. We can change those things because they don't affect our physical being.'

Marianne's movements distracted me from the conversation. She leaned forward to check on Lucas again; he slept, peaceful. He stealthily wrapped his hand around her leg and snuggled his head further into her lap. I thought it might have irritated her—him being so close given past disdain, but she seemed content.

What is your game with my brother, Marianne?

'Tell us about The Protectors,' Thomas asked, rupturing my thoughts and drawing me back in. 'We need to know everything.'

Karina looked right at me. I wasn't sure why or what she asked with her eyes, but I was nonetheless captive. 'I have been tightly bound for so long it seems impossible to consider uttering their secrets.'

'But you will ...' Thomas prompted.

She gulped audibly, eyes shimmering with unshed tears. 'I never thought I'd be on the opposing side of The Protectors. I've always conformed—always done what my father has asked of me and protected our secrets from our enemies.'

'Surely you can see now that the real monsters are those that have been sheltering you?' Eric said, voice low and controlled. 'Look what they did to Lucas—to the person you call your friend.'

Karina bowed her head, the tears breaking and falling to the floor in glistening streams. After some time, she looked back, speaking as if I was the only one in the room. 'It's hard for me, Elena,' she breathed. 'I have always been so loyal, but everything I held in high regard has crumbled.'

I whimpered, sympathetic to her plight. I wasn't sorry she'd finally realised the IMI were shady bastards. What I was sorry for was that everything she believed to be good and true was tarred with lies and deceit. Her entire life was a lie, wasted to a cause that never truly existed.

Marianne spoke up, though she kept her head lowered and eyes firmly fixed on Lucas as she continued to stroke his cheek with tenderness. 'Elena undoubtedly understands where you are coming from, Karina. When I first met her and Lucas, they both felt strong ties to the IMI. It was only once their eyes were opened did they start to make their own decisions. You have that choice now too.'

'I know that helping Lucas was the right thing to do, but what is righteous justice? Will spilling their secrets elicit terrible backlash?'

Everyone frowned and studied the other. 'What do you mean, Karina?'

'Are you going to send an army of vampires back there and kill everyone?'

Eric shook his head. 'Of course not. Talking to you has enforced our beliefs that a lot of you are kept in the dark about the IMI's true intentions. It would be unfair to punish the mass for the actions of a few.'

Karina blinked, unsure she'd heard correctly. She'd expected vampires to be vicious, unemotional and violent creatures, not rational and capable of reason. 'You mean that?'

'Yes.'

'The IMI talks about vampires in a horrifying light. We are taught to believe that if you encounter one on their own and they look threatening—kill first and ask questions later.'

'Just like humans we have many faces, Karina, but we do try to be civilised.'

She nodded thoughtfully, finally shifting from her suffocating confines to the space nearer Thomas—still quite a distance from my reach. 'So what do you want to know?'

'What made key members of The Protectors head for Antarctica?'

She shrugged. 'A lot of us really don't know. I only found out from Alba yesterday what she knew.'

'Who is Alba?'

'She's the human nurse that helped me free Lucas. She said we were brought there so we could be inoculated against vampire and vânător attacks.'

'We believe The Protectors are trying to become more like us.'

Karina's lips puckered, barely hiding her disgust and scepticism. 'Why would The Protectors want to do that? We already have magical powers.'

'The serum has been made from Elena's blood. Did you know that?'

Karina glanced briefly at me, a little shocked. 'Why?'

'Elena is the daughter of the oldest and the very first vampire in existence. Her blood is pure, untainted and what we believe to be the basis of a serum the IMI created to turn any being into a variation of what we are.'

'What is there to gain from being like Elena?' She grimaced. 'Sorry. No offence.'

Whatever.

Eric ploughed on. 'Elena's strength, imminent immortality and self-healing capabilities are all very appealing to someone who is already quite powerful.'

Karina waved her hands in protest. I couldn't help but notice the state of them; bruised and badly cut across the knuckles.

227

Eric was determined to make his case. 'Lucas found out about the serum through letters sent between George and the head scientist, Chester. After Elena escaped the IMI and the torture they put her through, Lucas started doing some digging and—'

'You were tortured by the IMI!' Karina shrieked, creeping forward to look me over. 'Are you serious?' She seemed to have forgotten her fear of me in light of current events.

'It was how they came to extract copious amounts of her blood.'

'So you are trying to convince me that the IMI has developed some sort of formula that transforms a Protector into a vampire?'

'We even think that Roshan—the alpha vânător stalking Elena—is trying to get his hands on it to strengthen his packs,' Nicholas finished.

'It's unthinkable,' Karina groaned. 'I don't believe that everyone would agree to the inoculation if they knew what it could really do to them.'

So it hasn't been administered yet?

Eric echoed my sentiments.

'I don't think so. I mean, I only found out about it yesterday, but wouldn't I have noticed a difference in people?'

'What about Lucas?' Thomas asked.

Karina looked at him anew, uncertainty brewing in her eyes. 'I don't know. Even Alba didn't know what they were giving him.'

'Do you think he might know if he's been affected and with what?'

'It's possible. Lucas was trying to leave the facility when Chester and George approached me about stopping him.'

'It didn't cross your mind to question it?' Marianne growled, looking up from Lucas long enough to give her an evil stare.

Karina recoiled, shying away from everyone again. 'Of course I questioned it! It's just ... You wouldn't understand the sort of pressure ...' She shook her head, unwilling to finish.

'Maybe we should try and wake Lucas up,' Caleb suggested.

I growled, placing a paw across his chest and shaking my head. Lucas needed time to recover and as his sister, I was going to give him anything he required.

Nicholas coughed, drawing everyone's attention. 'I'd be curious to hear your account of Lucas's current wellbeing. Surely after watching him grow up and the upheaval of recent events in

Antarctica you have seen the effects of whatever change might have gripped him?'

'Well, he hasn't been the same old Lucas for a while. He really threw himself into training and study and started going to the gym. He bulked up quicker than I would have thought possible; shaved his head and simultaneously abandoned friendships with the rest of us. I don't know if his moodiness or these changes in habits and physicality had anything to do with the IMI, though it does seem suspect now ...'

'Elena leaving was obviously traumatic,' Nicholas tried to reason.

Caleb begged to differ. 'By then he would have known about her escape from the IMI and what they did to her. My bet is that he was preparing.'

'Preparing?' Nicholas queried.

Caleb grinned. 'Preparing to join Elena to kick Protector ass.'

I wondered if my eye roll translated to my wolf face.

'Regardless,' Karina said, 'I could see something was wrong, but ...' She shrugged. 'The adults whispered a lot about his transformation, but I was always too scared to ask.'

'Transformation?' Everyone echoed.

'Besides his rapidly altered physicality, I secretly started watching Lucas's training sessions. The rest of us had always trained separately from both Elena and Lucas. I'd thought it was because Elena was a freak, but seeing how competent Lucas was with spells and defence—I knew he was different, just not sure how. He was more advanced than some of the adults, spells easily wielded in his mind alone.'

Nicholas cocked his head to the side, looking at me through narrowed eyes. 'Could it be possible that the IMI got to him before they got to Elena?

They've obviously been planning the serum for a while. Maybe Lucas was plan A?'

I barked, completely in agreement. I knew for a fact he'd been tampered with. The letters between Chester and George weren't just authentication of the serum and my personal involvement, but proof that Lucas was very much a lead character in a movie I was still unfamiliar with.

Nicholas was determined to explore this idea further. 'Is Lucas capable of anything above and beyond the limitations of the spells you know?'

Karina's face spun a mask of confusion. 'What do you mean?'

'You said he doesn't need to utter a spell—his mind controls the action. Do his abilities extend beyond this?'

'I'm not sure I understand.'

'Is Lucas performing spells you've never seen?'

Karina seemed to consider the question carefully. 'It seems that Lucas can do anything he puts his mind to.'

'Like telekinesis?'

Oh shit ...

All eyes soon fell upon me. I was suddenly very much aware where Nicholas was going with this line of questioning. Could it be possible that two, physically unrelated siblings were more intricately bound than first appearances?

Karina answered for me. 'I don't think he's telekinetic.'

'But you're not sure ...' Nicholas prodded.

'No.'

'Is it not possible that he now has that gift because of the serum they have concocted from Elena's blood?'

'Well something has changed,' Marianne murmured. 'He doesn't smell like a vampire, but he doesn't smell like he used to either.'

They all started sniffing him like he was a hot cinnamon doughnut at a county fair. 'You are right,' Thomas agreed. 'He still has a Protector scent, but there is something else—something not unlike Elena's scent. There was a shadow of it when we first met, but now it's a lot stronger than before.'

What? Meaning it's always been there? Meaning that Lucas has always had my blood inside him?

How the hell is that possible?

Still sandwiched next to Lucas, I pressed my wet nose against his skin, inhaling. One of the benefits of being in this form meant that I could finally take advantage of all of the senses I lacked in human form—recognising them was key.

Oh ... Oh ...

His blood *did* smell like my blood. There was no doubt. What had The Protectors done to him? Or better yet, what had Susan and George been hiding from us both?

Karina crawled a little closer again, curious by our assessment. 'Why would Lucas share Elena's blood? Whatever the IMI gave him surely wouldn't alter his DNA?'

'We really need to talk to him about this—about everything,' Marianne whispered. She seemed hesitant to talk louder. The fact that she continued to nurture my brother without complaint rattled my pigeon-holed idea of her.

As if he knew he were the hot topic of conversation, Lucas began to stir. He rolled over, stretched his legs and arms, hands reaching and fingers groping air until he found her breasts.

Marianne's wide eyes rolled up to meet mine, embarrassed and possibly shocked by my sleepy brother's antics. I knew better. 'Hey, Blondie,' he mumbled. 'I had the best dream about you.'

'Hmmm,' Marianne grumbled, guiding his hands from her breasts and back down to her lap. 'I can see that.'

He decided to go fishing under her dress instead.

Jesus...

Caleb started to laugh. 'I think I'm going to like him.'

Marianne trapped Lucas's wandering hands within her own; there'd be no more hide and go seek. Problem was, his next move included trying to bury his face in her lap instead. I was going to have teach my brother some general etiquette, but since Lucas was already asleep again, the lesson would just have to wait.

* * *

The flight back to Hobart was nothing short of frustrating. With Lucas out for the count and me unable to communicate, it was left to Karina and the others to fill the void. I had so many questions, yet I could only listen, passing the time as Caleb and the others filled Karina in on current events.

Karina wasn't as helpful in her return information. She had been kept in the dark as Lucas had, unsure of the IMI's current and future plans, but grateful to finally make up her own mind about the current state of affairs.

I watched Karina carefully as the others gave detail on the war, my involvement and the Vânători. I saw shock twist her features often and occasionally shame for the small part she believed she played in the fall of the alliance.

I had never really been a big fan of Karina's; a goody-two-shoes and intellectual snob, that opinion was slowly shifting. I was still livid that she'd sedated my brother and inadvertently made him subject to experimentation, but also forever in her debt for helping him escape.

When the plane finally landed, we were all antsy about what might have been waiting for us. Lucas and Karina's absence would not go unnoticed and recovery of assets seemed almost certain. Chester had tried to keep me under lock and key—the same obviously true for my brother. Would they let the both of us slip from their grasp again or would they come after us with the full force of their powers?

No immediate danger awaited us other than my continuing state of canine. Caleb spent the drive back to the hotel making dog jokes and now the valet was giving me shit too. He complained about my un-collared state and suspected lack of control over my bowel movements. I was compelled to leave a present for him in the lobby, but I'd be proving his unfounded accusations.

'Do you want to hear another joke?' Caleb bated. I was too busy watching as Marianne disappeared into the hotel, Lucas bundled like a small child in her arms. It should have been me helping him. Instead I was forced to endure Caleb's poor humour and the valet's ongoing looks of disdain.

'What do you get if you cross a cocker spaniel, a poodle and a rooster?'

Seriously?

'A Cocker-poodle-doo.'

'Caleb ...' Eric warned, 'this isn't the time.'

'Not funny? Okay. What happens when it rains cats and dogs?'

Apparently my low growl and exposed teeth did little to deter the advancing punchline.

'You can step in a poodle.'

So not funny.

Caleb tapped his chin thoughtfully. 'You know, I went to this zoo once and they had no animals except one dog.'

I was pretty sure I knew what was coming.

'It was a Shit-zu!' he yelled over his shoulder, making a bolt for the lobby before I claimed an appendage.

'That was actually a good one,' Nicholas remarked.

Eric shook his head. 'No, it wasn't.'

Meanwhile, Thomas still argued with the valet about my domesticity and general over-sized nature teamed with hotel policies and procedures. Thankfully he switched to compulsion and the valet was more than pliable about my entry into the building. All I had to do was get through reception.

'Elena,' Eric started, 'I'm going to go ahead and open the elevators. Nicholas will make sure you can get through reception by holding the door open long enough that you can run through without being noticed.'

It was a good thing that as a vânător I could move nearly as fast as the Vampires. I still wished I could figure out how to change back into a human without a bit of shut-eye. I missed my legs and my upright posture.

Thomas and the others were already in the room when the rest of us arrived. Marianne had carried Lucas to my room, placed him on the bed and made sure to tuck him under the bedcovers. He stirred, groaning a little as he rolled onto his side, but managed to get comfortable enough to settle down again.

'He sure is tired,' Caleb remarked, head poking through the bedroom door.

'That's because he's been force-fed sedatives for the last few weeks,' Karina answered. 'We found him hooked up directly to an IV. He probably just needs to sleep it off. Hopefully he'll be better in the morning.'

I jumped up onto the mattress next to him, settling in for a long one. If Lucas was sleeping, then so was I. Besides, I needed my body back pronto and the only way I knew how was through slumber.

Eric and Nicholas seemed content with my decision, leaving the room immediately to embrace their own pursuits. Caleb and the others lingered momentarily.

I knew Karina was motivated by guilt and a lifetime of friendship with my brother, but Marianne? What was her affinity with a human she often described as a blood bag? Was it possible that Marianne had a thing for Lucas, their friendship progressing much further than I ever truly realised?

She must have noticed my dark eyes upon her, because her head finally snapped in the direction of the door, feet carving a path of exit with no backward glances. Did she feel my scrutiny? I suspected as much, but liked that she was wary of my reaction, especially when it came to Lucas.

Caleb followed, leaving and starting a conversation with the others in the next room, but Karina lingered, awkwardly shuffling from foot-to-foot. She straddled the doorway to both rooms, glancing at me and then at the Vampires beyond. She looked conflicted and scared. It was in that moment I realised she was truly alone—an orphan, just like me.

She was amidst the supernatural, away from everything familiar and comfortable. She had to decide right from wrong and who in this moment she should stay with; the werewolf and the chemically altered Protector or a room full of vampires?

Decisions, decisions.

I tilted my head, ears flopping to the side in an attempt to look non-threatening. I sheathed my claws and retracted my fangs, barking softly in what I hoped was an encouraging manner.

When she persisted on standing there, unmoving and uncertain, I gave up, snuggling closer to Lucas and resting my head on my paws. The sooner I went to sleep, the sooner I'd be back to being me. Karina could take that time to adjust to her new surrounds. It couldn't be easy being surrounded by creatures you'd been brainwashed into believing were the enemy for so many years.

A few minutes of quiet deliberation did her good. She edged her way towards the bed, sliding onto the mattress with extreme caution. She watched for a while for signs of movement, then proceeded to unzip her boots and place them neatly at the end of the bed. She then stood, grabbed the excess blanket from the end and folded it to form a neat little bed on the floor.

'Thank you for letting me stay, Elena,' she said coyly, walking to the closet to grab a pillow and another blanket. 'We haven't been the best of friends, but I'm sorry and hope we can change that. I used to think you were loud and obnoxious; I didn't understand you were trying to be heard.'

She settled down onto her makeshift bed and peered up at me with wide green eyes. 'I promise I'm going to start listening more and thinking for myself.'

I had about a million things I wanted to say to her right then, but since she couldn't hear any of them, I merely nodded.

'Goodnight Elena.'

Goodnight, Karina, and thanks for giving me back my brother

CHAPTER NINETEEN: TRAUMITISED

My lids fluttered open, tantalised to continue the action once I heard the sweet sound of chirping birds outside and my vision filled with the heart-wrenching sight of powder blue eyes framed by dusty, blonde lashes.

'Hey, Dickhead,' Lucas murmured, brushing a stray lock of hair from my eyes.

I couldn't begin to describe how much I had missed my brother's voice, even if the first thing out of his mouth was a stupid pet name he'd adopted for me when we were younger.

I followed suit, yawning loudly. There was no point breaking with tradition now. 'Hey, Dumbass.'

He flicked the end of my nose and grimaced. 'As much as I'm glad that you're here with me now, Elena, I can't begin to tell you how much it grosses me out that you are lying next to me ... naked.'

Naked?

I glanced down, groaned and scrambled to pull the covers up to my chin. 'You could have covered me.'

'That would have required looking in that general direction, so I kept my eyes closed until I was certain you were awake.'

'The nakedness isn't intentional. For some reason—after a shift—I don't get my clothes back.'

'What are you talking about?'

'We have so much to catch up on it's not even funny.'

'Start with the naked thing before I go blind.'

'I'm covered!'

'The damage is already done. I'm freaking traumatised!'

My ever-widening grin extended to laughter. 'I *so* want to hug you right now, naked or not. I missed you so much, Lucas.'

'Do. Not. Hug. Me. I already have a mental image I can never erase. I don't need the brail version as well.'

My continuous cackling was enough to rouse Karina from sleep. 'What's going on?' She sat up at the end of the bed, rubbing her eyes and yawning. 'Oh, Elena, you're human again.'

Lucas jabbed a thumb in her direction. 'What's she talking about?'

'It relates to the whole naked thing.'

'Oh.' The furrowed brows and the bemused expression spoke volumes. A lot had transpired since we had spoken last.

'Elena turned into a vânător last night,' Karina said, languidly stretching her arms above her head. 'It was pretty scary. I thought she was going to kill us all.'

Lucas continued to stare at me blankly.

'Karina? Do you think you can give me and Lucas some time? We have a lot to talk about.'

'That's an understatement,' she muttered. She started to get up, but stopped as some sort of indeterminable concern settled upon her shoulders. 'Um, if I leave the bedroom and go out there,' she said, pointing in the direction of the suite's living area, 'am I going to be safe with the Vampires?'

'Only if you don't have any open vein sources!' Caleb shouted from the other room.

I rolled my eyes. 'He's kidding.'

'No I'm not.'

'Who is that?' Lucas said, propping himself up onto one elbow and glancing over his shoulder.

'Caleb. You'll like him. He's a dumbass too.'

'Right, well, I'll be in the other room with *them*,' Karina said, climbing back to her feet and straightening her clothes. 'If it, um, gets a little *too* quiet, will you please come and check on me?'

'Sure.'

Once the door was closed and everyone on the other side, I turned my attentions back to Lucas. 'I don't even know where to start.'

'Well, the fact that you're lying next to me alive and well tells me you escaped from Roshan. When Sebastian rang and told me what had happened, that Roshan ambushed you in Bucharest and bartered you for everyone else I was pissed.'

'It wasn't Sebastian's fault, Lucas. He tried to stop me, but you know me. I always gotta play the hero.'

'It was a stupid decision.'

'I bet any money you would have done the same thing.'

'I'm not as brave as you are.'

'Oh, so now I'm brave and stupid?' I said teasingly, jabbing him in the shoulder.

'At least you escaped.'

'Yeah, I escaped, but it took two weeks.'

Lucas gulped. 'Did he ...' He couldn't finish. No one that had ever asked that question could finish the sentence. The idea of being tortured and raped by an alpha wolf was just too terrible to contemplate.

'No,' I said, shaking my head emphatically. 'He found satisfaction in my blood only.'

'So you let him feed from you?'

'It was better than the alternative.'

He nodded, no more questioning or judgemental than I'd expected him to be. He'd always trusted my decisions and stood by the outcome. 'How did you escape?'

'I'm still not one hundred percent sure. I've lost that portion of my memory, but I saw the aftermath. It wasn't pretty, Lucas.'

'I figured you must have killed a few vânãtors along the way.'

I shook my head. 'This wasn't a few. This was a whole den—sixty of them.'

Lucas looked aghast. 'How did you do that on your own? I mean, I know you have been changing since the two blood exchanges, but how does little old you kill a den of wolves?'

'I got in a rage so thick that it brought out the darker side of me—the vânãtor. I don't remember, but I killed every member of Roshan's pack. Since that night I've turned two more times. Last night was one of them.'

Lucas frowned. 'I don't understand. Karina said she thought you were going to kill everyone.'

'I haven't learnt to control it yet—not fully, but it does seem to be getting easier with every shift.' I gestured to my body. 'But as you can see, I haven't mastered the transformation back yet either. I have to go to sleep to become human again and I lose my clothes which really sucks because I liked those boots I was wearing.'

'So shifting shreds your clothes or something?'

'Or something. Maybe it's like when you put socks in a dryer? You only get one of them back. You know what I mean?'

He was shaking his head. 'Not really, but I assume the point is; don't make Elena angry. She gets hairy, loses her clothes and then blinds me with her nakedness.'

'Close enough.' I touched the side of his face, uncertain as to the reason. Lucas and I had never been overly physically affectionate, but I think I needed validity that he was finally here with me. After months apart I needed to reassure myself that my struggle to find him had truly paid off.

'Where's William?'

Sighing, I dropped my hand. 'It's a long story and I'd much rather hear about you. You've changed so much. When I first saw you, I thought ... I mean I knew ...'

He rolled onto his back, staring aimlessly at the ceiling. 'They've messed with me so thoroughly I don't even know what I've become yet.'

I was silent for several minutes before speaking again. 'But you have a pretty good idea ...'

'I have some unconfirmed ideas, but I guess we'll know for sure after my birthday.'

It was my time to swallow a suspected boulder of indecision. 'Lucas, it's Thursday, February eight, two days *after* your eighteenth birthday.'

'Right. So I was under on and off for that long. Well, I guess I'm an adult now—mature as dad would say.' There was serious animosity coating every word uttered.

'Meaning?'

He sat up slowly, turning his back to me. I watched as he undid the first few buttons on the lab coat and slid it down the side of one shoulder. 'Do you remember this?' he said, touching the raised scar on the side of his neck.

'Not really. I know I bit you when we were kids, but I don't know why or what we were fighting over at the time.'

'I do now.'

I cocooned myself in the bed sheet and sat up next to him. I leant back against the headboard for support and waited patiently for his explanation on how and why it might relate to his missed birthday.

'You killed me.'

Well I wasn't expecting that. 'Surely I didn't hear you right?'

Lucas moved to face me, readjusting the coat. His face was ashen, lips pressed together in displeasure.

'You lashed out during whatever childish fight we were having and bit me, but you didn't just bite me, you drank my blood.'

'I was human then. Why would I have done that?'

'Your vampire side was dormant, but that doesn't mean your vânător side was. It's probably why you've always been able to smell blood and why you enjoyed drinking mine.'

'I thought the first time I ingested blood was after drinking John's blood.'

'I thought so too until I read our medical files.'

'And?'

'And apparently you fed from me—fed until you took me to the brink of death.'

I was shaking my head because I refused to believe that I would do such a thing, even at tender age.

He made a derisive sound in the back of his throat. 'Instead of taking me to hospital, the IMI opted to hook me up with a transfusion of your blood. They figured because it is so pure and not type specific, I'd be safe.' His serious eyes found mine. 'They used you like a blood bank, draining you repeatedly to keep me alive without regard for you. There were notes linked to ideas that your self-healing might have somehow been beneficial to us both, but in the end, I died, if only for a few minutes.'

'So they resuscitated you with a full contingent of my blood running through your veins?'

'I think the link between life and death and your blood may be the reason I've always been just that little bit different from other Protectors.'

I could feel my brow furrowing. 'Lucas, when I left Cairns you were perfectly normal.'

'As it turns out, I'm way too advanced for a Protector my age. I had no idea because we always trained separately from the others. I can do anything a Protector can do now and then some.'

I took a steadying breath. It was a lot to take in. 'Like what?'

'I can move any object with my mind without the use of spells, I don't know how or why I—'

'You're telekinetic.' It wasn't a question but a statement of fact.

Lucas looked deeply into my eyes. 'Elena. I could be anything now that I'm eighteen.'

'You're not a vampire and you're not a vânător. Marianne and Thomas confirmed it by the scent of your blood.'

'I suspect I'm a version of you.'

'Is it just my blood inside of you?'

It was Lucas's turn to frown. 'What do you mean?'

'I'm talking about the serum. Are you sure it wasn't fed to you intravenously while under sedation?'

He shook his head, adamant. 'When I was lucid, Chester made it clear to everyone involved that I was not to be tainted, that my adaptation to your blood was unique and the experiment would be irreparably altered if a synthetic source was added.'

'So the tubes Karina described coming in and out of you were what, filled with my blood?'

'Yes.'

'Shit.'

'I could think of a better word.'

So could I.

I ran my fingers through my hair, gripping it by the roots in frustration and then letting it free again. 'Okay, so what else has changed besides physicality and telekinesis?'

He shrugged. 'I don't know.'

'What about the serum, then? You must have gained some insight?'

'According to mum and dad it's still in the testing stages. It's too unstable with unpredictable side effects; exhaustion, depression, nausea—you name it. Beryx is Chester's test subject and from what I gather, not exactly a willing participant.'

'Wait. Hold the phone. Did you say Beryx is the test subject?'

'So I've been told, but it makes sense. He is abnormally strong and fast and his body is killer.'

'As in predatory?'

'No, as in incredibly ripped and hard to the touch. Don't ask me what else he can do because I never saw him again after our first throw down in the training ring. I have to tell you though; the only way I could beat him was with magic. In hand-to-hand combat he practically creamed me.'

'And the serum is definitely only in the initial testing stages?'

'Like I said, as far as I know.'

'Then why the hell did Chester drag key members of the IMI to Antarctica?'

Lucas was as perplexed as me. 'I don't know, to perpetuate change with the strongest and most capable members?'

I disagreed. 'Then why leave Peter from the Cairns faction at home. He excelled in martial arts and trained nearly all of us.'

'Perhaps they were offered a choice.'

'Do we even know what that choice is?'

'Mum and dad said the goal is to make The Protectors like you—immortal, infallible.'

'And the rest who opposed were magically brainwashed to forget about the serum's existence and their missing faction members?'

'I suppose so.'

'Susan and George just handed you this information?'

'No,' Lucas said with a nervous laugh, 'not even close. I told them I wanted to leave the IMI and to be rid of the lies and deceit. They finally came clean, but I think because they thought I'd never actually escape.'

'And then they drugged you.' I punched a pillow; completely ineffective, but a good mood stabilizer. A few loose feathers and dust motes exploded and finally stilled as I gave the violence away and slumped further against the headboard, wearier than I'd ever been. When would it all end?

'Elena, there is still time to stop them before the serum gets out.'

'What about you? How do you feel about going up against the IMI?'

'I don't feel anything. I'm numb to the whole experience. All I can think about is what they've done to me—to us.'

'I'm used to being thrown in the deep end of the pool, Lucas, but that doesn't mean you have to learn to swim to keep up with me.'

Those powder blue eyes locked on mine. 'E, the deep end is all I know now. My knees still knock together and I'm shit scared about ninety percent of the time, but I'm your big brother and I have to get my act together. This shit isn't going to go away. You're shape-shifting now and drinking blood. I'm telekinetic and God only knows what else. Facing The Protectors and making them pay is already marked on the God damn calendar!'

I steadied Lucas's trembling forearm. His enthusiasm for justice was infectious and dangerous when ill-considered. 'We have to figure out your deal before we march on back into ice city.'

'That might be a luxury we can't afford.'

My fingers tightened on his skin. 'You've already changed so much since I saw you last. We need to know, Lucas, what your strengths and weaknesses are.'

He shrugged himself free, irritated.

'Sorry,' Marianne interrupted, swinging open the door and wandering into the room. 'I know you two are catching up, but I thought I'd let you know that we've booked the jet back to Rome. They want to take off within the next few hours.'

Lucas's whole demeanour shifted and he quickly smiled. 'Hey, Blondie. It's been a while.'

Marianne tossed her blonde curls around her shoulders, determined to remain composed. It wasn't until her eyes had flit around the room three consecutive times and she started picking at her fingernails did I realise she was nervous. She coughed and managed another sweep of the room, careful to avoid my gaze. 'Yeah, I was starting to think I wouldn't hear your annoying voice again.'

'I'm pretty sure you missed me.'

She scoffed. 'I just missed the adoration from a misguided blood bag.'

'You haven't called me that in a while.'

Her sapphire eyes fixed on him, shoulders stiff and hands curled into fists by her sides. 'It's been a while since we've spoken.'

'Too long.'

Lucas folded his legs over the edge of the bed and pulled himself up slowly. He staggered a little bit, but soon righted himself on the headboard, straightening up and moving towards her.

Marianne didn't move an inch—didn't even flinch when he almost fell. She kept her eyes on him and her body rigid, face completely devoid of any real emotion. She reminded me of the vampire I had first met—hardened and calculating, uncaring and arrogant.

I felt like an outsider walking into a movie half way through and trying to determine the plot. Something was going on between these two, but I was clueless.

I didn't even know they were friends until recently, let alone friendly enough to embrace one another, which was exactly what they did next.

Marianne's rigidity melted as her slender arms encircled him and squeezed tight. She buried her face against his neck while he whispered in her ear. She nodded, taking in my open-mouthed expression before dropping her arms and exiting the circle of his embrace.

What the hell?

Lucas cupped the side of her face, eliciting yet another troubled expression from me. 'I never imagined you'd be part of my rescue party. This tells me a lot, Blondie.'

She took a rather uncharacteristic, uncoordinated step backwards, hitting the doorframe. 'Don't call me Blondie. You know how much I hate that.'

'Why did you come?'

'You know I couldn't have left you there.'

'Why not?'

'You know why.'

'I want you to say it.'

I didn't. I didn't want them to say anything else. Marianne was a first-class bitch hung up on William, yet all subtext of this reunion led to me wanting to tap my ruby slippers and wave this conversation the hell goodbye.

'We're friends,' she finally murmured. 'You may be a blood bag, but I still care about what happens to you.'

'Why?'

Her lips tightened into an unhappy line. 'Because friends look out for friends.'

I couldn't see Lucas's face and I wasn't sure I wanted to. 'Hmm. I can see I still have my work cut out for me when it comes to making you realise you totally want me, but at least I know you care.'

Vomit made an appearance in my mouth.

'Lucas ...' she said, voice breaking.

'I'm out!' I gathered the sheet around me and jumped from the bed. 'I'm going to get ready. I'll leave you two alone.'

'I-I was just leaving,' Marianne said, stuttering. 'I didn't mean to i-interrupt.'

'You didn't,' Lucas said, taking another step towards her.

'And I'm outta here,' I said, grabbing my backpack off the floor and slamming the bathroom door behind me. I did not want to see what might have been coming next.

Ugh!

When I re-entered the room—some twenty minutes later—Lucas was perched on the end of the bed, head between his hands. I wondered how long he'd been like that while I'd luxuriated in the shower.

He looked up the second I approached. 'At least you have clothes on now.' His attempt at humour did not mask his brewing concern.

I dropped my back pack and sat next to him. 'What's wrong?'

His answering smile was dim at best. He snaked and arm around my shoulder to compensate. 'I'm fine, just thinking about the last few months. I feel like we've been cheated—forced to grow up quicker than we should.'

I wasn't sure how to react. My own feelings on the topic were still mostly unresolved. 'We could have lived in blissful ignorance back in Cairns, but then I wouldn't have met my father or anyone else along the way.'

'That's true, I suppose.'

'And, you wouldn't have learnt the truth—which by the way—you still haven't shown me the freaky crap you can do yet.'

He smiled wryly. 'Freaky crap? This coming from the blood donor?'

I squealed as my body left the mattress. Levitation was a good trick but not exactly unique, but since every other object in the room had also begun to defy gravity, I stopped questioning the extent of what he might be capable of with my cynicism.

'You didn't need a spell for this, did you?'

Lucas shook his head. 'Nope.'

Curiosity gripped me now. 'What about shields?'

He frowned. 'I don't understand.'

'Instead of moving objects you can see; can you manipulate particles in the air to create physical barriers?'

He lowered me and everything else back to its initial resting place. 'I don't know. I never tried. I guess I thought my new powers only related to what I can do as a Protector.'

'If you have my blood, then you can probably do everything I can do.'

'I hope this doesn't mean I'm going to turn into a wolf too.'

I snorted. 'What's that supposed to mean?'

'Nothing, I just think between the two of us we have enough quirks to deal with.'

'You and I are changing all the rules, Lucas. Who knows what's coming or what else you might be able to do, but so far it isn't all bad, is it?' I gestured to his body. 'I mean—technically speaking— you look hot. The shaved head is a big change, but your new body and kick-ass power aren't bad.'

'Elena, I recall you going through this *woe is me* phase when mum and dad told you that you were half vânător. Cop me a break for feeling betrayed and confused.'

I rubbed soothing circles across his back. 'Sorry, I just wanted you to know it's not bad being different.'

'It is when the parents you thought were supposed to love and protect you turn out to be the ones that made you different in the first place.'

'I'm the one who bit you.'

'You were just a kid; you didn't know any better.'

I sighed. 'Look, not that I'm defending Susan and George here, but I'll bet they didn't know I would bite you and simply reacted accordingly.'

He dropped his arm from around my shoulders and patted my knee, forcing a smile. 'Don't worry about it. I'll deal.' He pushed himself to his feet and headed for the bathroom. He stopped in the doorway, turning to face me again. 'Will you show me how to work on that barrier thing?'

'Sure.'

'And will you tell me why William's not here?'

'Are you going to tell me what the hell is going on between you and Marianne?'

'Not likely.'

I waved him off. 'Then you have your answer too.'

He closed the bathroom door behind him, putting an end to a conversation that neither of us were truly prepared to have.

For now.

* * *

'Lucas, this is Eric, Nicholas and Caleb. You already know everyone else.'

One-by-one Lucas shook their hands. He stopped at Caleb, breaking out the big guns and smiling broadly. 'Thanks for the clothes man, I really appreciate it.'

'No problems,' Caleb answered. 'We're about the same size and I can see you're appreciating my taste.'

'He'd be the only one,' Marianne murmured, Thomas ribbed her.

I studied the Nine Inch Nails shirt and black denim jeans with ripped knees—not so stylishly paired with big, black combat boots. He didn't have Caleb's pink hair or black fingernail polish, but was well on his way to looking the part. I shuddered. 'When we get you home, we'll take you shopping and get you a heap of new clothes.'

Lucas—now on another tangent—smiled and embraced Thomas. Serious man-hugging ensued with back slaps and an abrupt pull away.

'It's good to see you again,' Thomas said, now kneading his shoulder. 'We were starting to get worried about you.'

'I appreciate the rescue party.'

Thomas looked over at me, sapphire eyes sparkling with mirth. 'Your sister is a very determined woman.'

Lucas laughed. 'She always has been. You should have seen how creative she could be whenever she used to get grounded.'

The Vampires looked baffled.

'Punished,' Lucas corrected.

I touched Karina's shoulder tentatively. She jumped regardless, still clearly on edge. 'You know, if it wasn't for Karina, I doubt getting you out of there would have been so simple.'

She smiled shyly. 'Thanks.'

Lucas studied her face, consideration etched on his features; decisions about her loyalty no doubt plagued him as they had done with me. He shook his head dismissively, focusing back on Thomas. 'Are you still based in London?'

Karina's face dimmed. Betrayal was hard to forgive or forget.

Thomas nodded. 'We are here now because of the multi-coven gathering and our urgency to hear news of William. Then of course we learned from Caleb that Elena was returning to Australia to look for you and we figured we would at least try to help one of our friends.'

Lucas gnawed his lower lip, confused. I'd skipped over a lot, including the gathering and news of William. 'What is a multi-coven gathering? And what the hell has happened to William?' He shot me a particularly irritated look.

'So I missed a few details. Sue me.' I collapsed onto the sofa. Lucas's burning gaze left little to the imagination. I clearly had some explaining to do and he wasn't going to let the matter drop until I did.

I refrained from groaning. 'A multi-coven gathering is exactly as it sounds—different covens of vampires coming together to discuss current issues. In this instance, Lucius addressed the impending war between vânător and vampire and the breakdown of the alliance with The Protectors.'

'So the breakdown of the alliance has fuelled the Vânătors to rebel without consequence?'

'As we speak, fighting has broken out at the borders of Italy. As far as we know they are pushing to destroy Lucius's coven.'

'I thought you said your dad couldn't be killed?'

'He can't, but the Vânătors don't know that.'

'So what does the war have to do with William?' This time my brother glanced at Marianne. She held his gaze for a few painful seconds and then averted her eyes.

'Nothing,' Thomas continued. 'William's role was to help his brother hunt down the Alphas and kill them.'

'His brother?'

I laughed. I couldn't help it. I kept forgetting how much Lucas had missed and how bizarre some of those things were to repeat. 'Sebastian is William's brother. Sebastian was chosen for his unparalleled tracking skills and William for his experience; three hundred years of hunting vânătors under his belt.'

'Wait, Sebastian and William are related?'

'Tell me about it,' I muttered.

He stood there, blinking at me for the longest time before he burst out laughing.

Not the reaction I had been expecting, but equally as amusing as the irony. 'Okay, what are the odds of that? And how's that working out for you?'

'Don't even get me started.'

'Elena admitted she's in love with Sebastian,' Caleb interrupted.

If I could have locked him in an inescapable room with an approaching sunrise, I would have.

'So what about William?' Lucas persisted. 'I thought you two were going to work it out?'

When had my feet become so interesting? I couldn't take my eyes off them or stop wondering how far I could shove them up everybody's nosey butts. 'Can we talk about this in private?'

'Once you see Sebastian in the flesh, you'll understand the infatuation.'

'Did you just call me shallow?' I barked, my head whipping up to level an angry gaze at Caleb.

He quickly recanted. 'I was just pointing out that Sebastian has certain qualities that are difficult to miss.'

'So you're saying I'm only interested because his ass looks great in leather?'

'He does wear leather well,' Nicholas commented.

I glared at him too.

'So William is out of the picture?' Lucas asked.

I took a deep breath, attempting to channel calm. 'I don't know, I don't know, I don't know. There. Does that answer anything for everyone?'

'Elena, don't ignore what you feel for Sebastian,' Caleb pressed. 'I thought you got past this?'

'I'm not having this conversation again.'

Lucas waved his hands in dismissal. 'We can talk later. Just tell me the progress on finding the Alphas.'

I breathed a sigh of relief. 'Progress is good. I spoke to William and Sebastian yesterday and they told me they're all dead except Roshan. Sebastian thinks that Roshan will look for me now, so heading home would be a good plan.'

'You mean he wants to use you as bait,' Lucas surmised. I could tell any warm emotions he may have had reserved for Sebastian were fading fast.

'It's not a bad plan, Lucas—kill the Alphas, kill them all.'

'It's not a plan.'

There was no point in arguing with the truth.

'Okay,' Lucas said, defeated. 'I missed everything.'

We all murmured various versions of agreement.

'E's turning into a werewolf now, William and Sebastian are siblings and Roshan's the last alpha standing. The IMI and what it stands for is defective, the serum is still in infancy, I'm a giant question mark and a war has broken out. Great. Anything else I missed?'

'Sebastian could be the Archangel Michael,' Caleb added.

Everyone groaned except Lucas who slapped a hand against his forehead, still shaking his head as if it was all just a little too much. Perhaps it was. I'd never really laid it all out like that. 'The Archangel Michael, really?'

Caleb nodded emphatically.

'And William?'

'We don't think so.'

'And what about fairies, are they real too?'

Ahh, sarcasm, my favourite fall-back. 'Yeah, sure. Why not?'

'Seriously?'

Everyone glanced at me curiously, eyes narrowing, inquisitive about this latest revelation. Given the current state of supernatural evolution, it was narrow-minded to assume that otherworldly creatures were non-existent. Five of us were vampires. One of us was technically a witch. I was a half-breed, and Lucas was undetermined. Acting doubtful about the existence of fairies was simply negligent, especially since there was one of them no doubt prancing around at home.

'I'll tell you what, Lucas,' I said, climbing up from the sofa. 'When we get back to Rome, I'll introduce to the biggest fairy I know.'

'So you're serious about this?'

The others looked perplexed.

'Sure. Marcus is a little bit of an asshole, but he might actually like *you*.'

Now on the same page, everyone who knew the thrall rolled their eyes and started to laugh. Karina and Lucas were of course titillated by the thought of meeting a real live fairy.

I patted them both on the shoulder. 'Don't worry. You'll understand when you meet him.'

CHAPTER TWENTY: ADMISSIONS

'**A**h … no,' Lucas argued, wrinkling his nose at Thomas's outstretched arms.

'I won't hurt you.'

'I know,' Lucas agreed, 'but we're guys. Guys don't let other guys hold them.' He peered into the darkened tunnel entrance, hidden beneath the dumpster in the alley behind Synth Corp. 'Can't I just walk?'

I gave Lucas an impatient look. It was hard enough getting Karina to comply with our transportation efforts. I wasn't a big fan of being toted around either, but it was efficient, especially when using the tunnels.

Lucius denies entry to the villa to anyone not previously known to him. The tunnels mark multiple kilometres of underground access, opening onto what is known as the 'visitor entrance'. This entrance is marked by a door manufactured from the toughest steel—impenetrable to a vampire. Humans don't know about the tunnels, but accidents do happen and getting caught in one is a death sentence. The lights are only activated to accommodate vampiric speed. To a human on foot this would mean going it alone in the dark and we all know what can hunt you in the dark …

'Why can't we drive like normal people?'

'When Lucius learns to trust you, he will let you know the villa's location. Until then, he's protecting himself and everyone else in the household.'

'I'm with Lucas on this one,' Karina said, side-stepping me and backing up towards the dumpster. She didn't appreciate the idea of being carried by a vampire. 'Isn't there another way?'

I groaned. 'I give you my word that no one will hurt you. You're going to have to start trusting me, Karina. You're going to be living with us now and vampires are a part of that equation.'

Karina struggled. Eric and Nicholas stood particularly still, trying to look nonthreatening. For the most part they pulled it off.

'Which one would you choose?' she whispered.

I smiled, couldn't help it. In the last twenty-four hours Karina had turned her back on everything she believed in; helped a fugitive and divulged secrets. Now I was asking her to throw caution to the wind, climb into a vampire's arms and trust that her neck would remain intact. I had to give her points for effort.

I opted for a different approach, endeavouring to appeal to the teenage gene I only recently developed myself. 'Which one do you think is cuter?'

If looks could kill. Nicholas and Eric did not like being objectified. Understandable for sure, but they could deal if it got Karina and Lucas back to the villa without all this bullshit.

'Um, neither of them are really my type.' She grimaced. 'No offence.'

'She likes them trapped and helpless, don't you, Karina?'

'Lucas!' I chided. 'Now's not the time to stir the waters again.'

He of course ignored me. 'Were you even attracted to me at all?'

'Did I miss something?' Marianne asked, looking to me for answers.

I shrugged. 'I think we've all missed something.'

After a twenty-hour flight, I was baffled there was something left to talk about. Whatever happened between them played with Lucas's emotions. He hadn't said anything nice to her since the rescue.

Karina's discomfort shifted another notch. 'I like you, Lucas—I always have. Just, um, not like that. What happened between us—'

Lucas slammed the rubbish bin next to her head. It made all of us jump, especially those of us who knew Lucas wasn't prone to acts of violence. 'Answer my question.'

Karina's resolve was steely. She straightened and leant forward to consume Lucas's vision. Brave or stupid to tamper with his currently unpredictable nature. 'You may not be my type, Lucas, but I do find you attractive. I wouldn't have kissed you if I didn't.'

Marianne hissed, unexpectedly punching the wall next to her. Dust, brick and concrete rained down to the ground in chunks, leaving behind a fist sized hole in the exterior of my father's business. It was starting to look like Lucas wasn't the only meathead in the alleyway.

'You're paying for that,' I said, pointing to the damage.

Her nostrils flared; not a pretty sight. She stomped her foot, hissed again and then dropped down into the entrance of the tunnels. The darkness swallowed her, but her envy remained. I was starting to think that Marianne might be a hypocrite—gnawing at me about William, but secretly pining for my brother.

The prospect was just too foul to consider.

On a positive note, Lucas had been distracted by her tantrum and forgot about preying on Karina for the mistakes of her past. She'd since slipped into Nicholas's arms, opting for the lesser of two current evils.

Thomas took the lead, clapped Lucas on the shoulder to draw him back to the present and held his arms out. 'Come on, Lucas. If you don't climb aboard within the next ten seconds, I'm carrying you regardless. The war waits for no one.'

Thomas was right, the war was upon us; Lucius needed support and I was going to be bait for Roshan. Dicking around in front of Synth Corp was not a productive afternoon.

Caleb rolled his eyes, echoing my sentiments. 'I'm just going to meet you all at the villa. This conversation is going nowhere and Sebastian awaits.'

The mentioning of his name choked me with excitement and robbed me of breath. My skin itched with anticipation, my mouth went dry and my heart started pumping, thrumming in time to the butterflies that fluttered in my stomach. Worst of all, my head was filled with the memories of our last kiss—a constant stream of images that would undoubtedly transform me into a bumbling idiot. Talking was dangerous. Admissions of any degree could ruin everything between us.

By the time I'd shaken the reverie, Eric held me in his arms and we were travelling through the tunnels. Karina and Nicholas were in front, barely visible in the dimming light and Caleb and

Marianne were nowhere to be seen. Behind me, Lucas was with Thomas, screaming like a little girl.

When we reached the door to the Romanesque holding cell in the basement of the villa, Lucas jumped shipped and attempted to shove Thomas into a wall. Unsuccessful, Thomas and Caleb laughed; Lucas undoubtedly embarrassed.

I dropped from Eric's arms and banged on the steel door. Someone in the house would have heard us.

Marianne stood huddled in the corner, arms folded across her chest. She looked troubled, but her current feelings were of little importance to me right now. My heart thumped for the sight of Sebastian.

The fountain above us slid to the side, scraping across the terrazzo that Marcus had recently restored. It was followed by the sound of pounding footsteps on the stairs beyond.

'It's Marcus,' Eric said, retreating.

'Marcus?' Lucas echoed, now curious.

The steel door was unbolted and opened. Marcus stood on the other side dressed in long, black dress slacks and his favourite designer loafers. He paired them with a white button down shirt revealing more chest hair than a bear skin rug.

I looked at him more critically. 'Are you wearing eyeliner?'

'You know, Elena, you are the very reason I never had children.' Bitterness filled his words.

I chuckled. 'It's good to see you too, Marcus.'

'Who said I was pleased by this reunion?'

'This is *Marcus*?' Lucas asked, mild surprise etched on his features. He was eyeing the vampire critically from head to toe.

'Who is this?' Marcus demanded, suddenly putting on the smile he reserved for people he actually liked. 'Is this your brother?'

'Yes, Marcus, this is Lucas. Lucas, this is Marcus.'

'Wow. You look just like a vampire,' Lucas said, marvelling as he walked around Marcus slowly. He reached out, touched Marcus's chest and then touched his hair, rubbing the silken locks between his fingers. 'You even feel like a vampire.'

I slapped Lucas's hand away. 'Stop poking him.'

Marcus's face reflected a certain amount of confusion. 'Of course I feel like a vampire,' Marcus drawled, blinking narrowed eyes. 'Should I feel any other way?'

'I honestly don't know,' Lucas said, studying Marcus with awe. 'I've never met a real live fairy before.'

'Oh this is *too* good,' Caleb said, bursting into laughter.

Eric cradled his head in his hands.

Oh boy. I'd forgotten about the fairy comments from earlier.

I grabbed Lucas's arm and quickly pulled him past Marcus and up the stairs before the fairy finally caught on.

He was currently perplexed, but I had only seconds before he made the connection.

Behind us, Marcus roared so loudly that the chandeliers above the courtyard began to shake.

'He's not a very happy fairy, is he?' Lucas said, peeking over his shoulder.

'Not unless he gets a discount at Prada.'

I attempted to keep running towards freedom, but Lucas pulled me to a stop, pointing back at Marcus. 'Hey, look at that. He has fangs like a vampire too.'

I grimaced. 'He *is* a vampire, Lucas. He's one of the thralls.'

'But you said he was a fairy!'

I slapped my hand over his motor mouth. 'A figure of speech.'

Marcus screamed obscenities at me, thankfully the others had him restrained. Judging by his filthy temper they could be holding him in check for a while.

Lucas punched my arm and bit the hand that gagged him. 'Great. Thanks a lot. You just made me call a pissed off vampire a fairy. Good job. I'll be sleeping so much better tonight knowing that he's down the hallway from me.'

I wiped Lucas's slobber from my palm. 'I'm more worried about my neck than yours, Lucas. Do you always have to say everything that pops into your head?'

'You could have told me!' He scowled. 'What's next? Bar fight between William and Sebastian when William finds out you're in love with his brother?'

'Can you shut the hell up? Even the walls have ears in this place.'

'I can safely say that will not happen.'

I spun mid-stair, gobsmacked to see Sebastian standing only inches behind me. His words whispered hot breath across my skin, yet his eyes were specifically trained on my brother. There wasn't even a glance in my general direction.

He offered his hand to Lucas. 'I am not a fan of bars or fights if I can help it, but you are right. There will be some animosity with this latest admission.'

Lucas shot me an apologetic look as all three of us finally ascended into the courtyard.

I tried really hard not to pick up the nearest shovel and bury myself. I was mortified. The only thing that stopped me from throwing my hands in the air and running off screaming like a little girl was the fact that *his* brother watched from the sidelines, shooting me every distinguishable expression of angst.

Shit.

William looked at me for the longest time, mute. His emerald eyes spoke the oldest tale of betrayal and unrequited love. I felt like a shithead and wanted to kick Lucas in the shins for opening his big mouth yet again.

I averted my gaze from judgement, too cowardly to face another second of his probing. What do you say when you've stomped all over their heart?

'It's good to finally meet you. Elena's told me a lot about you,' Lucas said, snaking around me to shake Sebastian's hand.

'All good I hope?'

Lucas shrugged. 'Mostly.'

William cleared his throat, drawing Lucas's attention. I still couldn't look back—cowardly to the core.

'Hey, Will, how's it going?' Lucas dropped Sebastian's hand and headed for William. They clasped hands tightly and pulled each other in for one of those 'man hugs' that my brother considered acceptable masculine contact.

'It's good to see you, Lucas. I am glad to see that you are well.'

Lucas thumped his chest. 'I've been working out, drinking protein powder, got a haircut—that kind of thing.'

'You look good.'

He shrugged again. 'Thanks.'

I watched Sebastian, my eyes always impossibly drawn to him. Today I was more than happy to see him, but my interest in studying him was based on other motivations. I tried to picture him as an angel. I tried to picture him as a lot of things, but all my mind perceived was the question: why wouldn't he look at me?

'So you have Elena's blood inside of you?'

What?

I'd missed half the conversation. Lucas was recanting all the details regarding his time with the IMI and I was distracted by Sebastian's lack of attention and his … assets.

Clad in black leather pants, it was hard not noticing the snug fit. His t-shirt clung to his broad chest and muscular arms, hinting at the definition of perfectly toned abdominals. Unblemished skin, a chiselled jaw, high cheekbones and the most delectable lips you have ever seen completed the messiah package. I supposed being an angel meant you wouldn't have rolled off the assembly line looking less than perfect.

'I smell another Protector,' William said, jogging me from my long-standing avoidance and general lack of contribution to the conversation.

'Yeah, that's Karina,' Lucas said, scratching his head nervously. 'She kind of helped me get out of the IMI. Granted she got me trapped there too, but—'

'She got you out.'

'Well … yes.'

William's eyes found mine, lingering only for one miniscule second before they skated on by, focusing on something behind me.

Karina made me jump, brushing my arm as she emerged from the darkness of the tunnels below, eyes wide and mouth slightly ajar as she spun around on the spot, studying her latest surrounds. 'Wow.'

I took her hand and manoeuvred her in front of me. I was using her as a buffer between me and William and it seemed to be working, his curiosity regarding her presence abundant.

'This is Karina?' William asked Lucas, side-stepping him for a better view. 'Why have I heard this name before?'

'She was one of The Protector children at our Cairns faction,' Lucas answered, eyebrows drawing together in contemplation as he watched William approach her.

'Why don't I remember you?' William said, stopping in front of her, emerald eyes searching her face for an answer.

Uncertain, Karina glanced at me over her shoulder and then back at William. I could offer no insight. I had no idea why she'd be so interesting to him. 'We d-didn't actually m-meet,' she stuttered, her grip on my hand loosening.

He smiled and it was filled with genuine warmth, not an ounce of it directed at me. 'I would definitely remember meeting you.'

My whole face suddenly dropped, my throat dry and coarse like sand paper.

Oh my god! Is he hitting on her? In front of me?

Lucas and I shared a look, the shrug of his shoulders and drawn brows confirming that he was equally confused. I had no right to be annoyed by this exchange given my recent activities with his brother, but it was impossible not to feel ... jealous.

Karina smiled shyly, her dark lashes fanning against her smooth pale cheeks, acceptance of flirtation if ever I saw it. 'You were in your vampiric form and in battle at the time. I stood behind my father during the fight against the alpha John and his pack. I don't remember seeing you like a human.'

'Well, despite that, I am William—William Granville and I am very pleased to make your acquaintance.' He picked up her hand and placed a gentle kiss on the top of her flesh.

What the hell is going on here?

Karina withdrew, smile faltering. Too far? 'Nice to meet you too.'

Lucas and I found a new realm of incredulity. Call it whatever you will, but the guy who had professed his undying love for me time and time again was practically drooling over Karina and judging by the look on Lucas's face, I definitely wasn't imagining it.

Instead of relief, I felt jealous. My feelings were unjustified. I didn't want to be with William, but I wasn't sure I was ready for him to lay the charm on someone else. I knew what those lips had done to me and the thought of them touching someone new tied me up in a few knots I wasn't quite sure how to undo. 'Come on,' I said, tugging on Karina's elbow. 'I'm going to show you guys to your rooms.'

'May I escort you?' William asked Karina. He held out his arm for her. Chivalrous and decidedly unsettling.

She released me, but remained momentarily still. Unease debated with her features once more, but then she tentatively reached out and smiled he slipped her arm through his.

Oh for ...

'Lucas,' I muttered, ambushing my brother for secret dialogue. 'Can you believe this shit?'

I steered him towards the formal stair case that led to the second story. He murmured in my ear that he was equally surprised by William's change in demeanour.

When I looked back over my shoulder, the two of them were talking, seemingly enjoying one another's company. Sebastian had not followed as I expected. He'd settled into one of the courtyard chairs and was staring at the garden. He still hadn't looked at me; an assumption I now believed based entirely on Lucas's blurt. I never should have admitted to anyone how I felt about Sebastian. Feelings make you vulnerable to pain and rejection. I should have known better.

What an idiot.

'Maybe William's trying to make you jealous?' Lucas whispered as we ascended the stairs.

'It's working.'

'I thought you weren't into William anymore.'

'William has always been special to me. He was the first vampire I ever met, the first person who ever accepted me for exactly who and what I am.'

'So you *do* love him?'

'Not loving William romantically doesn't mean I don't find him hotter than hell and wish I could have my way with him.'

'Um, boundaries ...' Lucas muttered.

'Sorry. It's just that William and I had great times together, you know? His blood is inside me now. He's always going to be there, swimming through my veins and stirring things up.'

'Are you going to tell Sebastian how you feel?'

I elbowed him in the ribs and he hissed in pain. 'I think you already did that for me. Haven't you noticed that he can't even look at me now?'

'He is a guy; he might just need to process.'

'No way. It's over before it even began.'

'You're being too hard on him and yourself.'

'No. I'm realistic.' I grimaced. 'I should have kept my walls up.'

Lucas wrapped an arm around my shoulder. 'Walls stop you from enjoying the view outside, E.'

I shrugged the insightful comment off. 'I don't need a view; I've got too much else to worry about. First things first, getting you settled.'

To distract myself from errant thoughts, I gave Lucas a quick rundown of all the upstairs bedrooms, echoing some of William's comments about the villa. Anything was better than wallowing in self-pity. Lucas seemed only interested in one bedroom—Lucius junior's. With brightly painted figures of soldiers and animals on the timber surface; it was the same room that had caught my attention on my first night in the villa. I knew now that the bedroom belonged to my father's murdered son and that he preferred to keep the room locked, the painful memories hidden away.

While William continued regaling tales of the villa's history to both Karina and Lucas, I peered over the railing of the balcony onto the open-air courtyard below. Sebastian was still there, sitting with his back to me, long legs resting on the chair in front of him. He was the very picture of ease, yet I knew from the slump in his shoulders and the way that his thumb rubbed the top of his hand that he was severely agitated.

'So which room is mine?' Lucas asked, tugging on my t-shirt.

I pointed to the last two available. 'Take your pick. They are the only ones left.'

'Well, actually,' William murmured, smiling at Karina. 'One of them is my room.'

My lips twitched. 'So you're moving back in?'

'Time will tell.'

'Wait. I thought you hated Lucius? In fact, I thought you hated Sebastian too? Now that we're over, I'd thought you'd want to leave?'

Karina gasped. 'You two were an item?'

'We've been intimate.'

'Jesus, Elena,' Lucas moaned. 'Do you have to be so graphic?'

'I didn't realise,' Karina said, shaking her head. 'I thought the rumours about you being involved with a vampire were untrue.'

'Not so much.'

William set those green eyes upon me. 'We could have been a lot more, but since I now know that you are in love with Seb—'

'William,' I interrupted, 'You left me after our exchange and I didn't see you for months. It never really even started. It was just always meant to be fun.'

'Just fun ...' He bitterly mimicked my usual line of explanation for our trysts. 'So trivial compared to the ties I thought we shared.'

'We'll always be tied, just not romantically.'

William left Karina's side, looming close enough that we were almost touching. His cool breath whispered against my ear. He leaned closer, lips brushing flesh and said, 'then why are you upset by my lack of attention?'

I shoved his chest. 'Because you're rubbing my face in it.'

'That's rich coming from you.' William gripped my violent arms and backed me up until I hit the pillar of the balcony. Restrained, he pressed his body against mine, engulfing me with his scent before I could protest any further. 'Rubbing *your* face in it? You said on the phone to me in Hobart that we are done. Why are you now jealous?'

'I'm not ... jealous,' I lied. 'I'm surprised.'

'That I could be attracted to anyone but you?'

'No,' I mumbled, struggling against his hold. 'I'm surprised you couldn't wait for the dust to settle before openly throwing yourself at my friend.'

'As opposed to what you and my brother do behind closed doors?'

'That's not—'

'The same thing?' William pushed another wave of his essence upon me. Spices and sandalwood slithered across the surface of my skin and slipped down my airways, filling my lungs with the compulsive need to listen and understand. He pressed himself painfully against me, wedging my body so tight between his and the balcony I gasped for air. 'From the first moment I laid eyes on you, I knew that I loved you. I've never met anyone who takes my breath away the way you do. I've also never met anyone so confused by her own thoughts and feelings. I love you, but something has to change. This thing you like to call *fun* between us is not so fun anymore.' He savaged my wrists between his fingers, bruising and unrelenting. 'So I have to let you go,' he whispered, voice catching ever so slightly. 'I have to look for another opportunity to be happy.'

I yanked my head back to look into his eyes. 'I want you to be happy, William.'

'You do?'

How could he deny the truth in that statement and the sincerity on my face?

'Do you want to be happy with Karina?'

He smiled, a small rumble of laughter rolling around in his throat as he bent down to brush his lips across my forehead. 'Let's just take this break-up one step at a time. I'm not ready for you to pick out dates for me just yet.'

'Sorry.'

Smiling again, he said, 'I think we should try that 'friends' thing you keep mentioning.'

'Why? Because it's now convenient for you?'

'No, because it's the only way you and I are ever going to end this cycle of fighting, kissing, making up and then doing it all over again.'

'I was just getting used to that.'

'Really?'

'No, but being friends is going to make living under the same roof a challenge.'

He chuckled, his cool breath fanning my cheek. 'You know how much I like a challenge. I tried to tame you, but that was like trying to ride a wild bull bareback.' He sighed. 'In the end I'm starting to think that maybe Araqiel had it right all along.'

'So you do know the angel?'

He ignored me. 'I just wished I'd listened to him when he'd told me to let you go, deliver you to Lucius. Maybe I could have stopped so much harm from befalling you, maybe things between us would be different—less strained.'

I blew a raspberry, hoping to deflect the serious talk. 'You're just saying that now because you found someone else that takes your fancy.'

'I'm not ready to look just yet, Elena.'

I bowed my head. 'I'm sorry, William. I'm a freaking disaster.'

He surrendered my wrists and folded me in his arms, his scent slowly evaporating. 'Don't apologise. I didn't really give you many choices, did I?'

I sniffed. 'To be fair, you were difficult to resist.'

'Some people more than others.' He bobbed his head in Sebastian's direction.

I shook my head. 'I didn't mean for it to happen.'

He placed his fingers against my lips. 'I know better than anyone that the heart wants what the heart wants.'

'William, I'm so sorry,' I whispered against his chest for the second time in as many minutes.

'Has everyone forgotten there is a war going on outside?' Sebastian said in irritation, appearing beside us. Lucas wasn't irritated, merely as uncomfortable as Karina appeared to be having to watch re-runs of the William and Elena show.

'We were just showing Karina and Lucas to their rooms and then we were going to leave,' William answered, kissing my forehead one more time and stepping away from me.

'Where are we going?' Lucas asked, glancing between the triangle that was my love life.

Sebastian addressed Lucas directly, once again ignoring me entirely. Anyone would think I'd killed his cat! 'I am sorry that we do not have more time to make you feel welcome, but the frontlines are becoming over run and it is difficult to hide the evidence from humans. We need you and your friend's abilities to cloak what we do not wish to be discovered.'

Lucas nodded, all business. 'How big an area are we talking about?'

There was a long pause before Sebastian spoke again. 'Milan.'

'Milan!' I gasped. 'That's an entire city! When did the Vânători manage to break the front lines?'

'They are jumping past our defences. By the time we hunt and track them, they are already escaping into the city.'

'That sounds bad,' Lucas agreed.

Sebastian nodded, clapping a hand on my brother's shoulder. I noticed he winced and made a mental note to ask him later if it related to the scar I'd given him as a child. 'That's your room over there. There are a few of my clothes that you can use that might be more comfortable and warmer than what you are wearing now.' He paused, looking at his younger brother. 'William, settle Karina into Elena's room. We'll work out a more permanent solution after the war is over.'

Sebastian grabbed me roughly by the arm, turning away from everyone and dragging me down the hallway towards his bedroom like some rudimentary caveman. 'We'll meet downstairs in a few minutes.' He shoved me through his bedroom door and slammed it shut behind us. It wasn't exactly a buffer for vampire hearing, but its symbolism was not lost on me. The last thing I saw was Lucas's concern. The others would undoubtedly fill him in.

'What the hell has gotten into you?' I said, stumbling over the black shag pile rug.

263

'You!' he roared back at me.

'Me! You're angry with me? Why? I'm the one who should be pissed at you. You haven't even acknowledged me since I got back!'

He crossed the distance between us, gripping my face tightly between his palms. His eyes were a swirling mass of silver, like tiny diamonds winking back at me from behind long dark lashes. They were beautiful. Not the reflection of anger or irritation I had seen in the past as storm clouds of grey. They were like Christmas tinsel, a perfect recreation from every dream I had ever had of him in the past—hints of his angelic nature perhaps?

'What happened to your eyes?' I asked, momentarily forgetting we were supposed to be yelling at each other.

His face softened, angry brows melding into compassion. 'You happened to them. It's why I am so angry with you.'

'Oh, so you *are* pissed at me?'

'Most definitely.'

'We were fine when we talked on the phone last.'

'There has been a major change since then.'

I pulled his hands from my face and sat down on the edge of his bed. 'If this has something to do with what Lucas said downstairs then I—'

'Don't you dare take it back,' he chided. 'I've waited too damn long to hear it.'

'So what now? You're pissed at me because I have those feelings for you?'

Sebastian reached out, gripping the bedpost and crushing it like a dried twig until there was nothing left but dust. 'I'm angry because I had to hear it come from your brother's mouth.

I'm angry because everyone else seems to have known the truth before I did.' He grabbed the remaining bedpost, snapped it off at the base and hurtled it across the room, sending it flying through the open French doors.

'I didn't tell you because I wasn't ready.'

He was livid again. 'So it's okay for you to discuss your feelings with everyone else, including my friends downstairs who coincidentally congratulated me on scoring with the boss's daughter?' His fingers curled into fists and his eyes began to glow. 'Not to mention other insights you have provided them with.'

'Okay, that's just gross and what insights are you referring to?'

His gaze nearly ripped me apart. 'I think you know.'

'You can blame Araqiel for that.'

'So you know?'

'So it's true?'

He shook his head. 'I wanted you to know who and what I am, but I also wanted to hear how you felt from your own lips.'

'What do you want me to say, Sebastian? The others finding out was not my intention. I was cornered and the words just came out.'

'What words?'

I shrugged. 'You know what I'm talking about.'

'I want to hear you say it.'

I folded my hands across my chest, all defiance. The posture was a challenge to maintain as he put hands on either side of the bed next to me, leaning close. My heart skipped a beat and I'd started to sweat even in the cold. Judging by the smirk on his face, he knew the effect he had on me.

'Why must you always play this game?' he said, lips only an inch or two from mine.

'What game?' I answered, trying hard to catch my breath and calm my racing heart.

'The game where you pretend that you are impervious to any real emotions. It's time to act like a grown up and admit what you feel.'

'Why? So I look like an idiot for falling for a bloody Archangel?' I jabbed him in the chest. 'Why don't you tell me how *you* feel? It's not like we've ever had *that* conversation before—like so many conversations you've apparently skipped over.'

He leaned forward just that little bit further, forcing me to slip backwards and have to brace myself. 'You want to know how I feel about you?'

'Sure. Let's lay your emotions bare and see how you feel.'

Sebastian leant so far forward that I was forced back into a horizontal position, his weight now settled above me. 'Okay, I'll tell you.'

'Go on then.'

'I need something from you first.'

I rolled my eyes. 'Of course you do. What is it?'

He settled his thighs on either side of mine and pressed himself against me. I couldn't even describe the impact his positioning had on my underwear. 'I need a kiss.'

I laughed. 'And you think I'm the game player.'

'If you kiss me, Elena, I'll tell you exactly how I feel.'

'This happens every single time, you know.'

His warm breath—uncharacteristic in vampires, but common with Archangels—settled across my slightly parted lips 'What does?'

'The minute we get remotely close to honesty; you have to find a way to deflect.'

Sebastian chuckled low in his throat. He rested his cheek against mine, lips touching the side of my fleshy lobe. 'Isn't that what you are doing now?'

I shuddered as his tongue darted out to trace the tender skin. 'I don't want to tell you how I feel because I want to make sure that my feelings are for someone I can trust.'

Sebastian pulled back, brow furrowing. 'You don't trust me?'

'In the end Sebastian, I don't even really know you.'

'How can you say that? What you feel is the truth.'

'The truth? Seriously? When were you going to tell me you had wings?'

'It is irrelevant. What I am has no bearing on how we feel about each other.'

Another deflective answer.

'Then I'm not discussing this any further.'

Sebastian flipped the switch to outraged. 'So even though everyone else heard you say you love me you won't speak of it?'

'Not until I know everything about you—everything you've kept from me.'

'So let's talk now.'

'I thought you said we didn't have time?'

Sebastian cursed. 'You're right. Your father needs us.'

I rescued my hands from under our combined weight and placed them on his shoulders, resisting the urge to trace fingertips across his collar bone. 'So get off me.'

'I'm not sure I want to.'

Honestly, I don't want you to either.

'Regardless, it's time.'

Sebastian groaned and rolled away. 'I can't keep going on like this.'

'Me neither.'

He shook his head again. 'What is wrong with us?'

I stood, reaching out to take his hand in mine; warm and soft and large enough to envelope my own. 'What's wrong with us, Sebastian, is the space in between.'

He sighed. 'We really do need to talk, don't we?'

'Yeah, we do.'

Sebastian dropped my hand and stroked the smooth skin of my cheek. 'Promise me that you'll be careful tonight. Promise me that you won't do anything stupid to get yourself killed.'

It was a strange change of subject, but I went with it. 'I'll try not to get killed, but I can't make promises about not doing anything stupid. You know it's kind of like second nature to me.'

'If you are in doubt, just run. Protect yourself and protect Lucas; don't worry about the rest of us.'

'Is it really that bad out there?'

'It's not good. Something is wrong about all of this.'

I touched his hand gingerly. 'Make sure you take care of yourself too.'

He smiled at me, lowering his hand. 'I always do.'

I turned my back on him and headed for the door. It was the safest option given that all I wanted to do was throw myself at him and spend the next few days making out until I needed to come up for air. The problem was, I needed to know who I was in love with. Was it Sebastian, the arrogant and seductive vampire that I had come to know? Or was it the Archangel Michael that had boxed Lucifer in hell and constantly watched over me in every cycle of life?

'Where are you going?' Sebastian asked me.

'I don't know.'

'Then don't leave just yet.'

I fingered the doorknob, twisting it in my grip until the door cracked open. Outside the sound of silence greeted me. Perhaps I should have left, let sleeping dogs lie, but I had to know. I rested my head against the jamb and rolled back around to look at him. He said nothing, just stood there, eyes now glowing silver, marking him as the angel we all suspected him to be.

'Michael?'

'Yes, Elena?'

That settled it. Sebastian had answered to the name Michael. Unconsciously or not he'd revealed himself to me—the first step to understanding who and what he was.

I smiled, suddenly more confused than ever before, but also more sure of him and of us. I was in love with an angel. Stranger things have happened and probably still would, but for now I could wait. 'It's nothing, Sebastian. I'll see you downstairs.'

CHAPTER TWENTY-ONE: SCENTS

Sebastian's eyes searched the night like a hungry predator tracking his prey. Ever vigilant in his study of the horizon, my human eyes were unable to find focus. He ducked left and right to avoid oncoming obstacles—invisible to anyone but a supernatural being. His powerful jaw and the column of his throat were visibly tense and tightly-clenched teeth emphasised tendons and blood vessels pressing against the surface of his skin. His usually soft, full lips were set in a thin line as his body pushed speed barriers; mine debated the dependency of skin, the wind a punishment I was forced to endure.

His eyes had lost their sparkle; the silver gone from their depths completely. They had turned black; reminiscent of his vampiric form—a persona I was now struggling to understand given the halo. The biggest mystery: why choose to be a vampire when you're already an angel?

Had I been disapproving of his angelic nature in the past or did it come back to those stupid rules Sebastian harped on about? Why choose darkness over light given the repercussions of this existence?

Watching from the crook of his arm, wind whipped through his hair, pushing it from his face and highlighting perfect cheekbones. He had a chiselled jaw meant to be nibbled on and lips made solely for kissing. I should have known he couldn't have been a

269

vampire—vampires were super-hot, but Sebastian was off the Richter scale.

New question: why the hell was the Archangel Michael so interested in me?

I'll admit I'm not ugly, but I don't think I'm Cindy Crawford. I have a great body and really nice skin, but my legs are too long—much like a Praying Mantis. My teeth are straight and white, but my smile is definitely crooked. My hair is long and soft, but almost always untended—reminiscent of a bird's nest. My lips are too plump, my fingernails almost always chipped and broken. I snort if I laugh too hard and swearing like a trooper is just a highlight. I also think my boobs are too small even though a handful is considered more than enough, but since I have small hands, I find that truly depressing.

The point is, he's an angel and I'm just me; Elena Manory— emotionally retarded dickhead extraordinaire with a really great ass. Whoop-dee-fricken-doo.

'You seem distracted,' Sebastian observed. His hair blew across his face, momentarily covering his coal black eyes from me.

'I'm just thinking.'

'What were you thinking about?'

'Parliamentary affairs.'

'You were not.'

'Land taxes?'

'Not even close.'

'Brazilians?'

'Nuts, country or the wax job?'

'I don't know, you choose.'

He grinned. 'I'll take the latter.'

'You're a pervert.'

He laughed. 'Hey, these are your thoughts we are discussing.'

'I'm not so sure anymore.'

Lucas and Thomas ran past; a welcome distraction. I had thought about telling Sebastian what was really on my mind, but decided it wasn't the time. Plus, with Lucas screaming like a little girl again, there was no way to have a serious conversation.

'Your brother seems interesting,' Sebastian commented.

I liked his choice of words. 'He's that and a little bit more.'

'He doesn't appear to enjoy the benefits of vampiric speed.'

'I'm not a fan either, you know.'

'You're not complaining.'

'I've had worse.'

There was a lengthy pause; Lucas told Thomas he was a parasite who was going to get him killed.

'Has he changed much since you saw him last?' Sebastian queried.

I attempted a nod, forgetting my head waged war with oncoming winds and execution of any gesture was a waste of time. 'He was skinny and nonthreatening before and now he's taller, bulked up and shaved all his long blonde hair off. He seems harder too.'

'What do you mean?'

'It's as if the whole situation has taken some of his innocence. He may be my big brother, but I've always had to take care of him. I'm not so sure that's the case anymore.'

'From what I gather he's been through quite an ordeal. He seems pretty together for someone who has been experimented on and had his parents betray him. He's had to grow up—work things out for himself. The fact that he's trying to move forward makes a bold statement that he's simply become an adult accepting of his circumstances.'

I felt the wind smear one of my escaped tears across my cheek. 'It doesn't seem fair. I had all of you to help me.'

'You had no one when Roshan took you,' he reminded me. 'Elena, even you have grown since I met you. Life has a funny way of changing us.'

'I'm just worried he's turning into me.'

Sebastian frowned. 'That's not exactly a bad thing, Elena. You've proven that your dual natures can be controlled. Lucas will be the same.'

I sniffed. 'I think he's worried about what my blood has done to him. I don't want him to resent me.'

'That will never happen. It's obvious to all of us just how loyal you two are to one another.'

'Do you think?'

'He wouldn't have stayed with the IMI so long and endured what he did if he wasn't loyal. And, you wouldn't have defied your father, flew across the globe twice and run head-first into a dangerous situation if you didn't think he was worth it. We could all benefit from the lesson that you two unknowingly teach.'

'Thanks, Sebastian.'

'No problem.'

We stopped talking for a while, the effort to shout above the wind somewhat tiresome. Doubt niggled at me again. 'Do you know that Lucas can control his powers with his mind now?'

'We spoke a little on the phone while you were held captive by Roshan. He was starting to perfect certain skills then, but yes, I have since been informed of his ... gifts.'

'That's not a Protector trait. My blood has given him telekinesis.'

'Are you sure?'

'Lucas said when we were kids I bit him during a scuffle and then fed. I killed him, Sebastian.'

'But they resuscitated him?'

'Yes, but with my transfused blood inside him.'

Sebastian sighed, re-adjusting my positioning. 'You are a direct descendant of Lucius. The fact Lucas died and was revived with your blood could certainly be the reason things are happening to him now.'

'Why now? Why not then?'

'There could be a number of reasons: sexual peak, puberty, a traumatic event. It could even be in the mind. Let's face it, your abilities grow the more you practice. Perhaps Lucas focusing solely on his training at the IMI and perfecting his craft has unlocked this latent ability.'

I chewed my lower lip, frowning. 'I had blood exchanges in order for that to occur.'

'Lucas is a magical being, not a supernatural.'

'Plus, he recently turned eighteen.'

'I suspect that only completed the transition. Lucas has probably been gifted his whole life.'

'Maybe it's because he was born of two Protector parents.'

'Perhaps. Your father's blood is the blood of Lucifer. It runs through all vampires' veins and through you—now Lucas. The potential for change is strong and certainly capable of gripping Lucas on his eighteenth birthday as it does for the rest of us.' He looked down at me briefly and smiled. 'He is unique like you.'

Sebastian pulled me tighter against him and picked up the pace. Over his shoulder I caught a glimpse of Karina curled tight in William's arms. Her eyes were squeezed shut and hands knotted into fists in his shirt. She was clearly frightened, but trying to be brave ... unlike Lucas.

William winked at me and then whispered something in Karina's ear to soothe her. His hands cupped her thighs and upper arms gently, his posture reassuring in light of the hastened pace in which he moved. She cracked her eyes a fraction and forced a smile. Envy was still annoyingly present within me.

'Are you really jealous about William and his growing attraction to your friend?' It was as if Sebastian was reading my mind.

'A little.' There was no point lying. I preached about truth and honesty between us, surely Sebastian understood that William and I had a past?

'Do you still have feelings for him?' he asked stiffly.

'William is special. I think he always will be.'

'So you love him.' A bitter statement if ever I'd heard one.

'It's just a word. Words mean nothing without meaning behind them and to be honest, I'm sick of the soul-searching involved.'

Silence for several seconds.

'I will stop asking.'

I rolled my eyes. 'Don't pretend you didn't hear our conversation earlier.'

His lips twitched ever so slightly. 'So strictly friends hence forth?'

'Here's hoping.'

Sebastian gave me a wry look.

'It's going to be awkward between us for a few years, but friends is all we can be.'

Seemingly satisfied he said, 'Could you ever just be friends with me?'

'It's complicated.'

'Until we talk.'

'Yes—until we talk.'

'When did you know that you had fallen—'

'Careful,' I interrupted.

He paused, now grinning. 'When did you know you had succumbed to my charms?'

I made a face, secretly delighted we were bantering like old times. 'Who said you're charming?'

'Humour me.'

I took a deep breath, deciding to *humour* my dark warrior. Tonight could be the end of us all and I'd never get a chance to tell Sebastian that I cared. I was not about to profess my undying love, but I'd remind him that his kindness and protective nature had not gone unnoticed or underappreciated.

'Okay,' I said, drawing on that breath again. I felt so silly, like a bumbling idiot and I'd barely said a word yet. 'I think from the onset I knew that ... I mean knew you were ... are ... have always been in my—'

Dreams.

'Thoughts?'

'Sure, thoughts.'

'I thought I might have breached your defences when I kissed you for the first time.'

I thought back to that moment on a darkened street corner in Cairns when he'd made my heart stop and my legs quake. It was the best and most surprising kiss ever and I'd do it again in a heartbeat. 'It wasn't the kiss.'

'Perhaps I need more practice?'

I didn't want to stroke his ego too much. 'Maybe.'

He shuffled me around again, holding me closer to him. 'You better hold on tight now, I'm going to jump.'

A second later Sebastian left solid ground. Air rushed over me like a blanket of steel, plastering hair to my head and stealing breath. As my stomach leapt into my mouth, the pressure altered and we were sailing downwards again, falling back to earth. My hair became a shiny cape, my eyes fighting to stay closed. My lips were somewhere near my cheekbones and I think I swallowed a damn bug.

We landed soon after, connecting with the pavement with calculated precision. I barely felt the jolt of impact. William and Karina landed thereafter, Karina cradled carefully in his embrace— an improvement on his past efforts. He whispered in her ear it was all over; she opened her eyes. He was so close yet still so comfortable with her proximity that it got me thinking.

'Tell me something,' I said to William as Sebastian set me down. 'How is it that Karina's scent doesn't entice you?'

'She is a Protector.' He looked at her and smiled. 'Their blood smells unappetising, possibly something to do with their magic.'

'That's convenient,' I muttered.

'Well I'm glad,' Karina answered, relinquishing her grip on his shirt as he to set her down. She took a quick inhalation of her asthma puffer. I'd forgotten she required the device. 'It would have *sucked* if you kept trying to bite me.' She giggled. 'Get it? *Sucked?*'

William politely chuckled. I looked away so she wouldn't see my eye roll.

'Ahhhhhhhhh!'

Marianne, Eric, Caleb and Nicholas landed with ease behind us. A fast approaching and especially vocal blur known as my dumb-ass brother, landed with Thomas a second after that. Lucas fell off Thomas's back, knees hitting the pavement a second before the entire contents of his stomach were relieved.

'Sick,' Caleb muttered, side-stepping the foul-smelling muck. 'I've never heard so much screaming from a human male in all of my life.'

'Surely that cannot be true?' Marianne flashed pointed canines and smiled. 'After all, we are predators.'

Caleb scoffed. 'Even before the ban on human feedings, I never did like to play with my food.'

Lucas retched again, slowly climbing to his feet when done. He looked positively pale as he wiped his mouth with the back of his hand. 'Cop me a freaking break,' he muttered. 'I usually drive cars and catch buses like normal pe—'

'Quiet' Sebastian hissed.

It wasn't Sebastian's admonishment that silenced us, but our sudden attention to the scene before us. Nicholas and Eric observed in stony silence. Marianne stood next to Karina, open-mouthed. William and Sebastian stood on either side of Lucas while Caleb cursed.

We'd all been distracted by ridiculousness until now.

'This is a disaster,' Marianne said, stepping beside me.

'I didn't realise there were so many.'

'We're too late,' Eric murmured.

'I fear you may be right,' Nicholas agreed. 'This was not part of the plan.'

Lucas exhaled loudly, his breath marred with the stench of sickness. 'Good, because I had no idea what you were hoping I could do with ... *this.*'

I took a good look at '*this*' and tried to disregard the hopelessness of the situation. There were bodies everywhere;

vampiric, human and vânător. To top it off, the sprawling city of Milan with its bustling nightlife, packed restaurants and shopping delights were quite literally alight with the glow of looter's fires. The sound of screaming, howling and crackling debris accompanied the picture of a once safe metropolitan city burning alive.

'I don't think we can fix this,' Sebastian murmured. 'People have already seen the Vampires and the Werewolves. The rest of the world undoubtedly knows what has happened here too.' The point was made when a group of teenage boys took happy snaps of the supernatural entities lying dead in the street.

'So what do we do now?'

'The only thing that we can do—fight.' Sebastian took my hand and squeezed it tight. 'Can I talk to you for a minute? We may not have much time left.'

I nodded, slipping my fingers through his. The others rallied to devise a strategy for attack while Sebastian pulled me down a side street hidden from view. 'Do you remember what I said earlier?'

'Don't get killed. Don't do anything stupid.'

'Right.' He was clearly agitated, something playing on his mind.

'What's wrong? Well, besides the obvious ...'

'I have a bad feeling about tonight. Something tells me I shouldn't have brought you here.'

'As if I'd stay home with Marcus.'

He didn't smile like I thought he might.

Deep breaths Elena, you can say it.

'Look, relax. Nothing is going to happen to me because I'm pretty sure I have an Archangel watching over me.'

He stiffened, undoubtedly pressed to say something equally ambiguous, but I stopped him by pressing a finger to his lips. 'Don't say anything. Don't ruin what I already know with one of your agendas aimed at deflection.'

We stared into each other's eyes for the longest time, my finger still resting on his lips. I was trembling, unease skating across the surface of my skin, chipping at the bravado I'd built.

Sebastian brushed shaky fingers through my hair, settling the palm of his hand against my cheek, caress tender. He kissed the finger I still pressed to his lips, nibbling the tip before moving my hand so he could speak. I fought the urge to close my eyes and lean into him. It would be so easy to succumb to this moment of intimacy.

Sebastian's lips parted and I retreated, once again surprising him into silence. 'Look after yourself, Michael,' I said, squeezing the hand that cupped my cheek. 'I'll see you on the other side.'

Before he could mutter a single word, I hastily kissed him, savouring the feel of his mouth, the smell of his essence and the warmth of his skin. I relished that chaste kiss like my life depended on it and then shattered the moment, taking leave before he second-guessed my next move.

'Elena!' he yelled after me. 'Where are you going?'

He could have caught me, stopped me in my tracks, but I suspected he knew where I was headed and what I had to do. We each had our own paths and Sebastian knew mine was tied to the Vânătors. As much as I wanted to fall into his arms and share words always unspoken between us, I wanted my life back more. The only way that would happen was to kill the last alpha— Roshan.

I ran as fast as my legs could carry me, hoping to save my conscious mind from the lure Roshan's scent held. He was so close I could almost taste his breath on my tongue. I would not stop until I had control—until I could turn the tables.

'Lucas, we're leaving,' I yelled as I ran past the group, signalling for him to follow.

He was slow on the take-off, stumbling over his own feet, clearly confused by the abrupt change in plans.

'What about us?' Caleb shouted after us.

'Fight!' I yelled back.

Lucas attempted to stop me, hurling questions about our separation from the group, but I was on a mission. 'What has gotten into you?'

'The urge for retribution.'

'Hey! Where are you two going?' Marianne said, materialising beside us, jogging to keep pace.

'The fight's that way,' I said, pointing behind us. 'We'll kill more if we split up.'

She couldn't argue logic so gave a reluctant nod despite her pouty lips arguing without further question.

'Make sure William looks out for Karina. I'm not sure what she's like under pressure.'

'You sound like you're saying goodbye, Elena.' She looked to Lucas, fear momentarily clouding her eyes. 'We should come with you.'

'No ... I ...' How could I explain that there was no one I trusted more or wanted at my back than my brother. The others would watch over us, but would they die for us? The simple and most honest answer was probably no.

'This is madness, Elena,' Marianne chided. I had to get rid of her soon, her questions were many and our enemies legion.

'I have my reasons.'

'I'd like to hear them,' Lucas shouted from the left.

I shook my head. 'Just tell everyone that if they encounter a big black wolf tonight, don't kill it, it's probably me.'

'I get the feeling you're about to do something stupid.'

'No, Marianne. I'm doing what I should have done in Paris. Now go back to the others and let Karina help you.'

She clucked her tongue, disapproval dripping from every pore. 'You're going to get yourself killed.' She gave Lucas one last lingering look and then broke away, presumably returning to the others.

'So what *is* the plan?' Lucas asked, now keeping pace.

'I haven't got one.'

Lucas snorted. 'Typical. At least if we'd stayed with the others we might—'

His words were lost between his lips and God's ears; a vânător leapt from a side street in front of us and crushed admonishment in its tracks. I barely had a chance to whip out my fangs; Lucas had already thrown him through a brick wall and brought a house down on top of him.

'Impressive,' I remarked. His reflexive instinct and magical defence were stunning examples of his recent acquirements.

'Let's not get too ahead of ourselves.'

'I'm not, but I know now we can definitely do this by ourselves.'

'Do what?'

'Kill Roshan.'

His face dropped, expression gutted.

'We are running blindly around a foreign city littered with werewolves and you're telling me we're going to kill the Alpha?

You've always been reckless, but I really don't want to die after just escaping the IMI.'

I sniffed, uncertain how to react or feel regarding his lack of confidence in us. 'You can protect yourself better than anyone; you won't die.'

Lucas forced me to stop running, gripped my chin and urged me to look at him. His eyes were narrowed slits, too aware of my now quivering jaw and trembling lips. 'Then why are you so scared?'

I wrestled free and kept walking, desperate to avoid his scrutiny during my rattled state. The prospect of a showdown with Roshan scared me, but was an inevitability. To be defeated, forced back to his den and ordered to submit to his every whim made me physically ill. Roshan was my Kryptonite—my weakness. Human or vampiric, his scent called to me. Only in wolf form was I invulnerable, but in wolf form I was also at my most dangerous and unpredictable. That's why I'd chosen Lucas to help; the only one who could shield himself against *me*.

'Elena, wait,' Lucas muttered, jogging to catch up and resigned to whatever fate awaited. As always, I admired his bravery in the face of adversity.

Roshan was so close now that he'd become a shadow—a stain of overwhelming darkness. The essence of raw earth, sweat and pheromones sung to my wolf soul like no other. It bent and transformed my will to resemble theirs and I hungered for the feel of a pack I had every intention of killing.

I wondered if he felt me too.

Several more wolves slinked into the street around us, their footfalls almost impossible to hear in the war-ravaged city. For a brief moment I considered us out of our depth. Outnumbered by at least four, Lucas dispatched them as quickly and efficiently as the last one—minus the structural damage. I attempted his creativity for killing and tried to wrap one around a bus stop. It wasn't as formidable as dropping a house on its head, but it did the job.

I grabbed onto Lucas the second we appeared alone, pulling him close and whispering in his ear. 'It's Roshan.'

'What about him?'

'He's close.'

'What about the others?'

'They're safe. If he's trying to avoid detection and find me, he will try to avoid all of them.'

'Are you strong enough to kill him? Because if he locks onto my scent and decides I'm as big a risk as a vampire, you could be on your own.'

I grimaced. 'I might be if I could resist his scent.'

'Great. So if we find the guy, you're going to be useless?'

'Until I turn vânător. Then his alpha sway doesn't work on me, but it's difficult to shape-shift. I have to be in the right frame of mind to do it. Then if I can do it and I can resist Roshan, we end up encountering problem number two.'

Lucas sighed. 'And that is?'

'Well, I think if I kill Roshan—given past alpha deaths and vânător reactions—I might be incapacitated for a while or die, but I think that's a remote possibility.'

'I'm not liking this plan of yours, Elena.'

'You're the only one who can help. If I can't control myself after the shape-shift, I might try killing more than Roshan. It's why I wanted to get away from the others. I can't be trusted. I hunger for all blood, Lucas, not just human.'

'So it's okay that I get shred to pieces?'

I punched his shoulder, marvelling at how he didn't collapse or whinge about my heavy-handed touch. He really had changed. 'You can shield yourself telekinetically, levitate, blind me and turn me to stone. I think you have this one covered, Lucas.'

At least he was nodding now. 'Okay, so what's the plan? Find Roshan? Then what?'

'Well, you're not going to like it, but you have to let him toy with me for a bit. I need to get angry so I can shape-shift.'

Lucas scoffed, crossing his arms over his chest. 'You think I'll let that happen?'

I nodded. 'Lucas, we can't lose this good opportunity to kill the last alpha standing.'

'You're asking a lot of me; watch my sister play bull rush with a werewolf and neither of us get eaten.'

'I know.'

He sighed again, uncrossing his arms to pull me in for a quick hug. 'Okay, E. Let's do it your way, but if I see something I don't agree with, I'm going to kill him myself.'

I hugged him back, burying my face against his burly chest, marvelling at how he'd developed. 'I would prefer to kill Roshan, but at least I know you can cream him with an apartment building if need be.'

He patted the top of my head. 'Fine. You can kill the big bad wolf, but like I said—'

'I know. You'll kill him if things get rough. Thanks, Lucas.'

He squeezed me one last time and then released me. 'You know; I have a feeling everything will change after tonight.'

I forced a smile as we started walking again. 'Everything will be fine.'

'How can you be sure?'

'It can't be any worse than the mess I left at home.' I was lying through my teeth.

'Marcus?'

I laughed. 'Oh yeah. I have some serious apologising to do.'

Lucas scoffed, shocked. 'You? Apologising? Shit, this I have to see.'

'Then we better hurry up, kill the Alpha, win the war and hurry home.'

Lucas continued to grin. 'Not asking for much, are you?'

I laughed, so nervous I could throw up. 'All in a night's work.'

CHAPTER TWENTY-TWO: DONE DEAL

Araqiel closed his eyes, waiting for emotion to claim him. He expected some semblance of the humanity he'd witnessed over the millennia to take hold and squeeze his heart with pain or fill his eyes with moisture, but there was nothing. All that lingered was the calm before the storm; a stiff breeze tousled his long blonde hair and the sun above warmed his angelic skin.

When he opened his eyes he looked at his hands; fingers curled around an ancient piece of parchment held by the Seal of the Fates and accompanied by the Quill of Destiny. The Time Contract had existed since the sands of time; fought over by good and evil for a chance to change the past and re-write the future in either image. Now the hands of light held the contract for the first time in over two millennia and it was all his doing.

Araqiel was torn in more ways than one; not by guilt, remorse or happiness, just an understanding that his choices had led him to this moment—a moment he had to choose between the fate of all humanity and a brother he held in high regard.

Michael.

The Archangel was scheduled to die; his reign on earth ending indefinitely; his last chance of incarnation dashed and future prospects of escaping Purgatory grim. Lucifer now knew Michael lingered in the human realm and was willing to hand over the Time Contract in exchange for Michael's life.

Araqiel had signed on the dotted line, sealed his brother's fate and hoped Michael would one day soon understand that with events as they stood, this was the only way.

'You have the Time Contract, Araqiel. Why do you linger?' Nakir asked.

Araqiel studied the angelic council member, judgement absent in his inquisitive eyes. Was it possible that his kin finally saw the bigger picture—the role Elena would play and Michael's key to ultimate freedom?

'I'm thinking of my choices.'

'It's a little late to think through alternatives, my brother. You have sealed Michael's fate. He will never again walk the earth and he will never leave Purgatory. Heaven is but a distant and impossible dream for him now.'

'Perhaps,' Araqiel answered, certain they were still unaware and that explaining his complete plan would only serve to promote further scepticism. 'Michael will understand what I've done eventually.'

'Not even we—the council members—understand your reasoning, Araqiel. Our father—as you know—is also baffled by this choice. You tread a very dangerous line between light and dark.'

'My intentions are only for the greater good.'

'Yes, but what evil must you perform in order to achieve your goals?'

Araqiel countered. 'I risk all that we are on the goodness of the human spirit. It is mankind that has the power to change darkness into light and darkness will be conquered by beasts of their own making.'

Samael—one of the demonic council members eavesdropping—snorted, saliva spraying from his whiskered snout. 'You dare to threaten us in this place of neutrality?'

'I make no threats,' Araqiel rationalised, 'I make promises. You will soon see light triumph even if darkness must reign first.'

Samael slammed his slimy fists against the table. 'You may have the Time Contract, angel, but it does not alter the darkness of the human condition. You can turn back the clock to the beginning of time and you will still find humans that beg for our favour.'

'I do not dispute the unpredictability of human nature, but you do underestimate their finer qualities.'

'You speak of love,' Nakir murmured.

'Love!' Samael spat. 'What a ridiculous sentiment! You are hoping to use the Time Contract based on a decision stemming from love?' He started to laugh, his goat head bouncing like a dashboard monument. 'Then we have made a worthwhile deal. Only pain comes from loving someone.'

Araqiel shrugged, avoiding the crimson eyes still looking upon him with abject loathing. 'I agree that our deal is worthwhile.'

'Now,' Mammon interrupted, eyes narrowed and red skin glistening with sweat, 'Is everything in place?' He swept his tail from side to side, its forked end brushing the rough ground at their feet like a tattered old broom.

Both angelic council members Nakir and Munkar bowed their heads. They had no desire to witness this conversation, yet bound to ensure fairness amongst them. Both angels were firm believers in steering clear of human affairs. Purgatory was run with neutrality—the place where fate was decided after a life ended. Mammon and Samael were not so. They enjoyed messing with fate and those in the human realm, persuading borderline souls towards moral corruption. There were so many easily consumed by the lure of darkness.

'Before I give you Michael's exact location, I must know how you plan to kill him.'

'Kill him?'

'Do not play coy, demons. I have the Time Contract, but if you plan on torturing my brother, I will hand it back and the deal will be off.'

Mammon growled, snapping his fingers. A second later a vampire appeared. He shook his head, confused and guarded by the disruption. He'd been elsewhere a second ago and now stood before five strange entities in a place of unknowns. Three moons marked the sky above him and the whisper of prevailing winds sent shivers across skin previously impervious to weather. 'What is this?' he commanded, now clearly overwhelmed. 'Where am I and who are you?'

Mammon snapped his fingers again and the vampire was instantly transported by magic unknown to his side. His already pale skin turned ashen, his hands trembling. He had no idea where he was or who he was dealing with. 'Stay still,' Mammon commanded of him.

'Who are you?' the Vampire asked once more, his bravado returning slowly, caution still guarding his actions.

'Hold your tongue,' Samael ordered.

The Vampire rubbed fingers across his eyes, perhaps uncertain to his current state of existence. Staring at Samael, his disbelief was evident and assumptions he'd been slain during the war now growing. Where else would he encounter beasts with hooves and mostly human bodies slicked with sweat and stained with blood but the hellish depths of the underworld. And the all-white beings sitting adjacent? The Vampire couldn't conceive this a reality.

'What is this?' Araqiel asked, leaning across the table to get a closer look at the visitor. He was glad he had not left immediately after receiving the contract. He should have known the demons would play a secondary hand and he was not unfamiliar with the vampire they'd summoned. His name was Julius; enemy of Lucius Valerius and a vampire interested in the bloodied death of Elena and her friends.

'This is our champion,' Mammon answered, licking his lips. 'He seeks revenge on his own kin, seeks to rule the human world and paint it with blood. Who better to kill Michael?'

'No,' Araqiel said, shaking his head. 'This vampire started the war and is driven by inner conflict.'

'Who are you?' Julius asked, studying each council member critically.

'I said, hold your tongue!' Samael hacked, threw his head back and spat a thick globule of drool onto the vampire's face. It rolled across his cheek, moving rapidly until it formed a tight seal across his lips. Julius began to pull at the impenetrable barrier, his fingers searching to pry it loose—to no avail.

'That's better,' Mammon gloated, slapping Julius across the back. 'Now listen to what we have to say.'

'We have summoned you,' Samael cut in, 'to kill the Archangel Michael.'

Julius's eyes widened. He was entirely uncertain of the mixed group and the reasons he'd been embroiled in this gathering. What quarrel did he have with an Archangel?

Araqiel prayed for strength and patience. 'This vampire knows not of our existence or our struggles. He has his own agenda—'

'You will not talk your way out of this, Araqiel. We have waited patiently and honoured the deal. You have the Time Contract, now give us Michael's location and let us be done with this.'

'It is not that simple.'

Mammon whipped his knife-like tail and slashed the bondage capturing Julius's lips. 'Do you want to kill the Archangel Michael?'

Julius wiped the residual filth from his mouth, glaring at Samael. 'I fear I am delusional at present. It has been some time since I fed and I think it is possible that I am seeing things.'

'This is no dream,' Mammon answered. 'You are in the presence of your brothers—demons from hell. We have a task we know you will perform well.'

Julius locked gazes with Araqiel, curiosity present. A cursory glance at the bowed heads of Nakir and Munkar soon followed. 'I have no quarrel with an angel.'

Araqiel smiled at the well-considered response and neutral request of position. Why would the vampire get involved? Samael and Mammon's grunt of disgust served to further fuel Araqiel's amusement. 'If you do not convince this minion to kill Michael,' Mammon snapped, 'then we shall send something far worse than a vampire to complete the task.'

Knowing what other creatures Lucifer kept in the fiery pits of hell, it was truly a small mercy to be offered death by this vampire. The question begged: how could Araqiel twist this change in plot to his advantage? 'What compensation do you seek in order to complete this task?' Araqiel asked Julius.

Julius didn't hesitate. 'Revenge, but again, who are you and why have I been selected to kill a being whose existence has been fictional until now?'

'Your questions, thoughts and opinions are irrelevant,' Samael snapped. 'We are the council members of Purgatory and our request is not a pleasantry. Unless you wish your meaningless existence to end here and now, you will shut up and do as directed.'

Araqiel wasn't stupid and knew that the resolute and defiant part of Julius would carve his own path when let loose again and thus continued his questioning in order to achieve the best result for *his* ultimate plan.

'You want revenge against Lucius Valerius?' It was an obvious choice given their history and Julius's manoeuvring of the Vânätors into combat against the covens.

287

'Yes. He has been the bane of my existence.'

'What is happening here?' Samael chided, narrowed eyes darting back and forth.

Araqiel shushed the nosey demon. 'You have chosen your champion; it's my right to question his intentions as the holder of the contract to ensure the job will be done right.'

Samael and Mammon growled once more, irritated by the angel's thoroughness and unending quest to turn every agenda whether touched by light or shadowed by dark into his advantage.

Araqiel continued to ignore their feeble attempts at distraction. 'Lucius is unique in his ability to cheat death; however, it's possible to kill Sebastian Marcellus, but you must leave Elena Manory alone.'

Julius pulled a face, human in its contortion of annoyance. 'I must have my vengeance! Lucius took my wife, robbed all vampires of the life we deserve and thus I will take from him what he values the most—his beloved daughter. I care not to hunt for this ... Michael you speak of.'

'To punish Lucius you wish to kill Elena and Sebastian?'

'I care not whether Michael, Sebastian ... anyone else lives or dies. I only hunt Elena.'

'You cannot kill Elena ... at least not yet.'

'What?!' the angles cried in unison. 'The contract was for Michael!'

Samael and Mammon looked equally perplexed.

Araqiel had no time for patience or in-depth explanation of his reasoning.

'So I can kill Elena, but not yet? Julius pressed. He still had not drawn his own conclusions and neither had the stupid demons—small mercies.

'These are my terms. If you wish your vengeance, then kill Sebastian and take your leave. I will come to you at the moment when you may pursue your ultimate end game—killing Elena Manory, but if you take matters into your own hands before then—I will kill you myself.'

'And if I refuse?'

'Do you really want to cross any of us?' Araqiel said gesturing to everyone seated at the table.

Samael solidified the point by roaring in anger and Mammon slammed his fists on the table top once more, the surface groaning in protest. 'We do not hunt Sebastian!' Samael yelled. 'We are after Michael! Why do you beg such nonsense?'

Nakir—particularly quiet until this moment—raised his head, a single tear rolling down his cheek. Araqiel hoped that understanding was finally upon him, but it seemed that uncertainty still covered his innocence like a blanket. 'Sebastian *is* the Archangel Michael.'

Everything stilled; Purgatory became a deafening silence that roared within everyone's ears. The breeze ceased to tousle Araqiel's hair and the moons above forgot to shine for but a second, plunging the realm in a darkness of indescribable uncertainty.

Julius was the first to speak. 'Sebastian Marcellus *is* the Archangel Michael?' The repetitive information did little to alleviate the stunned reactions of all within earshot.

Silence stretched on for a further minute, fate now totally exposed and open to interpretation. When the moons and breeze remembered their place and the lost souls stumbling nearby continued their aimless quest in search of judgement, breath was exhaled and clarity obtained.

'Michael cloaked himself with the very darkness he chose to fight for two millennia. He grows weary of the games and understands that his time has come.' Araqiel's response did not ease Nakir and Munkar's greatest fears.

Mammon had beads of fetid-smelling sweat drip onto the table top and form a putrid puddle. 'He has been under our noses this entire time moonlighting as a vampire?' It wasn't exactly a question, more a statement coated in stunned accusation.

'I accept your deal,' Julius said, surprising everyone present. 'I seek no compensation other than my revenge. I will do as you ask and I will kill Sebastian.'

'And you will wait for my signal in regards to Elena?'

Julius's eyes fluttered, rage barely contained. 'I do not like it, but I will.'

'I do not understand,' Munkar interrupted. 'You have fought tooth and nail to protect this girl. Why now do you seek her death?'

'I do not, but I must prepare for alternatives.'

Samael sneered, irritated he was yet to conclude the finer details of Araqiel's master plan. He detested that intellect had deserted him and thus not solved the angel's desire for the Time Contract,

Michael's exposure or Elena Manory's role, but given his standing of neutrality, he was not to pursue the matter much further.

'What alternatives?' both angels pressed.

Araqiel shrugged and shook the Time Contract within his hand. 'I have had thousands of years to reflect upon my choices; thousands of years to observe humans and the emotions that drive them. I have waited so very long to help change what even the strongest of us had hoped to avoid. Now I have my champion as the darkness has theirs. Time will tell which of us will be victorious in the end.'

'It will not be the light,' Mammon admonished.

Araqiel smiled, light from the three moons above shimmering through the feathers of his slow spreading wings. 'Well, since I do have the Time Contract now, we will see, Demon. We will see.'

CHAPTER TWENTY-THREE: TRAFFIC

Have you ever been witness to a traffic accident? If you haven't, you wouldn't understand what lay before me now—the streets of Milan were a portrait of preventable disaster. Accident—clearly not the right word to describe the carnage around me, but it did offer a clear image of the human condition and current state of affairs. It was a good metaphor representing the choices and impulses during times of tragedy and our actions.

I was facing my fears.

Maybe I'm naive to compare a traffic accident and city-wide bloodshed as relative, but it's only my point of view—a recount of how I view the actions of others and then analyse how mine might differ. For instance, at the beginning of a traffic accident, people at the back caught in the aftermath have no idea what's going on. They sit in their cars, honking horns and scanning radio stations looking for answers via news casts. Most don't care about the cause, only its resolution. It's not wrong to be a bystander, held back by lack of knowledge or motivation. Not knowing offers you little option to move forward, but what if you seek it? What if you look for answers and find them? Do you have the courage to offer help?

Now there are those waiting for traffic to clear; radio stations have been scanned and curiosity is abundant. Some will eventually leave their cars, edge their way closer while others will remain oblivious.

Curiosity grips most of us and concern does take a more permanent hold when hearsay becomes truth. Whether it's war or a traffic accident, carnage is still carnage—people are still people. If you walk through that throng of bystanders and find devastation, action soon speaks louder than words.

I think I make choices beyond the bystander's ambitions and as Lucas and I began to encounter the terrified citizens of Milan running rampant through the streets, I'd already decided I would not stand idle!

Tormented screams came from every direction; the unaffected were confused and cautious and those lucky not to have encountered their nightmares, pulled their collars around their necks and buried hands in their pockets, quickly leaving the scene. People in surrounding houses and businesses closed their doors and turned off the lights, choosing to remain oblivious. Screams from their fellow man, howls from the Wolves and the ear-piercing hisses from the Vampires tortured the night, but they were content to turn away.

I kept judgement in reserve. This was far worse than any traffic accident. The war between supernatural beings had spilled into a world nowhere near ready to accept the mythical creatures immortalised by film, television and books. This was a world happy to keep nightmares unspoken—a world that not more than a week ago, believed terrorists the ultimate enemy.

I did judge The Protectors. They should have been fighting alongside us, making sure that humans were safe. They had turned a blind eye and left us to scramble from the burning wreckage of a war that should never have started. The Protectors had a lot to answer for. They had played us like fiddles in a well-orchestrated show and now the sound of that symphony tore through the night in painful bursts of torment and defeat.

Humanity would never be the same now our secret was out.

Lucas and I increased our pace, jogging towards the city centre where most of the screaming originated and the scent of Roshan was the strongest. I tried to swallow my fear and embrace it, knowing what waited for me in the distance. Every choice I'd made led to this moment and it would culminate tonight.

I jumped, fright gripping me; several vânători leapt over the hood of the car beside us. A foreign object was embedded in one of their teeth, but it wasn't until it was tossed against the wall of a

292

nearby building did I see it was in fact a vampire. Turned and without the abilities of a born vampire, she was badly injured and seriously outnumbered.

Rubble rained upon the ground, collecting on the pavement around the vampire as she struggled to climb back to her feet. Blood was everywhere; her leg looked partially mauled. Not having the ability to self-heal as a born vampire was a detriment; the ten vânători present now circled, sure to end her life quickly.

'Are you ready?' I said to Lucas. 'Things are going to get rough now.'

He flexed his neck muscles. 'Bring it.'

We didn't waste a second longer on pleasantries. We ran full speed towards the Vânători. I used telekinesis to collect stray rubble to hurl with damaging force. It swirled and shot faster than bullets, pounding the side of their heads. Lucas worked on similar techniques using street debris and spells before impaling some on street signs. The kills fell to the ground in piles of fur and blood, but it didn't dissuade the rest of the pack from taking us on.

Stupid.

They forgot about the wounded vampire, focusing their intentions entirely on us. They stalked, muzzles pulled taught to reveal razor sharp fangs coated in blood and bits of torn flesh. On another day I may have been intimidated, but not tonight—tonight I was forced to forget my fears with so much at stake. Lucas obviously felt similar; lips set in a hard line, eyes focused and breathing controlled—all techniques learned with the IMI.

As the Vânători circled, I reached for my Vampiric soul. My fangs lengthened and senses sharpened. This was the first time Lucas had seen me this way. It didn't scare him, but it threw him off guard long enough to be assaulted from behind. He hit the deck hard, but was more than capable of taking care of himself.

My eyes flicked between the grey masses of fur determined to kill us both. Attacking first seemed ideal, so I leapt with calculated precision. I surprised myself how fast I could move, catching the wolf around the throat and slamming him to the ground. Broken bitumen sprayed on impact and ruptured his internal organs as blood spurted from his snout. Death found him in seconds.

Another came thick and fast, but I dodged the attack, grabbed its back paw in mid-flight and swung it like wet washing to connect with the building where the vampire waited. She made light work of him with her talons, finishing him off by tearing out his throat.

The wolf that sneak-attacked Lucas now staggered around blindly. Two others had also stupidly pursued him and were now targets for T.V antennas; they rained from the tops of nearby houses, spearing them one by one. I was concerned by Lucas's talent and flare for original methods of murder.

One attempted a getaway, but tonight I was faster, trapping him down an alley with an inescapable barrier of telekinetic energy. I found him next to a dumpster, clawing at my defences. He turned faster than anticipated, snapping his snout and catching my arm in his vice-like grip.

I cried out, teeth puncturing through to bone. I followed with a punch in the head—right between the eyes. It reverberated through my arm, making me wince, but had the desired effect. His eyes rolled back before he dropped to the ground unconscious, the tension his teeth had on my arm easing enough to pry free.

I then bent down, secured his head between my hands and twisted. What made me angry was the fact I was becoming a proficient killer thanks to these monsters. A year ago I was acting out with my best friend Kayla and hating on boys. Now my innocence had become a word from the past, an echo of the person I used to be.

'Elena!'

I spun, Lucas stood at the entrance to the alley, a scuff mark on his chin and t-shirt covered in dirt and blood, but he was otherwise okay.

'Are you alright?' he said, racing towards me. He quickly assessed my arm. 'That doesn't look so good.'

'I'll be fine. How's the Vampire?'

He shook his head. 'Not good. Her leg is a mess.'

We jogged back to the main street and over to where she leant against the brick wall, a dead vânător in her lap. She looked up, eyes dilating and fangs unsheathing as my blood called to her nature. She licked her lips.

'Don't even think about it,' I scolded. 'If you're thirsty, feed on the wolf. I don't have time to fight you off as well.'

'I'm sorry,' she said, looking away apologetically and plugging her nose. 'It's just that you smell so good.'

I rolled my eyes. 'I know.'

'You should try avoiding further injury,' she murmured. 'I've been practicing restraint for a few centuries, but I can't say the same for other vampires.'

'I'll take my chances.' My arm was almost healed, but it was obvious she was vulnerable to the smell of fresh blood and therefore unpredictable. I kept an eye on her regardless. 'Is there somewhere we can take you? The sun will rise in a few hours. You don't want to be stuck in the open.'

She still held her nose. 'It's just my leg. I will be okay. Go now. Don't waste time with me.'

We offered one last lingering look and then shrugged. We had done all we could here. So we raced along back streets again, bodies were everywhere—humans caught in the crossfire. I had no idea how Lucas and Karina's powers as Protectors would have been able to hide this carnage.

'There are so many bodies,' Lucas noted, jumping over several crowding the pavement. 'When mum and dad first told me I might one day encounter war, I never expected this.'

'Who can expect something like this? It's like a horror movie with no intermission.'

We skidded to a stop, almost taking a tumble as a child sprinted past. She ran as fast as her legs would move, tears streaming down her face and blood soaked clothes. I made motions to go after her—take her somewhere safe, but then saw what she was running from. Up ahead another pack of vânâtors and a few vampires were engaged in battle. They looked like they could still use our help.

Another human shot past; his face a mask of terror. He was suddenly accosted, knocked sideways by another vânâtor who threw him into the next street and bounded after him. I couldn't have saved him even if I wanted to; humans don't bounce after landing on their head.

'Don't let them get away!' one of the Vampires shouted. Three extremely large wolves broke rank ahead and were headed directly for us.

They were upon us in seconds, sniffing warily and analysing our scents. Sharp fangs appeared, but they weren't rearing for attack. Were they scouts for Roshan—otherwise known as the shadows that had been following us?

We lunged; Lucas relied solely on his abilities, rarely having to touch the wolves in combat. I didn't mind getting my hands dirty, but my initial punches were deflected by quick movements I neglected to predict. He moved with the speed and precision of the Vampires and it was difficult to maintain superiority.

I sucked in air tainted by the smell of acrid smoke and blood. I cracked my neck and flexed my muscles, concentrating. Lucas had run ahead to help the other vampires.

The Vânătors he'd dispatched were shish-kebabs on the windscreen wipers of a nearby car. Surely he was running out of ways to skewer a wolf?

My vânător stopped evading me, senses on high alert and aware of what I now conjured. Several cars hovered towards us, telekinesis coming easily now. The vânător was confused by the levitating cars and decidedly wary, but failed to run as I'd expected.

His hackles rose, the hovering vehicles pulling into position directly above him. He dodged left as the first car dropped, pre-empting the movement perfectly. He then moved right—another car crashing at his feet. He now inched forward, getting closer as he ducked and weaved every car that plummeted around him. At arm's length, I seized him by the throat and squeezed, clutching at life. He definitely hadn't seen that one coming.

Front paws left the ground, lashing at my forearms, slicing through flesh and drawing blood. I hissed in pain, but flatly refused to let go; I would heal. He attempted to launch with his rear paws, but thanks to my exchange with one of the Alphas late last year, we were equally matched in strength.

Up ahead, hissing and the dying sound of a howl could be heard—the Vampires and Lucas finishing off the last of the pack. That was nothing compared to my roar of pain as claws suddenly tore open my chest, cleaving it right down the centre. Blood erupted like a cascading inferno of molten agony, eliciting ongoing screams of torment. One hand clutched my chest, holding everything inside—pain, blood and nausea—the other crushed the wolf's oesophagus, the fight leaving him slowly as he gasped and wheezed for breath.

I discarded the furred piece of malevolence, defeated by the pain and revelling in a sick form of pleasure from his timely demise. I now secured both hands to my gaping wounds, waiting to be healed again.

Through blurry, tear-filled eyes I noted the ground by my feet coated in the sweet slickness of my life force—so much of it I expected to attract half the battle to my location. As it was, the nearby vampires edged closer. My scent was everywhere, virtually impossible to resist. Their eyes were black as pitch, skin translucent with blue veins that throbbed with anticipation. It angered me that they could not focus. Thinking about their thirst during such an arduous time seemed selfish and redundant in light of the night's possible outcome.

'Don't come near me!'

'But the blood …' one of them whispered, licking parched lips.

'Lucas, stop them or I will.' I was in no mood to pick and choose my enemies. Roshan was close and I could barely keep my internal organs in situ.

The Vampires were immediately suspended, swimming through the air and trying to find traction where Lucas held them captive.

'How's that?' he asked.

'Great. I need to replenish what I've lost so I can heal quicker. I don't want them sneaking up on me.'

'What are you going to—?'

I'd already buried my fangs in the side of my dead vânător's neck, his still-warm blood oozing into my mouth. Lucas gagged and I drank fast, greedily slurping liquid life-force to fill my veins and repair the damage.

'That's freaking disgusting,' Lucas groaned. 'We've been reunited for two or three days and I've already seen you naked and now carving up a wolf buffet.'

I gasped as I withdrew my fangs, the last of its blood warming my insides. I wiped my mouth, surveying my chest which now was whole, my arms also free of claw damage. I couldn't say the same for my shirt.

'Are we done?' Lucas asked, wrinkling his nose in distaste. 'Can I put the Vampires down or are you going to eat them too?'

'Hilarious. You know, however gross you think it is, it's one hundred times better than Susan's cooking.'

Lucas snorted. 'Eating mud is one hundred times better than eating mum's cooking, but even eating mud is not as disgusting as drinking blood.'

'You just don't know any better.'

'Can we get down now please?' one of the vamps asked.

Lucas rolled his eyes and promptly adhered to their request. Now free of the shackles, they still just stood there, staring at me in morbid fascination.

'What are you?' one questioned.

'I'm Elena Manory—Lucius Valerius's daughter.'

'He doesn't have a daughter.'

'Says you.'

'Smell her blood,' one argued. 'The Valerius line is right there.'

'And what are you?' another asked Lucas.

'I'm the great and powerful Oz.'

'You smell like a Protector, but you also smell like her.' He pointed at me, face blank and words without accusation or hidden meaning. I could have been as exciting as a mid-week sale at the supermarket for all his words implied.

'We need to keep moving,' I interrupted. 'Do any of you have weapons on you?'

'I have a knife,' one answered. He handed it to me, his nose twitching as our proximity intensified.

'Thanks. It might stop me from getting clawed to death next time.'

They all smiled, unconsciously focusing on my bloodstained shirt again. I didn't think it was because of my winning set of cleavage either.

'Has anyone seen Lucius?'

It was a unanimous 'no'.

'He's probably with your coven in the thick of it,' the first one instructed, gesturing behind me. Smoke spiralled in the air; the cries of the wolves strongest in that locale. 'Lucius told most of us to patrol the outskirts and catch strays.' He looked away as if ashamed. 'We're not as well-trained at fighting as some of the older vampires.'

'At least you are here,' I encouraged. 'You could have left, but you didn't. I won't forget your efforts and neither will my father.'

'That's very kind of you,' he answered.

'Hey, thanks for the knife. It's been a while since I had one of these.'

'Keep it.' He flashed his fangs at me. 'I have no real need of it.'

I sheathed it in the top pocket of my jeans and gave him a gander of my own extended fangs. 'Neither do I, but I also don't have switchblades for fingernails.'

The Vampires examined their taloned fingers and started to laugh—a comforting sound in all the madness.

I grinned. 'Keep up the good work and watch your backs.'

Each respectfully inclined their heads and backed away, disappearing into the night.

'Well that was fun,' Lucas muttered. 'You got dinner and I got a show.'

'Will you stop it? I'm a blood drinker. Get over it.'

He mumbled some sort of smart ass comment as we gave chase to our agenda again. Lucas kept pace easily, feet noisily pounding the pavement in comparison to my footfalls. I focused on that slap of rubber, pushing aside mounting fear as the next street across revealed more bodies and several wolves feeding from carcasses. I had no idea if we could take them all at once or be slaughtered trying.

They sensed our approach, perhaps Lucas's elephant stride gave away our position. I clutched my new knife and whispered a silent prayer to the powers that be. Angels were out there—Sebastian and Araqiel proof. Surely one would hear my cry for help as I was fairly certain that an attack from this many vânători wouldn't end well for us. Even with Lucas's new skills, we were outnumbered. Where was Roshan? Why was he avoiding me and seemingly putting so many obstacles in my path? Was he scared to face me again?

The Wolves didn't wait for us to engage, they leapt simultaneously; a lot of sharp teeth were coming our way.

Is it too late to kiss my ass goodbye?

Spinning the blade in my hand to establish a better grip, I soon threw it directly into the eye of the closest one. Its pointed tip pierced through viscous fluid and lodged somewhere entirely too disgusting to describe. The beast went down hard and fast.

The other wolves were not dissuaded. Even as I levitated multiple items of debris to act as weapons—cars, bicycles, fire hydrants, street signs—I could only slow my assailants down. Lucas resorted to old tactics, blinding them and throwing some of them through walls. Others not impeded were upon us only seconds later, throwing us to the ground and snapping their jaws inches from our faces.

Fetid breath wheezed around me as they fought the hierarchal battle to get first bite. I rolled free as two engaged, snapping their teeth and taking swipes at each other's flanks. Another swiped me with his paw, but I caught it, snapping it to the left. He howled and then whimpered, licking his injury. Any wolves not trapped by flying debris, locked in a fight over territory or battling Lucas, immediately isolated me and attacked.

I screamed as appendages were ruptured and tongues greedily lapped at the blood running freely from my open wounds. I had to do something; every second I grew physically incapable. Sooner or later I would turn wolf, capable of overthrowing any enemy in my path, but I'd possibly be urged by blood and ultimately hurt Lucas.

I tried to maintain focus, summoning telekinetic energy and once again using local rubble from the busted buildings and cars as weapons. They yelped as I punished them with anything within grasp or view.

A street sign speared one through their stomach; another flattened with a car—the third hit in the head with a fire hydrant. The fourth was scrapped by a member of his own pack, greedy for a taste of my blood and flesh.

To the right, Lucas bled from a nasty gash on his forehead. His right arm was mottled with bite marks and he was breathing heavily. He'd managed to get upright and fight the incoming wave of terror, but I could see now that he was truly scared. He couldn't heal like me.

I ignored the odd angle of my right foot and various other injuries and continued to lash out. The wolves were faster in most instances and anticipated my moves. With ten now crowding around and digging their teeth in wherever they could, it was almost impossible to find a solution. At least Lucas was okay—albeit scared.

It was time to close my eyes and focus on putting my vampiric part to sleep and allow the vânător to surface. I ran the risk of being maimed in the meantime, but since the wolves were no longer afraid of me as a human, I had to try despite the repercussions.

I waded into the darkness within, digging deep through fear and doubt and harnessed the wild and virtually unstoppable part of me. Pain and anguish surfaced, stoking the hatred flames that seared within.

A growl of epic proportions shattered my concentration and renewed a sense of terror. Fierce and determined, it was like no other; this growl demanded authority and respect—instilled fear.

Roshan was finally here.

He was twice the size of the others, his coat shiny and dark. He smelt like the earth and the sweat of a hard day's work. He stood out from the pack, his presence like a shadow upon us all and his scent an unwelcome reminder of who was in control. He commanded authority with his razor-sharp teeth—a warning to those that would defy. His hackles were skyward, his body trembling with ire as he snapped his snout at those closest. They quickly relinquished their hold on me—Lucas joining the submissive pack and backing away.

I was wincing in pain and limping, but resolute—relieved when Lucas remembered his place and stumbled back to stand at my side. He wrapped an arm around my waist for support, concern for our welfare etched upon his features. He too was bleeding badly and there was sweat all over his face, his hands shaking as he attempted to mop it away.

'Everything will be fine,' I reminded him in a coarse whisper.

'You're bleeding out.'

'Not for long.'

Roshan moved closer, arrogant in his command as he swaggered past his pack; a few growls of reprimand a reminder to keep their distance. He stopped in front of me, his alpha scent already warm in its embrace and pushing for the abstract sensation to want to pursue his touch.

'Now would be a good time to do something,' Lucas urged.

'I can't,' I sobbed. 'His alpha sway has already gripped me.'

'Then I'll kill him.'

Roshan growled, eyes gravitating to Lucas.

'No,' I almost shouted, hating that he'd drawn the Alpha's attention. 'Protect yourself, Lucas. I can handle Roshan—trust me.' I tried to push him behind me, forcing Roshan to refocus on me, but Lucas was a stubborn shit and remained resolute.

Meanwhile, Roshan's limbs twisted and contorted, lengthening before shrinking into fleshy pink counterparts of the human body. Hair fell from his form, leaving smooth and glistening sweat-slicked, tawny-coloured skin. His spine straightened and ribs snapped, re-aligning inside his chest. He stretched his neck, rolled his head around his shoulders before a curtain of raven hair spilled from his scalp and cascaded down to his waist.

I'd forgotten how mesmerising the transformation from wolf to man could be.

His now amber eyes settled upon me. As I searched their depths there was something I'd never noticed before—something that renewed my self-confidence and boosted hope. Caution was present, the underlying emotion before fear itself. The angry red scars on his arm were a reminder of how truly vicious I could be.

'Elena …' He accentuated my name slowly and concisely as if he'd missed hearing the word on his tongue. 'You are as beautiful as ever.' He took a tentative step, reaching to touch me.

I flinched as his hand grazed my cheek. A variety of emotions poured through me—heat, longing, fear, disgust. I wanted him to touch me yet I wanted him to burn in hell. How weird it was to be at war with your own desires.

Lucas was stiff beside me, his whole body alight with blue flames, once again drawing the Alpha's attention. Roshan surveyed him from head to toe. 'I remember you.'

Lucas gritted his teeth. 'I remember you and everything you've done to Elena.'

'This is my brother,' I interrupted before Lucas went too far. 'If you hurt him, Roshan, you *will* be hurting me.'

'He is touching you,' Roshan snarled. His nostrils flared as he surveyed the arm that Lucas had laced around my waist. I no longer needed the support to stand, but it was a comfort to have him near

'I'm healing.'

Roshan frowned, collecting my bloodied arms for his inspection. 'My pack has hurt you,' he stated, smoothing his fingers over the relatively slow-healing wounds. I winced.

Lucas's grip perceptibly tightened, but I shot a warning look. Whatever emotion echoed inside him was manifesting on his skin. I had seen Protector's hands alight with blue flames before, but I had never seen their whole bodies encased. Emotions amplified magic and though I was not affected by its reach yet, I wasn't sure of his control.

Roshan took a measured step back, tugging on my arm in an attempt to pull me with him. Lucas held tight, but Roshan's scent was a deal breaker. It could wrap around me like ropes of restraint, pull me like a puppet in any direction—he wanted me away from my brother's flaming protection.

Lucas was insistent, holding me closer still. 'Stay with me, Elena.'

'I can't, Lucas.'

'You're not even trying.'

'You don't know what it's like to have no control.'

'I do actually,' he said, face darkening. 'Just hold onto me and I'll get us through this.'

'Let me go to him. I promise it will be alright.'

'Yes, let her go, Magical one,' Roshan echoed. 'She does not want me to hurt you, so do as she says before I change my mind.'

Lucas's nostrils flared. 'I'm not afraid of you.'

Roshan laughed, running his fingers over the flesh of my palm. 'Perhaps not, but you should be afraid of her.'

Lucas studied my profile as though suddenly unsure of his words. 'She would never hurt me.'

'I won't have a choice if he tells me to, Lucas. Just let me go.'

'You would never give up on me.'

'This isn't about giving up. It's why I chose you, Lucas. I knew you would be able to let me do my thing and not interfere. I knew you would trust my judgement.'

He shook his head, warring with his conscience. One last lingering look begged me to change my mind before he dropped his hold. 'Don't make me regret this, Elena.'

Before I could react, Roshan pulled me into a crushing embrace.

His arms were around me, warm and oddly comforting as he buried his face against the top of my head, breathing in the scent of my hair. 'I have missed you. It has been many lonely nights without your body by my side.'

'I will not be your pack mate, Roshan. You have limited power over me now.'

His grip loosened enough that I could look up into his eyes and see his smiling face. 'Yes. I am aware of that now.'

My eyebrow rose ever so slightly as he lifted one of my arms to his face and gently licked the blood clean from my arm. He did not dig his fangs in as I would have expected. 'What do you mean by that?'

He traded one arm for the other. I was almost healed, blood barely trickling across my skin. 'I saw who you really are,' he answered between languid licks of my searing flesh. 'You are wolf and vampire—strong and determined.' He released my arms and cupped my face. 'You are my equal.'

'I am nothing like you.'

His smile widened which only served to feed my doubt and disturb me further. 'My, Elena, you are exactly like me. It is why I must protect you from the Vampires.'

'The Vampires won't hurt me.'

'They do not realise what you are.'

Now I was horribly confused. 'What are you talking about?'

Roshan leaned in, warm breath caressing the surface of my lips. Deep inside a fire ignited, burning hot and glowing with eager anticipation. My wolf was attracted to this creature, wanted him to kiss me and make me his; my vampire was repulsed.

He brushed plump lips across the top of mine; tentative at first they sought permission. I had enough willpower left to resist, closing my mouth to his invading scent, but helpless to resist his hands finding solace on my rear, cupping the firm flesh and pulling me against him. 'You are special. You are one of a kind.'

'I'm h-half b-breed,' I stuttered as his scent claimed superiority and the delicate caress of his lips soon sought full access.

I was lost.

Our limbs came together like puzzle pieces, my hands finding purchase on the hard muscles of his chest, delighting in the feel of him beneath my touch.

His mouth melded—rough against mine and tormenting as his tongue delved inside. He groaned, writhing against the traitorous body that had begun to enjoy the intrusion.

We parted minutes later, the shock and disgust on my brother's face was enough to dampen any unfulfilled desire within me. Roshan's breathing was hampered and my lips were swollen and aching for more. My limbs were weak and toes tingled. I hated this reaction. It was wrong on so many levels to be attracted to an animal, particularly an animal without conscience or desire for betterment.

'My Elena,' Roshan breathed, 'my beautiful pack mate.'

'I'm not your pack mate.'

How many times do I have to keep telling him that?

'Oh but you are. You will realise this soon. You are special.'

I shoved against his chest. He barely moved. 'You keep saying that. What the hell do you mean?'

He chuckled. 'Elena, you are an alpha. You are the first female of our kind and therefore a controlling member of the packs.'

'What?' Lucas barked.

Roshan growled at him.

'I'm an alpha?' I repeated in disbelief.

'Yes,' Roshan said, still growling at Lucas's intrusion. He turned away from him, seeking another kiss while I stood baffled over the admission.

'Wait. You couldn't possibly be that stupid.'

Roshan nipped at my lower lip, drawing blood. 'What did you just say to me?'

I ignored his injured ego and my sore lip. 'Are you telling me that if something were to happen to you, I would command the Vânǎtors?' I looked at Lucas who was gaping at the pair of us. By the tilt of his head and matching cocked eyebrow I knew he was also piecing this vital information together.

Roshan's eyes narrowed, brow puckering. His hold on me was tentative at best. His amber eyes turned black. Ordinarily I would have shown caution, but now I smelt *his* fear. 'You cannot kill me.'

'Oh, Roshan ... do not tempt me.'

He shook me roughly. 'I have control over you!'

'You may control my body, Roshan, but you don't control my mind.' I was smiling as he had done, the seed of doubt dwindling and now replaced by the tree of knowledge.

'You are drawn to me.'

'That doesn't mean I can't kill you.'

Roshan spat on the ground beside my foot, a daring look in his ebony eyes. 'You cannot kill that which binds you.'

I finally found the rope in the darkness inside that held my vânǎtor conscious. I grabbed it tightly in my mental hands, preparing for what I knew was coming. 'Do you want to make a bet?'

CHAPTER TWENTY-FOUR: FREEDOM

Staring someone down isn't as easy as you might think. You have to concentrate and not permit outside distraction. You must maintain eye contact, try not to blink and keep a straight face. You cannot be intimidated and most of all—you cannot show fear.

I'd learnt this technique watching Crocodile Dundee with Lucas. The buffalo taming skills interested me enough to try it on the neighbour's cat. Of course it scratched the crap out of my face, but with a little bit of practice, I had it licked by the time I approached the guy at the liquor store. The point is, I wouldn't let Roshan get the better of me now.

Lucas was in his sights—the plan to undoubtedly use him as leverage; a smart plan that would almost certainly work. Even Roshan with his limited knowledge of our relationship could see I would protect my brother at any cost.

'If you touch him, you *will* be sorry,' I said, maintaining that all important eye contact.

'Another empty threat, Elena?'

The tethers of his alpha sway attempted to worm their way under my skin. I used that pressure to fuel the beast within and gain even greater control. I was finally free of his bonds, had acquired mental clarity and total unity with my beasty balance. At any moment I would release the leash that tamed me and let the creature within free.

'What can I do?' Lucas prompted. He stood back, keeping his distance from mine and Roshan's battle of wills.

'Go find Sebastian and tell him everything. I've got this, I promise.'

'He's not going anywhere!' Roshan disappeared and then reappeared again right behind Lucas. He grabbed him by the neck and pressed a long, pointed claw against his jugular. 'If you try to help him, Elena, I *will* slit his throat.'

This was the problem fighting vampires and werewolves; they were too damn fast.

'Let him go. It's me you really want.'

'I already feel your resistance and thus I order you not to kill me.' A second wave of essence spilled over me. Harder to deny than the first, my eyelids fluttered and knees quaked.

My lips trembled and my body yearned for his touch, but I maintained the control I'd fought so hard to achieve.

I allowed him to believe he owned victory and fell to my knees as if succumbing to his timbre. 'I will not kill you.'

Yet.

'You will not kill me.'

'Yeah, I heard you.' I fought not to roll my eyes. He was practically dousing me in his scent, the stench barely hiding the indecision and fear that slithered across his skin.

My stage performance must have been convincing, he threw Lucas against a brick wall. He landed with a crunch, cried out and slumped to the ground with a sickening *thud*.

'Lucas!' I climbed back to my feet and ran to his side. 'Are you alright?'

'I think my arm might be broken.' He sat up, gasping in pain as he clutched the offending appendage to his chest. The other vânători playing spectator began to close in—Lucas now injured and vulnerable.

'Can you get up?'

Lucas grunted and used the wall against his back to help shimmy himself upright. I grabbed his other arm to help, but he cried out; that one was covered in teeth marks.

'I'm sorry.'

'I'll be fine. Just kill this stupid mutt before I do it for you.'

Roshan's amusement rang clear. 'If either of you think you are fast enough to kill me, then you are mistaken. I am the sole survivor of my alpha brothers. There is a very good reason for that.'

'Yeah, you ran away while your pack howled for help,' I muttered under my breath.

Lucas was shaking, sweating profusely and cursing about the pain, but his eyes stayed completely focused. He watched those vânătors so closely that when he closed his eyes and suddenly disappeared, I was as taken aback as everyone else.

'Where did he go?' Roshan commanded.

'I don't know.'

'Don't lie to me.'

I searched the spot where Lucas had been. 'I honestly don't know where he is.'

Roshan threw his head back and roared. 'I can still smell him!'

Realisation dawned. Lucas may have been in the middle of indescribable changes at present, but he was still a Protector—born with magic like the 'Revatarus' spell. Ordinarily that spell only worked on inanimate objects, not individuals. Lucas was definitely perfecting a craft unchanged for the last three hundred years.

'Find him!' Roshan snapped at the other wolves. 'His scent is fading!'

They attempted some semblance of a search party, skirmishing the wall where Lucas had been. They clawed at debris and sniffed the pavement looking for his scent, but they wouldn't find him.

'He has to be here,' Roshan continued. 'He would not leave you.'

'Oh, he's gone,' I said, grinning.

'Bringing vampiric help will make no difference.'

'He's not bringing help.'

The Vânătors continued to sniff in circles, clearly confused. Roshan was fuming.

His teeth lengthened and skin turned an awful shade of grey. His human hair fell away and fur sprouted in uneven patches. He grabbed me, the bones in his fingers in a state of transformation, shrinking and reforming into clawed paws. They found my shoulder and spun me so he could bury fangs into my neck, hunting tendons, pain and my life blood.

I focused on the pain. I wanted it to rule me, but not cripple me. I wanted him angry and vulnerable, careless in his disregard for my abilities.

While Roshan continued to take deep pulls on my veins, leaving me light-headed and typically weak-kneed, I envisioned that rope in my consciousness. Instead of using it to calm the dark-natured part of myself, I detangled myself from human form. I severed the connection with my vampiric soul and fuelled the malice I needed to make the change.

I imagined my limbs succumbing to the transformation, clothes disintegrating and my naked body free to embrace the wolf within. Bones broke and rapidly reformed; downy fur now in abundance.

My eyes changed colour; vision sharpening and my nose cracked and reformed into a snout that grew several lengths of razor-sharp teeth. Clawed paws touched the street, my feet and legs now shifting to accompany a body on all fours. Before I knew it, I was wolf; primed for the kill and eager to look upon my prey.

I snarled at the Vânătors surrounding us, asserting the authority Roshan had spoken of. Whether it was because I was a werewolf now—stronger and faster than even Roshan himself—they abased themselves under my command, moving so quickly that I looked twice to make sure they'd scattered.

Roshan's fear was like city fog; bilious and pore-clogging, assimilating with every fresh pocket of air. He was the prey and I the predator, two alphas set to engage in a battle to the very end.

I moved in, a low growl rumbling in my throat. He appeared unaffected, but scents do not lie; he reeked of anguish. He wouldn't run or show weakness, yet I sensed that was exactly what he wanted to do.

Some straggler wolves hidden behind dumpsters and cars, clambered to the tops of buildings and howled, alerting other kin. The imminent showdown was upon us and a new leader would prevail. They lingered to know their ultimate fate.

Distracted by the growing crowd, Roshan charged. He clamped teeth around my neck and we were suddenly tumbling into the side of a restaurant. Glass shattered, tables flew and yet he hung on to me for dear life. My claws found traction and I leapt, taking his body through the ceiling and into the upstairs premises. We kept going until we crashed through the terracotta roof tiles and plummeted down the side of the building.

We both hit hard, Roshan releasing me. Blood dripped over my front paws, but I knew I'd be okay. My advantage was I could self-heal—the very ability he lusted after.

The spectator wolves kept pace; their interference was nil. They merely wanted to watch.

I attacked first this round, but Roshan propelled himself off the side of another building and in the other direction. His enormous paws breached the cement under his grip, spraying debris in my eyes. I barrelled into onlookers, rolling over myself and quickly turning in time to catch Roshan coming from behind.

I ducked, lifting my claws to strike his flanks. They tore through flesh and ripped away tendons and fur—fresh blood splattered my face. Roshan howled, limping as he landed, quick to disappear again.

I caught sight of him fleeing via a nearby rooftop. I bounded after him, using a few wolves as a step ladder to launch onto the adjacent building. I clawed at the render and used my talons to grip every jutting angle I could find. I even used my teeth on window ledges to help support my weight as I pushed myself vertically up an impossible incline. I was going to have to learn how to jump.

The rooftop was covered in TV aerials, air-conditioning units and storage sheds. From this vantage point I could now see the Piazza Del Duomo. It was littered with terrified people running in every direction; vampires chasing after crazed vânători and fresh bodies piling up like rubbish. Fires had escalated out of control and human authorities tried neutralizing the situation with guns. In the distance I could hear air support and wailing sirens. Things were so far out of control now that stopping Roshan and gaining control over the packs was my only option.

With that in mind, I threw my head back and howled as loud as I could. I wasn't sure if I was doing it right, but from this position it carried across the rooftops and down into the piazza where everyone suddenly stilled. Fires still raged out of control and tore through sacred monuments and historical cathedrals, but everyone remained motionless.

I howled again, throwing everything I had into it. I thought about power, about control and about being an alpha. I figured since I couldn't speak wolf that if I howled with the emotion I wanted to portray then hopefully the message would be received—it worked.

Responding calls of the wild filled the air from every corner of the city. I had no clue what they were communicating, but I hoped it was the echoes of support.

Uh oh.

The stillness that had preceded my first call soon turned into rapid movements from every vânător in the vicinity.

From my vantage point I spied the blur of their bodies moving through streets and alleys; grey fur streaked the night over rooftops and cars. I felt their collective presence drawing nearer. I allowed this connection to roll over me and tie me intrinsically to the incoming wolves; I also used it to find Roshan.

I moved like the wind, jumping off the edge of the building and diving onto the next. My hind legs destroyed a lot of terracotta, but I was making progress. As I dove from the building and landed on the pavement—spewing bitumen everywhere—wolves got out of my way. They followed—flanking, but never attacking.

I raced through the streets in a blur; diving over bodies, ducking and weaving past screaming humans and attempting to avoid gunfire from the police. Even the burning buildings as they started to collapse around me proved ineffectual at slowing me down. I had my eye on the prize now and I would not let anything stop me.

I could see Roshan.

As I steamrolled into the centre of the piazza—stirring up whatever pigeons remained—I saw my father. Lucas and the other thralls also stood under one of the porticos surrounding the square. They might have been engaging the human police or vânătors at the time, but now everyone stopped to watch me as I chased after Roshan, a mass of werewolves nipping at my heels.

My focus was temporarily blighted by Araqiel. He sat perched on one of the turrets of the Milan cathedral, wearing his trademark white suit—feathered wings billowing in the breeze. I was uncertain if his presence in the midst of war was a good sign or bad.

Focus, Elena. He whispered in my head.

Of course this was the perfect opportunity for Roshan to attack. I was completely distracted by the fair-haired angel and wondering where Sebastian was. Roshan had changed course and was coming straight at me. It wasn't until we were flying backwards and into the cobblestones did I realise I was a love-sick idiot.

I tore up pavers like they were made from flimsy paper. Debris was abundant and rained upon us as we rolled, trying to find purchase on one another. His claws found my stomach, tearing it open and making a right mess of my black silky coat.

I buried fangs in the side of his leg and tore a large chunk of flesh from bone—the same leg I'd clawed earlier.

He howled—so loud the packs joined in. They had started to crowd the square, hordes of vampires hot on their tails. Neither group currently fought, perhaps pointless when the outcome of the war depended entirely on which one of us survived. I hoped it was me.

Roshan launched; we sailed higher than the cathedral turrets. I looked again for Araqiel, but he was gone. We hit the ground moments later, etching another car-sized crater in the piazza that erupted sizeable chunks of concrete and cobblestone.

I wheezed as precious breath was forcefully expelled, my lungs seizing from lack of oxygen. My back felt shattered and my legs were twitching uncontrollably, but I still refused to give up.

Roshan went in for the kill, aiming to get his teeth in my throat, but I managed to slap him into the side of a portico. As the columns began to crumble from impact and cascade around him, I rolled onto my side and climbed back to my feet. My spine screamed in protest and my ears were ringing. Breath was still a challenge to catch and to top it off, someone had started shooting at me. In fact, the army had arrived and were shooting at *everyone*.

At least they were indiscriminate.

Turned vampires and vânătors started dropping like flies. They weren't fast enough to outrun a bullet and couldn't heal like the rest of us. Thankfully the army didn't have a supernatural handbook and hadn't loaded their weapons with silver bullets— most of us would live.

The piazza came to life as the born vampires rallied to everyone's defence. They destroyed weapons and discarded their tanks by turning them into twisted piles of metal. They immobilised the infantry by relinquishing all guns and brought down a helicopter shooting aimlessly into the square. There were explosions as the helicopter fell from the sky and crashed into the cathedral, destroying centuries of history.

Roshan was slowly dislodging himself from the fallen building rubble. When he emerged and tried slinking into the shadows, I caught his crushed hind leg between my teeth and tossed him back into the centre of the square.

I was on him again like a fat kid with a cupcake, sinking teeth into every portion of his hind legs until they were so badly mauled he could do no more than crawl across the piazza. He relented and rolled onto his side, legs a bloodied pulp, yet remained calm, his breathing even and eyes upon me. Suddenly victory didn't taste so sweet.

I levelled my gaze upon him. The human part of me pitied and feared him. My vampiric entity longed for his death and the part that was pack mate almost surrendered to him. Then I considered my time as his captive. I thought about the way he'd used my body, forced me to touch him and kiss him and the way that he'd robbed me of free will. I also imagined three centuries of women being raped and abused to expand his packs and the countless lives taken to satiate his feeding habits. He had never shown me mercy and had never shown any to his victims; Roshan had to die.

I didn't think about what I had to do next. I secured his jugular between my powerful jaws and squeezed until I pierced though visceral matter and bone. He bucked and gagged beneath me as blood spilled from his body like it no longer belonged. It slid across my tongue—just as sweet as I remembered, but for the first time ever, I did not drink. I wanted his death to be clean, but most of all—I didn't want him inside me anymore. I wanted to be free of Roshan.

The last gasping breath claimed him and blood filled the remains of his lacerated throat. I closed my eyes and waited. After three hundred years of existence, his heart beat for the final time. I tasted fading power in his veins as his body went limp. Roshan was dead and I was finally free.

When I opened my eyes again, the pain finally hit. My skin grew itchy and began to burn. It started as a mellow heat that swathed my appendages with warmth, but soon morphed into something significantly more painful as my body abruptly burst into flames.

I wasn't the only one.

My ear-piercing howl was met with pained cries from the packs; we dropped to the ground, writhing uncontrollably, begging for relief. We clawed at our own skin, praying it would soon end, the fires would abate and our flesh would be restored.

Fur disintegrated and insides liquefied; limbs were only attached because the bones held firm. Blue flames roared skyward from my body, the smaller flames of the Vânǎtors exacerbating the excruciating heat. People called my name, running fingers through my fur, completely oblivious to the pain they caused. I wanted them to kill me, not stroke me.

I prayed for my heart to stop so that I would no longer endure the relentless torture. Wishing for death felt like failure after everything, but all I wanted was peace—a pleasure found when the flames finally died or death claimed me.

By some miracle, my flesh was doused by an unseen force. Where skin had felt like molten heat, it was now chilled. I stopped howling, the pain retreating. I remained still, uncertain this reprieve was ongoing.

My friends and family looked down at me, worried expressions etched on all their faces. From the corner of my eye, Roshan's lifeless body was being swallowed by a pool of his own blood. It stretched its crimson essence to touch my paw and to gather around the feet of those near. He would never awaken or find a way to pursue me as he had done for months. I was now the only alpha left—the only one capable of controlling the packs and ending this war.

I rolled gingerly onto all fours, everything cracking due to the sheer bulk of me as I straightened my back and flexed my muscles. I ignored the voices of those closest and surveyed the Vânători that had begun to congregate again. They had recovered as I had, shaky and unsure, but they looked to me, perhaps sensing I was the last ounce of structure they could depend on.

Lucas knelt next to me, took my head between his hands and forced me to look at him. I growled without meaning to, the others taking a perceptible step back. Lucas remained unfazed, believing the truth that I would never hurt him. 'Stand proud, E,' he said, rubbing the fur next to my ears. 'Put your head back and howl at the moon. Let them know who's boss.'

'Hurry,' my father added. 'I can hear more humans approaching; they send much more permanent solutions to kill us. Go to higher ground, show the pack who is in charge and lead them from this place as quickly as you can. We do not have time to fight anymore.'

I acknowledged Lucius by bowing my head and then licked Lucas's face—much to his disgust—before I turned towards the awaiting packs. They appeared inquisitive, noses twitching as they took in my scent. Some sniffed my coat and then backed away—

skittish. Others began to flank me. At the back of the packs some crawled along the ground, whimpering.

I wondered what Sebastian thought right now and if he believed I had the strength and courage to lead these animals. Was he proud of me? Was he worried that I'd stuff everything up?

A cursory look over one shoulder and a scan of family and friends now converged around the cathedral stairs, proved Sebastian absent. Strange, considering he rarely took leave unless requested by Lucius himself. It seemed odd that he would be absent from such a poignant moment in time. Something wasn't quite right.

I turned back to look more closely at the huddled group I'd left behind. My wolf vision took over, turning darkness into light and though the wolves sensed my unease and attempted to follow, I barked an order to stay put.

I could not see clearly into the huddled mass. They no longer watched my retreat or paid care to the Vânǎtors still lingering. I started to listen instead, ears rigid and focused. Burning buildings, continuing gunfire and the screams of the innocent made it difficult to competently hear.

'I don't understand why this happened,' Tiberius wailed. 'It is a silver dagger, but his heart does not beat. He should not be reacting this way.'

What?

'Sebastian has never been like us. You know this, my friend.'

'I believe he is dying and I don't know how to help him.'

I threw my head back and howled with everything I had inside of me. I did not do it to appease my father or strengthen ties with the wolves. Something terrible had happened to Sebastian and they had chosen to keep me from him. I was furious.

The Vânǎtors howled with me, echoing my pain and anger as I took off, running directly back to the group. The wolves followed, hot on my heels and ready to attack if I bid it.

I didn't need some ceremony under the moon or a gathering of the packs to know they were now mine; I could feel it with every new breath as the alpha I took—bonds growing stronger.

They formed a tight circle around what I now assumed was Sebastian. They dodged my approach, not bothering with reprimand merely offering pity—except Lucius—he was always irritated when I defied him.

'Elena,' he growled. 'Get the packs away from here—fulfil your duty as alpha.'

I snarled at him until my hackles rose and fangs lengthened, attack pungent in my mouth. He may have been my father, but I was ready to end him if he did not get out of my way soon.

'You must address the pack,' Lucius urged. 'There isn't much time.'

'The pack is already behind her,' Lucas yelled. 'Just let her go to him. It might help.'

'You do not help the situation young, Lucas.'

'Can it really get any worse than this?' he answered, gesturing all around. He had a valid point.

Lucius sighed. 'He asked me not to tell you. He didn't want you to—'

I barrelled through the group, determined. Sebastian sat propped against a doorway, eyes closed and covered in blood. His beautiful face was paler than usual, hands resting loosely by his sides. A silver dagger protruded from his chest, gleaming under the call of night. Tiberius was slumped beside him, face buried in his hands.

A minute passed where I did nothing but stare at Sebastian, horrified. I couldn't move, my paws rooted in fear. It never occurred to me that I might lose Sebastian this night. After reaching a point where I could accept love, I was terrified to be robbed of it—terrified to lose what I now held dear.

I shifted, moving those final few inches until my nose touched the side of his face. He was cold—uncharacteristic for his touch was usually warm. That worried me most—his lack of response secondary.

'He's dying.'

I lifted my head; Araqiel leaned casually against the open doorway of the cathedral. His arms were folded across his chest, one leg leisurely resting in front of the other. He seemed unconcerned by current events, even expectant. Was this part of some grand master plan from above? Whatever the reason for his ominous presence, I consoled myself with the knowledge I would move heaven and hell to save Sebastian if that's what it took to keep him with me.

'Relax,' Araqiel said, perhaps sensing my unease. 'No one can see me, not even Michael.'

I wish I could tell him to help Sebastian or piss off. I don't have time for this shit.

Why isn't anyone trying to help him?

Can I pull the blade out myself?

'I can hear your thoughts, Elena and no, pulling out the blade will not be helpful.'

You can hear me?

'Have I not always come to you in your thoughts?'

Help him.

'I cannot.'

I snapped and barked at everyone crowding around.

Then why are they not helping?

'Michael is a puzzle they cannot solve.'

I reconsidered the knife. Its silver origin was why it was capable of piercing his flesh, but it was still just a knife. If I could figure out how to remove it, he'd start to self-heal. He didn't need his heart to live the way I did. Did he?

I could use my teeth ...

'I have said that pulling it out will make no difference ...'

So why aren't you helping him? I was certain my mental voice reprimanded with ire. *You're supposed to be his brother.*

'I cannot interfere with Michael's life on Earth.'

But he's an angel like you.

Araqiel waved a finger. 'Not exactly.'

Then what is he?

'He chose to be a vampire. He exists as you do, but is not without some of his old powers.'

I glanced back at Sebastian. He looked terrible. There had to be a solution.

He's mostly vampire. If I pull the knife out everything will be okay.

'The knife is the least of his problems. He has been poisoned by what has marred the blade.'

You cannot poison a vampire!

'Yes, but you can poison an angel with innocent's blood.'

You know what? I don't really give a shit what he is anymore. Help me fix this!

'Why?'

Are you serious?

My patience was wearing thin and I had begun to shake with fear and rage. Tiberius had scattered, his bloodstained face wet from tears. He now stood with Lucius, confused like everyone else by my random snarling and particularly aggressive behaviour towards a vacant doorway.

'I wish to know why you want to save him.'

Because he's dying!

Araqiel uncrossed his legs and wandered over. He knelt beside us, oblivious to my enraged state. 'But Michael has been lying to you about who is since the day you met.'

Do you think that matters right now? All that matters is that he lives.

'Yes, but why?'

Because I love him!

Araqiel's face exploded into a smile so bright I had to avert my gaze. 'What would you do to save Michael? What would you do to save anyone you loved?'

I didn't even have to think about it, the answer was more than obvious. *I would do anything.*

He tsk tsked me, disappointed I'd so quickly disregarded caution. 'Anything?'

As long as saving him does not put another life in jeopardy, I will do anything, but the only life I have to offer you is my own.

Araqiel ignored my answer and touched Sebastian's shoulder, leaning closer to whisper in his ear. I strained to hear the words passed, but quickly forgot their exchange as Sebastian's body suddenly bucked and glowed with iridescent light. It radiated from within—his heart the epicentre.

I shielded my eyes against the brightness with a paw, peeking through a second later to find Sebastian gone. For only a moment I'd been blinded and now he'd vanished without a trace.

Where is he! I screamed. *What did you do to him?*

Shouts of disbelief echoed around the crowd, everyone rushed in to uncover the mystery of his sudden absence. The Vânǎtors tasted my anger, fuelled by emotions that radiated from my very core. I was so caustic and animalistic that even Araqiel had the good sense to wipe any smile from his face.

I lunged, cornering him by the cathedral door, unsure if my fangs would perforate angelic skin, but nevertheless willing to try.

'Be calm, Elena,' Araqiel said gently. 'Michael is safe.'

Where is he!

'Purgatory.'

What!

'It is the place between life and death—the judgement realm. Some souls will be relinquished by Lucifer—some to heaven. Lost souls possessing both good and evil stay on in Purgatory, awaiting future judgment.'

What does Sebastian have to do with Purgatory?

'Michael, as you know, has watched over you for many millennia. Now that his time on earth has ended he must go back to Purgatory, await your arrival and then await your re-birth.'

My shoulders slumped and my lungs hurt as if all the air had been squeezed from them. I knew there'd be no re-birth. I was born a vampire and thus obligated by the rules of Lucius's contract with Lucifer to reside in hell when I met my true death.

'Do you wish to see him again?'

My head snapped back to attention. *What kind of stupid ass question is that? Whatever it is I have to do, I'll do it.*

'Are you prepared to deal with the consequences of that choice?'

I'd never been particularly good at thinking things through. A smart person would take a minute to consider the ramifications of being sent to some previously non-existent realm, but then that wouldn't have been me. I was impulsive, head strong and sometimes ridiculously stupid for my own good, but I was in love. I was going to Purgatory and be damned the consequences.

Take me to Sebastian now.

Araqiel's expression was mostly blank, bar the slight curl of his lips. 'I did try to warn you that this would happen.'

What would—

Silver daggers were seemingly in abundance tonight—another now ruptured my chest cavity and plundered my heart. I didn't even see it coming.

My paws slid out from under me and a riot of confused thoughts travelled through my addled brain. Did going to Purgatory mean I had to die? Would I be coming back?

Oh my God … Lucas.

'Elena!'

My brother's grief-stricken scream shattered my entire world. Pandemonium broke out; wolves howled, vampires went on the defensive and my father roared in competition with the freshly released gunfire.

Araqiel laughed; he smiled so bright his teeth looked like shiny gems, glistening like stars in the darkness. They were brighter than his opalescent suit and the feathers he kept concealed at his back.

He echoed earlier movements, touching my shoulder, hand warm and soothing even though I felt numb and relatively indifferent. His sweet breath whispered across my cheek smelling like chocolate and vanilla custard. He leaned closer still, brushing lips that felt like rose petals against my furred ear. 'It's time to go, Baby vamp.'

I thought he might have said something insightful or poignant given his relevance. Instead he stated the obvious, laughing in the face of my death, crowding my view of those that might truly mourn my passing.

With my last breath, I looked upon my brother whose eyes were glistening with tears, his arms flailing wildly as Marianne and Caleb held him back. He fought to reach me, his cries an echo through thoughts laden with guilt. Circumstances were once again separating us for reasons not yet fully realised. I wanted to tell him everything would be okay and I'd be back, but I never did read that fine print. I had no idea if I would.

In the midst of madness, I'd shifted and now reached for him with my human hands—death stealing my wolf persona. All other versions of my soul had also disintegrated. I was naked again too, Lucas undoubtedly crying because he'd seen my boobs. At least, that's what I was telling myself as everything began to fade.

'Are you ready, Elena?' Araqiel asked. His hand still rested on my shoulder.

I barely noticed the knife in my chest or the pain. I was apart from everything now, even my own body. I was ready for whatever was coming, knowing this choice would lead me to Sebastian.

'I'm ready.'

'Then close your eyes, Elena and take a deep breath.'

'Is this going to hurt?'

'There's no more pain for you here.'

So I did.

I closed my eyes and drew in a breath so deep my head spun and senses dulled.

Then I was gone, my life and soul but a memory on the wind.

CHAPTER TWENTY-FIVE: DEATH

Lucas broke free of Marianne and Caleb or perhaps they let him go, as he rushed to his sister's side and pulled her lifeless body against him. The blade protruding from her chest butted against his ribs, the feel of her still-warm blood seeped through the folds of his sweater and t-shirt. 'Elena!' He screamed again with all the agony and emptiness he suddenly felt. 'You have to wake up!'

There was no answer.

A plethora of hope still bloomed within. It didn't seem right to give up, not after everything she had done to find him. Elena couldn't die now. She was supposed to be invincible.

'Lucas …'

What are you without her? What are you even going to do now that everyone you love has either turned against you or died?

'Lucas.'

'Not now!' He spat. Pleasantries were on the backburner. His sister had just passed and how the others felt was irrelevant. Lucius may have loomed and William edged closer for a chance to mourn, but Lucas was beyond sharing her right now. These people were related to her in weird and freaky ways, but he was still her family—her original family!

A strong, cold hand secured his shoulder, fingers exerting a gentle pressure. Lucas eventually looked up long enough to meet the speckled optics of Elena's father. 'Lucas,' he breathed again.

'Step aside. I want to help Elena, but there's only a small window of opportunity.'

Lucas wasn't ready to let her go just yet. She was all the family he had left.

Geez, Elena. Why did you have to go and die?

'Please, Lucas,' Lucius urged, tightening his grip on Lucas. 'You're not helping.'

'She's dead.'

'There's still time.'

Lucas warred with conflicting emotions. He could hear the words, but could not assemble meaning.

'Lucas, get out of the way!' William yelled, nowhere near as delicate of his feelings as he pried Elena from his grasp and deposited her into Lucius's outstretched arms. 'If he says he can help her, then just be quiet and let him do it!'

Lucas lurched, grappling at empty space. Elena now hung limply over her father's arms, head tilted back at a rather disturbing angle. 'Give her back to me!'

'Shut up, Lucas,' William muttered, grabbing the back of his shirt and hauling him away.

'Let go of me!' Lucas shouted, preparing to punish his friend with hastily deployed magic until he finally noticed William's distraught features. Tears of fresh blood streaked his cheeks and his lips were set in a grim line, eyes averted where possible. William was clearly heartbroken. If there was anyone among them that would want Elena to live, then it would be William.

Lucas stopped struggling. 'What are you going to do to her?'

Lucius adjusted Elena within his arms and walked her inside the church. Lucas expected he'd burst into flames, but that wasn't the case with this paradox. The Vânătors did protest her removal from their vision, but a roaring command from Lucius sent them scattering—still close enough to observe—far enough away to avoid damnation.

Lucas hurried to catch up, but the thralls he hadn't yet had a chance to meet tried barring his entry into the church. 'Let me through,' he snapped. 'That's my sister. You have no right to keep me from her.'

'It is a private matter,' one of the thralls answered. He bobbed his head in the direction of the curious vânători. 'Our ways are not something we like to advertise.'

'Do you think I give two shits about your vampiric customs right now? Let me through or I'm going to start doing some serious damage around here.'

'Lucas may come,' Lucius's said, voice echoing through the cathedral inside.

The others hesitated.

'Did you hear that?' Lucas muttered. 'Get out of the way.'

As they parted, he ran to catch up with Lucius who was already laying Elena's body on the floor near the altar.

There didn't seem to be any specific reasoning for this positioning, but Lucas offered no snide comments.

'I need you to trust me, Lucas,' Lucius said, motioning for Lucas to kneel at her head and support her weight. 'You may not like what you see, but what I'm about to do might help her.'

'What exactly are you going to do?' Lucas asked, removing the dirty sweatshirt he was wearing over his head and covering Elena's naked body with it. She was already looking so pale and well … dead-looking.

'I'm going to drain her of her blood and then replace it with mine.'

'You're going to try and turn her.'

Lucius nodded. 'It is the only choice now.'

'You're so calm about this.'

Lucius averted misty eyes. 'I am barely holding it together, Lucas. You do not understand what it means to lose her.'

Lucas swallowed the lump in his throat. 'I'm pretty sure I do.'

Lucius didn't respond, comparing sentiment was impossible. Instead, he pulled the sweater down and yanked the silver dagger free. He restored her semblance of modesty and then positioned Lucas's hands over the top of her seeping wound. 'I need you to pump her heart for me.'

'But it's already stopped beating.'

'I need my blood to circulate if it is to have any effect on her body. I cannot perform all actions by myself at the same time.'

Lucas did as he was told and immediately started pumping. 'Why didn't her self-healing work?'

'She is still technically human and thus a fatal injury can kill.'

'She was impaled to a tree last year.'

Lucius frowned, uncertain he wanted or needed to know the logistics. 'Then we should be grateful the impaling bypassed vital organs.'

'Did you see how it happened? Who stabbed her?'

'It was Julius,' Lucius breathed. 'He somehow got to Sebastian first and then …' He hung his head in bitter irony, unable to contemplate the error of his ways … again. 'I should have known better.'

'Are you talking about that crazy vampire that's been trying to avenge his wife for two millennia?'

'Yes.'

'I'll kill him,' Lucas promised.

'Get in line.' Lucius bowed his head to assess Elena's wrist, extended his fangs and then sunk them deep into her cooling flesh.

Lucas turned away, disgusted by the blood that dribbled down Lucius's chin. He sucked so ferociously and without remorse that if Elena had been alive she might have whimpered in pain. The only thing that kept him pumping her chest and not throwing up was the thought of her coming alive.

When Lucas thought he could take no more, Lucius wretched his bloodstained lips away. 'Keep pumping until I say to move your hands.' He licked his lips. 'I'm going to put my blood directly into her heart if I can. Once my wound heals over, start pumping until I'm ready again. Do you understand?'

'Yes.'

Lucius extended a fingernail to manifest a long, black talon. He slashed his wrist, a small grunt of pain escaping his lips. Blood pooled quickly and hastily dripped onto the cathedral floor, staining the sacred space with the blood of the damned. He groaned louder as he lacerated the wound deeper, severing veins and allowing as much blood as possible to escape his ageless body.

'Alright, move your hands and pull back the sweater for me.'

Lucas did as he asked.

His haemorrhaging wrist hung limply over Elena's gaping wound. Lucas wondered how much touched her heart and how much drowned her insides needlessly. Would the blood heal? Did it need to go directly into her heart to work? All questions he was dying to ask—all questions that seemed pointless when praying for a miracle in a church being desecrated by a ritual of the damned.

Within seconds the flow of blood began to ease—Lucius's healing had kicked in. He ordered Lucas to begin pumping again. In the meantime, he hacked and slashed his wrist all over again to feed her more blood.

They repeated the process several more times until Lucius wandered the path of freshly fed vampire to the pale and sickly complexion of a dying man. Not only did his physical appearance waver, but so did his strength and fortitude to keep his eyes open.

'This is killing you.'

Lucius shook his head. 'I can't die, Lucas. I'm not allowed to.'

'But you look—'

'I will recover as I always do.'

They kept going until Lucius slumped, too weary to keep his head up.

'Now what?' Lucas asked. Perspiration dripped down his forehead as he continued to compress. His shoulders and arms burned from the effort, but he would not stop until he was told.

'Now we wait.'

'Should I keep pumping?'

'Absolutely.'

'For how long?'

Lucius shrugged. 'The normal process is twenty-four hours, but Elena has died. I'm hoping my blood is pure enough commence the turning.'

'What's going to happen to her?' Lucas asked quietly. 'We never knew the finer details of this process.'

'It's complicated and I regret this being my only option.'

'Tell me … please.'

Lucius was torn, but understanding. 'I never wanted her to be a vampire. I wanted to keep her safe for as long as possible and off Lucifer's radar, but now that this has happened,' he said, gesturing to her lifeless body, 'I've had no choice but to try and turn her, make her into a thrall.'

'Lucifer's radar?'

'We are all the Devil's pawns, Lucas.'

Lucas shook his head. He didn't understand at all, but it didn't really matter. 'Sorry, go on.'

Lucius pinched the skin on the bridge of his nose, weary and incredibly troubled. 'Usually the body shuts down completely,' he said, continuing on. 'The person loses all sense of sight, smell, taste and hearing. It's not unpleasant, like going into a coma. After that, fever grips and sweating out the impurities of the human body occurs.'

'Then what?'

'The internal organs shut down one-by-one.'

'Is she going to be in pain?'

'I don't know. Technically she bypassed those stages by dying.'

Lucas was utterly exhausted, but continued compressions, breathing hard and using the conversation as a distraction. 'Don't you need those vital organs even when you're a vampire?'

'No. The only thing that keeps us alive—if that's what you want to call it—is the life force of others—blood. It is why our skin is cold and our bodies rigidly hard to human touch. Nothing inside us operates. Not even our hearts.'

'So Elena is already dead, her organs have shut down and her heart has stopped beating. What's next?'

'That's usually when her vampire blood would take effect, but because she's of mixed heritage, I don't really know what will happen. Now that I have given her my blood as part of the exchange, it should spread through her arteries, repairing damage. Her muscles should harden and her sight and hearing will improve dramatically. If everything goes according to plan, her extra chromosome—what we call the *predator gene*—will not only endow her with the thirst, but irresistible charisma, beauty, poise, speed, agility and of course, the power to hypnotize her prey.'

'And then what happens?'

'After all of that, she hopefully wakes, gasping for first breath. Her senses will come to life, but then so does the all-consuming thirst. It will not be safe for you to be near if she wakes, Lucas.'

'She knows me; she won't hurt me.' He was adamant about that.

Lucius remained doubtful. 'All she will see in those first few seconds of breathing new life will be your arteries pumping with blood that she needs in order to survive.'

'She is also part vânător. Won't that mean you and everyone else will be in danger?'

'I will be able to restrain her,' he answered assuredly.

Lucas looked back at his sister. She didn't appear any different. Her skin was still pale and sickly, her eyes vacant and lifeless as she stared up at him. 'Is anything happening yet?'

'No. Not yet.'

Lucas nodded and kept at it. His shoulders were screaming in agony, his breath almost a wheeze, but he'd never stop unless told. 'Do you know what happened to Sebastian?'

Lucius studied his bloodied hands, contemplating each slender finger in turn. 'I have long held suspicions about Sebastian. He is not like us and recent events have led me to believe that he could be—'

'An angel,' Lucas finished.

Lucius whipped his weary head up, a renewed sense of energy sparkling in the speckled depths of his eyes. 'What did you say?'

'Elena was told by another angel called Araqiel that Sebastian is the Arch angel Michael—or something like that.

'So it's true?' Lucius appeared awestruck and then slipped into quiet contemplation. The Archangel Michael had lived under his roof for two millennia. How had he never conceived of such a possibility?

'He's certainly something. He was stabbed like Elena, but disappeared in a halo of blinding white light. I'm pretty sure that's not normal for a vampire.'

'It's not,' Lucius agreed. 'Whether born or turned, when true death finds us, our bodies become ash on the dawning of a new day.'

Lucas took a minute to think about that. 'So where did Sebastian go?'

'I am uncertain.' A softness touched Lucius as he stroked the length of his daughter's cheek. 'I have a feeling that she knows, though.'

'Why do you say that?'

'Because her self-healing just kicked in. I can hear the change within her, but her mind has not yet come back.'

'What does that even mean?'

Lucius covered Lucas's hands to halt his efforts. 'It means that what we did here worked.'

'But ...'

'But I cannot see or hear her thoughts. Her consciousness is not inside her body.'

'I still don't get it.'

'It means she will live, Lucas, but she might not ever wake up. Unless her soul can find its way back to her body, she'll stay wherever it is she went.' He looked up as the cathedral doors blew off their hinges and the sound of gunfire exploded into the pre-dawn night. 'Whatever the case, we must leave now and get Elena to safety.'

'Agreed,' Lucas said, using his gifts to send the heavy doors back through the opening and into the oncoming barrage of men with guns. It hit them hard, throwing them backwards into their comrades who tumbled, releasing surprised gunfire into the sky.

'Tiberius!' Lucius roared.

A vampire similar in appearance to both Sebastian and William suddenly appeared at Lucius's side. Bloodied tears marked his face as he continued to mourn Sebastian's passing. 'Yes, Lucius.'

'Take Lucas back to the villa. I cannot carry them both.' He scooped Elena back into his arms again.

'But Lucius ... the war. The humans are back in force and the Vânǎtors are getting away.'

'The war is lost my friend. Elena was our last hope of controlling the packs. The humans know of our existence now and they will not stop until we are all dead. All we can do is go home, re-group and figure out how best to equip ourselves with this next stage.'

'I will quickly let the others know to spread the word.' Tiberius disappeared for not more than a few seconds before he was back again. 'May I?' he said, holding his arms out to Lucas. Lucas reluctantly nodded. Now was not the time to get pissy about manhandling.

Tiberius picked him up like laundry, bundling his lengthy torso against his chest and holding him close. His whole frame shuddered as he sucked back a fresh wave of despair.

'I'm sorry about Sebastian,' Lucas said quietly. He didn't know what else to say. He hadn't known Sebastian all that well, only that his sister was in love with him which honestly said a lot about the person he must have been.

Tiberius nodded. 'Thank you.' His sorrow-filled eyes flicked to Elena as Lucius carried her towards the door. 'I too am sorry about your sister.'

'Lucius said she will live.'

'I am glad of that.'

'Her consciousness is still missing, though. We think she went to look for Sebastian.'

Tiberius sniffed and offered Lucas a warm smile. 'Do you think so?'

'I'd like to think that she didn't just die and lose her soul without reason.'

Tiberius's brows crinkled, confusion evident. 'Why would she do that? Why would she risk everything for my son?'

Lucas suddenly felt like the smartest person in the room. He thought about his own personal reasons for staying with the IMI, enduring the heartache of their experimentations and wanting to believe the deceit. He thought about Elena's trials to find him, her disconnection from a family that spent years lying to her and her woes with the Alphas. How could the answer be so obvious to him, but not to anyone else?

He eyed the two-thousand-year-old vampire with careful consideration. 'Do you really not know?'

'How could I know what motivates that girl? She is so unpredictable.'

'Yet somehow predictable in the end,' Lucas added. 'Tell me, what would you do for love?'

'Love?' Tiberius grumbled. His brows knotted further as he considered the question. 'What does love have to do with anything?'

'It's the reason your son is gone and the reason I believe Elena is with him.'

Tiberius shook his head, sceptical. 'Meaning?'

'She fell in love.'

'With my son?'

Lucas rolled his eyes. 'Try to keep up.'

CHAPTER TWENTY-SIX: PURGATORY

Sebastian groaned—pain, thirst and hunger assaulted nearly every sense he had. The hot sun beat upon his back and coarse, dry sand covered his face and mouth. The tiny particles crowded his swollen tongue, tasteless and gritty against his parched flesh. An acrid taste at the back of his throat stopped him from swallowing, urging him to spit all debris clear. His eyes ached from the glare of a sun he had not seen in two millennia and his bones protested like he'd been thrown off a cliff, his skin chaffed and burnt.

He'd never felt better.

Coming back to Purgatory had its downsides—endless days alone and indescribable torment from the demon council members, but misery had its pleasure; here he could feel human again.

An angel felt no true emotion, physical pain or pleasure. To remain impartial is to remain void of anything leading to consequence or sentiment. Sebastian had fallen from grace to sample such intrigues—becoming human more than just a curiosity. There was nothing to gain or lose as Michael the archangel, but there was always something missing.

As a human and even as a vampire, he'd experienced the varied ways of life, enchanting in different ways. Human life was finite—precious, but it was for this reason he cherished it. Every memory, every new experience, every taste, every pleasure—it was all wondrous. A vampire led life in magnification, loaded with time and opportunity to fulfil dreams, but forced to sacrifice the simple pleasures of food and daylight.

Everything comes with a price, but a price worth paying.

Sebastian wiped his face, spitting out another lump of unwelcome sand from his gritty mouth, coughing from the dryness in his throat. It had been over two thousand years since he'd used his vital organs; he'd forgotten how wonderful it was to need breath and taste life.

He looked around, not the least bit surprised by his current location. He'd been to Purgatory more times than he could count and had visited this desert wasteland. He detested this unfriendly sector, finding lingering souls loitering to warm the darkness in their heart or punish their bodies with the abrasive nature of the sun. Sebastian preferred any other area of Purgatory, certain Araqiel had been cruel in leaving him here. Finding the Lakelands would take time—the only sector he could fathom spending eternity.

Sebastian rolled onto his back, straining to see the sun and the three rising moons above. He supposed it didn't matter where he was. His last chance on earth with Elena had perished and thus the purpose of his existence had ceased. Vampirism had destroyed all opportunity to be re-born again and his soul too tainted for heaven and too pure for hell. He was stuck here.

I'm dead. He thought numbly. *I'll never see Elena again.*

He closed his eyes, relishing the sun's warmth upon his skin; two thousand years was a long time without warmth. He crossed one leg over the other and rested his hands behind his head. There really was no hurry to move. He had eternity to make his way to the Lakelands, set up some semblance of a home there. Earth was a dream he would have to forget.

'I see you're back again, Michael.'

Sebastian cracked one eye slowly. Samael—the demon of death—hovered above him. He hadn't changed; tall, ugly and meaner than a rattle snake. He had the head of a goat, the body of a man and feet moulded into hooves. His eyes were the colour of blood and his breath smelt like sewerage. Sebastian expected a welcome party, but not quite this soon.

'Samael,' Sebastian muttered. 'It has been a while.'

'Just over two thousand years,' the beast replied. 'Though I don't know how you hid for so long.'

Sebastian shrugged. 'I am well practiced.'

'Not anymore. We know everything now, Michael.'

'And ...'

'And we also know about the girl. Tell me, will she be following you here? I've heard she's quite the target.'

'I'm not sure I understand what you're getting at.' Sebastian fought to remain calm, knowing he could never show fear or unease.

It worked.

Samael stamped his foot, snarling. 'Do not jest. We know about your re-birth deal with Elena.' His demeanour instantly changed and he started to laugh. 'But that won't be happening anytime soon, will it?'

Sebastian feigned a nonchalance he did not feel. The demon could not see the tide of pain that threatened to engulf him. 'I am the only one who has seen death today, Samael. For this alone I imagine that Lucifer is quite happy.'

Samael shook his head. 'You know how he feels about you, Michael.'

Sebastian pushed his angst to one side and started to smile, proving he too could play the games that the demons expected of him. 'I do. My brother has never been anything but forward with his intentions. Now you tell me, what does Lucifer have planned for me now that I'm back in Purgatory?'

'Lots of things.'

'Such as?'

'Pain and suffering.'

His smile widened. 'At least be original.'

Samael flexed his fingers. 'I will—'

'Let me guess,' Sebastian interrupted. 'Lucifer can't do anything until I choose to meet him in battle again. In the meantime, you're going to pretend you have power over me.'

'We do have power over you.'

'Then you forget who I am and what I am capable of.'

Samael screamed with rage and then spat on the ground next to Sebastian's head. Its festering filth was corrosive upon the already burning sand. 'You cannot hide in Purgatory forever! Mammon and I will see to that. We will follow you wherever you go—torment you endlessly until you agree to meet with our master!'

'No. I think I'll stay here.'

'Then you are a coward.'

'No,' Sebastian said, sitting up slowly. 'I am no coward. Lucifer is exactly where I left him—trapped in hell. I won't give him an opportunity to fight his way out any time soon. That would be ill-conceived.'

Samael snarled. 'Then perhaps I will just take you to him myself?'

Sebastian laughed. 'Did you miss my earlier lecture? You have no power over me, Samael. It is the one place the two of us can co-exist without causing damage to any world including this one.'

'I will find a way to avenge my master's punishment!'

'Well, you have eternity to do it. Take your time. I'm not going anywhere.'

Samael stamped his hoof-like foot and threw his head back, screaming at no one in particular. 'Will you not fight Lucifer to end all this?'

'No.'

Samael screamed again—a child to the end. 'I will torment you, Michael. That is a promise.'

'Do your worst.'

'Eventually someone will take pity on you—release you from here and send you back to earth where you are vulnerable.'

Sebastian scoffed and tried not to laugh at the demon's stupidity. 'So your plan is to torment me here and if I don't agree to fight Lucifer then you'll find a way to send me back to earth?'

'Yes.'

'So you can kill me again?'

'Yes.'

'Right. So we'll be back where we started—in Purgatory.'

Samael took a while to think it through before repeating his earlier tirade of screaming and stamping his foot, finally seeing the flaw in his most illogical plan.

Sebastian saluted him. 'Well, until then, Samael. Now if you don't mind, you're blocking my sun.'

'Blocking your—' He stopped mid-sentence, his blood red eyes wide and full of hatred. Steam hissed from his nostrils and his teeth ground together, grating like stones on concrete.

Samael leant down, secured Sebastian's ankle and tossed him as far as he could throw him. The torment would begin now. 'The sun won't help you in the snow caps Michael!' he shouted after him, laughing.

Sebastian was suddenly gliding through the air at dizzying speeds, the prospect of an ill-fated stop within his near future. There was no hope of changing course or slowing down until he arrived at Samael's intended destination. He had to remember that in this world he was an angel trapped in a human body—a body not entirely invulnerable to suffering if the mind is weak.

He caught glimpses of the desert; sand dunes painting the backdrop to small shanties filled with souls currently communing. Wild camels gathered around an oasis and further afield, canvas tents and market stalls caressed the landscape for miles.

In the distance, the world shifted from sun-bleached sand to the autumn fields. Parched land gave way to browning grass that gave the sparse trees with crimson leaves room to spread their strangler roots. These solid trees were used to erect tiny hovels, nature providing the palette in which the souls here painted their buildings in riotous colours.

The Autumn Fields had always been pleasant. Sebastian spent a few turns there, helping plant a few of those trees and dig a well to provide water for the transient town members. Souls didn't need to eat or drink in Purgatory; to be hungry, thirsty, hot and cold or even tired was simply a state of the human mind. It merely made the dead feel better to somehow still feel alive.

Past the Autumn Fields was the bordering world of Forest Ridges; abundant with trees and plant life, undulating hills and tiny rivers and streams, it was easy to see why so many souls migrated here. Always perpetually on the cusp of spring, flowers were almost always in bloom—a general air of happiness and wellbeing constantly present amongst those that lingered.

Sebastian smiled as his flying body crossed the threshold into the Lakelands. This had always been his favourite place. Spectacular aquamarine waterfalls cascaded over glossy white rocks and into the lakes and catchments below. Set amongst the highest mountains and ridges in Purgatory, accommodations were carved into the rock faces and accommodated souls that dared to live at such extreme heights.

Over the next ridge, Sebastian spotted the snow-capped mountains. It had been long since he'd felt the frigid air caress his skin. He wanted to touch the snow and feel the heat of such fierce coldness—feel it dissolve on his tongue and melt in his hair.

As the mountains drew closer still, Sebastian curled into a ball, knowing the landing would be unpleasant. From this height and the speed at which he travelled, he was bound for a rocky outcrop.

Sebastian braced for impact and as his back hit a rock, his feet rolled over his head. He knocked his arms several times on the sharp ledges around him, remembering to pull them in at the last minute and dispel thoughts of pain manifesting. He finally came to a standstill, body bruised and a little bent out of shape, but nothing that wouldn't heal in a place that saw no death. He tasted blood for what it really was—salty and metallic and not at all appetising.

He laughed. It was good to feel alive—ish.

Sebastian willed the frostiness of the falling snow away; it was cold and you couldn't ignore the weather in Purgatory completely, but the power of belief stopped him turning into a shivering mess.

He surveyed the snow-capped landscape. It was a barren wasteland filled with rocky outcrops, damp caves and freezing temperatures. Conflicted souls lingered here; they saw no happiness in life and no relief from death—neither good nor bad, they were difficult to judge. They sought no desire to warm their hearts in greener pastures or heated deserts. Escape from nothingness was irrelevant, but relevance applies to the individual. Sebastian felt the pointlessness of escaping one prison for another, but in the end, would he ever truly be happy without her?

'I doubt lingering on such thoughts will make you feel better.'

Sebastian observed the cuts on his hands and massaged the bruises on his legs. He had expected at least one visit from the angelic council members. 'Hello, Nakir. How is Munkar?'

'He is good, though I have not appeared to you to talk of our brother, Michael.'

'Do you come to bait me just as Samael has?' Sebastian looked up in time to see the angel frown.

'You are our brother, Michael. We would never wish to upset you.' Nakir sat down next to him. He unfolded his large, white wings and wrapped them around Sebastian to keep him warm.

'Then what is it that you want?'

Nakir focused his sparkling silver eyes upon him. 'You have lost your last opportunity, Michael.'

'I know. Thank you for reminding me,' Sebastian answered bitterly.

'You have to help her seize hers now.'

'Seize what?'

'Her opportunity.'

'Nakir, what are you talking about?'

The angel fluffed the feathers of his wings and smiled. 'I speak of Elena. She comes here looking for you.'

'What? How is that even possible unless she—'

'Love makes all things possible, Michael,' Nakir interrupted. 'You should know that better than anyone.'

Sebastian shook his head in disbelief. 'Elena is in Purgatory?'

'She travels here as we speak. Araqiel opened a doorway.'

'But for her to come here ...'

'Yes, brother, she had to die,' Nakir finished for him.

'Then I have failed,' Sebastian murmured, agony squeezing his vocal chords. 'All hope of regaining footing during that war rested on Elena's shoulders. All hope of Elena returning to earth or even to heaven has failed because of her Vampirism. She belongs to Lucifer now and there's nothing I can do.'

Nakir rested a firm hand upon his shoulder. 'You did not fail, Michael. Lucifer does not have as firm a grip as you seem to think. The relationship that you and Elena share is unprecedented—a love that stretches through even time itself. No one could stop her from making this journey. Even now she thinks only of finding you and that might be enough to save you both in the end.'

'I will not allow her to use the Time Contract to selfish ends.'

Nakir chuckled, unconcerned by possible abuse of the most powerful contract in existence. 'Her decisions have been made and so far I approve of what I see. I wish you had sight as you used to, Michael. You would be proud of her and how far she has come in opening herself to loving those around her.'

'So she will choose right?'

'Araqiel believes in her.'

Sebastian inhaled deeply, the winter's chill burning his lungs and clearing his mind. 'She really does love me.'

'Oh yes,' Nakir agreed. 'But if you love her in return, then you must help her to get back again.'

'She has died—'

'Her body lives. The master vampire polluted her veins with his blood. She will rise again if you help her to outsmart the demons on the council. You know you have our vote.'

Sebastian bowed his head, forcing the tide of selfish reasons for wanting to keep Elena with him to the back of the pit manifesting the darkest of his thoughts. 'If she does go back, I will never see her again.'

'It is a sacrifice that we make for the ones we love, brother. Once again you know this and as I said, her choices may see you both united once more.'

Sebastian reluctantly nodded. 'How long will I have with her?'

Nakir squeezed his shoulder once more and then released him. 'In one week her soul will be summoned for judgement.'

'What if I can't convince Samael and Mammon to send her back?'

'You know what runs through her blood. Elena has the power to change a lot of things, Michael. If her love for her friends and family is what drives her decisions, she can put an end to this misery we see on earth.'

'So we must sacrifice our love for everyone else …'

'All's fair in love and war, my brother.'

Sebastian scoffed, kicking a loose mound of snow over the ledge of the cliff face. 'It really isn't.'

Nakir appeared amused. 'You have had so many lifetimes with this girl. What is it about her that is so special?'

Sebastian sighed, leaning further into the warm crook of Nakir's wing. 'No one sees me as she does. Even when hiding who I truly am, she sees past everything and touches my soul. She always chooses me—just me. Her love is more addictive than the blood I've craved all these years.'

Nakir nodded, but Sebastian was certain he would never understand until he comprehended the truth depth and complexities of human emotion. 'Is it attraction?'

'Everything about her speaks to me; the breath from her body, the words on her lips and the smile in her eyes. She's the sun—the warmth I longed for, for so many years in heaven.'

'But she is always reborn different.'

'Physically, yes, but she is always the same inside, Nakir. The first time I saw her was around 8500BC. She was part of the early settlement near Cramond in Scotland—part of suburban Edinburgh now.'

'I remember it well.'

'She ran with hunters and gatherers, wary of outsiders like myself, yet drawn to my inhuman qualities. Her name was Eimhir then; beautiful and unique—her interest in me more than mere curiosity. I would have studied her as we do all humans, protected her when necessary and left when my good deeds were done, but she knew what I was. She made me want for something I had never wanted before—to see life through her eyes and feel as she did.'

'What happened?'

'I touched her hand just once, knowing it was forbidden, yet unable to control the warmth she bloomed within me.'

'She made you *feel*.'

'For the first time in my existence I recognised longing, my skin burned from her touch and my mind was fearful of wanting more.'

'What finally made you throw everything away, Michael?'

'She found me sitting by myself in a glen that night. She'd slipped away from the watchful eyes of her father, walked right up to me, kissed my lips in a way that made them tingle for hours and then disrobed herself right in front of me.'

'I get the picture.'

Sebastian swallowed, the memory still fresh. 'I had never felt a woman's complete touch until that night. I realised I could no longer go on being what I was, especially not when I had felt the truest meaning of heaven.'

Nakir scoffed, tormented by a sentiment beyond his understanding. 'You are comparing the pleasures of the human flesh to the kingdom of heaven? Oh, Michael. How the mighty have fallen.'

'You could never comprehend, Nakir. It was everything to hear the sound of her voice murmuring my name, to feel her warm breath on my skin and sample her flesh against mine. I felt everything in those moments; she opened my eyes to what I was truly missing.'

Nakir looked sideways at him, eyes brimming with concern. 'Are you going to be able to let her go now?'

Sebastian curled bruised fingers through his hair, balling them into a fist at the roots. 'I have to. I have no right to dictate to fate and what it has in store for all of us.'

341

'You are still wise, Michael, though I do not understand how you can choose a human existence over an angelic one.'

'You don't know any better.'

'Then I pray that you and Elena have another opportunity to be together in another life soon.'

'I have one week with her. It's more than most people have.'

The angel closed his eyes, reopening them a moment later. 'She just landed in Forest Ridges. How about I give you a little head start? I'll deal with Samael later.'

Sebastian's hands began to shake. It was not the cold that afflicted him, but the thought of seeing Elena again, spending a week alone with her. 'Thank you, Nakir.'

And just like that, Sebastian was flying through the air again, leaving the cold behind to seek out his destiny in the forests beyond, sailing over ice and rocky outcrops, straight towards the love of his life.

For now, Purgatory was as close to heaven as he could get.

EPILOGUE

Fear not death, for the sooner we die, the longer we shall be immortal.
Benjamin Franklin said that.
I remember reading the quote once during a brief jaunt through a history book Susan had force-fed me during home school studies. You never can tell when you're going to learn something, poignant now considering the circumstances; I was dead or at least I *think* that's what happened to me.

The last thing I remembered was a silver dagger and my brother's face; he was crying. He'd always been a bit of a sook, but I'd never seen him cry before so it was a pretty good indication that I was now worm food.

I didn't feel dead. In fact, I felt very much alive, even aware of the pain surrounding my purported death. I had a connection to whom and what I was and could sense what was happening, but couldn't *feel* my body—touch it physically.

I guess that made me a ghost.

I also had ongoing—pardon the pun—stabbing pain in my heart which funnily enough I was going to link an ill-placed silver dagger. Each breath my phantom body took became laborious. I wheezed and gasped, finding that pulling in oxygen in the dark space of nothingness I currently existed was impossible. Was it too late to tell Araqiel I had changed my mind, the pain of this unknown indescribable?

343

No wait. I love Sebastian. I would do this a thousand times over to save him.

Okay that was hasty. I'd do it maybe twice; the third time would definitely be under coercion.

Now fever gripped me, a warm heat in the centre of my heart. It was surprisingly soothing at first, spreading throughout my veins, muscles and flesh; like immersion in a nice warm bath or drinking hot chocolate on a cold winter's day. The cynic within knew that pleasantness could only be temporary; good things didn't happen to me without bad things vying for equal rights.

The heat grew in intensity, soaring to ungodly temperatures that saw me screaming in a darkness where no one was listening.

I tried to convince myself that pain was an illusion, a rite of passage into Purgatory. After all, I couldn't see or find my damn body in this place, so why could I feel anything at all?

Sensations continually flooded through me. The fever subsided, but many newer symptoms made an appearance. I deduced that if my organs were a sludgy mess, then I shouldn't be aware of their basic functions ceasing to exist.

At first it had been my kidneys, a strange sensation morphing from heat to an icy chill. Then another laborious breath led to pain in my lungs. Pressure expanded across my chest and all through my tissues. I could taste blood in my mouth—blood in my throat. I was suddenly swamped in the warm stickiness of it.

It leached into my muscles and tissues, my head suddenly wrapped in lashings of cotton wool. My liver then solidified, the very centre of the core frozen solid. Icy tendrils—so far removed from the heat I'd endured—licked the side of my lungs and reduced my intake of oxygen. I suspected blood had reached my lungs, slowly drowning me.

I had never feared death, but I did now fear the path in order to get there. I was so alone and the angel promising me hope was nowhere near and, since he'd displayed general lack of care during cross over, I wished upon him a severe bout of Syphilis.

Another burdened breath proved my body unresponsive to oxygen. I tried again—nothing. I started to panic, aware that burning sensations spelled the imminent start of respiratory failure. Then the ice cold sensations claimed the rest of my body, invading any organ untouched. They hardened and stilled, icy tendrils spreading to my throat and sealing my airways. Like little delicate spiders, my thoughts were extinguished one-by-one.

I held Sebastian's image in my mind and forced myself to remember that I was going to Purgatory to find him—that I'd died twice so I could bring him back.

Remember him ...

'Sorry I'm late,' Araqiel said, switching on a dangling light bulb above. 'There was a little bit of a delay on the Ley-lines.'

I blinked, straining bleary eyes at the nonchalant angel who had the audacity to put me through hell before he got here.

'That wasn't hell,' he said, reading my thoughts. 'If you were in hell you would have wished worse things on me than a sexually transmitted disease.'

I glowered, mentally violated. Given the indifference he now showed, I wasn't entirely sure that wishing him the burden of an itchy crotch was enough.

'No harm done,' he said, all innocence. 'You feel fine now, do you not?'

No harm done? I wasn't sure how true that was, but I certainly felt better. I was also distracted now too that the lights were on; Purgatory had fitted me with Manolos and a cute little Gucci dress. Anything was better than gallivanting naked or remaining trapped as a werewolf.

I focused on the room now; it was small, no bigger than a bathroom—quite the claustrophobic nightmare. There were no windows, only one door and everything was white. 'This surely isn't Purgatory?'

'This is the waiting room.'

'Waiting room?'

'A place where the soul waits for their spirit guide to take them to Purgatory.'

'So you have a waiting room for the waiting room?'

Araqiel frowned. 'I'm not sure I follow.'

'Isn't Purgatory the place where you wait to be judged?'

'Yes.'

'So ... you wait here to go there and then you wait there to go somewhere else. It sounds like a lot of double-handling to me.'

Araqiel crossed his arms in front of his chest, smirking. 'The waiting room moves, holding the soul until an appropriate Ley-line opens to take you to Purgatory.' He rolled his eyes as if this was something you learnt in grade school. 'You can't just hail a taxi. The spirit world works a little differently, Elena.'

'I don't know what you're talking about.'

'Ley-lines? You've never heard of—' He took one look at my face and stopped talking. 'Never mind.'

'Please just take me to Sebastian now.'

'We are waiting for a Ley-line to open up. Did I not just say this?'

'After the day I've had, I'm hoping it's a magic rainbow that takes me straight to Sebastian. I didn't just die twice to sit around in some dumb waiting room's waiting room.'

'You haven't *technically* died.'

'I was stabbed in the heart with a dagger and then I was ... well, I don't know what the hell that was that you just pulled me from.'

'Yes, you were stabbed in the heart, but we have your father's blood to thank for small mercies.'

'Speak in English.'

'Your father helped execute your change to vampirism. What you felt in this room was an echo of your metamorphosis.'

I just knew that I was frowning again. 'So why am I still here?'

'You wanted to come to Purgatory and find Sebastian.'

'So my body is back in the real world in the grip of transformation and my soul is what, this version of me?'

'Yes.'

'That aside, why is Sebastian here? We both know he's special.' I shook my head. 'How was he killed if he's angelic? It's not like him to be so careless.'

'We all have a path we must follow.'

'Who killed him?'

Araqiel scratched his chin, quietly contemplating his answer. 'A vampire known to you as Julius.'

'This all happened because of one stupid vampire's intent to avenge his crazy murderous wife! I can't believe the shit timing.'

'Elena, watch your language.'

I rolled my eyes. As if I cared about saying *shit* after all the *shit* that had happened recently. I could have said a lot worse; I *wanted* to say worse.

'Don't even think it,' Araqiel warned.

Censoring on a massive level I said, 'Is it a coincidence that Sebastian was murdered by Julius?'

'There are no coincidences.'

I groaned. 'Angel or demon; you move us all around like pawns on a chessboard. Lucius was right about you.'

'Yet I gave you the choice to be with Michael again.'

'I'm starting to wonder why.'

Araqiel dared to look offended. 'You bargained your life for love, therefore I offer you one week in Purgatory with Sebastian to resolve your issues.'

'Issues? We don't have—'

'In one week,' he interrupted, 'you will appear before the council for judgement. How that goes is entirely up to you.'

'Whoa, wait. I thought I could stay here with Sebastian—find a way to bring him home.'

'No, Elena.'

'I can't save him and I'm going to hell?'

'Michael doesn't need saving. He's an Archangel.'

'I should have read the fine print.'

'I tried giving it to you, but you were insistent about coming regardless.'

I was about to scream a barrage of obscenities, feeling hopelessly sick to my stomach at the thought of never seeing Sebastian again and spending eternity in the southern sauna. I'd truly believed I could save him. When had I grown so naive?

'You have a week. Make the most of every moment, Elena and think long and hard about your life and those who are in it and how best you can help all of them.'

'You make it sound like I could come back.'

'Perhaps you can if you play your cards right.' His coy expression only raised suspicion. Here I thought I'd become a crispy critter and now he suggested otherwise.

I sighed. 'What good will going back do? The war is out of control and humans know of our existence.' I bowed my head, pain of a new variety tugging at my heart. 'I left a bloody big mess behind and no idea how to fix it.'

'Don't fret, there's nothing that can't be altered.' He snapped his fingers, breaking out into what I believed was another ill-timed smile. 'The Ley-line's opened.'

'And?'

He wretched open the door, a cacophony of bright swirling colours greeted me. I was temporarily blinded, hiding beneath my hands as the rainbow of prisms leapt into the room, drowning all the white with indescribable luminescence. 'Take my hand. You can't run around in these lines by yourself. You never know when and where you might end up.

'Did you just say *when*?'

Araqiel nodded, all seriousness. 'Ley-lines have been known to unexpectedly throw people back and forth through time. Now hold on, this might sting a little.'

Sting?

With my hand now firmly in his, he jumped through the opening, dragging me with him like a circus acrobat in heels. He landed steadily while I stumbled, falling onto a tangible puddle of coloured light; a weird conveyer belt of stickiness about three feet wide that adhered to my skin like warm toffee. It travelled above the earth, zipping quickly above the scenery below, colours whirring past in a blur. My hair clung to the surface, my head bent at an awkward angle and my fingers from one hand were now stuck under my butt.

The belt moved faster, jostling me to the side as we swerved around a corner. I fell in the opposite direction, my face now buried in a bubble gum pocket; my new heels were buried, fingers still up my butt and face about an inch deep in the sticky surface too. I looked like a complete idiot.

'What are you doing down there?' Araqiel asked, spinning on the spot like he was strutting his stuff at the disco. I thought of a very graphic and inappropriate retort, sure to be as descriptive with the insertion method as I could be.

Araqiel's features darkened. 'Who taught you that language?'

Before I could answer, the conveyer belt surged in a new direction, all colour and light extinguished as we were transported into a space so dark that I shrieked when Araqiel reached for my free hand again. His fingers closed around mine and I was suddenly unburdened; my other hand was no longer wedged under my unmentionables, my shoes were free to tap dance and my face unobstructed.

Then we were free falling, the darkness transitioning into the rainbow of colours once more. Another sharp tug to the right, then upwards saw us tumbling in a completely different direction. We landed on the conveyer belt again, Araqiel helping me stand properly this time round.

'How do you even know where you are going?'

'I've been travelling these lines for many millennia.'

'Angelic public transport.'

'More or less.'

'How do you use them?'

'Are you well versed in astrophysics and quantum mechanics?'

'Oh, yeah, for sure.'

He detected my inner sarcasm and avoided further explanation. 'Let's just say it's complicated.'

'But you can go back in time …'

'Not on purpose and certainly not the likes of you—non-ascended being, mortal, vampire etc.'

'So what happened to Sebastian—?'

'Is destined. The opportunity to traverse time can only be given to those that have pure intentions. No selfish motivation can play part. Do you understand what I'm telling you?' His eyes were suddenly intense, ever watchful for my reaction.

I chewed on my bottom lip, contemplating the possibilities. Changing time would alter everything, but at what price?

'It's called the butterfly effect.'

'Yes, exactly.' There was newfound respect in his tone. 'A butterfly flapping its wings in one part of the world could lead to the creation or absence of a hurricane in another.'

Before I could comment on his particularly knowledgeable account of the Ashton Kutcher film, he pulled me up, yanking my arm to the left. He let go and I was suddenly falling again, landing face first in yet another sticky conveyer belt moving in the opposite direction.

Like an idiot trying to pull free of quicksand, I pushed against the surface to free my face and ended up shoulder deep with my butt up in the air. I could breathe the rubbery substance as if it were air, so that knowledge stopped me from panicking.

'Are you ready, Elena?'

Ready? I thought to myself. *Ready for what? A life jacket?*

The toffee floor evaporated, leaving nothing but blue sky beneath me. I shrieked, grappling for the last few vestiges of sticky substance to hold onto, terrified of the imminent free fall. 'Pull me back in! Pull me back in!'

'It is safe,' Araqiel cooed. 'There is no need for this degree of alarm.'

'I'm going to fall!'

'Yes, into Purgatory.'

I looked down again—clearly a mistake. The conveyer belt had moved, bringing us closer to solid ground. A dense forest filled with pines, spruces and the dribble of freshwater streams was my landing pad. It was yet another opportunity for me to be skewered by a tree.

'This district is known as Forest Ridges. Michael will find you here. Now let go.'

'You've got to be fuc—'

'Language, Elena.' He shook a finger, decidedly annoyed by my absent self-censorship. 'It will not hurt.'

'Have you been impaled?'

'You can't die in Purgatory. Pain is a state of mind.'

'What the hell is that supposed to mean?'

Araqiel sighed. 'I'm going to have to spend a couple of hours cleansing my soul after listening to your potty mouth.'

'Oh for—'

The bastard dropped me.

I plummeted, the Ley-line snapping closed behind me, Araqiel waving like I would return the friendly gesture. I returned a gesture involving my hand, just not the one he expected.

I tumbled, flipping head over foot, screaming as the pointed tips of the trees approached. I saw my life flash before my eyes— my body a piece of meat to be harpooned. I would have pine cones coming out of my eyes and pine needles piercing my finger nails. If by some miracle I missed the trees, then I could look forward to slamming into the ground. I'd always wondered what my insides might look like.

I really hated my vivid imagination sometimes.

I took a deep breath, pushed the imagery aside and did what any normal girl in my position would do—I kept on screaming. I screamed so loud and long that if Sebastian were down there waiting, he'd know I was coming.

Soon I would see Sebastian and unravel the details of his angelic persona. I'd finally begin to comprehend the silver-eyed vision from my dreams and hopefully understand his role in my life and what he truly means to my heart.

So, it was time to be brave. I was plummeting to yet another death and that meant quibbling about thoughts of *I love you* were quickly becoming trivial in light of the next few seconds. My rather uncomfortable landing loomed clear in my mind and yet I still spared a minute—not to kiss my ass goodbye—but to wish Araqiel the nastiest case of herpes ever.

Amen.

Coming Soon

The Delivered

Volume 5
of
THE HUNTED SERIES